RAISED IN FIRE

Also by K.F. Breene

FIRE AND ICE TRILOGY
Born in Fire
Raised in Fire
Fused in Fire

FINDING PARADISE SERIES
Fate of Perfection
Fate of Devotion

WARRIOR CHRONICLES
Chosen, Book 1
Hunted, Book 2
Shadow Lands, Book 3
Invasion, Book 4
Siege, Book 5
Overtaken, Book 6

DARKNESS SERIES
Into the Darkness, Novella 1
Braving the Elements, Novella 2
On a Razor's Edge, Novella 3
Demons, Novella 4
The Council, Novella 5
Shadow Watcher, Novella 6
Jonas, Novella 7
Charles, Novella 8
Jameson, Novella 9
Darkness Series Boxed Set, Books 1-4

RAISED IN
FIRE

BY K.F. BREENE

Contact info:

www.kfbreene.com

Facebook: www.facebook.com/authorKF

Twitter: @KFBreene

CHAPTER 1

A LIGHT BREEZE ruffled Agnon's oily black feathers. The being sat on a hillside, soaking in the pleasant heat of the afternoon sun. Below it, nestled into the golden hills of Northern California, ran a dull gray track. Metal boxes of all shapes and sizes moved along it, bending and twisting with the contours of the land.

Such stupid creatures, humans. Nothing but walking carcasses waiting for their expiration date.

Agnon closed its eyes and homed in on its duty. It had been sent topside for a specific purpose. Rumor had it the Great Master finally had an heir, a daughter powerful enough to rule the vast kingdom of the underworld in his stead—and if Agnon succeeded in validating the rumor, its superior would bestow a higher level of power unto it.

It was getting ahead of itself. It was mere hearsay. Silly babbling from the unworthy, who gained their pale knowledge from witches playing at magic.

Witches.

Delusional creatures. They thought their chalk and

their books could contain someone as powerful as Agnon. They chanted and they danced, issuing commands they had no business voicing.

The being shuddered in annoyance and dug its claws into the soft dirt of the hillside.

Regardless, they served a purpose. The being would allow them their misguided conceptions of power. For now.

From the north flew a nearly solid blot of black, twisting and turning against the deep blue of the sky. The throng drifted apart for a moment, revealing the hundreds of individual birds that massed into a whole. It immediately regrouped and changed direction, heading Agnon's way.

The being could feel the evil emanating from the inky mass, even from the distance. The *aswang* was old, and it was strong. At least the witches had gotten one thing right.

The birds thrummed by Agnon before altering course, circling.

"*Go*," Agnon shouted. "*You have your orders. Find Reagan Somerset. Infect her.*"

The throng twisted again, now heading east.

The *aswang* thought it would be passing its evil to a new host. And maybe it would, if the girl Agnon sought was nothing more than a powerful human bound to this world. But if the *aswang's* seed couldn't take root,

Agnon would have the first sign that its purpose topside was of utmost importance. That the Great Master had a capable successor.

It was well known that the Great Master longed for a disciple. Only once had it nearly happened, but the mortal elements of the son's body had finally withered away. That would not be the case with this new find, or so it was whispered. The girl had the blood of gods on her mother's side, as well as her father's. That was the secret elixir. She could survive.

If she was genuine.

Rumors of this magnitude had surfaced before. Once in every few human life spans, actually. Mages more powerful than their peers. Humans with the unique ability to summon fire. To feel the pulse of magic. To unravel spells.

In each case, the Great Master had gotten his hopes up. Found the human in question. Taken him or her to the heart of the Dark Kingdom.

The result had always ended in mortal death.

Agnon had been sent to scout the truth of the rumor before the Great Master was informed of the possibility. It was better for all involved. If true, a select few would reap impossible rewards. If false, no detriment would ensue.

Pausing for a fraction of a moment to feel the sun warming its back, something that lasted an hour in human terms, Agnon spread its great wings and launched into the sky.

BELOW, IN ONE of the cars winding along the California highway, a child looking out of a car window saw a great black bird sail above. "Look, Mom! What kind of bird is that?"

"What's that, honey?"

But it was too late. The winged creature was already gone, beating the air with its magnificent wings, shedding blue magic in its wake. Waiting for the *aswang* to infect the girl.

CHAPTER 2

I DANGLED MY hands to the sides of my chair and stared up at the beige ceiling. My gum popped as I chomped it, taking out my boredom on the watermelon Bubblicious.

"Reagan, we got something."

I turned my head without raising it from the back of my chair. I wasn't even slouching at this point—I was trying to lie down without actually dropping to the floor.

Clarissa, the healing witch employed by the Magical Law Enforcement office, or MLE, filled the entryway of my cube. Her frizzy blond hair had long since escaped the bun in which she'd tried to contain it. "We got something. Wanna come?"

"What is it?" I asked, my tone flat.

Her blue eyes blinked within black-framed glasses. She grinned and shook the sheet of paper clutched in her hand. "A partial beheading. They have no idea who did it."

A jolt of fire ran up my spine, but I didn't let it push

me to sitting. Not yet. I'd been fooled one too many times by promises of magical mayhem wrapped in mystery, only to arrive on scene and discover the MLE agent had embellished the situation. More often than not, it would take all of fifteen minutes to solve the case, and then I'd have to loiter off to the side while the agent did paperwork. It was annoying, especially when the car ride was long and the agent was unnecessarily chatty. Like Clarissa.

Using the papers that Darius, the vampire whom I'd worked a case with a while ago, had made, saying I was a legal—though completely fictitious—person, I'd gotten a full-time job in the MLE office as a peacekeeper. I'd figured I would be out running around, dodging spells and fighting for my life.

Instead, I sat in this boring cube with a mountain of paperwork and an uncomfortable chair. Occasionally I got to get out of the office, sure, but we were encouraged to use our words to pacify the situations, not our fists.

What did I know about using words? That wasn't my style at all.

What a bunch of hooey.

If it weren't for the regular paycheck, which kept me from dipping into the stash of cash I'd earned from completing the job for Darius, I would've walked away by now.

Well, that, and getting my chance to show up Garret the douche, the single most annoying peacekeeper in the MLE. It was going to happen. I wanted to be the rightful king of the office, the agent everyone thought was the best.

I just needed that chance.

"Who was beheaded?" I asked, watching Clarissa for signs of lying. She was a wily one when she wanted someone else to do her work.

"An older witch. The human police on scene thought it might've been done by a sword."

"What else?"

She hesitated. "What do you mean?"

"What else is there to the case? A sword attack is pretty tame. Was the victim held by a hook in his navel over a simmering pot of mysterious potion or something?"

Things I'd learned about myself during the two months on the job: I got really gruesome when routinely bored.

"Or maybe the aggressor is still on scene somewhere, waiting to strike again?" I continued. "Because that could be a good time."

"Psycho." My annoying coworker Garret's voice carried through the gray cube wall separating our desks. It was my boss Captain Lox's terrible humor to put our desks so close together.

My hands curled into fists despite my best efforts to remain calm. "I wasn't talking to you, Garret."

"Good. I don't want your crazy rubbing off on me," he said in an elevated voice. Someone in our cube farm of an office snickered. "You should just shove off. We don't need your kind around here."

"And what kind is that, Garret? Competent?"

"Vampire lovers, that's what kind. You should go back out onto the streets where you belong."

"I am not a vampire lover, you donkey. I am stalked by the buggers. Not my fault."

"Whatever, freak," he said.

"Sticks and stones, Garret. Sticks and stones." I rolled my eyes. "Speaking of sticks, did you take my advice and head to the gym? I worry about you. One wrong move and a leg might crack. Feebleness has a cure, my dear boy. Movement. You should try it."

"I move plenty, or hasn't anyone told you who reigns as king around these parts?"

See? He always had that on me. It instantly invalidated every rebuttal.

"Anyway," Clarissa said in a slightly shaking voice. The office personnel got a little on edge when Garret and I disagreed. Our past was fraught with...incidents. "There isn't any potion or anything, no. But he might've shown signs of struggle."

"Might've?"

"Well, he was sitting in a chair when it happened—"

"Nope," I said, turning my head back toward the ceiling.

"They think it was a magical sword that holds power—"

"Nope," I said again. "I was hired on for the more dangerous, robust cases. This was assigned to you for a reason. It sounds pretty tame. You don't need me."

"C'mon, Reagan, please? It'll take you two seconds to solve the case. It's girls' night out tonight. I don't want to miss it. Do you know how long it's been since I've gotten out of the house without kids? *Please.* I really need this."

I hated sob stories that involved missing a party. They pulled at my heartstrings.

The slide of my boots across the clean desk surface preceded the thunk of them hitting the ground. No clumps of dirt flaked off. Yet another sign that the job was too slow.

I missed my bounty hunter gig.

"You'll come?" Clarissa said, bouncing up and down. Being that she was mid-forties and had birthed a few kids, there was a lot bouncing up and down with her.

"Yeah, sure, but I'm leaving directly after. I'm not going to hang around while you do paperwork."

"Pushover," Garret drawled.

I gritted my teeth, trying to keep a surge of violence at bay. Captain Lox had told me I couldn't physically assault Garret. If I had a problem, I was supposed to take it through the proper channels. That was apparently how offices in the Brink ran, and MLE was trying to do things by the book. This was explained to me after our first "episode." Garret had harassed me (office language for being a dick) shortly after I started working at MLE full-time—he'd said *you've got a big ass*, and I had (understandably) punched him in the mouth, shaking loose a tooth. We'd both had to sit through hours of videos on why each of us had behaved badly. On that occasion, everyone more or less agreed he'd deserved it, but I had been warned that when he *didn't* deserve it, I'd get a red flag in my file. Three red flags, and I'd be fired.

Three flags had come and gone rather quickly. The captain had quietly boosted my flag limit to five.

I was now sitting pretty at four and doing pretty good, if I said so myself. When Garret was absolutely unbearable, I waited until after hours, followed him in the shadows, and *then* punched him in the mouth.

He'd had a lot of trips to the dentist in the last couple months. It hadn't kept him from continuing to badger me.

The hot and sticky air coated my exposed skin the moment we left the cool of the air-conditioned building. I grimaced as I followed Clarissa to her car, and slipped my phone into the leather pouch at my waist. It jostled a bunch of casings filled with spells that were weak and mostly useless. The office kept us stocked up, and even though they weren't great, they were free. I'd keep putting my hand out for free spells, no problem.

"I'll debrief you while we're on the way," Clarissa said after we were in and she'd started up the engine.

"You don't have to. I can just take a look for myself when we get there."

"This one is tricky, though." She gave a little laugh, condescending in nature. It was very mage-like of her. "It has some serious magical elements. The mage work will surely be above your expertise, since, you know, you aren't a mage."

She'd said that before. I didn't bother to argue. It wasted time.

Instead, I stared out at the darkening sky, letting my mind wander as she drove us to the crime site. Being a secret department within the Brink law enforcement, we were often called in after the "real" detectives had taken their pictures, written their notes, and noticed all the little details. All but a select few thought we were psychics and mystics, and even those select few often made a show of rolling their eyes when we came on scene. It was quite the change from the bounty hunter days, let me tell you. There'd been no rolled eyes on that detail, but there'd been plenty of shifty eyes and shiftier perps. Chases had been the norm rather than the exception.

Perp. Since when did I call them that instead of a mark? This job had changed me for the worse. Made me soft. Made me follow rules.

"What was that sound for?" Clarissa asked as we parked beside a patrol car.

"What sound?" I asked, pushing open the door of her old Honda.

"The *yelch* sound. Is it the smell of my car? I've tried to clean it, but I can't find the source."

I was no stranger to the lingering smell of decay that was Clarissa's car. It smelled like a poopy diaper had been dropped between the seats and left to rot. Being that her oldest was beyond diaper-wearing age, I couldn't even speculate what had created the foul odor. But like everyone else familiar with the smell of her car, I knew to religiously breathe through my mouth when getting a ride from her.

"No, it wasn't that. It's nothing," I said, waiting for her to drape her satchel filled with magical supplies over her shoulder.

"Oh good. I *thought* it was getting better. That's great to hear."

I ignored the comment so I wouldn't have to lie.

"You have to leave the weapons in the car. We can't

take those in." She pointed at the sword on my back.

"I have a license to carry." I patted the gun strapped to my leg.

"Okay, but..." She pointed at my sword again. "The license doesn't encompass a sword. I'm pretty sure we're not supposed to carry those."

"I don't see the problem. I'm a nerd. Nerds love swords. Everyone knows that." I tsked and smiled good-naturedly. "We're the weird stepchildren of the police department. They won't question us."

Without waiting for an answer, because I knew they *would* question us if given half a chance, as they had tried in the past, I stalked forward. People got confused with moving targets. One thing was for certain: I did not plan to take off my weapons. Anything could happen, and hopefully would. I didn't want to have to run away because I had nothing to fight with.

A police officer stood in front of an open doorway blocked off with yellow tape. Upon seeing us, he put his hand out. "No one is permitted inside."

"We're the special investigation unit." Clarissa held out a paper badge encased in a canvas slip—the kind with a plastic viewing area and strings that could be worn around the neck. The MLE office wouldn't even splurge for plastic badges; ours were printed via laser jet.

I didn't bother carrying mine. It made me feel ridiculous.

As expected, the policeman rolled his eyes and stepped to the side, lifting the tape marginally. Clarissa bent with stiff joints that seemed older than her years, and struggled to get under the tape.

"Really, guy?" I pushed him aside and pulled the tape off the doorway. "Who raised you, a pack of cavemen? Give her a break."

"Hey!" he said, puffing up and reaching for his cuffs.

"Yes, see how that works out for you." I grinned manically. I could get a new identity, but could he repair his shattered ego after he got beaten up by a girl? I doubted it.

He must've seen the crazy in my eyes: my natural urge for action coiled into a tight ball and straining for release. Wisely, he jerked his head for me to get going.

I saluted him and walked through the doorway, leaving him to worry about the tape.

"I have really stiff joints," Clarissa said apologetically when she stopped in the entryway of the moderately sized house. "The doctor said that dropping some weight and exercising more would help. Easier said than done."

"I hear ya." I took in the surroundings, feeling a light buzz of residual magic. Either someone had done one or more larger spells in the area a while ago, or a lesser-powered spell more recently. From where I was standing, I couldn't tell what kind of spell, or what the magic might've been used for. Hopefully I'd get a better impression once we moved further into the house.

Clarissa scoffed and took two small orbs from her satchel. "You're skinny, young, and eat whatever you want. How do you *hear* me?"

"Theoretically. Are we going to enter this place or what?"

"Yes, just a minute." She pulled out a bay leaf and a baggie of mustard-colored powder, the two fundamentals of a spell used to determine the type of residue magic left at a crime scene. It was MLE office issued, and seemed to work pretty well for all power levels.

"Okay, here we go." She straightened out and walked forward with her head held high, seemingly confident. Halfway through the dim interior, she turned left within the sitting room filled with older-style furniture, heading for another doorway.

I stalled. The residual magic was a little stronger in this area. I moved through the space, feeling the hum with outstretched fingers. I didn't need a handful of spices to tell me what had happened here. I just needed to pay attention, both to the magic and to people who might notice this rare trait of mine. Feeling the magic in spells wasn't an unheard-of talent, but only extremely powerful mages were capable of it. I didn't need meddlesome questions that I didn't plan on answering. *More* meddlesome questions, I should say.

A spell blanketed half the room. From what I could gather, it was a searching spell. But what was it looking for?

I hastened to catch up with Clarissa, who'd already stepped through a sliding double door, only one side open. Tangerine light glowed in the living room beyond. When I followed her, I found the body sitting in a chair facing a blank, boxy TV, his head leaning unnaturally to the side and blood all down his front and shoulder. His mouth hung open and his eyes only showed the whites. Residual magic thrummed through my veins, revealing its secrets.

Clarissa spoke to a detective I half recognized as the main contact point between our department and the normal human one. He was *in the know* as to what we really were. I suspected that was why I hadn't witnessed him rolling his eyes. Although I hadn't been in his company much, so maybe I'd just missed it.

Another detective, a younger guy, stood off to the side, glowering at Clarissa. As soon as he noticed me, his scowl swung my way. He clearly *didn't* know our real function, and probably wanted that fake magical whack job (Clarissa) and her ridiculously dressed cosplay friend (me) to *adios*. He had real work to do, damn it!

I did love putting words into the detectives' mouths. After all, their expressions were pretty clear tells.

I stepped closer to the body.

"No." The younger detective's hand firmly wrapped around my upper arm. "We can't have you tampering with the evidence."

Somewhere in his later twenties or lower thirties—I wasn't great with identifying ages—he was an attractive man spoiled by a patronizing smirk. I squared off with him. "I've seen more dead bodies than you can possibly imagine. Back off. I know what not to touch."

I'd never been very good at staying professional when I needed someone to back off. At least I stopped myself from saying I'd *created* more dead bodies than he could possibly imagine. Though, in my defense, they usually weren't human, and if they were, they deserved it.

"J.M., let her take a look," the head detective said. That was why we were there, after all.

I brushed by and leaned over the body, noticing the marks on the older man's neck. "A sword makes sense," I said, pointing at the wound. "Someone used more than one strike. He was hacked at with a dulled sword. Maybe rusty, maybe not. If you let your sword go that dull, you aren't taking care of it. Attacked in anger, I'd bet. Passion. Not romantic passion, but the perp was possibly a loved one of some kind."

I pulled my sword from its sheath without thinking, and certainly without warning anyone first.

"Whoa, whoa, whoa." J.M. held up his hands. "What's going—"

"Let her work," the head detective barked.

Huh. This was the first time one of the human police had let me wave my very pretty, though very deadly, sword around. I might grow to like this guy.

I didn't wait for him to take the directive back. Sword in two hands, I went through the motions of chopping at the guy's neck. Then switched to one hand to see how my body positioning, and the sword positioning, might change.

"Two-handed, definitely," I said. "Two-handed, and the person swinging the hardware wasn't very strong. A woman would be my guess, but maybe a scrawny guy."

"What gives you that impression?" J.M. asked, bracing his hands on his hips. The lead detective had a notepad out.

"I mean, look at the hacking she had to do to *nearly* behead him." I mimed the motions. "There's all this torn skin around the wound." I mimed the attack a little more and then stepped to the side, getting a better angle and more power. "Yes, look, she must've ended up here. She kept her distance—she didn't bend over the guy and create downward cuts. That says woman to me. Women know they can be overpowered by a man, in general, so as a rule they keep their distance. Men just go forth. I could be wrong." I shrugged. I wasn't one of those women, so this was all guesswork.

"But that guy looks like he just sat there and took it." J.M. gestured at the body, arms rested on the armrests and feet on the floor like anyone sitting in a recliner watching TV.

I glanced back at the lead detective. "I have some theories, but they are in the realm of divinity and crystal balls." I sounded absurd, but that should get the point across. It was time to talk magic.

"J.M., I got this," the lead detective said to the younger guy. "We're looking for a sword. Search the house again and talk to the neighbors."

"But I—"

With a *look* from the lead detective, J.M. pinned me with a flat stare before turning and stalking from the room.

"He's not ready to know what I know," the lead detective said quietly. "Hopefully someday, because he is driven and intelligent, but right now, he's too hotheaded for his own good."

I nodded politely, which was miraculous, because not only did I not care, but it was also quitting time and I wanted to go home.

"Right," I said to get the show on the road. I sheathed my sword and glanced at Clarissa. "Hey, I think there was a spell used in the sitting room." I gestured that way. "Can you check that out while I talk to him?"

"How do you know there was a spell?" she asked, confused.

"I, uh..." I dug in the leather pouch wrapped around my middle. As I did so, I felt my phone vibrate. Tilting it toward me, I saw an unfamiliar number.

I pushed the button to still the phone and held up an empty casing for Clarissa to see. "I used a spell that I got...from a friend."

Clarissa's brow furrowed and her head tilted. "I've never heard of a spell that can determine if magic was used."

"You do it."

She held up her bay leaf and baggie of powder. "Like this, yes. It takes time and practice. You can't encase this type of spell. It doesn't work that way." She narrowed her eyes at me. "Are you trying experimental magic? Because you do know that is forbidden in our line of work, don't you?"

I tried to look sheepish. It was as difficult as sounding polite. "Sorry. I'd used one before and it worked, so I figured, you know, the homeowner was already dead, so..."

She rolled her eyes. "That's not how we do things, Reagan. Let me see it." I moved to hand over the empty casing. She dodged the offering. "No, I meant, let me see a loaded shell."

"Oh. I don't have any more. This was my last one."

Her expression turned disbelieving. And it should've. When someone said it was their last piece of gum, how often was that legit? Rarely.

"Ladies," the lead detective said. "Can we get moving?"

"Sorry. Yes. Reagan, I'll talk to you about it later." Clarissa sniffed, turned up her nose, and walked from the room.

"Effective," I muttered, putting away the empty casing and letting my palm hover near the wound.

"You're a terrible liar."

"Note to self: do not lie to the lead detective."

"You can call me Sean."

"Right. Sean." I'd totally forget. I already knew it. Then next time I met him, it would be awkward because I'd have to ask for his name again, and he would undoubtedly remember mine. I hated the black hole in my memory that always swallowed names. "Okay, Sean," I said, trying to use his name as often as possible in hopes it would stick. "Let's get freaky, shall we?"

"What's that?" he asked, taken aback.

"Magic, man," I said quietly. I didn't want Clarissa to hear, and Sean wouldn't know how rare my abilities were. "Get ready to write things down."

I felt my phone vibrate again. Trying not to let it distract me, I focused on the magical hum of the body's neck, then moved closer so I could feel that of the drying blood on his clothes. Finally, I used two hands to feel the pulse from around the chair, including where the body's hands rested.

"How long ago did this happen?" I asked.

"Three hours. At first we didn't know it was magical in nature, or we would've called you sooner."

"What tipped you off?"

"The sword. Normal people don't walk around hacking people's necks with swords."

"You're not from New Orleans, are you?"

"No." He shifted. If I hadn't known better, I'd have said he was uncomfortable. "Seattle. Why? Is it the West Coast accent?"

"All kinds of crazy stuff goes down in New Orleans..." Dang it! What had he said his name—

"Sean!" I smiled in triumph. Moving on. "A sword doesn't make it magical."

"It did in this case."

"Touché." I backed away and started wandering around the room, feeling the same type of spell blanket as in the sitting room. "You're looking for a mage. Someone moderate to high in power. These spells all have the same beat, so I'd bet they were all done by her. Or him—I'm still not sure about the sex. That mage doesn't use a sword often, I'll tell you that much, and the weapon was older, but it was most likely hers. She wouldn't commit murder with a loaner, and a new one would be sharp. She's been doing magic for a while, which means she'll be at least, the very least, mid-thirties. I'd bet forties or greater, though, judging by the intricacies of the spell. She's had time to work on her craft."

"His daughter?"

I glanced at the older man sitting dead in the chair, probably mid- to late seventies. "That was a jump, but...could be."

Sean pointed at a framed picture on the mantel of the man, an older woman who was probably his wife, and a younger woman who didn't look like either of them.

"Maybe, I don't know. I'm just giving you the facts. Anyway, she did a spell to keep him in place. See his hands? They were clawing at the chair, but his arms clearly couldn't move. His legs couldn't either. He was magically pinned to this chair. Usually holding some-one like that is done for information. She was definitely looking for something in this house. The blanket spell in the sitting room, and here in the living room, points to that.

"If I'm wrong about looking for something, though, then she was giving threats. Except you don't chop at someone's neck to deliver a warning. That's just stupid. She probably would have beaten him if that was her aim, and there's no sign of that."

"Can't a person kill with magic?"

"Absolutely. Which is why I think this was done out of anger, or passion of some kind. She is powerful enough, and knowledgeable enough, to kill with magic. But instead, she hacked away at his neck." My phone vibrated again. I gritted my teeth. "The last thing, and then I'll leave you to your deductions"—so I could yell at whoever was repeatedly bothering me—"is that blanket spell. A treasure hunt, perhaps. Looking for—"

"I know what she was doing in there!" Clarissa emerged from the sitting room. Her eyes twinkled. "The perpetrator was trying to find something."

"What do you think that might be?" Sean asked her.

Leaving them to chat, I wandered into the kitchen. No magic. Jogging now, I headed into a back bedroom. The searching spell was even thicker in here. Headier. She'd used more power, probably suspecting this was where her treasure was hidden.

Just real quick, because my curiosity was burning, I did a look-n-see, immediately finding the disturbed closet. She'd torn the thing apart. There was no way to tell if she'd found what she was looking for.

Back in the living room, I took out my phone. An *SOS 911* message, signed Smokey—how did he get my number?—a voicemail, and a text message from the captain. *Call ASAP. We got a nasty one. I need the whole team on this one.*

"Oh it's happening," I said with a surge of excitement. "I'm finally going head to head with Garret."

"What's the matter?" Clarissa asked, the triumph over her discovery melting away.

I hooked a thumb over my shoulder. "The perp might've found what she was looking for in the closet in the bedroom. Or maybe it was supposed to be there and wasn't. I don't know, but I gotta go. We got something. Something big. Garret better step aside—a new king is in town."

"Wait a minute, Ms. Somerset. I have a few questions." Sean took a step toward me.

"I was just helping out," I said as I tapped into voicemail. "Clarissa knows what's up. She can hold the fort."

"I have to go, too." Clarissa's face turned white as she held her phone to her ear. "Dear God. There is an *aswang* in the city."

CHAPTER 3

"W HAT'S AN *ASWANG*?" I asked as I led Clarissa out of the house. Adrenaline spiked in my blood.

"It's a type of...demon, I guess you could call it, from Filipino lore. Not a true demon, like from the underworld, but...evil. Filipinos think of it as evil. I only know about the creatures from books. I've never actually seen one. They are immensely powerful, and eat babies and the organs of adults."

"Holy crap, they eat babies? That's messed up." I grimaced. "Well then, that is definitely a green light to kill it. Right? I can kill it?"

"You've just seen the horror of violence in action, and you're eager to go kill something?"

"Is that a trick question? Because I feel like you should know the answer to that based on my personality..."

"Fine. Whatever. Okay, so you'll be going into the heat of battle. That's your job. You signed on to be the front line—"

"I'm not complaining," I said, patting my gun. "I'm in it to win it."

"You're worrying me."

"Wise. What should I expect?" Not that it really mattered. I'd run right at the beastie with a snarl turned smile regardless of how vile it was. That was what I did. It was what I excelled at.

Hell, it was why MLE had hired me. We both climbed into the car.

"If we are being called, it has tried to feed. They like intestines the best, I've read, and will move from person to person if they have the option, getting their fill. They like preying on the weak."

She leveled me with a serious look from behind the wheel. "They are hard to kill, Reagan. You have to stab it in the back with a sword."

"How is that hard to kill? Sounds pretty easy to me."

"Not as easy as you'd think. They can shape-shift. Some might look like large wolves. Others might turn into a flock of birds. They travel extremely quickly, almost as fast as a vampire, I've read. And they spook easily, taking flight or running when they think they're outnumbered or can't get an easy feed."

"Got it. I need to be quick like a bunny, so I can stick a sword in the creature's back before it flies away."

She blew out a frustrated breath and checked her phone. A glance at the address told me we were headed into the heart of the French Quarter. Talk about easy prey. Get a drunk person, of which there were a great many, on their own, and the creature could have its fill.

"If it bites or scratches you while in its humanoid form," Clarissa continued, stepping on the gas, "you'll die if I don't get to you fast enough. They kill really easily."

I doubted it. I was absolved from most evil, especially the demon variety. Daddy Dearest had given me a lot of his powerful gifts. Not like I could tell her that. I'd just have to hide any wounds I took until they healed over.

"Okay, then. Don't get killed, move quickly, and kill the thing." I nodded decisively and entwined my fingers in my lap. The adrenaline pulsed in my blood now, something that would make me as fast as a vampire, increase my strength, and keep me moving. I was made for action, not a cubicle.

"You really are crazy," she muttered. "Or ignorant of the extreme danger you're about to face."

"Neither. I'm just good at my job." And a different breed—literally—than the others in the MLE office.

In the French Quarter, she tried to navigate around the milling crowds, jeering and laughing as they swigged drinks and slung beads.

"It'll take us forever to get through here," she said, pounding on the wheel.

I fired a quick text message to Smokey. *Working. What's up?*

Almost immediately I got a message back. *Supernatural creature was in cemetery. Eating stomach. Changes into flock of birds. It's gone now, but might come back. Tourist just found it. Cops called.*

"Oh man," I said. "That thing made a stop across the street from my house. That ain't right."

"It did?" Clarissa asked with wide eyes, her gaze dipping to my phone.

"Yeah. This just got personal."

I reached for the door handle.

"What are you doing?" she asked.

"It'll be faster on foot. The captain gave me coordinates."

"But wait, I didn't tell you about—"

I jumped from the car, shut the door behind me, and hit the hood twice, telling her I was clear. I would figure out whatever it was she hadn't told me. Before now, I'd always had very little information when I went in hot. The outcome was usually the same—tag and bag my mark.

I jogged along the sidewalk, weaving in and out of people and keeping my eyes open. Some supernatural creatures could hide in plain sight. Since I hadn't confronted this particular creature before, there was no telling what it might surprise me with.

I crossed Bourbon Street. There were way too many

people there. Instead, I worked toward the slower areas near the sighting. I wasn't actually far from Darius's home in the Brink. Ghost and vampire tours would be meandering around, not to mention people staggering home or heading to their lodgings. For a supernatural, it was a good place for a little dinner.

I turned down a quieter street, dodged a horse and carriage carrying a man explaining French Quarter architecture to two tourists, and slowed. Laughter, a shout, and someone talking too loudly drifted toward me. Shoes scuffed against cement. Someone belched. Welcome to New Orleans, where the party never ended. My kinda town.

I gripped the hilt of my sword and pulled it free, ignoring the surprised expression from a passerby. There was no need of a gun or even magic. If the creature needed a sword to the back, by golly, who was I to say *boo?*

I walked a ways, not hearing anything foreign. No screams. No flocking birds. I typed a message to the captain, asking for new coordinates.

It's MIA. We're hunting, came his reply. So he was on scene as well. That was rare. This thing had to be a doozie.

I did love a challenge.

Bring it in and we'll get you partnered off, he sent. Their whereabouts came next.

"Um...*nope*," I muttered to myself. Working with one of the other agents would only slow me down.

"Dude, have you seen the display?" a passing guy asked me, holding a pink plastic container half filled with a cocktail.

I slowed and gave him my attention. His friend laughed and pointed the way they'd come. "It was gnarly. Seriously. Some guy in a costume went after some other guy. They staged the whole thing so people could see."

"It was awesome!" The first guy, younger twenties and with a shining upper lip from his drink, grinned. "Blood and guts all over the place. You should check it out. They're probably still going."

I saw a cluster of people gathered in front of a doorway down the road, all with wide eyes and open mouths.

Bingo.

"I will, thanks," I said.

"Wait, was that a sword?" I heard one of the guys ask as I broke into a jog.

"Gross," a woman said as I neared, her eyes big and a smile curling her lips. "That's really great makeup."

"It's got to be a costume," another said in a hush.

I stopped beside them, peering into the open doorway protected by a small chain. The sign dangling from it told tourists it was a private residence and not to enter, and warned of a camera watching.

I'd been past this residence a million times, and if the occupants were home, this door was usually open. They liked to be one with the Quarter.

Bad move, it turned out. It had made them easy pickings.

At the back of the room, hunched over a still form lying on its back, was a creature with a leathery torso and muscular legs ending in huge wolf paws. Blood spread along the cream-colored linoleum floor. Pretty gross.

"Well, 'ullo, lovely," I said in a horrible British accent. "'Ave you come for tea?"

The creature's head jerked up, and the crowd jumped as one. Blood dripped from its remarkably human face.

And I thought the vampire monster form was gross, with the swampy look and the claws. This thing was way worse.

"Scatter, you guys," I said to the bystanders around me, slashing the chain with my sword.

"Are you a part of it?" someone asked as the creature straightened up.

"No, but you might be if you hang around." I launched into the room. A chair tumbled as I pushed it out of the way.

The creature lashed out at me. I dodged, letting the

long talons on the ends of its three-fingered hand sail past my face. It screeched like a bird of prey before blasting into a swarm of birds, much too close together to be natural.

"Holy shit," someone exclaimed. "How did he do that?"

"Magic," someone else said as the mass of birds swirled around me, scratching at my head.

I sliced my sword through the air, hitting one or two birds before the swarm rushed through the house. Without delay, I followed, jumping over a couch and seeing an open back door. Maybe it hadn't snuck in through the front after all.

Once outside, I watched it swoop into the air, rolling and swirling, like ink in water, before heading west. I took two fast steps and leapt onto a small storage shed before launching myself onto the wooden fence. I ran along it, my balance perfect in the heat of the moment, before jumping onto a rooftop and taking off across the city after it, using the jammed-together houses as a kind of multileveled sidewalk.

In the distance, barely discernible, I saw the swarm dive downward. The creature didn't plan to go far. Good.

At a gap in houses, I dropped down and ripped out my phone.

"Captain," I said, barely out of breath. "I've got a

sighting. That sucker flies."

"What's your twenty?"

"Heading east. I'm at Ursulines and Dauphine. It touched down four or five blocks away. It turns into a half man...thing, and a half big-legged wolf...thing. That's when it isn't a flock of birds."

"Reagan, if they're old enough, they can change sex at will. They can also adopt a true human form, though usually disfigured. These things start out human. Stay vigilant. I'll meet you there. And whatever you do, don't engage on your own."

No promises.

CHAPTER 4

A CAR HONKED as I darted out in front of it to cross the street. When I hit the sidewalk, a tourist stepped in my path with his hands raised, beads swinging from them. "Show me your tits," he yelled.

I punched him in the throat.

He made a choking sound as his hands fell from the sky. Served him right. I wasn't that kind of girl.

I pushed him out of my way as his friends screamed with laughter.

Idiots.

A deep-throated shout caught my attention. Then another from the east. A lithe and agile wolf ran up ahead. One I recognized. It was a shifter. A real shifter, not an *aswang* turned shifter. They also helped police the Brink, which was what we called the human world, from supernatural creatures.

Boy, hopefully there weren't more of those *aswangs*, because that might get confusing for the poor shifters.

I crossed a grassy area where homeless were gathered. To the right was a collection of jazz bars where my good friend Red, a weak shifter and an excellent source of information, always hung out. Another shout drew me forward, into an area blanketed by darkness. I could see in it just fine, one of my (not as special) traits.

"Don't go that way," a homeless man said in a scratchy voice. "They got trouble up that way."

A surge of adrenaline had me pushing faster. "Thanks," I said, not heeding his words.

After another half-dozen steps, I saw a body crouching with his hands held out. Getting closer, I realized it was the captain, his attention focused on a space between a house and a fence.

I stopped in front of the house. "Hey," I whispered.

He started, and something in his hands crackled. He blew out a breath and cocked his head, looking at his fists. When no magic issued forth, he glanced my way. He pursed his lips like he was saying *shhhhhh.* He jerked his head toward the space he'd been focusing on a moment before.

I eased my head around the corner, where there was similar tableau to the horror show in the Bourbon Street house. Another poor sap had had his number drawn. He was a big guy, too. As for the creature, this time the torso was a woman's, still leathery. The bottom half looked the same. It was sucking an intestine like it was a piece of spaghetti.

Wow. That was one of the grossest things I'd seen in

a long time. It was the stuff of nightmares.

"What's the plan?" I asked softly.

"We're trying to get in position. We're still waiting on a few of our people." Nodding toward the walkie-talkie attached to the side of his belt, he said, "Take this. It's for you. I have my earpiece in."

I glanced at the space between the house and fence, then darted to the captain's side of the space and grabbed the walkie-talkie. It went into my pouch, since I couldn't very well hold it while fighting. Unfortunately, my pouch was only so big, and the bulky, out-of-date equipment made it hard to close.

"Do you have the entrapment spell?" he whispered.

Probably. I had no idea. I wasn't good at keeping track of that stuff, since I rarely used it. I nodded anyway.

"Get it out. On my mark, we'll all throw it at the thing. It's the only way to prevent it from getting away."

I made no move to dig through my overburdened pouch. It would make too much noise and take too long. "Why don't we just kill it? I can sneak in there and get it done. The trick is not announcing your presence before you lunge at it. Lesson learned." I winked to show I'd learned my lesson after the last hiccup.

"This is too dangerous, Reagan. One swipe and you're done. We wait and do it as a team. The others should be in position soon."

That creature probably wouldn't be there long enough for this crew to get into position—I knew how slowly they worked—and we couldn't let it get away. The thing had taken out at least two people, possibly three if it had found someone in the cemetery. Besides, I was much too impatient for those shenanigans. "Okay, here's a better idea. You guys get ready. I'll run in there. If I don't kill it by the time you're up and running, you trap it. *Then* I'll kill it. Good?"

"Reagan—"

His tone said he was going to say no, so I got moving before I could hear the order to stay put. The trick was, you couldn't get into trouble if you didn't hear the command.

Hopefully. It was worth a shot, anyway.

I ran around the house until I found a way onto the roof. I broke a shutter, but I got up there. I'd need to remember to leave a note.

On top of the abnormally steep incline, I made my way to the side of the building where the creature was still feasting. Once there, I looked down at it, hunched over its prey like a fat guy at a buffet. Good gracious, what a mess it was making. It was really going to town.

A muffled voice sounded from my pouch. The creature jerked up and looked around.

Crap!

I backed away from the edge before the creature

could see me, quickly took out the walkie-talkie, then threw it as hard as I could. The distant racket of plastic and metal breaking apart a ways away melted into the sounds of the city. Back at the edge of the roof, I watched while the creature continued its look around and then dove back into its main course.

The walkie-talkie chatter probably meant they were in position. Hopefully, because this was about to kick off in a big way.

I'd sheathed my sword before climbing the roof, and it would have to stay there for now. If I climbed down one-handed, I'd risk falling on my head, and jumping from this height with such a steep incline would probably have the same effect. Knocking oneself out was not the first step to winning a fight.

I gripped the edge of the roof with my fingers, hurled myself over, and then hit the side of the building with my feet and pushed off. I spun in the air like a cat and landed with a bounce-step. Sticking the landing would've been cooler, but I definitely got style points.

The creature jerked up again, a screech gurgling through the blood in its mouth.

You are the worst!

I didn't want to risk saying it out loud in case the thing burst into the flock of birds. I probably didn't have long as it was.

I ripped out my sword and lunged forward.

The creature straightened and swiped. I met its two-fingered hand with my blade, lopping it off.

"Killing those birds took out part of your body, huh?" I said, dodging a swipe from its other hand. "Good to know." I stabbed forward, getting the side of its stomach.

It screeched again and turned away, its form going blurry. It was about to change.

"Trap it," I yelled, jumping at it. I sliced downward, catching its shoulder. A talon scraped my leather pants as the creature howled and twisted.

I jumped up and wrapped my legs around its neck, then ripped my body to the side and around. Its neck cracked. I let go with my legs and fell to all fours. My sword clattered away.

The creature's head at an unnatural angle, it came at me, its good arm swinging. Its human face shifted into the glower of a grotesque monster with huge fangs. I'd gone and pissed it off.

"Holy beekeepers, what *don't* you turn into?" I rolled to the side and grabbed my sword as magic buzzed around us.

"Get out of there, Reagan, we've got it," Garret yelled from atop the fence behind me.

I dodged a foot trying to smash me as the creature righted its head. "Fast healing. Dang it. I don't like this thing very much. At least it's mostly slow."

"No, you're just damn fast," the captain called. "Get clear."

"You're blocking my catch!" Garret threw a casing. A spell erupted out of it and blocked off the thing's upward escape. Another burst of magic materialized, putting up a wall. Then another, a second wall.

"This is mine," I said, trying to get around the thing and stab it without also tearing down the spells with my magic-filled sword.

"Get clear, then put up your wall," the captain yelled.

"I don't have that spell handy," I said through gritted teeth.

The thing realized what was happening. Its edges went blurry again as it paused, changing. *Hello, weakness.*

I took a quick step forward and stabbed. My blade sank into its mid-back.

The *aswang* howled in anguish. It writhed, folding in on itself before turning back to face me. Its jaws opened, inhumanly distended, issuing forth a growling gurgle. I had no idea what was happening, but its breath could put Clarissa's car to absolute shame. I nearly passed out from the fumes.

Garret yelled my name. Before I could take another step back to get clear of the stench, something small and black worked out of the creature's mouth. Almost like a wisp of smoke, a little bird flapped my way. I brought up my sword to kill the magic, an easy feat, since it was moving so slowly, but without warning, a green fireball blasted into the space between the creature and me.

Weak magic that seemed to come from Garret, but strong enough to somewhat damage normal human skin, it raked across my face and ate away my eyebrows. Luckily, I wasn't a normal human, and soaked in the delicious heat, feeling the burn deep inside of me, my own special magic answering the fire's call. When it had died away, I saw that the little bird was gone.

Survival mode kicking in—I'd need to explain why the green fire hadn't burned me—I yanked at my pouch's zipper, grabbed an empty casing at random, pinched it, and only then realized it wasn't actually empty.

Donkey balls!

I threw it away from me, no idea what it was in my haste.

Another wall went up, the same spell the others had used. Hopefully no one would notice it had happened after the fact.

I staggered away and dug around for an empty casing. Clearly putting my hand out for all those free spells hadn't been a good idea after all. Hindsight.

I put my hand to my face, racking my brain for an excuse I could give for being unharmed. That magical fire had killed the little bird, so it should have been plenty strong to blister my face. People couldn't know my skin was fireproof. That kind of thing raised eyebrows.

Not on me, of course, since I no longer had any, thanks to Garret. It was a good thing Callie, my mage friend, was so good at regrowing them.

"Reagan," the captain said as he ran up, out of breath.

The creature writhed on the ground before crumbling to ash. So it was definitely dead, then.

"Are you okay?" Captain Lox gripped my shoulders and peered into my eyes. His brow furrowed as his gaze roamed my face.

"I used a spell to ward away the fire," I blurted.

The furrow deepened.

Now on to important matters. "That kill went to me, right?" I asked. "That was mine, not Garret's? I was the one who stabbed it."

"Yes," the captain said, releasing me and taking a step back, his confusion still evident. "You killed it. But without us, you probably wouldn't have, so you'll only get a fraction of the bonus. The rest will be divided."

I waved that away. "Divide the whole bonus; I don't care. I just want it in the books that I got this kill. Over Garret."

"It will be." The captain nodded.

"And my name will go in the books as saving Reagan's life," Garret said, sliding down the fence and hitting the ground too hard. He staggered and wind-milled his hands, just managing to stay on his feet.

Dang.

He stalked over, all swagger and ego. A smug smile graced his pointy face. "You're welcome."

"Wait...what?" I asked, cold dripping down my middle.

"An *aswang* transfers its evil by issuing forth a tiny black bird," the captain explained, writing something in his book. That had better not be Garret's name under the title *Reagan Savior*! "That bird nearly made it to you. Had it succeeded, it would've forced its way into your mouth or eye and turned you into one of its kind. It's not a real bird, obviously, but magic. You would've transformed, and we would've had to kill you. Speaking of"—he pointed at my leg with the jagged end of his pencil—"it didn't scratch you, did it? I don't see a hole in your pants."

"No, it didn't scratch me." I shook my head. "I was just about to kill that bird thing with my sword. I wouldn't have ingested it. That doesn't count. Garret, of all people, did *not* save my life."

"Not even a magical sword can cut through that type of magic," the captain said without inflection.

I opened my mouth to tell him that *my* type of magic, which was stored in the sword, surely would have cut through that bird thing. It could cut through anything, especially dark, underworld-type magic. I *was* underworld-type magic.

No words came out.

There was absolutely no way I could admit to any of that. Nor could I tell the captain that if the bird thing *had* infected me, its evil wouldn't have taken root. I'd had plenty of experience casting demons out of my body. It was part of my lineage—a lineage I couldn't share with anyone unless I wanted to enslave myself to the land below.

No, I couldn't tell the captain, but I really, really wanted to. This sucked so hard.

"You were right there without the means to kill it," Garret said, grinding the point home, standing beside me with his chest puffed out in triumph. "It would've turned you into one of its kind. I've seen it happen. It's immediate and not pretty. Face it, I saved your life. And what do I get for saving your life?"

"Don't be a putz, Garret," the captain said without inflection.

"That's right, I get a bonus. And honors. And a write-up in our newsletter." Garret smiled and hooked his thumbs into his belt loops. "I'm a hero. Hail to the king."

My hands curled into fists. He had me. And now, in

the eyes of the office, I was indebted to him.

"You're welcome," he said, flicking my last nerve with his smug, douchey smile.

Before my mind caught up with my body, my fist hit his nose. The *crack* made everyone blink in surprise. He staggered back and reached for his face. A moment later, blood gushed over his lips.

"Oops," I said. I meant it.

"That's a red flag," the captain said nonchalantly, not looking up.

I sighed. That fifth red flag had probably been inevitable. I clearly wasn't cut out for a routine-driven, normal life.

Clarissa hastened up, out of breath and clutching her satchel. "Reagan, are you hurt? Did it scratch you?"

"It scratched her leather pants. It didn't pierce them." Captain Lox closed his book and finally looked up. "I've half a mind to have everyone wear leather. It's a good idea."

"Maybe tum'one s'uld ass her why her face isn't fried," Garret said through his fingers, his eyes watering and half closed.

"Why her face isn't fried?" Clarissa asked, squinting at him. "Is that what you said? Let me see your nose."

"Reagan got blasted in the face with magical fire when Garret burned the *aswang's* transformation bird," the captain said, looking at the ashes on the ground.

"Oh my gosh!" Clarissa's hand drifted to her chest. "Oh thank God, Garret. Quick thinking. I didn't have a chance to tell her about that. She would've been a goner for sure. Oh wow, that must've been a close one."

My nails dug into my palms.

"But…" Clarissa studied my face. "Oh, I see, your eyebrows are gone. But your face doesn't look blistered or burned in any way. Was the spell old? It must've created a decent amount of heat if it burned your eyebrows. I'd think you'd have light blistering, at the very least. I can heal that, of course."

"Oh. Uh…" I shrugged. Time to lie. "A cousin made a fire-retardant spell. You know, *that* cousin. The one I mentioned when I helped you with the case earlier today. He lives in Canada." They couldn't possibly know I had no living relatives. Except my dad, but he didn't count.

"Da one you lost yer birginity to?" Garret asked. He wheezed out a laugh, still holding his face.

"Do you want a broken limb to accessorize with that nose?" I asked him. "But yeah, turns out the spell works on skin but not hair. I'll, uh…have to tell him that."

"I thought we had an understanding about experimental magic," Clarissa said with disapproval.

"It saved my life, didn't it?" I turned toward home.

"No, *I* taved yer life," Garret yelled after me.

I was walking away when Garret asked Clarissa to

see to his nose. Other MLE staffers were showing up as I exited the little side alley. Their response time was terrible. If I hadn't acted when I did, prompting the captain and Garret to act with me, the creature would be long gone.

Something that would be overshadowed by Garret's assumed heroics. What joy was mine...

Now to deal with Smokey. If he'd seen what I had, which was likely, given the text message and his many calls, he might be a little frantic. Not to mention that if he was dumb enough to talk to the cops, he might need to be bailed out. It was the day that wouldn't end.

CHAPTER 5

I COULD FINALLY afford a car, but I still hadn't gotten around to buying one. Instead, I took cabs or one of the rideshare services that were like cabs, only nicer.

One of those services, Lyft, dropped me off down the street from my house so I could check in with the local neighborhood watch, which consisted of Smokey, No Good Mikey, and occasionally ex-boxer Mince.

It didn't take long for Smokey to come hustling my way, his face drained of color and a trickle of blood down his neck.

Alarm rolled through me. I picked up my pace, yelling out, "It didn't scratch you, did it?"

"Reagan," he said as he neared, out of breath. "Thank God. That thing was disgusting. I didn't get pictures, but I can describe it in detail. Where are your eyebrows?"

"They flew away with that creature you probably saw. Did it scratch you?" I pointed at the line of blood originating from a small dot on his neck.

He absently brushed at his skin. "No. Some idiot

mugger thought I had money. But the bird claws scraped at me. They didn't draw blood, but I felt them. Why? Is that bad?" He pushed in closer and stuck his cheek out for inspection.

"If you're still alive, you're probably fine."

"Wait," he said, shadowing me down the street toward my house. "There are a bunch of police down there. Maybe you should sneak in through the back. I've been avoiding them."

I shrugged. "I'm not worried about police. I don't have anything on me they'd be concerned about."

"Except your gun."

"I have a license." Illegally obtained, but nonetheless real, just like the papers that had legitimized me in the supernatural world.

Darius was nothing if not thorough.

"The sword?"

"I'll say it's a *Lord of the Rings* sword. No one questions extreme nerd-dom. It's crazy without equal."

"*You* are crazy without equal."

He had a point there.

"Fine," he said, slouching beside me. "So anyway, first I saw a huge bunch of birds. Little black birds." He cleared his shaking voice. "Wait. Let me just start from the beginning."

I listened as I closed the distance to my house. Once there, I leaned against the railing beside the two steps that led up to my porch while looking at the cemetery opposite us. In a normal neighborhood, there'd probably be a cluster of people hanging out around the cemetery gates, trying to peek in and see what had happened. Not in this neighborhood. People minded their own business where cops were concerned.

Glairing lights glowed from behind the stone wall. Yellow police tape crossed off the opening, and I could just see someone within standing sentry.

"Did you tell the cops what you saw?" I asked Smokey.

"No way. How could I? First they'd want to know why I felt it was my duty to police the cemetery. Then they'd want to know how come I couldn't ID the killer. To the first question, I couldn't very well tell them that I was on the lookout for witches or other supernaturals. And the last…well, we both know I'd sound insane. I haven't even told Mikey. I don't know what to tell him, other than that something is going on in the cemetery and you know what it is. Sorry that I had to throw you under the bus, but…"

"It's fine. So you didn't talk to the cops at all?"

"No. I don't do well when questioned."

"Good." I sighed and rubbed my eyes. I was tired and hungry. "Well, I killed that thing, so you're good. It won't be coming back. But if you see birds like that again, get to cover, or get to where there are more people. It tends to pick off the loners, apparently."

"I got really lucky, Reagan. Really lucky. It's made me question…" He hesitated for a moment. "I've been thinking about moving out of this neighborhood. Vampires are one thing, but stuff like this…"

I patted his bony shoulder. "That thing killed two people in the French Quarter. Trust me when I say that of all the neighborhoods in New Orleans, you're probably safest in this one."

"Why is that?"

"Because I live here." I patted him again and turned toward my house as a white Crown Victoria pulled up alongside the cemetery. I glimpsed the man getting out of the passenger side, did a double take, and then noticed the driver, who was stepping out of the other side of the car.

Damn it.

"Get gone," I said to Smokey.

He didn't need to be told twice. He was slinking away even as the younger detective, whose name was lost to the black hole, crossed the street.

"Long time no see," the younger detective said with a smile. He was a handsome devil and he knew it. That cocky grin of his slipped when he stepped up onto the sidewalk next to me. "What happened to your eyebrows?"

I ignored his question. "You guys here to look at the

murder?" I pointed at the cemetery as Sean crossed the street after him.

Suspicion crossed the younger detective's face. "Yeah. What do you know about it?"

"My department ended the threat not that long ago," I said, taking a seat on my porch steps. "There were two more victims in the French Quarter. I bet you'll get the call soon."

"Your department ended the threat?" he asked. "Aren't you guys psychics?"

"Yeah. We consulted our crystal balls, so we knew just when to drop the piano out of the window." I clapped my hands together. "Splat."

"They think it's a serial killer," Sean said as the younger detective shifted in confused annoyance. "This was the first. At least, that's what I've heard."

"A serial killer who does fast work. Of the three victims that I know of, yes, this was the first. Before this, though..." I shook my head. "I have no idea. The creature that did it is called an *aswang*. Clarissa gave me the basics after we left your last crime scene. It was old, hungry, and really gross. I have no idea where it might've come from, or what it was doing here."

"Wait." The younger detective held up his hand, blinking repeatedly.

"Is this what you do, then?" I gestured to the young buck without shifting my gaze from Sean. "You just take the new guy around until he finally pieces it together?"

"Piece what together?" the younger detective demanded. I could see his anger boiling just below the surface.

"Never mind, J.M.," Sean said, not sparing him a glance. "Go check in with the others. Get a feel for what happened. We have a lot of ground to cover tonight."

"No, wait. What is it I'm supposed to be piecing together?"

Sean straightened his shoulders and turned to J.M. Something in the older man's bearing read: *Do not mess with me, or I will rip your spine out of your mouth and beat you with it.*

I grinned, because I hadn't expected this type of alpha standoff from Sean. J.M., sure, but not Sean. He seemed too sweet.

I waved the whole thing away. "Let him stay. You might not think he's ready, but it's better to bring people on when they're younger and can bounce back than when they're older and easier to break. Besides, if you're going to keep bringing him around to these kinds of crime scenes, he'll be a target. He should know what he's getting into."

"Okay, this is starting to piss me off," J.M. said in a rough voice. "I want answers, and I want them now!"

Sean turned back toward me slowly, his body taut. I had a feeling the two of them would have more than a few standoffs down the road. J.M. didn't seem the type to blindly do as he was told. It was something we had in common.

"In answer to your question, Reagan," Sean said, taking out his notebook, "yes, we wait until they start piecing things together. There are probably better ways, but I hate sounding as crazy as I feel." He readied his pen. "Do you want to tell me what you know?"

I relayed what I'd heard from Smokey, telling them that he had seen the whole thing, but he shouldn't be questioned by the normal police, for obvious reasons. I made a point of telling them about the bit of blood on his neck, and how it had gotten there, because they'd be sure to notice it. I then went through what I'd seen in the French Quarter, ending with the showdown.

J.M. turned more incredulous as my explanation continued, until he was looking at Sean and me with obvious doubt and disbelief. Also humor. He clearly thought we were pulling his leg.

"At least this case will be easy to put away," I said when I'd finished. "You can get back to the other one."

"You guys can't be serious," J.M. said with a chuckle. "I mean, I've heard about making light of the grisly crimes, but this is ridiculous."

"Go look at the body," Sean said in an even voice. "I'll be right there."

J.M. sighed, then shook his head and turned away.

"It's too early and he's hardheaded," Sean muttered. "He'll resist until the very last."

"You'd be surprised. The body he's about to see is grrr-*oss*! Look up an *aswang*. You'll see."

Sean put his notebook away. "Head to bed. I won't need anything more from your department. I'm sure Captain Lox will have this all written up in the morning."

"Yes, he will. What about that other case? Did you make any headway?"

"In two hours?" Sean smiled and scratched his shoulder, turning sideways on the sidewalk to watch as J.M. ducked under the police tape and headed into the cemetery. "My hunch says it's the daughter. We haven't found the murder weapon yet, but we found a few fibers for the lab to analyze. The crime wasn't calculated, so there are bound to be over a dozen slip-ups. We'll solve it. Thanks, by the way. You're much quicker and more thorough than the rest of the agents at MLE. You'll make captain someday, I have no doubt."

"Good God, that sounds horrible. Don't jinx me." I stood with a grimace. "Besides, I think I'm fired. I punched my weasel of a coworker. That was my last strike."

"What'd he do?"

"He was gloating over saving my life even though he technically didn't. It's the little things."

"Well, good luck with that. I'm sure I can get you a job working on the other side of things if you're interested."

"You guys would certainly frown on the type of work I excel at. Namely, killing things. Thanks, though. And good luck with the young buck." I climbed my steps, threw him a wave, and let myself into my house.

The keys clanked as they tumbled into the bowl by the door. My air freshener was doing its job, filling the entryway with the smell of clean cotton. I glanced at the renovated living room off to the right, which boasted the best furniture money could buy, accentuated with wall decor that must've cost a fortune.

I turned into my totally revamped kitchen, now sporting granite countertops and the latest appliances available. A small, round table made of some sort of barn-looking wood sat in the corner. *Shabby chic*, or so I'd been told by Marie, the extremely elegant vampire who essentially worked for Darius.

The deal I'd made with Darius a couple months ago was that in exchange for helping him bring in the person terrorizing the unicorns, I'd get a boatload of money and a house of my choosing, fully paid for. I could've picked any house, anywhere—a mansion in the Garden District, a chateau in Beverly Hills, the sky was the limit.

Much to Darius's dismay, I'd chosen the one I had

been renting (and had half ruined). Why not? It was plenty big for just me, and it came with a neighborhood watch. You couldn't beat that.

My landlord at the time had seemed intent on resisting the purchase, but he'd undergone a sudden change of heart. Darius was in the habit of getting what he wanted.

I had fully expected to wait for the insurance company to fix it up before I bought it and made it my own, but again, Darius had had other plans. Without my consent, he'd fully renovated the whole place, top to bottom, forcing me to move into a hotel as he did so. Half of the house had been fine, but that hadn't escaped his perfectionist's eye. He'd updated my bedroom and the guest room, and even put in an extension, which ate up half of the backyard. Not to worry, he'd also bought out three-quarters of the backyard from the guy behind me, and pushed my fence back accordingly. I didn't even know that could be done, but I did enjoy the extra space.

Then Marie and her army had come in and gone nuts. I could've had some say in what direction she took, but that lady had more style in her fingernail than a ten-year subscription to *Vogue*. The result? I was living in small-scale luxury in a rough part of town.

I'd expected the vampires to get lost at that point. The terms of our deal had been fulfilled on both sides.

Per the contract, they were supposed to leave me alone. Sure, I'd expected them to check in from time to time to make sure I wasn't spilling the beans about their unicorn secret, or even telling the shifters—their archenemies—everything I knew about vampire habits, but that didn't happen. Instead, they hung around. Constantly. Even if I didn't physically see them for a couple days, there was always evidence they'd come around to check up on me.

I did not appreciate it. Not only was my privacy at stake, but people were starting to think I was a vampire's pet.

I most definitely was *not* a vampire's pet. What did people take me for, insane?

Besides, how many ways could a person say *get lost?* I was pretty sure I'd tried them all. It wasn't my fault they'd taken to hovering around like ghouls.

I flicked on the lights even though I didn't need them to see, and headed toward the fridge. Bracing myself, I opened the door and immediately squinted. The thing was like the inside of a disco ball. Bright white light assaulted me from a few different places within the well-stocked interior. Blue shone at the back, letting me know the filter was in fine working order.

Not like I would need to change it. The second it was out, it would be changed for me. If I ate all the cheese? New, expensive cheese would show up the next night. Cleaning the fridge? Done for me. Cleaning the rest of the house? Taken care of when I wasn't home.

Yes, the vampire presence in my house was pretty obvious. I was living with an army of invisible butlers. And while that sounded super cool, and might've been a lifelong dream once upon a time, I also knew they were reporting my every move to their master. Darius. The most persistent, overbearing vampire I'd ever met. He treated me like we were bonded and I was fragile, even though no way were we bonded, and I certainly wasn't fragile. He acted like he was still under orders from Vlad (elder vampire supreme) to protect and look after me, and he did it with the diligence and the attention to detail that had kept him alive through so many troubled periods throughout history.

Did I mention I'd tried to bar the door? Didn't matter. With their "breaking and entering" magic, as I called it, they could undo any lock I tried to use, then waltz in against my wishes, rearrange everything, look through my stuff, stock my fridge, and wash, fold, and put away my undies. My undies!

Did I say overbearing? I meant suffocating.

Had I paid for the service, okay, but he was doing this after I'd expressly asked him to leave me alone. To give me some space. To stop trying to break into my magically protected closet and poke through my stuff, for criminy sakes!

"Reagan, part of protecting you is to protect you from yourself. I just want to know what it is you are hiding," he'd said.

I'd tried to punch him, but he was danged fast. Instead, I'd said, "Fat chance," slammed the door in his face, locked it, and pretended I didn't hear him unlock it immediately after. Then chuckled darkly.

That vampire was tap-dancing on my last nerve.

What was nuts was that his actions were not standard operating procedure for vampires. I'd asked around. Even people who were bonded, which basically meant they shared a special link with a vampire, didn't get this kind of attentiveness.

The only thing I could figure was that Darius was trying to put me in a gilded cage. He knew what I was, which meant he also knew I was his meal ticket to becoming the most powerful vampire in the world. He probably thought all the help and gifts would keep me happy, which would keep me put.

He didn't know me very well.

If he made a move on me, I'd kill him. I would probably need help, because he was old as hades, and an exceptional adversary, but I had backup. Callie and Dizzy, two high-powered mages, had become my family. They also knew my past, they'd helped hide me when I was a baby, and they knew vampires were not to be trusted. The three of us could get me out of most any bind.

Hopefully. That theory had yet to be tested.

I rubbed my forehead as I stared into the fridge. It had been a long, kind of terrible, day. I took out some high-quality cheese, salami, and grapes. Whoever did the shopping got only the best, and clearly the most expensive, stuff. Not like I could taste the difference. My magic was powerful, but my palate was weak.

From the equally stocked pantry, I grabbed some fresh French bread. After I'd picked out a bottle of wine, a knock sounded on the door.

It was either the cops or Mikey wanting to know what was going on. Maybe even Mince looking to gossip.

I set the full plate onto the counter, flicked on the hall light so I didn't seem weird, and answered the door.

My stomach flipped over and tingles spread across my skin.

Stupid, handsome vampire.

Darius stood at my door in a black button-up shirt that hugged his muscular chest and pulled taut across his broad shoulders. The vee of his upper body led down into trim hips encircled by a black leather belt, holding up formfitting jeans that probably cost as much as some people's rent.

When dealing with normal people for days at a time, I always forgot how incredibly hot Darius was, and how incredibly powerful. He moved with a raw magnetism that entranced the eye. It was probably because I'd taken blood from him once, but his proximity made my body vibrate in worrying ways. If I didn't keep my wits, I was liable to reach out and run my hand up that bumpy torso, or reach around and grab that perfect ass.

Great googly-moogly, I needed to stay away from this vampire. He was decadent sin in a mouth-watering wrapper.

"What's up?" I asked, blocking the doorway.

His eyes roamed my face. "Your eyebrows have gone missing again."

"You've always excelled at observation." Just as I, apparently, excelled at losing my eyebrows.

"Yes. I heard about the *aswang* and, more importantly, Garret allegedly saving your life." He paused, watching my reaction. I was sure he saw what he was looking for. That sore spot might not go away for a while. "I thought you might like some company."

Who was he in contact with at the MLE office, I wondered?

"No. I'm okay," I said. "Thanks, though. I know I've said this before, a few times, but could you please tell…whoever it is that I can do my own shopping and laundry? I'd rather not have someone in here when I'm gone." There. That was a nice-guy approach. I hadn't tried that one yet, maybe.

"Don't be absurd," he scoffed. "Only simpletons perform those duties for themselves. Clear the way. I'll make you dinner."

Nice-guy approach was out. I didn't much like saying *please* to him anyway.

He waited for a moment, clearly thinking I would move of my own volition.

"Seriously, Darius, I'm good," I said, staying firmly rooted in the doorway. "I've already pulled out some stuff for dinner." I pushed the door closed a little more. "Thanks for checking up on me, kinda, but I've handled much worse. As you know."

"Come now. Don't be obtuse." Darius moved faster than thought. One moment he was in the doorway, and the next I was staring at the void of my front porch.

"That's breaking and entering," I said lamely, shutting the door.

When I entered the kitchen, he was swapping out the wine for a more expensive bottle. The things I'd taken out had already been put away.

"Go and take a bath," he instructed as he rolled up his sleeves, exposing toned forearms. "Relax. Take your time. Dinner will be ready when you return. Would you like a glass of wine to take in with you?"

I opened my mouth to argue, but that did sound good. It wasn't like I'd be able to get him out of my house, anyway. He'd be making dinner whether I wanted him to or not, and I'd eat it, because he was an excellent cook and I was really hungry.

"Snack?" I asked, giving in.

"Of course. I'll bring something in."

CHAPTER 6

NOT LONG AFTER I'd sunk into the large tub in my completely redone bathroom, Darius knocked softly on the door. Since the tub and shower were separate, I didn't have a shower curtain to pull closed to conceal my nudity.

"Hold on," I said, sitting up to reach for a towel. Before I could grab it, the door swung open.

Darius carried in a silver tray laden with snack foods and wine. I crossed my legs and jerked my arms over my chest.

He set the tray on the tiled ledge near my head and perched next to it, looking down at me. "You have a beautiful body, Reagan. You should allow me to appreciate it."

"No."

His gaze roamed my face, like it had when I'd opened the door earlier, then shifted down to my neck, where it lingered. Hunger flashed in his eyes. Last time he'd looked at me like that, I'd shot him in the leg. Pity I hadn't thought to take my gun to the bath.

"Nope," I said. "Not going to happen. And you're starting to make me uncomfortable, which is the opposite reason of why you're here."

"I apologize." His gaze skimmed down my nude body, the heat in his eyes burning now. "I fed just two days ago, and already I want more," he murmured. "Of you, specifically. What is this hold you have on me, Reagan?"

"No hold. I'm a naked chick and you're a creepy dude. Your reaction is pretty standard."

He shook his head slowly and reached for my face. I would later ponder why I didn't flinch.

He feathered his thumb along my jaw. "If there is one thing I know from all my years as a vampire, it's that there is nothing standard about my reactions to you." His thumb grazed the edge of my bottom lip, burning my flesh. His hand fell away. "I will see to your supper."

A moment later, he was gone and my body was on fire. Literally. The bath water steamed and started to bubble, my power reacting to my desire.

The guy was too hot for his own good. That was the bottom line. All vampires became more attractive after they were turned, but he was just ridiculous.

An hour later, after I had recovered from my temporary insanity (mostly), soaked, relaxed, and put on a robe, I sauntered into the living room feeling like a whole new me. Darius was lounging on the couch, reading a book. A delicious aroma tickled my nose from the kitchen. I started to salivate.

He looked up when I came within a few feet, and held up the book. "This is garbage, but I can't stop reading it."

"Great." I fell onto the couch and sighed.

"Will you be dressing for dinner?"

"I am dressed for dinner." I plucked at my robe. "This counts."

"Are you hungry now, or would you like to make love first?"

"Nice try, Fabio."

He laughed and rose gracefully. "I never seem to catch you in the right mood."

Thank God for that.

As he was moving into the kitchen, a firm rap sounded at the door. He paused and looked back at me, his expression blank.

"I'll get it," I said, getting up. "Since, you know, I live here."

A raw edge came to his voice. "Are you expecting someone?"

"Would I be traipsing around in a robe if I was expecting someone?"

He didn't comment.

I wrapped my fingers around the handle and pulled

the door open a crack.

The younger detective—J.M.!—stood on my porch facing sideways and with his hands in his pockets. He'd lost the confidence and ego from earlier. In fact, he looked a little hunched over, as if bowed by uncertainty.

"The denial stage is over, huh?" I asked as I opened the door wider. I crossed my arms over my chest. "That was fast."

Shock smacked into his expression the moment he turned my way. His gaze dipped to my robe and his jaw went slack.

I did a quick check to make sure nothing had popped out. Nope, all was right. Granted, the robe was a silky number that Marie had bought me, along with a bunch of other uncomfortable-looking clothes I had no desire to wear, but I was thoroughly dry when I put it on, and the garment left nothing exposed from my neck down to past my knee. Since I also currently lacked eyebrows and my hair, unbrushed, was pulled up into a bun, there was nothing hot about the situation other than the beholder's imagination.

Annnnnd that just solved the riddle.

"Sean explained what my department really does?" I asked him, pushing the door a little further closed and half hiding behind it. There was no reason to give him any ideas.

"Yes. I didn't believe you guys. It sounded crazy."

He scrubbed his fingers through his hair and tore his gaze away. He turned sideways again, staring vaguely into the distance. "Crazy."

"If you weren't born into it, how would you know?"

"You were born into it?" His gaze was imploring.

"Yes."

He nodded and looked away again. "I saw all three bodies. I saw the pile of ash in the French Quarter. I saw a man change from a wolf into a human—"

"You did?" I shifted, bracing a hand on my hip. "How'd that come about?"

"A *wolf* into a *human,* Reagan," he said, his eyes haunted. "What the hell?"

"Yes. It can take a second to get used to it."

He exhaled noisily and shook his head. "The wolf-turned-human said he followed that *aswang* as best he could, but he wasn't able to get his crew there in time to help. Plus, you guys were already on scene. But he wanted to extend his offer to help in the future should we need anything."

"No, he did not!" My nails dug into the wood. "Those sneaky little bastards. Trying to move in on *our* setup. Well, my old job's setup, anyway. They're trying to get more legit as magical police in the Brink. Oh man, the captain won't be pleased. If the shifters offer you their muscle, that'll cut jobs from MLE. Oh no, the captain will not be pleased at all."

"Magical police, Reagan?" J.M.'s eyes were tight.

"My bad. Look, you'll come to grips with it eventually. I mean, you've gotten this far in a couple hours. That's huge."

"How could I not? I saw that guy change."

"Most people would think an animal did it."

"The rest of my department, yeah. Sean spun that tale and they ate it up." He shook his head. "Look, Reagan, would you go to dinner with me? I'd love some insider perspective on this."

No was on the tip of my tongue, but his gaze was imploring me to help him. To give him a hand up out of the pit he'd fallen into. I felt bad for the guy, since I was basically the reason he'd landed in this mess. If not for my impatience, Sean would've let him keep his sanity for a while longer.

"Sure," I said with a sigh. "When?"

Gratitude and longing both crossed his face, and I felt a weird pang. Like maybe going out with him wouldn't be so bad. "Whenever you want. Tomorrow night?"

A seething presence took up real estate behind me. J.M.'s eyes widened.

Ah yes. I'd forgotten about Mr. Overprotective there for a second.

I glanced behind me, confirming that Darius stood there. His face was shut down into a hard mask, and his bearing was clearly intended to display his size and power.

"Don't mind him," I said, turning back. "He's like a stray cat."

"Is this your—" J.M. gestured at Darius.

"Yes, I am her—"

"Nope," I said. "I don't know what he was going to say, but—"

"You are my—"

"Nope." I cut my hand through the air to stop him again. "He's a vampire who is cooking me dinner. Strange, but true. There is literally nothing else going on here, trust me. He will leave right after dinner."

J.M.'s eyes drifted to my robe.

Dang it. Timing was never on my side.

"Anyway." I shrugged nonchalantly. "Give me your phone and I'll put my number in it. You can text me." I quickly inputted my digits and name and handed it back. "Talk to you tomorrow."

With a furrowed brow, he nodded, said goodbye, and then slowly worked his way down the steps. He glanced back before he crossed the street. His car had to be the Mustang parked on the other side. This hadn't been a business call, though I'd already guessed as much from the lost look in his eyes.

"Well, that was weird." I closed the door.

"Reagan, that *human* cannot treat you how you

need to be treated," Darius said.

"Number one, it isn't a date, it's a counseling session to help him come to grips with magical stuff. Number two, I would ask how you think I should be treated, but you'll just—"

"Like the priceless treasure you are."

"That's what I thought you'd say, but while I might be priceless, my worth to you is definitely quantifiable. You know what you'll gain by using me, which is why I suspect you are guarding me so closely. But that *human* doesn't want anything except comfort. He can't use me, especially since I just got fired. Or am about to be fired, one or the other. He's looking for normalcy. So am I. Save it."

His jaw clenched.

"Truth bomb," I muttered, leaning against the wall. Silence descended, thick and heavy. "Let me guess," I ventured, "are you going to trash my dinner and storm out of here?"

"Don't be ridiculous. You're hungry." He stepped aside graciously and put out his hand, motioning me into the kitchen. "Or would you prefer a stand on which to eat your meal in front of the TV like a modern-day barbarian?"

I tapped my chin. "Well, when you put it like that, in front of the TV sounds great."

Mere seconds later, my eyes widened when he

brought in a TV tray laden with a gourmet place setting. A heaping plate took up the center, with a glistening steak resting on mashed potatoes and accompanied by string beans. A small bowl of salad and a piece of baguette sat to one side, and an array of silverware spanned out on the other—two knives, one for meat and one for buttering the bread, and two forks of different sizes. A glass of red wine sat next to a sweating glass of sparkling water, and a crystal vase holding a single red rose adorned the other corner.

"I had roses in my kitchen?" I asked as my stomach growled. That snack hadn't been nearly adequate.

"No. I had Mr. LaRay bring one while you were in the bath."

Moss LaRay was Darius's driver, and even though he didn't like me very much, he'd saved me one time from a bunch of younger vampires. Darius did nothing by halves, and poor Moss had to accommodate him when it came to me. No doubt he hated me more for it.

"Thank you for this," I said, and meant it.

He sat down beside me and flicked on the TV. "Is there anything in particular you'd like to watch?"

"No, I don't care. Silence is fine, if you want. I just wanted to see if you'd go through with it."

The screen went black and Darius set down the remote.

"I never asked. Do vampires eat?" I cut off a morsel

of the steak and placed it delicately on my tongue. When Darius cooked, the first bite should always be savored, because it always surprised and delighted, no matter how much you had expected to enjoy the decadent meal. "This is unbelievable, Darius, as always."

"We can eat food, if we must. Otherwise we couldn't exist in human society. It isn't enjoyable, however. It reminds us of the real sustenance we crave. It is a battle of wills to eat food amongst humans, one that only middle- or higher-level vampires can sustain."

"Do you miss it?" I indicated my plate.

"At times I do. Food was one of my loves, many lifetimes ago. Eating pales in comparison to taking blood, however. To the taste, and to the connection and intimacy."

"Do certain people really taste better than others?"

"Taste and feel, yes."

"What do you mean, feel?"

"Some resist the pleasure they are feeling when I am drawing on their vein and often moving within them. They either tense or reserve themselves. It makes for a less enjoyable transfer for all parties."

"You prefer willingness, then."

"Of course, but more than that. Complete surrender of both parties. I've explained this to you before."

"Right, yes." I prevented myself from wiping my brow. *Why is it so hot in here?* "How'd you get turned into a vampire? You'd said once that you were ambushed. Was that when?"

He rose gracefully. "That is a story for another day. Would you like more wine? The whole bottle, perhaps?"

"If you could hold as much alcohol as I can, you'd suck this wine down just as quickly, don't tell me you wouldn't. It is delicious."

"Bottle, then?"

"Well, if you're offering…"

CHAPTER 7

THE NEXT DAY I marched into the MLE office with a surly attitude and balled fists. If I was going to be fired, I'd do it with my usual gusto. And maybe I'd kick down a door for kicks. I'd rather kick Garret, but that wouldn't fly. People would think I was ungrateful—or more ungrateful, since I'd already punched him. The last thing I needed, in addition to everyone thinking he'd saved my life, was for them to think he was nicer than me. So far the split on who liked whom better was tied in the office. I needed to keep it that way for the sake of dignity.

"Oh look, there she is." Garret stood and rested his elbow on the corner of his cube wall. A gloating grin slid up his face. "Does the air smell sweeter today? Do the colors look brighter and the food taste better? I've heard that's what happens when people have a near-death experience."

I flexed my arms to keep them at my sides. I absolutely could not punch him again. I could not.

"I never did hear a thank-you for saving your life,"

Garret continued as I drew closer. Other people popped up out of their cubes, watching.

"Sure you did," I said through a tight jaw. I didn't, but the others didn't know that. "Last night. I wasn't aware that heroes stooped to the level of gloating."

The smile slipped from his face. Clarissa, in the cube across from him, nodded slightly.

Ha! Point to me.

"But anyway, thanks." I patted his shoulder as I passed, making him jump. "Good work out there. It's good you had my back after I stabbed that thing."

He'd gotten the credit, deserved or not, so the only way to make him still look like a douche was to admit it. Oh well, there were worse things in life. Tomorrow I'd figure out what those were.

"He in there?" I asked the unimpressed secretary outside of the captain's office.

"Yeah. He's waiting for you." She waved me through without looking up. That was probably bad news. Usually she told me to make an appointment on the intranet and get away from her desk.

I knocked. The captain had installed a reinforced metal door to his office after the last time I'd kicked it down. I'd have to find another door to kick in. Why let go of my favorite act of violence just because I'd been outsmarted?

After a moment I turned the handle and walked in.

He glanced up from his desk before leaning back and clasping his hands on his stomach. "That was a civilized entrance."

"What can I say? I got a new chance at life, so I turned over a new leaf." I crossed my arms over my chest, silently refusing to take the chair in front of him. I preferred to get fired standing up, thank you very much.

"Shut the door," he said, opening his desk drawer. In a moment, he'd pull out a red card stating my infraction. I'd been here before.

I did as he asked, and resumed my stance.

As expected, the square of red made an appearance, followed by a normal-sized piece of paper. He laid both down in front of him and leaned back again. "Let's clear the air, shall we?" He motioned me into the chair.

"Sure." I stayed where I was.

"I know Garret didn't save your life."

Surprise ran through me. Then alarm. How could he know that? "But he did," I hastened to say. "You said so yourself."

"Sit."

"No, I'm good—"

"Sit," he barked.

I did as he said, half wondering what was going on, and half dreading finding out. I didn't want to have to kill this man to protect my identity. I liked him, for all the grief he'd caused me over the years I'd worked for the MLE as a bounty hunter.

"You have a terrible poker face unless you're actively trying to keep something to yourself," he said, staring down at his desk. "After Garret firebombed the threat, it was clear you believed, without a doubt, that he had not saved your life—even *after* I explained how an *aswang* transfers its power. You aren't one to blow smoke, or get indignant and deny the obvious truth."

"I just admitted that Garret did save—"

He held up his hand. "You also didn't use any sort of experimental magic. That bullshit lie was obvious. The fire didn't burn your skin. That's not possible, that I know of. Not just that, but the way you handled that *aswang* speaks of a completely different magical person than I typically employ. You're not like them. You're not like anyone I've ever met. I long suspected that, but now I've seen it with my own eyes. I don't know what you are, Reagan Somerset, but I know it's more than a leather-clad woman with a fanny pack and no eyebrows."

I groaned. "For the last time, it is a *pouch,* not a fanny pack. How come no one sees the difference?"

"There is no difference. That's why no one can see it. Anyway, we'll table the issue of your unique powers for now." He pushed forward the red card. "You know what this is, and why you're getting it."

"Because I punched my hero in the nose, yeah. Some bitch I am."

"Yes, some bitch is right. Garret is a twerp most times, so I get the feud. Regardless, it was completely out of line. As you know, I've raised your tally to five red cards. Most people only get three."

"Yep."

"Usually, we allow an employee to lose a red card after a clean year of service. You've received all five in two months."

"But it's been three weeks since the last one. I'd say that's progress."

"Are you trying to talk yourself back into the job?"

"Nope." I shook my head. "I'm just pointing out my awesomeness."

"Garret has two red cards on file. He's gotten three in the six years he's worked here. The first was in his first year for hot-dogging. The second—"

"Let me just stop you right there to express how much I honestly do not care."

His eyes twinkled and the corner of his mouth tweaked into a half-smile. "Be that as it may, my point is that Garret is the next highest red card holder, and that is largely because of you."

"I'm inspiring."

"Something like that, yes." The captain picked up the red card. "Despite your affinity for collecting these, most people don't cross the hard lines easily. It takes willful disobedience. I, myself, collected four in my tenure on that side of the desk." He pointed at the chair I was sitting in. "That was in four years. I was great at what I did, but I was unruly."

"I hope this doesn't turn into a job offer."

He shook his head and flung the red card across the desk so that it landed right in front of me. "Eventually, it probably will." He tapped the white sheet of paper. "This is a pardon for all five red cards. A full pardon. Not increasing your number, like last time, but wiping them out altogether. This comes from my superior."

I felt the knot work into my brow. "Why?"

"Because you have extremely powerful friends." He pushed the sheet across the desk. "I'll need your signature on both. You know how it goes."

"So...wait." I grabbed the piece of paper. "In addition to *not* losing my job, I also get to start over?"

"I doubt I'll ever be able to fire you, no matter how often you punch Garret. As I said, you have some powerful friends."

"That's absurd. I don't have any frie—" The words dried up as it hit me. "Darius."

"Mr. Darius Durant. An extremely influential elder vampire." The captain nodded slowly. "Since you were hired, he's made this office his project. He has no real affiliation with us, but his donations and business sense give him the ear of our board. He's actually helped out in restructuring, which has saved the organization a lot of money. What he wants, he gets. Without anything being written down, it has come to the board's attention that one of the things he wants is your happiness. That translates into: what Reagan wants, Reagan gets." The captain held up a hand. "That wasn't written anywhere, as I said, but that's what the board has unofficially decreed."

Anger boiled up my middle. This was going a step too far. I did not need my life messed with on this score. Food in my fridge, laundry, dinner delivered—I didn't like it, but those things saved me money and aggravation. Sometimes it was even kind of nice. But *this*? No. This was a level of controlling that did not fly. Not at all.

"Anything else?" I asked with a rough voice.

"Yes." The captain shifted in his seat. "You used to keep a pretty low profile. I was a little surprised you let me bring you on, to be honest, but you had the paperwork, so fine. But now, after seeing what I've seen, and knowing it won't be long before everyone else sees it, too—you are possibly walking a dangerous line. Possibly, because I don't know what you're hiding." He held up his hands. "And I don't want to. But you have the attention of a ruthless elder vamp. His type, as a rule, don't get involved with humans to this degree unless said human is extremely valuable. That means something if nothing else does. Given the contract from that big case you solved for the vampires, you don't have to work. Not regularly, anyway. I can't fire you, Reagan, but I'd strongly suggest you think about whether this job is really the right place for you."

I stared at him for a moment, speechless. "But then Garret would win," I blurted.

The captain laughed and shook his head. "I think you have bigger things on your plate than worrying about your feud with Garret."

"Yeah, but none quite so infuriating." Though Darius was starting to get close.

Purposefully, I lifted the piece of paper and ripped it in two before flicking the red card back at him.

"So you quit, then?" he asked.

"No. I got fired because I earned the final red card allowed me." I stood and moved toward the door.

"What are you going to do now?" the captain asked.

"Right now, I will attempt to kick this bitch down." I gleefully faced off with the door. "After, who's to say?"

Anger sped up my heart and rushed through my body. I kicked his door. The metal bent. I kicked it again, and a third time, before grabbing the handle and ripping it toward me. It wouldn't come away. "Damn it, captain. Good call on this door."

"You almost got it."

Panting, because it was hard work, I kept going. I

looked like a complete idiot, but this was going to happen. I anticipated the sweet rush of kicking a door open.

"It would probably be easier from the other side, you know," the captain said. Very helpful, the captain.

"I got it." I kicked again, this time near the hinges. Metal squealed. After the next kick, it groaned. "Screw you, door!"

"It's the vampire you should be taking your aggression out on, not the door, but you'll get there. With age brings wisdom."

A bit nosy, too, the captain.

I jump-kicked, putting all my power behind it. Finally, the thing bowed in. Like a ruler bent too far, it snapped.

"Ha! There was wood on the inside."

"Normal people wouldn't be able to kick down that door, you know. The salesperson was very clear on that. Hence the subject of this entire meeting."

"Don't talk logic now, captain. It's too late." I yanked on the handle. The metal knob came off in my hand. I grabbed the side where it bowed away from the frame and ripped. Finally, it pulled free, launching toward me.

I didn't get out of the way in time. The corner hit my shoulder, sending shooting pain down my arm. Undeterred, or maybe unwilling to show that the door had fought back, I gave it a kick before stomping on it.

"There," I said, wiping sweat from my face. "I hope that was expensive."

"It was. Very. Shall I charge it to Mr. Durant?"

"No. Charge it to the board, and blame it on Darius. From me." I waltzed out, knowing I would not look cool after that, but not caring. There was something about kicking in doors that was intensely gratifying. Like meditation.

"Well, I guess the reigning king will retain his throne unchallenged," Garret said with a satisfied smirk, still leaning against his cube wall.

"Were you fired?" Clarissa asked with sorrowful eyes.

"Of course she was fired. That's five red cards. *Five.*" Garret shook his head and pinned me with gloating eyes. "You should've been fired after three. Law enforcement isn't the place for you. Leave this job to the heroes."

"Man, you suck," I said, passing him by. I didn't have the strength to punch him. That door had taken a lot out of me.

I stepped into my cube and looked around. I'd barely used the now-dusty computer, much to the annoyance of the rest of the office. A few pens stood in the holder, and a blurry picture of a sasquatch was pinned to the gray wall of the cube. A joke, because

Clarissa had said I needed some personal artifacts. I had nothing to take out of there.

"Well, it was boring while it lasted." I shrugged and turned away. "Good luck, everyone. I guess you'll see me if a mark you can't handle comes through."

"Yeah, right, like that will happen." Garret snorted in disdain.

"Dude, that was my job before this, remember? It did happen. A lot." I made a fast movement toward him. He flinched, fear crossing his face, before he realized I was just playing. He straightened up with a glower. Someone snickered.

It was definitely the small things.

"Check ya later." I threw up a peace sign on my way out.

Now what?

CHAPTER 8

B EING THAT IT was daylight, Darius was sleeping. I'd have to wait until nightfall to kick his ass, and I had plans that night, assuming J.M. hadn't been frightened off. Given the way Darius had oozed menace last night, I wouldn't blame the poor detective for running the other way. Another reason why I was going to teach that elder vamp a lesson he wouldn't soon forget.

With nothing else to do, I figured I might as well practice my special brand of magic. My mage friend Callie was convinced that I needed to use it as much as possible to get my power to blossom. Whether that was true or not—it could be a matter of growing into the power, like the fae did—I figured it couldn't hurt to keep working at it.

I exchanged my tank top for a leather halter and put a leather cap over my head. Dizzy was working on a fireproof spell for my hair, but so far, it wasn't coming along well. He now sported burns ninety percent of the time.

At least Callie was able to magically restore eyebrows and hair. Speaking of which, I needed to pay her a visit before my dinner tonight, assuming it was on, to get my eyebrows fixed.

I stepped onto my back porch and closed the door tightly behind me. I didn't want any air conditioning leaking out.

I plucked one of Dizzy's shielding spells out of my pouch, pinched the casing, and threw it at the back of my yard. I did another and threw it at the right side. After fishing around for one more like it, I realized that was it. I had two. That meant the people on the left side of my house would both be able to hear and see me.

I leaned over the side of my deck to see if Mikey was out on his back porch. Nope, all clear, which made sense in this heat. Looking down the row of houses, I didn't see anyone out. Again, in midday and in this heat, that stood to reason.

I wiped sweat from my brow. It was annoying that I could withstand fire, but weather still affected me. Of all the injustices in the world…

Taking a deep breath, I let my power burn through my body as I slowly moved my hand through the air. Fire sprang up on the stone ground, spreading in the pattern I willed it to take, as quickly as I willed it to happen. This part of my power was second nature. Easy.

I feathered the flame higher, changing its heat and intensity, keeping it away from the wooden fences. The color shifted between yellow, orange, red, and blue. Next, I influenced different places in the yard to burn at different temperatures. This was a bit harder.

Sweat was dripping down my forehead from the strain as I created revolving fireballs. Orbs of blue, orange, and red moved around the yard like a school solar system. I blinked my eyes against a droplet of sweat. If only the yard was air-conditioned.

I clenched my fists. The orbs of fire blinked out and the flames dwindled. Taking a deep breath, I focused on the rocks in the middle of my yard. Ranging in size from small to half my height, they represented the newest power I'd tapped into. Telekinesis. Lifting things with my mind.

This ability had come as a surprise. I'd discovered it while knee deep in whiskey one night, bored as hell in my burned-out living room (before Darius fixed it up), making orbs circle each other like fairy lights. I'd felt a hankering for another sip of whiskey, but my glass was across the room. Clearly a ghost must have moved it, since I couldn't remember putting it there. Deciding I didn't much care about ghosts—they were easy enough for experienced mages to banish—I made a move to get up and get it. But the orbs flared, and suddenly there came my glass, floating through the air.

It was then I realized two things. I could move things with my power, so the myth about demons doing that while in a human host was probably true, and also, I did actually care about ghosts. A great deal. Because at first I didn't realize *I* was moving the glass, and it scared the holy bejeebus out of me. I tore out of the living room for my sword, and the orbs winked out and the glass dropped, shattering across the floor.

At the time, I was more relieved I didn't have a ghost than excited I could move stuff with my drunken mind.

From then, it had been *on*. I had a new thing to practice.

Turned out, making things move with my mind was way harder than making an orb of fire.

In the bright sunlight, I stood on my deck, staring at the smallest rock and keeping my hands at my sides. Pulling on my power, I imagined lifting the rock. It merely wobbled on the ground.

I pulled harder, feeling a strange numbing at the base of my stomach. The rock rose slowly into the air until it was three feet or so off the ground. Still focused, legs trembling, I moved it minimally before trying a larger one. That done, though not as successfully, I tried the next biggest, and then the next, until I was straining with the last and heaviest of the rocks.

The cold in my gut surged, pushing at my fire. I furrowed my brow as the biggest rock wobbled, an improvement on my last practice. The way my magic was acting, however, felt like a step backward. The fire in the yard, which had sprung up during my exercise with the first rock, had dwindled to nearly nothing.

I wiped my forehead and relaxed. All activity in my backyard stopped.

Though a little off balance from the feeling in my gut, I hadn't yet practiced levitation, and I steeled myself to do so. I didn't understand that new cold sensation, but I was confident my fire could fight it.

Maybe hopeful was a better word than confident.

Determination setting in, I shook out my arms and rolled my shoulders. I wasn't far from using a boom box to blast "Eye of the Tiger."

The thick air hung heavy around me. Distantly, a dog barked. Somewhere, a rattling, buzzing air conditioner clicked on.

Here we go.

Fire raged through me as I amped up my power to the red line. My heart thumped in my chest, feeding off the surge in adrenaline. Rushing sounded in my ears.

Slowly, I lifted my hands like Magneto in *X-Men*. Like Magneto, my feet lost connection with the wood under them, and I rose into the air. Heat rolled over my body, sweet agony. A foot off the ground, and I was still in my comfort bubble. I pushed a little harder and lifted a little higher. Two feet now. Three. The burn of using this much power ate through the pleasure of it.

Now for the hard part. Even drunk and totally committed, I had a hard time with this one.

Biting my lip, focusing with everything I had, I flexed my body and *willed* myself forward.

My muscles started to shake. I could barely hear through the pressure in my ears. It felt like there were weights on my shoulders, holding me down. Keeping me immobile.

Breathing heavily, fists clenched, I *willed* myself forward again. It felt like I was trying to move through a wall.

Gritting my teeth now, determined to make some sort of headway, I squeezed my eyes shut, held my breath, and gave it everything I had.

Air wafted against my face. At first I thought I'd gasped or exhaled, but I belatedly realized I wasn't breathing at all. I'd moved forward!

Drenched in sweat, tremors running through my legs and arms, I tried again. And lurched again. It was then I noticed that the numbness now pulsed inside me, dull and cold, throbbing up my esophagus. Strangely hollow, too, like an echo through a vast, empty chamber.

"What in the holy fuck?" I heard.

My eyes snapped open and everything came crashing down. Rocks I hadn't realized I'd lifted hit the ground. Orbs of fire fell, winking out as they did so.

Flame, which had been crawling across my backyard, pulsing in all colors, sank until it extinguished. I followed, hitting the wooden steps of my porch and rolling to the bottom, thunking my head against the hard stone. Good thing my noggin was hard.

My neighbor, No Good Mikey, stood on his back porch looking into my backyard. His face was devoid of expression, but his eyes were rounded and his fingers had a white-knuckle grip on his banister.

"I'm a circus performer," I blurted, sitting up. I rubbed the knot that was quickly forming on my head.

He shook his head slowly. "Nope. Try again."

"I do magic. I learned it in Vegas and I'm practicing for a comeback tour. Neat tricks, right? I'll crush it."

He wiped his hand over his face. His gaze landed on the rocks spread around the yard. I'd even gotten the big one off the ground. A first. I needed to figure out what that cold sensation was. That seemed like the key.

His gaze shifted to the sides of my yard protected by the shielding spells, something he could clearly see from his vantage point. The air was filled with a sparkling purple haze reaching high into the sky. From the other side, it wouldn't be noticed. In fact, the eyes would slip right past it, hiding the things behind the spell in plain sight.

"Have you done this before?" he asked through a tight jaw. He was clearly trying his damnedest not to freak out. He had balls of steel, that guy. If only he were magical, we'd make one hell of a team.

"Would you like the truth, or something that sounds good?" I asked.

"Don't fuck with me."

"Right. Yes, I've done this before. Not to this extent, because practice makes perfect and all, but..."

"Those rocks aren't part of some shitty OCD decoration scheme?"

"Not really, no. Though thanks for pointing out my poor taste in decorating," I said sarcastically.

"I haven't heard or seen this before because..." He motioned at the shimmering purple air.

"I was better at keeping it under wraps, yes. I ran out of the..." I hesitated. "Hell, I'm just going to say it. Spells. I ran out of the spells. I only had two, and I needed three."

"I ain't never seen a witch in that cemetery light shit on fire without touching it, not to mention throwing shit around like that," he said in a strangely accusatory voice. He swore a lot in general, but when his brain was bending, he apparently pushed it to the next level.

"Say, listen, why don't we take this conversation indoors? People like you aren't supposed to know about people like me. It could get me in trouble and you dead."

As though I'd flicked a switch, Mikey bristled and

straightened out, turning his meaty shoulders toward me. His hands flexed and then curled into fists at his sides. All hint of *I'm freaking out* left his eyes and demeanor.

"I'd like to see them try," he growled.

We'd definitely make a helluva team. And Darius wondered why I didn't want to move...

"Well, I wouldn't. I'd have to kill them all, and then we'd both have to move."

"Open your front door. I'm coming to you. I don't want you to burn my house down like you did yours."

"That wasn't me, and you know it."

He was shaking his head as he turned. I distinctly heard, "Looney tunes," before he disappeared around the edge of my house. I heard his back door slam shut.

If only I'd heard it open.

Weak and shaky, I moved into my gloriously air-conditioned house. I heard the knock at the door, two fast raps, and ignored it. I needed to put something on that wasn't drenched in sweat. A moment later, I heard another two raps, followed by the handle jiggling. I assumed my door was opened directly afterward.

"You gonna let me in, or what?" Mikey called through my house.

"Clearly you just let yourself in," I yelled back, peeling off my leather pants. That material was the absolute pits in the summer weather of Louisiana, but it did prevent me from buying a bunch of new clothes. "Don't let the air conditioning out."

"Girl, you need a lesson in hosting," I heard him mutter.

I threw on some yoga pants and a T-shirt before heading out to find Mikey standing against the closed front door. He was looking around the new digs with a straight face.

"So?" I asked, gesturing at the living room. "You like?"

"Fancy," he said. He'd seen the place when it was a half-burned ruin, and he was the reason the second half hadn't also gone up in flames. Since then, we'd gone back to normal, which meant he did his thing, I did my thing, and our paths didn't often cross. "Didn't peg you for the type that bought that kind of stuff." He jerked his head toward the closest oil painting on the wall.

"Surely you must've seen the outrageously gorgeous woman who was hanging around after the remodel was done." I paused by the archway to the kitchen, waiting for his answer.

"Yeah, I saw her."

I'd bet. Every man in the neighborhood had probably noticed her, even though she hadn't strayed far from my house.

"She did all this." I gave a sweep of my hand.

"And you let her have free rein."

"Obviously. What do I know about decorating?"

He huffed out a laugh as he filled half of the entrance to the kitchen. "About as much as me, I reckon."

"Exactly. Want something to drink?" I asked, getting myself some water. Part of me wondered if I needed water to live. For that matter, did I need food? I got hungry and thirsty, but I felt the need to breathe, as well. I'd proven that I didn't need to, so maybe I didn't need those other things either. Maybe the pain of not having them could be endured.

Truth be told, I didn't much want to find out.

"I'm good," Mikey said, crossing his arms.

"Want to sit?" I pointed at the table in the corner of the kitchen.

He shook his head, so I leaned back against the counter. He wasn't much for formal conversation, I gathered.

"Did Smokey tell you what he saw in the cemetery?" I asked, trying to figure out a good place to start.

"Yeah. Sounded insane."

"It is insane, yes. Most of the witches who come to the cemetery aren't very...magical. Some aren't magical at all—they just wish they were."

"This is going to be the worst conversation I have all day, I can already tell."

"All month, at least." I took a few gulps of my water. "But some of those witches are real. They can do crazy stuff with plants and spells and whatnot. That *aswang* Smokey saw was magical, and very dangerous. The people he suspects are supernatural are, indeed, supernatural. There are lots more, as well, all around. You've met more than one in your lifetime and had no idea they weren't—" His eyes glimmered with a warning and his body tensed. I changed the word I'd planned to use. "—normal." He relaxed somewhat.

"So you're one of those witches who is... Who can really do stuff?" he asked in a rough voice.

"I'm not a witch, no. And here's the tricky part of our relationship." I finished my water and refilled my glass, trying to figure out how to say this delicately. "Even as far as magical people go, I'm not normal. I'm not like anyone else, which is very dangerous for me. Only a few people have ever seen the things you saw, and those few could get me in big trouble. Now, you couldn't get me into hot water directly, but loose lips might get heard by the wrong sort of people, and then I'd be up shit creek, do you hear what I'm saying?"

"I know how to keep my mouth shut."

"Yes. I know you do. But occasionally someone might come around asking questions, and I can't have anyone knowing the answers to those questions. Do you hear what I'm saying?"

"I know a threat when I hear one."

"Good, yes. Because this is definitely a threat. Usually I would kill you without question, but what can I say? You've grown on me. I'd hate to move, and it would suck even worse to be a suspect in a murder investigation. Cops are annoyingly hard to shake. You've put me between a rock and a hard place."

A smile spread across Mikey's face. He looked out the front window in the kitchen. "What a strange fucking day."

"Sometimes meeting one's neighbors isn't all it's cracked up to be." I sipped my water, watching him over the rim of my glass. I wasn't lying—I really didn't want to kill him any more than I did the captain. In all honesty, I liked him. He was blunt and grumpy and violent and completely honest. He was good people. My kind of people.

While I knew I shouldn't be expanding my bubble of acquaintances, after the incident with Darius and the unicorns, it had just kind of happened. And, to be honest, I didn't want my life to go back to the lonely way it used to be. It would probably bite me in the ass in the end, but that was nothing new. I knew this semi-normal life I had was on borrowed time.

"Smokey thinks you're one of *them*," Mikey finally said.

"Who, a vampire?"

"No. One of them magical types. He's onto you."

"Oh. Well, he saw me carrying a really big rock one

time. It was super early in the morning, so I didn't think anyone awake would also be sober. That was my bad. It's fine that he thinks I'm magical. My community knows it. It's the exact nature of my magic that is the secret."

The smile dropped off Mikey's face. "And what specifically isn't normal?" I felt my eyes harden—the less he knew, the better. He put up his hands in surrender. "I gotta piece through this. Right now, I want to tear shit up because everything feels so whack. Humor me."

"Usually that would be asking a lot, but I'm kind of asking the same of you, so fine. Everything you saw was not normal."

"The fire, and the floating rocks, and the hovering? All that?"

"Literally, all of that, yes. Some people can make fire, but not like that. Not in floating orbs."

"This shit is blowing my mind." He shook his head and shifted again, bowing a little. "It is literally blowing my mind. Smokey talking is one thing—he's nuts—but I *saw* this shit, yo. I *saw* it." He took a step back. "I need a moment."

"Yup." Warning tingles spread across my skin. I didn't like this turn of events.

As if hearing my thoughts, Mikey put his hands up again, though he was still bowed over. "I got no problem with you. Your shit is your shit. I'm good with that.

Just like my shit is mine, and I don't need you telling nobody my hours or what I'm up to. I get this." He motioned back and forth between us. "You've got my back, and I've got yours. Still, I'm having a hard time with what I saw. It was either incredibly dope, or batshit *crazy*."

"Crazy. Stick with crazy."

"Yeah." He blew out a breath. "I'm going to go think on this, and avoid all your friends like the plague. Hope you're good with that."

"Yes. Probably wise."

"Fine." He motioned back and forth between us again. "We understand each other."

"Okay."

"Okay. I'm out." He turned and headed for the door.

I stared at the empty space he'd just vacated. He should've had J.M.'s job, clearly.

CHAPTER 9

A GNON HEARD THE summons and forced its way into the weaker demon's path, pushing it down and taking its place. Grudgingly, Agnon let the form it had assumed while last walking the earth, that of a young man, dissolve away. The being materialized in an enclosure it recognized. The summons it had interrupted before—when it had made first contact with the witches and promised them a boost in power for their participation in its cause—had come from the same place.

The building was large, damp but spacious, and held rows of stacked boxes toward the back. A body lay clumped some distance away, the vessel of the energy needed to summon Agnon. Humans in flowing robes of black gathered around him. Their toes were well back from the blood-splattered chalk outline they mistakenly thought would contain a being as mighty as Agnon.

Silly creatures.

While they clearly knew Agnon was a different demon than the one they'd called before it had stolen the summons, they still had no idea of the power they'd brought to their doorstep. The being occasionally loved working with imbeciles. In this situation, especially, it made the task so much easier.

It stayed perfectly still, facing the self-proclaimed leader, a male human with moderate magical ability.

"Great One, we have had news," the human said, wringing his hands. He was nervous and trying not to show it. Within his head echoed thoughts of fear, both for himself and for the woman to Agnon's right.

The being turned its head that way until it was looking just behind its shoulder. The woman startled, then frowned. She grabbed her robes. A thought echoed regarding a stolen necklace. What a strange thing to think of in that moment. Or maybe this secret was simply more powerful than all her others.

The being filed that knowledge away.

"It seems the *aswang* was destroyed before its power could be transferred," the human leader said, his fear amplifying. "The creature had fed before the confrontation, but still the woman dispatched it with ease. She did have some help, though it was minimal."

"How did the transfer fail?" Agnon asked. More than one person flinched. The being hadn't adopted speech that was pleasing to the human ear.

"Another human killed it with a magical blast of fire. The transfer did not have a chance to make it to the woman."

"Did the fire touch the woman?"

"No. She had a spell that blocked it. But she was close enough to lose her eyebrows, I hear. The transfer would've happened if not for the fire."

"You are such stupid creatures." The being clasped its hands behind its back.

"I'm sorry, Great One, I do not follow you."

"You are mages. Do you know of a spell that can block fire from harming the skin, but does not also protect the hair?"

All the mages exchanged glances. An echo of a thought came from a human on the left. The puny specimen worried his fellow mages would discover his lack of knowledge and power.

If a body was needed for a menial task, or to recover strength, Agnon would use this human first. His deteriorated body wouldn't be missed.

"There is talk of experimental magic," the human leader suggested.

It was a wonder this group of mages had managed to summon a demon at all.

"If what you heard is correct, it seems she is unaffected by fire," the being said. "This is noteworthy. We must get closer and test her."

The leader smiled. "We have connections. We can bring her to us and maintain the home field advantage."

"Then. By all means." The being lowered its head a fraction, giving its assent. Agnon would need to make preparations. If she was who it sought, the mages would not stand a chance against her power.

CHAPTER 10

T HE NEXT MORNING, I awoke to my phone vibrating. I rubbed my eyes and glanced at my nightstand, expecting to see it there. Instead, I spied it across the room on my dresser, not in arm's reach.

It could keep on vibrating.

The red letters on my clock said nine o'clock, on the dot. Soft light filtered in through the sheer white curtains.

I stretched, debating getting up. There was little chance I would sleep any longer, but really...what else did I have to do besides lie in bed?

Last night had been a quiet affair, if you didn't count the time I'd spent sneaking around the house, trying to catch Darius's minions. They had tried several times to get in unnoticed, and each time, I'd caught them and chased them away with my sword and a few well-timed spell casings. I'd scared the bejeebus out of them, even though they must've known I was lying in wait. One vampire had even screeched. I called it a win.

J.M. had texted that he had to work late. Our dinner

was postponed until Saturday, when he had a guaranteed day off. That had left my evening free for a confrontation with Darius, but I'd been tired and lazy at that point. Chasing his minions had felt like a better use of my time.

"What shall I do today?" I asked myself.

I needed to get a cat so I had something to talk to. At least then I wouldn't seem insane as I wandered around the house, muttering to myself.

After another moment, I heaved myself up and headed for the shower. Maybe I'd break into Darius's house in the French Quarter and rearrange all his crap. He'd probably hate that as much as I hated him sticking his nose all the way into my business. Add some spray paint, and he would be absolutely livid.

It would serve him right.

Shower done, I finally grabbed my phone, only to see another missed call and a voice message.

Seriously, who actually called people anymore? Now I had to physically put the phone to my ear and listen to a voice message. The horror!

Scratching a part usually covered in public, I trudged into the kitchen and opened the cabinet where I kept the coffee. It was getting low.

Maybe I should've let the minions in. At least until they restocked.

"Reagan, this is Detective Sean Smith. Call me if you

would. I have a question for you."

Could he not have texted it? All the telephonic hoops he was making me jump through just to ask me a question...

"Detective Smith," came the voice on the other end.

"Hi. This is Reagan. Somerset. Calling you back."

"Reagan, yes. Hi. Listen—" The line made sounds like he was shifting his phone. "The supernatural branch of the Seattle PD, the branch that I work for here, has a case they need help with. Their resident MLE office is stumped. Long story short, this looks like a serial killer. We think the killer started here, but those cases were unresolved. The same style killing seems to be happening in Seattle now. The PD thinks they look like cult killings, which really just means it falls in the magical department."

"What does that have to do with me?"

"They heard our MLE office is one of the best, and they reached out to me to get my opinion. I told them about you. You're a natural."

"I'm not a natural. I've only studied magic. Any good mage will be better, since they actually practice magic."

"Like I said, their MLE office is at a standstill. When the murderer struck in New Orleans, our MLE office didn't get very far either. That was before you joined them. But then, we didn't have much time." I heard the determination ringing in his voice. He didn't like leaving things unresolved. "Anyway, I agreed you'd be a good addition to the investigation."

"Bad news. I don't work for Magical Law Enforcement anymore. I was fired. Ish."

"I heard. Which is why I am calling you directly. The people in Seattle didn't want to stop at Captain Lox's *no*."

"I'm afraid I'm a little lost." I took down a coffee filter.

"Seattle PD would like to contract you as a consultant. All expenses paid, of course. Given your track record, I'd ask you to give it a few weeks, tops. If you can't solve it by then, it probably can't be solved."

I scratched my head. "You didn't work with me much, so you probably don't know that I'm not great at investigative work. I can figure out if magic was used, sure, but I'm not a true crime detective. I'm more along the lines of a...you know, bounty hunter. I didn't fit in so well with the MLE office. Hence my being fired."

"Even with your proposed handicap, you'd be a real asset. I've been working with the MLE for years, and I've never seen anyone as knowledgeable, or who works as quickly as you. Give it a few weeks, and if it doesn't work out, at least you got to travel."

I rubbed my eyes. It was too early for this. "What is the nature of the crime?"

Rustling sounded over the line, paired with voices drifting in and out of focus. Then a door closed and silence fell. "The victims appear to have been skinned alive," Sean said. "The killer struck twice here in New Orleans. Now, we had a great local magical team look into it..."

"Callie and Dizzy," I said. Callie had told me about this—a magical casing I'd found while working with Darius had looked similar to one she'd found while consulting on that case. "She said the perp was skinning the victim in order to get large amounts of energy to call a demon."

"That's what they concluded, yes. I will furnish you with the file and their findings. We found a few clues—hair fibers, fingerprints—but everything came up empty. The fingerprints weren't in the system. Whoever did this is off the grid. Or, at least, not in our databases."

"And the scenes in Seattle are the same?"

"They have found two bodies, which fit the killer's MO exactly, and one of the crime scenes, which also matches up. They haven't found the second scene, since that body was just dropped, but we can assume the perpetrator used a similar circle."

That might mean the mage had found a home for his or her circle—a place where it could be reused. It was safer not to start from scratch if you knew your circle worked. The problem was, it would make things more difficult.

"I honestly don't know what help I'll be," I said. "Like I said, I'm a lackluster detective, at best."

"And like I said, you're a natural. I'd love to get your two cents if I could. I want this case solved as much as the people in Seattle do."

I scooped coffee grounds into the machine. "What's the weather like in Seattle this time of year?"

A FEW HOURS and a talk with the captain at the MLE office later, I'd decided going to Seattle would suit me just fine. The hourly wage would be double that of my old job, with a bonus if I solved the case. They were calling it a bounty, but it was more of a contractor position, like Detective Smith had said. Whatever worked. Besides, I got to travel to a place I'd never been. With mild weather. Why not?

We'd agreed that I would fly out the next day, but as evening approached, I was sent new travel plans. It seemed they wanted to get a move on.

I packed a bag with my scuffed black leather pants and my non-scuffed red ones that Marie had gotten for me. A ton of tank tops, one of which was leather, and my toiletries, and I was ready to go.

The doorbell rang as I was checking the time. Six-oh-six. I had to get moving if I hoped to catch my new flight.

Wondering if Mikey needed another swearing session, I pulled open the door. Dizzy and Callie, dual mages, which meant that together they formed a unit that amplified their power, stood on my doorstep, their faces etched with worry.

"Hey, guys." I frowned. "You okay?"

Callie pushed past me. I stepped aside to let Dizzy in.

"I have a contact at the MLE office," Callie said as she paused near the kitchen entrance. Clearly she didn't much care for small talk at the moment. "I heard they're giving you our old case."

It wasn't like Callie to be territorial where it concerned me.

Unease rattled my heart against my ribcage. "Yeah. Hey, sorry. I didn't realize I was stepping on your toes. I recently worked with the detective, and he thought maybe it would help to have a fresh pair of eyes in Seattle. If I'd known you'd be upset, I would've passed. I still can, if you want."

"Don't be ridiculous. It's not that." Callie waved me away, adopting her bulldog expression that meant she was about to start bullying someone. I had a feeling it would be me. "Reagan, the mage you're dealing with is powerful. From what the police were able to deduce, he somehow kept his victim alive for over half of the crime. You know what the crime was, right?"

"Skin removal," Dizzy supplied.

Callie grimaced. "Yes, Dizzy, thank you. This mage harvested the blood and energy from a still-living victim. We think they might've used that technique to summon an *extremely* powerful demon. Do you hear what I'm telling you?"

"Why is my life crowded with demons these days?" I checked the time again. We needed to hurry this up. "All this time I've been able to avoid them, and ever since the vampires stepped into my life, it's been demon after demon."

"This is no time to play the martyr." Callie put a fist to her hip. "You're gaining power, sure, but a strong demon might overpower you. Your only hope might be to banish it. You shouldn't get involved."

"Hey, did I tell you that I managed to move yesterday when I levitated? And I picked up the big rock with my power." I lifted my brow and threw her a thumbs-up. "Cool, right?"

"That's great!" Dizzy clapped. "Well done. I knew practicing would really help."

"Now is not the time," Callie said to Dizzy.

"This is why no one will work with you!" he shouted. That was how he dealt with his wife's bullying. Yelling. "You don't appreciate people's efforts."

"People won't work with me because I tell them when they're being idiots. In our circle, that happens more often than not."

"How was Lorraine supposed to know that an Irish coffee wasn't made with vodka?"

"Because of the word *Irish*. Had I said a Russian coffee, sure, I'd get the confusion. But Irish? C'mon! Everyone knows they drink whiskey. Or beer. Had she used beer—"

"You still would've called her an idiot," I said. "No one in their right mind would put beer in coffee."

"You'd be surprised," Callie muttered. "Anyway, Reagan, stop trying to distract us. You can't put yourself in this situation. Catching this mage is one thing, but if he has that demon hanging around, it puts you in incredible danger."

"If the demon is that strong, they can't have him hanging around, though, right?" I headed back to my bedroom and grabbed my bag. "Only the highest-level mage could hold a demon like that for long."

"Even then, he wouldn't be able to hold it for long at all." Dizzy's solemn voice drifted down the hallway. "That's our concern. It is very likely the demon will eventually get out. One slip-up, or a conversation gone on too long, and the magic holding it could unravel and give it an opportunity to escape. That's the danger."

"The circles he was using here would've just barely been strong enough." Callie filled my doorway.

"Do you think he's ingesting the demon?" I paused

before leaving my bedroom, then threw a couple of hair things into my pack. Chances were, I'd forgotten a thing or two.

"No, thankfully. Any human body that demon took over would rot from the inside out. If it got out, though, it wouldn't need a host. It would have the power to adopt a form on its own. Only if it grew weak from keeping the form intact would it transfer to a host to regenerate and literally suck the life out of the human."

"Awesome." I tapped my sword, wrapped in a towel. Just to make sure it was in there. "Well, if it did escape, it needs to be killed anyway."

"There are people in Seattle who can do that."

"But they aren't doing it now, so…"

"She has you there, hon," Dizzy said.

"Don't help her. You're supposed to be helping me." Callie scowled at me. "We are talking about a high level-four demon here."

From what I'd gathered over the years, there were six levels of power in the underworld, with level six solely occupied by my father. There were three or four sub-tiers of level-five demons, but only two or three sub-tiers of levels four and three. As a whole, any level-five demon was extremely powerful. Level-four demons were obviously less so, but the upper echelons of four were still extremely dangerous.

I zipped up my pack. When did I back away from a

challenge? Especially on the backswing of Garret getting one over on me.

"Well, thanks for coming, you guys," I said. "But I have a date with a mild climate and a lot of trees. Maybe a rolling hill or two."

Callie followed closely behind me as I headed for the door. "Have we made any impact on you, Reagan?" she asked. "You really shouldn't go."

"I probably shouldn't—you're right. But they need help. Plus, I've been extremely bored since quitting MLE."

"That was yesterday morning," Callie exclaimed.

"But I haven't been working for two days. A very boring two days."

"You quit MLE?" Dizzy asked, following behind us.

"I told you that," Callie said.

"I was supposed to get fired, but Darius stuck his big nose in. So I quit." I opened the door and gestured them out.

"That was wise. You don't need that vampire infiltrating your life." Callie sniffed. "He's much too close as it is. Soon you'll start depending on him, and that is a very dangerous trap to fall into. You remember what happened with me and my vampire admirer?"

Did I ever. She'd killed him.

"Darius wouldn't be so easy to kill, hon," Dizzy said, exiting my house.

"I'm older now. Wiser. I have more experience. I could get it done." Callie nodded knowingly.

"I could kill him, but then I'd have to deal with hiding his body, and yada yada yada." I locked the door. "Hey, do you guys want to help me booby-trap my house?"

"Oh now, that would be fun." Dizzy nodded. "Who are we trying to maim?"

"Darius has people clean my house and stock my fridge and stuff. I told him to stop, but..."

"Here, we can take our car." Callie motioned me toward her "old" Merc, as she called it. It was not old by any means. The shiny Mercedes looked like it had just rolled off the lot, and could move fast enough to melt the passenger's face off.

"I have transportation coming," I said, checking my phone. "Any minute."

"Fine." Callie looked around. "This is not a great place to leave the car, though. We'll come back to it on blocks."

"Why would you—No." I cut my hand through the air. "You're not coming with me. It's too dangerous."

"At least she admitted it's dangerous," Callie said. "That's a start."

CHAPTER 11

"OF COURSE WE are coming." Dizzy rolled his eyes. "There is no way you can battle a bunch of mages and a higher-powered demon on your own. Plus, this is great timing. We've been in contact with that little mage from the mage battle a while ago, Penny. Remember her? She lives near Seattle. We were planning a trip out there anyway. We'll just get to it sooner than expected. Win-win."

I ignored his travel plans for a moment. "A bunch of mages? I thought you said it was just one?" I noticed the black Town Car turn the corner. A surge of adrenaline dumped into my body. It was still light out, but my gut reaction was that it had to be Darius. That was the last thing I needed right now. Luckily, as it drew closer, I saw a normal human driver behind the wheel.

"I think this is headed by one mage," Callie said, "but he, or she, will have followers. Dizzy and I know that from experience. Those with lesser power always flock around stronger mages. I have no idea how many there are, though."

The driver parked and stepped out, straight-backed and professional. Moss could learn a thing or two—not that he'd lower himself to be polite to me.

"Can you please pop the trunk?" I asked, stepping off my porch. I made a circle in the air with my finger.

"I can take that for you, miss," the driver said, coming around the car with an outstretched hand.

"Trust me, just pop the trunk. It's heavy." I did the finger circle again.

"If you wish." The man did as instructed, and stood by while I lowered the bag into the trunk.

"I'll just follow along behind, shall I?" Dizzy asked. "You ride with her, hon, so she can't ditch us, and get the plane tickets on the way."

"It'll probably be sold out so close to the flight." I waved Callie away. "Seriously, it'll be fine. I don't need help. And anyway, they're paying me."

"I find it interesting that you won't be talked out of going, but you assume we will." Callie pushed me toward the car. "Get in, you're wasting time. Besides, I've never been to Seattle. I hear it's nice this time of year."

"Actually, let's stop by our house." Dizzy pointed at my face. "It's only a matter of time before you burn off your eyebrows again."

He had a point.

"Dang it. Fine. But you'll have to take a back seat if

there's any danger."

Callie snorted and pushed me again, bustling me into the car without a word. The woman had skills. She turned to tell Dizzy to hurry up, and I saw the word *Bounce* written across the butt of her velvet orange sweats.

"It's just not right to put those sayings on girls' butts," I said, wisely not attaching an age to that pronouncement.

"Why? I got bounce yet." Thankfully, Callie didn't prove it.

After stopping at their house, dropping off their car, and getting more supplies, Callie, Dizzy and I sat in the back of the Town Car as Callie scowled down at her phone.

"I don't see any flights going to Seattle at this time of day. Are you sure it's not an a.m. flight?" she asked me.

"Oh. Uh..." I tapped into the email and handed my phone off.

She squinted down at the screen before shaking her head and handing it back. "That's too small. Make it bigger."

"Do you not know how to work a cell phone?" I did as instructed and handed it back.

"I don't want to mess with your phone. Some people have issues with that."

"We both know I'm not one of those people."

"You never know," she mumbled. "This isn't flight information. It says when to be ready, when you'll get picked up...and then there's hotel information. Good gracious. Are they paying for that hotel?"

"Yes. Why?"

"I've heard of the Edgewater. It's fancy."

I peered at the screen. The font was gigantic. "Get some glasses, woman."

"She thinks they make her look old." Dizzy glanced over at the phone.

"Well, this makes you look blind." I pointed at the screen. "It's probably a sister hotel or something. This is the MLE office. They aren't splurging. They don't even have the money to splurge."

"If you say so." Callie handed the phone back. "Driver, which airline are you going to?"

"You'll be going by private jet," he answered.

"Is this an FBI investigation or something?" Dizzy sounded confused.

I knew how he felt. "Whose jet is it?"

"I wasn't given the particulars, ma'am," the driver said. "I was just told when and where to get you, and where to drop you off."

"You really should question more often," Callie said in a low voice. "He could be taking you somewhere, right now, to kill you. And you don't even have your sword on you."

"I don't need my sword to use my magic," I said. "And besides, we're headed in the right direction for the airport."

"She's right, though, Reagan." Dizzy looked out the window. "You are too trusting."

"The email came from the captain. I trust him. Clearly he's got something worked out. This is all on the books."

"You belong to the magical world." Callie's voice was still low—an effort to hide her words from the driver, but it ended up a whisper-shout, still perfectly audible. "People sell out other people all the time. I don't care who it is—don't trust anyone."

"Even you?" I grinned.

"Of course not me. Is this your rebellious stage? Because I'm not liking it."

"I had that when I was a teen. This is just me taking the piss."

"That means making fun of you, dear." Dizzy patted Callie on the thigh.

"I know what it means," Callie snapped.

Dizzy and I smiled harder.

A half-hour later, the driver pulled right up onto the tarmac by a waiting private jet. Outside stood a woman in a flight attendant uniform with an aviator pin at her breast. Stairs led from the jet's open door down to the ground, and a red carpet led away from them.

A sinking feeling lodged in my gut as I got out of the car and retrieved my bag.

"This seems awfully luxurious for what we're doing here," Dizzy said with a furrowed brow. He took his suitcase from the trunk and stood beside me. "That's a big one, too. It can fly internationally."

"How do you know?" Callie looked wary as she looked up at the gleaming white jet cut with blue at the bottom.

"I've looked them up. I dream big." Dizzy hitched up his pants.

"Ms. Somerset, so good of you to join us." The woman standing beside the steps came forward with a red-lipped smile. "Will your friends be joining you?"

"Yes, they will. Whose jet is this?" I let her lead me to the stairs.

"Just go ahead and leave your bags here. I'll have those stowed for you."

I hugged my duffel a little closer. "Actually, I think I'll hold on to it."

"I'm afraid your bags have to be stowed. Please, take out whatever you need before you board." She nodded at us and moved away toward the driver.

"She didn't answer your question," Callie said, digging into her suitcase for her satchel. She flung it over her shoulder.

"We might not be able to take that in." Dizzy pointed at Callie's newly donned bag. "And we definitely shouldn't take a gun on an airplane."

That last comment was directed at me, but I slipped the weapon into my waistline anyway. "It's fine. No one has to know."

"Well, I'll know, and if you miss, I'll head straight down to the ground with you." Dizzy shook his head.

"Go," Callie said, pushing me. "I don't want to give them time to take away my spells."

"I feel like a fugitive." Dizzy crowded in behind me.

"Just go ahead up the stairs," the flight attendant called out. "We'll be underway within the half-hour. My assistant, Ms. Eddings, will make sure you are comfortable."

"I've always wanted to fly in one of these. I half worry they'll shut the door as soon as they have Reagan onboard." Dizzy looked over the banister and down at the ground. "Our own private runway, too."

"It's not a private runway." I pointed at the huge 747s lining up to fly out. "This is just our own boarding site."

"Our own boarding site. With no security!" Dizzy shook his head and smiled. "This is a good day."

"They might still be ferreting us off to kill us." Callie glanced over her shoulder at the black car creeping along the tarmac, heading back the way we'd come.

There went our ride.

"It would have to be someone very rich and power-ful to put all this effort into killing us," Dizzy replied. When I paused at the door, he motioned me onward. "C'mon. We can handle whatever it is. Let's just enjoy this while it lasts. I bet they serve champagne."

The interior was every bit as plush as Dizzy must've hoped. An oriental rug graced the entranceway. Four chairs filled out each of the compartment's four corners, arranged so the passengers could easily communicate. Pulled-back curtains stood between that and the next compartment, which had a beige couch on one side and two chairs with a table between them on the other. Just beyond this section was what looked like a bed in the back.

"I've died and gone to heaven." Dizzy stepped around me, moving toward the area with the more social seating arrangement. "What do you think, Reagan? Do you want a chair or the couch?"

"You guys can have the chairs. They're probably easier to get out of."

"So thoughtful." Dizzy sank into the chair with a smile. Callie and I were still in the entryway.

"Welcome," a woman said from the back, coming toward us. She pulled the curtain across the back compartment with the bed. Apparently we wouldn't be allowed to take a nap. "Please, have a seat. Can I get you something to drink?"

"Do you have champagne?" Dizzy asked with a smile.

"Of course. And for you, Ms. Somerset?"

"Water is fine. Thanks." I sat on the couch and turned so I could look out the window. The sun was kissing the horizon, throwing long shadows across the runway.

"Water. Thank you." Callie lowered into the seat opposite Dizzy, maintaining a firm hold on her satchel.

"Not champagne?" Dizzy's face fell.

"We don't know why we're on this jet. We don't even know why that door hasn't been closed up yet. Sobriety is a good idea right now." Callie adjusted and looked back toward the door.

"They are waiting for the other flight attendant. She said we'd be underway within the half-hour." Dizzy softly drummed on the tabletop.

"Why does one person need two flight attendants? They didn't know we'd be coming." Callie's lips tightened, but she didn't say anything else.

Time ticked by. The flight attendant gave us our drinks and provided us with appetizers, as tasty as one might expect from a fine-dining restaurant. The crew stowed our bags under the plane and fueled up the craft. Still, the door remained ajar. Finally, when I was about ready to call the whole thing off, the black car crawled toward us once again.

"Here's the secret third party," I said under my breath.

A man stepped out gracefully. I would recognize that silhouette anywhere—tall and powerful, with muscular, broad shoulders and a refined posture rarely seen in this day and age.

"That rat bastard," I mumbled.

"What?" Dizzy asked before hurriedly finishing his glass of champagne.

"I can't see. It's too dark." Callie hunched down in order to see out the window opposite her.

"Ah yes, Mr. Durant is here. We can be underway soon." The attendant's eyes glittered as she glanced out the window.

I shook my head, fire tingling across my middle.

Darius pulled his suit coat taut across his chest before doing up a button. He glanced up at the very window from which I was watching him. His face remained impassive. He must've known the anger he was walking into, but it didn't show in his expression.

"I am not amused," I said quietly.

"Do not ruin this beautiful plane, Reagan Somerset," Dizzy said, relaxing again. He held his glass up for the attendant. "Might I have another, please? Now that we aren't fearing death, I think all of us could do with some unwinding."

Callie shook her head at Dizzy in exasperation.

Darius paused outside to speak to the attendant who had been scurrying around. She nodded before continuing to direct the ground crew. After his unhurried walk up the stairs, he appeared in the plane, his body showing off his tailored suit to perfection. "I apologize for making you wait." He lowered next to me and flicked the button on his jacket open again.

"You buttoned it up just for the short walk in?" I leaned back, feeling anger pinging through my body.

"First impressions are key. Callie, Desmond, so nice to see you again. Will you be accompanying us to Seattle?"

"You bet your ass we will," Callie said, her bulldog expression firmly in place.

"What a lovely plane you have, Darius," Dizzy said. "I am in awe. Such luxury."

"Thank you." Darius clasped his fingers, his focus on me. "You have questions."

"Yes, but I'm not at all curious about how fast you can run," I said. "Do you know why?"

"I couldn't begin to guess."

"Because when I teach you a lesson for interfering in my life, running away won't save you."

"Fascinating. Horribly inaccurate, but fascinating." Darius regarded me evenly. "You quit the MLE office."

"Yes. Why, did you expect me to stay and then

thank you for bailing me out?"

"Reagan, I really think a glass of champagne would calm you down." Dizzy pointed to his glass as it was refilled. "You seem awfully tense. Ouch!"

Dizzy reached down to rub his shin where Callie had just kicked him, a piece of violence Darius and I had been at the perfect vantage point to witness. Judging by her scowl, she didn't care.

"You are too good to waste away in that office," Darius said. "I had hoped you'd realize that long before you did."

"Then why did you make it so I could stay?" I asked suspiciously.

"The short story is, you desired it, and I was in the position to make it happen."

"And the long story?" I asked.

His eyes flicked toward Callie and Dizzy. "Will need to come at another time. First I should probably explain what I am doing here."

I opened my mouth to protest, but yes, I needed that answer. I motioned him on.

Darius glanced at the attendant, who took Callie's empty glass. "Let's wait until we are underway before I explain."

"How did you even know I was going?" I asked. "This all happened in the daylight hours."

"My people received notice that the MLE office was

working out a special contract for you. Being that it was done in haste, my daytime attendants woke me. They are well versed in the matters I deem important. Loss of half a day's sleep was nothing. But that's no matter. Please, relax. Make yourselves comfortable. Once we are in the air and you are comfortable and sated, I will discuss the upcoming matter in detail. There is a lot to discuss."

"There is?" It didn't seem like it, though maybe he hadn't seen Callie and Dizzy's old case files.

He didn't answer me, but he did get me a cheese plate, which was just as good.

After takeoff, it took a solid hour for Darius to be convinced we were comfortable. That we all had plenty of food and drinks, and blankets should we need them. Finally, he waved his hand, and the two flight attendants made themselves scarce. Clearly he and Callie were in agreement about the inadvisability of trusting people, because he put up spells within our compartment to keep what we said private.

"Let's all get onto the same page," Darius said, crossing one long leg over the other. He leaned back and draped his arm behind me, over the back of the couch. I prevented myself from giving in to both of my impulses, equally as strong: scooting away like a Nervous Nelly, and scooting into his body. "Reagan, you are the most wound up. Maybe you should start."

"She has a damn good reason to be wound up, if you ask me." Callie shifted and yanked down her pink velvet top. "No woman wants a stalker. I don't care how good he looks."

"Honey, have some more whiskey. It'll do you good." Dizzy grabbed her glass and looked wistfully in the direction of the missing attendants. "Oh shoot. I forgot they were gone."

First things first. I hit Darius with a hard stare. "So you're here why?"

Darius eyed me steadily. "First and foremost, I cannot allow you to walk into danger on your own."

"Why is that?" Callie tilted her head.

"Yes, why is that?" I repeated.

"And I haven't been able to, I've realized, since you nearly died in my arms," he continued.

"I'm missing something, I think, and it's not just the champagne." Dizzy tapped the bottom of his empty glass. "I feel like I should've heard about that."

"I'll say." Callie stared at me with wide eyes.

"It was nothing." I waved it away.

"It doesn't sound like nothing," Callie said.

"There were things surrounding that situation that I can't talk about." Like the fact that unicorns were real and the vampires protected them. "So unless you also want to be stalked, it was nothing. Besides, Darius and I have been through this. It's not me you're worried about; it's my worth as an asset. The whole 'I'm price-less though not actually priceless' situation. Because since when do vampires care if a human dies?"

"Since you," Darius said softly.

"This is not good," Callie murmured.

"You guys, it's nothing. He doesn't know what he's saying." I rubbed my eyes. I sure hoped he didn't know what he was saying. The whole thing sounded nuts, because vampires, especially elders, did not behave like Darius. They just didn't. End of story. There had to be an ulterior motive.

Which probably circled right back to my status as an asset.

Didn't it?

I took a deep breath. At least Darius wasn't trying to prevent me from going to Seattle. That tiny distinction was enough to abate my anger. For now.

"What's your plan, then, Darius?" I tried to read his impassive face. Nothing came of it. Surprise, surprise. "Are you going to try to solve this with me, or just lurk around like the boogeyman?"

"I can help you solve it, if you'd like. As I recall, we made an excellent team."

"We were the worst team imaginable, actually. That point was driven home when you took off on your own with no explanation, then got captured and needed rescue," I said. His lips thinned. "But if I'm going up against a level-four demon and a bunch of mages, that monster form of yours might come in handy." I tucked a wisp of hair behind my ear. "You're not legit, though. The shifters there will be all over you."

"Do you think I went to all this trouble to help you, only to neglect such an important detail?" He tsked at me. "I added my name to the contract. It was easily done. The magical board is eating out of my hand. They will do anything for money, as corrupt as they are."

"Wow. You're something." I shook my head. "Okay, fine." I stuck my finger in his face, making him lean back. "But I'm taking the lead. This is my case." He nodded, but I didn't miss the humor sparkling in his eyes. "And I am keeping a low profile, got it? I'm there to find the mage who is killing people. I don't care about that demon. If it's around, their local people can handle it. I don't need it getting word of me. I'm going in as a normal, everyday magical person."

"Good luck selling that, Reagan." Dizzy chuckled and loaded a piece of bread with cheese and some sort of orange jelly.

"Got it?" I prodded Darius in the chest.

"I understand."

"Fine." I sat back, but jumped when I felt his arm— so warm and strong—nearly resting on my shoulders. My heart started racing. "And no hitting on me." I pushed his arm away.

"That might be harder."

"I will shoot you in the leg. You know I will."

"Does no one tell me anything?" Dizzy said.

"What is the other part of your reason for tagging along?" I asked.

Darius rose and crossed through one of the concealment spells. It disintegrated. He returned a moment later with a bottle of whiskey and one of champagne. While he refilled Dizzy's drink, he left the whiskey beside Callie's empty glass.

"Thank you," Dizzy said.

"Reagan?" Darius stayed standing.

"I'm good, thanks."

After he used another spell to restore our privacy, he resumed his seat. His arm came across the back of the couch. "As you know, Vlad is unsettled with the power the elves hold in the Realm. He has been working to increase our numbers, but also to create alliances. He hopes one of those allies will be Lucifer, and if not him directly, then a host of sufficiently powerful demons that can maintain their own forms in both the Realm *and* in the Brink—the Brink being the harder of the two, of course.

"I have always monitored Vlad vaguely, as he has done with me. It is important to be aware of what other political powers are doing. After hearing about his interest in the demons, however, I have watched him more carefully. In so doing, I learned about a collection of demons that had sprung up in a Northern Californian town. Like a whirlwind, the small town was plagued with vicious deeds and atrocities the area had never seen before in that magnitude."

"Why haven't I heard about that?" I asked, aghast.

"News coverage has been minimal. Many are blaming the occult. The effect lasted about two weeks. After that, the people who'd committed the crimes came out of their trance. Many of them were already incarcerated, but they had no idea what had happened, let alone what part they had played in it. Vlad's people checked it out and determined the demon responsible wasn't one they knew."

I shifted. "I thought you said there were a bunch of demons?"

"Dimensional demons," Callie said quietly. "Humans turned into demons by one powerful demon."

Dizzy moaned and shook his head. "I hope not."

"Did you not just hear the vampire?" Callie asked Dizzy. "He all but described them."

"Honey, don't be rude. Call him a man."

"But he's not a man. He's a vampire. Why shouldn't I call him what he is?"

"Fast-forward to the point, please," I said, rubbing my temples.

"A fifth-level demon sheds power as it moves

through the world in its chosen form. That power alters humans in the demon's image." Callie poured herself a finger of whiskey. "An experienced demon can prevent this, if it so chooses. Depending on the type of demon, the effect can make humans more villainous, lustful, deceitful, or even more loving. I once heard of a whole town that erupted in orgies. This demon, clearly, is swirling around our classic definition of evil."

"I honestly didn't know there were good demons," I mumbled.

Callie took a sip before replying. "People like to glorify the negative aspects of themselves in demon form. Demons are the scapegoats. But let's be honest, a great many of them are very bad creatures."

"Besides," Dizzy said, "they tend to make weak-willed people do uncharacteristic things. Forcing your will on others is never a good thing."

"Burn!" I pointed at Darius.

He looked at me quizzically.

"You know, because of the forcing your will on others thing. Namely me... Never mind. You're slow."

"It is not my inability to understand that is the problem," he said. "It is your inability to tell a joke."

"No..." That's all I had. A one-word rebuttal. "So what does that Northern California demon have to do with me?"

"Hopefully nothing," Darius said. "Demons that

strong, ones that can't control the power they shed, rarely come up to the surface. And if they do, they usually don't last long. Nothing brings magical people together faster than a demon threatening their way of life. I am hoping this particular creature went back down without any further issues.

"My worry is this: the mage we captured a couple months ago learned of you through an ingested demon. The demon was the one that recognized your power. If just once, upon banishing the demon, the mage forgot to bind it to keep her secrets, the demon could've communicated about you. I want to stay vigilant in the event that the information fell on opportunistic ears. Our worst-case scenario is that the powerful demon came to the surface as a byproduct of that situation."

Cold washed through my body. "I'm sure any demons that know about me would also know where I live."

"One would think. Still, it is wise to keep our eyes and ears open." I felt his thumb rub against my neck supportively. Everyone was quiet for a moment.

Dizzy shrugged, looking at the leftover food. "There's nothing we can do right now. We might as well enjoy the flight."

"It was probably just a demon up for a joy ride." Callie turned her mouth into a duck bill and nodded. "That's probably all there is to it."

I truly hoped so.

CHAPTER 12

"**I**S THIS ROOM to your satisfaction?" Darius asked, standing just inside the large hotel room he'd booked for me.

We'd gotten the same treatment leaving the private jet as we'd had traveling to it. Darius had called ahead to make sure Dizzy and Callie had accommodations, and now we were all checking in and getting comfortable before the next thing.

I had no idea what the next thing was. I realized I should probably figure that out in the next hour.

The curtains had been left open, revealing a yawning blackness beyond. I knew from the walk to the room (there had been no formal check-in, simply Darius stating his name and waiting for the staff to run around like chickens with their heads cut off) that one side of the hotel overlooked the water. I seemed to recall overhearing it was a bay, but I had no idea which one. I hadn't studied a map en route to our final destination. It seemed, however, that I would get to stare at the bay from the large windows of my room when I had nothing better to do.

"Looks great," I said, looking over the leather chairs that formed a triangle with a cold fireplace in a hearth of stone. "It's big." A modern desk sat against the wall with lit candles on its surface.

Actually, upon closer inspection, they were lights made to flicker like candles. Which made sense. Open fire posed a hazard. I knew from experience.

"Through here…" Darius crossed the room gracefully. "You can easily reach me."

He unlocked a deadbolt to a nondescript door that blended in with the wall. It led to the room next door— or so I realized when he used his magic to unlock the other side and pushed the door open.

"But this is a suite, right?" I gestured around me. "I didn't realize suites connected with other suites. That's kind of a weird feature. Super-rich people give their kids matching suites?"

Darius had already moved on with his examination. He stood in the threshold of my bathroom, which had a brick-red wall and a trendy sort of brown stone design that resembled my new bathroom at home. "That wall color is hideous."

"It's just a hotel, Darius."

"This is the vampire wing, designed with our special needs in mind. One of my children owns this establishment. I helped him get it off the ground. He keeps up the rooms to change with the times, but he has badly missed the mark on this. It is gaudy. I will speak with him about it."

I shrugged. If he wanted to waste his time, I'd get a drink at the bar while he made his complaint.

"Your room is commonly reserved for humans attending to their vampires." Darius looked me over expectantly.

"I'm not attending to anyone. But I sure hope room service attends to me."

"There is a young alpha shifter of a sub-pack in this town who has drawn Roger's eye." Roger was the head shifter of the pack that helped police supernatural activity in the Brink. "This alpha leads a pack to exterminate new vampires." Darius's lip curled aggressively. "I am on official business, focused on the issues concerning you, so I will not kill him and his whole pack, though they have killed one of my children in this area."

"Do you have children all over the world?"

"Yes. Hence my need of a private jet," he said, speaking slowly as though to an imbecile.

"Right. How stupid of me to ask."

"Yes." He paused. "The shifters might be sniffing around, getting under our feet."

"I have no reason to deal with them—I'm here on human police business. Besides, the only shifters I have a problem with are from the New Orleans pack."

"Reagan, you are rarely dimwitted. I'd prefer you didn't make a habit of it now."

I furrowed my brow at him, a silent rebuttal to his being an ass.

"They so seldom deal with elders that they might assume I can't control myself, and therefore, will watch and report," he went on. "I have to follow magical law to the letter to avoid an altercation."

"Darius, honestly, I was up all day, and now I've nearly been up all night. I'm human, remember? I need sleep. So could you please get to the point? And following the rules is not it, because you did that just fine when we worked together on the last case."

"Do you not remember my need for blood when we stayed at my house in the French Quarter?"

"So? Ask one of your friends to loan you a human for the night."

"That would not be following the letter of the law, something the local wolf pack will make it their business to know. Their leader, Devon, has the ear of Roger directly. He'll make sure my transgressions are made known and a witch hunt is organized."

"Well…not really a witch hunt, right? Since you're a vampire." I squinted at him, feeling the pressure of a ball about to drop.

"We are not supposed to feed on humans in the Brink at all. That violates the rule of not revealing what we are. We have to limit our needs to magical people. Something you seem to have blocked out of your memory of late. It does not change your promise, however."

A wash of tingles spread across my skin. Heat dripped down my core and puddled in a hot, sticky mess. I suddenly knew exactly where he was going with this.

"You promised Roger that if I needed blood, I could take it from you."

A rush of breath escaped my mouth. I tried to shrug, but the sudden rigidity of my body turned the motion into something Frankenstein's monster might do. My smile, intended to look blasé, probably resembled a grimace of pain, and the flush of heat in my face certainly gave away the pounding in my lady parts. All the sensual moments I'd ever experienced with Darius—his leans, his soft whispers, the flashes of hunger in his eyes, the few blissful kisses we'd shared—crowded in and invaded the conversation. My legs started to shake and a sheen of sweat coated my forehead.

"You filthy bastard," I said, balling my fists. "No wonder you were in such a hurry to fire up the jet and tag along on this trip. Worried about me, my ass. You knew the scent of my blood, teamed with the danger I will surely find, would make you desperate to feed—not to mention the fact that there's a pack of shifters prowling around. You were counting on it. Bing, bang, boom, you finally get to see if the curtains match the drapes."

A teasing smile wrestled his lips. "I already know they do, since I have seen you bathe."

"I meant, do I taste as good as I smell, you donkey."

"I am greatly looking forward to finding out, *ma chere*."

"Don't call me that. I'm going to make you wait until you're begging for it. You do realize that, don't you?"

"A type of teasing I can easily reciprocate once you finally give in."

"Oh no." I waggled my finger at him. "No, sir. I didn't say I would sleep with you; I said that I will keep you from killing a small village out of hunger by letting you feed from me. The two are mutually exclusive."

He gave me a knowing smile. "It is nearly impossible to resist. I don't think you'll want the strength to be one of the few."

"I know how hard it is not to give in, but for you, I'll make the effort—"

I cut myself off because his whole demeanor had changed. He'd gone from loose and easy, with a teasing smile and sparkling eyes, to balanced and squared off, his muscles taut and his eyes flashing with a predator's gleam.

"What just happened?" I asked. I glanced over my

shoulder, wondering if an intruder had broken in on the sly. I had been known to miss the obvious every once in a while.

"You have been with another vampire?" he asked in a rough voice. Menace crowded the room. "Was this recent?"

I let a smile drift up my face. "Aw, you're jealous. How cute." I patted him on the arm, ignoring the bulging muscles, and then proceeded to stoke the fires. He deserved it for knowingly backing me into this corner. For all I knew, he'd planned the whole thing. I wouldn't put it past him. "Yes, I have been. You remember, I briefly mentioned it when we were in the Dungeon. I had a wild couple of years right after my mother died. I gave in to curiosity, let him bite me, and spent a solid month throwing my hands in the air as the O-Express took me for a ride. It was a good time." My smile grew as the gleam in his eyes turned into something inhuman. Something monstrous.

I grinned. I knew what he was capable of, but he no longer knew my limitations. I'd grown in power, strength, and speed. Bring it on, swamp man.

"So yeah." I shrugged. "I know how good it feels when your special serum spreads through the blood. So good. And the things that vampire did—"

He put his hand up to stop me. Fangs elongated. "Please stop," he said softly. "Please."

"How about this. Don't jerk me around, and I won't mention the long nights I spent with his mouth trailing up the inside of my—" I stopped again as he flinched and then bristled. I laughed. "Look, I'll be an adult about this if you will. I made a promise, and I'll stick to that promise if you rein in the teasing sex crap. I swore to myself I'd never repeat the vampire situation, and I would like to keep that promise."

He took a deep breath, and I could see him fight for control over his primal, predatory side. The man had power in spades, and the more time I spent with him, the more I could see it.

He stuck out his hand. "I really have no choice, but it would be a shame to hold back on one of the most enjoyable parts of feeding."

"Ew." I didn't have to pretend to grimace this time, but I shook his hand anyway. "Don't say feeding. The idea of me being food is not pleasant."

"Would you like to sleep in my bed?"

I paused in my shake and yanked my hand back, my mouth open and my eyes wide. "*Really?* You couldn't even wait until after we finished shaking hands to start that up?"

"No, that's not what I meant." He held up his hands in surrender. "For warmth and companionship. I am offering closeness."

"That wasn't even a good save." I pushed him back

into his room. "Hopefully, we'll make it back before you need blood."

"If that's what you wish."

"I wish that, yes. You know, I'm not sure I get this new Darius. A soft spot on you is about as comforting as a brown spot on white carpet. I don't know how it got there, I don't know exactly what it is, but I'm expecting the worst."

He took a few steps back, giving me that danged teasing smile as he stepped from my room into his. This was a cat-and-mouse game, and I was way too stupid to play. It was a humbling situation.

"Good night. Or…good day, I guess. G'day. Mate." My Australian accent was the pits. "Anyway. See ya." I waved and moved to shut the door.

"Please engage the enhanced protections against the sun in your room," he said before I had the door completely closed. "As a special favor to me. If you are in danger for any reason, I don't want to fight the sun when joining the battle."

"Fair enough, but don't be creepy. Don't sneak in here, stand at the foot of my bed, and stare at me. I will firebomb you so fast you won't have time to dodge."

"Noted. And Reagan?"

I sighed, keeping the door open a crack. "Yup?"

"I apologize in advance."

"For what?" I asked, knowing there were eight hundred things he should probably apologize in advance for, and they all centered around that blood draw.

"I will find out who that vampire was, and kill him. I will not be able to live with the knowledge that another of my kind has consumed your blood."

I blinked a few times. "I'm not sure what to say. Please don't? That's insane? You have lost it, my friend, and need professional help?"

"If it makes you feel any better, I will blame it on the shifters so it does not come back to you or me."

"That does not make me feel better, no. Don't do either of those things. That's lunacy, Darius. Seriously, you've gone off the deep end, and it isn't good news." He winked at me and moved to close the door from his side. "Don't you dare! We need to talk about this—"

I surged forward, and got a door shut in my face. The deadbolt clicked over.

"Are you serious?" I wiggled the handle on basic principle. I thought about forcing the issue, but I was tired, and it wouldn't do much good anyway. Still, he should probably know what he was up against. "In the event that you don't have a personality change, *another* personality change, I should say, I will most likely kick down this door before this case is resolved," I yelled. "Know that."

I paused, listening. There was a random buzzing noise from something electronic across the room, but that was it. He didn't plan on yelling back at me through the door. I would say he was taking the high road, but he'd just informed me that he planned on killing a stranger just because one time, a while ago, I'd had a fling. Like...what?

He had definitely gone insane. That couldn't be good.

I headed to the bathroom and took a shower. I needed some sleep, and then tomorrow, I needed to find a mage without alerting his demon friend to my presence in the Pacific Northwest. I'd certainly had worse ideas than taking this case, but at that moment I couldn't think of one.

"A little late, Reagan," I muttered to myself.

CHAPTER 13

M Y BOOTS SQUEAKED on the floor of the police station. The large space was quiet, those with regular office shifts having likely gone home. A check-in desk spread out in front of Darius and me, and the woman sitting there had her eyes downcast at her work.

I'd decided Callie and Dizzy hadn't needed to come along since I wasn't sure what, if anything, I'd find on this first leg. This gave them time to accost that poor, untrained mage we'd found after the last battle a couple months before. That mage lived in a small town somewhere outside of Seattle, and little though she knew it, she would soon get two bullies on her doorstep. Dizzy might seem nice, but that was because he was the good cop.

Full night had fallen before we'd left the hotel. I'd had a long sleep, a large meal—charged to the room—and enough time to slip out of the blackout shades in order to sit on the small balcony and watch the setting sun. The weather was sublime, cool and moist without being humid, and the gentle lap of the water on the support beams under my section of the hotel had helped me relax.

Not long after sundown, Darius had engaged the mechanical mechanism to open the shades before stepping out to join me. Without a word, he'd sat down in the chair opposite me and looked out over the blackened waters, allowing me to enjoy the moment unmolested. Or maybe just enjoying it with me.

"Do you wish you could see the world in the sunlight again?" I'd asked quietly, letting my voice melt into the moment.

"That desire has reawakened for me recently. A new vampire misses the sun keenly. That sentiment goes away, however. In time. I do not have an explanation for the return of that desire, just as I do not have an explanation for how my primal side is reacting to your presence. I've never heard of such a thing."

"How is your primal side reacting? Or is it just the constant desire for my blood?"

He gave me a sideways glance. Silence took up real estate between us, and I started to think he wouldn't answer. I was probably better off not knowing. But a moment later, he did.

"For some reason I can't identify, I feel an overwhelming need to protect you. The primal side of me views you as mine, solely. I cannot pinpoint when this need took hold, just that it continues to grow stronger. I crave you constantly. I dream of you when I haven't dreamed in over five hundred years. I take blood from others, but nothing quenches my insufferable thirst. We are not tied through blood, and even if we were, the bond shouldn't be this consuming. Yet I am powerless to absolve my desire for you. In addition—"

"Oh good, there's more. I was worried the crazy was about to end."

"—you are incredibly valuable to me. Your abilities and lineage ensure it. There has never been anything as precious to me as you, be it as my beloved or as a bartering chip. My primal side wishes to claim you, but worse, my logical side realizes I must do that as a man claims a woman, as a husband claims a wife, in order to sustain your happiness. It is absolutely unheard of, not to mention absurd, for an elder to feel this way, yet…"

"I can see that this is sitting with you about as well as it is sitting with me."

He looked away. "Something is causing this, but I have no idea what. I would like to undo it, but I need to find the root. A vampire in my position needs to think strategically. Without emotion. You are making that impossible."

"Well. As is often the case with you, I'm sorry I asked." I stared out over the blackened waters.

"I wonder if it has something to do with what you are. I want to ask Vlad, since he has been around longer than most of us, but I fear it will give away your true identity."

I nodded and let the silence fall between us, until a new thought occurred to me. "He's been around longer than *most* of you? You mean, there are vampires older than Vlad?"

"Yes. A few. They don't engage much in political maneuverings, choosing instead to stay quiet, mostly in the Brink, letting time pass. They've let their minds go to sleep, it seems. They are content to live within the flow of humans."

"And you can't ask them?"

"I could. And they might know—one of them, at least—but they are unpredictable. It is not rare for a vampire to take a hundred years off, but then come back with drive and ambition. I don't want to create that problem. Vlad is bad enough."

"Being a vampire sounds exhausting."

"You are young and within your first lifetime. That sentiment is to be expected."

I didn't have anything to say to that, so I stalled for a moment longer, letting the cool breeze ruffle my hair, before summoning up the gumption to go to work.

The policewoman's eyes flicked up when I stopped in front of her. Her hard gaze took my full measure— what she could see from beyond the desk, anyway— pausing on my leather tank top. To her credit, she took my weird in stride without furrowing her brow or shaking her head. When she got to Darius, she only let slip a tiny moment of *holy crap that guy is hot* in the widening of her eyes and small smile before closing it down, resuming her hard, straight face. I was pret-ty impressed, I had to say.

"Hi, I'm Reagan Som—"

"Ms. Somerset. Hello." A man with glossy black hair, slicked back on his head, hastened toward us from the side. When he reached me, he stuck out his hand. "I'm Detective Allen. You can call me Oscar."

"Hi. I'm Reagan." His shake was firm but didn't last long. He glanced at Darius. "This is my...associate, Darius. He'll be helping me."

"Not likely," Darius said, shaking Oscar's hand before stepping back.

"He's a real charmer." I shrugged and threw up my hands comically. Apparently, despite what he'd said on the airplane, Darius would only be playing the completely unnecessary role of bodyguard. Whatever.

"Right, sure. Okay." Oscar gestured back the way he'd come. "Please, come with me. I was coming out here to see if you were waiting for me. Good timing."

The woman glanced after us for a moment, but went back to her work without comment.

"Just in here." Oscar led us to a small office at the back of an open space littered with messy desks. In his mid-forties, he carried a little extra weight, the kind you'd expect from someone with a slower metabolism and a settled life. This guy wasn't physically chasing magical people, that was certain.

"An office?" I asked, seeing him gesture toward a seat and choosing to stand instead. I hoped we'd be leaving soon.

"Yes. If you'll have a seat, I have the pictures right here." He picked up a folder from his desk.

"Pictures?" I stepped forward and put out my hand. He handed over the file. "What about the scene of the most recent crime? There have been two, correct?"

"Two, yes. With the recent one, the body was found in a dumpster in the Seattle port. We processed the evidence already. We've noted everything of value."

"How long ago did the recent crime happen?"

"About a week ago now."

I sighed. Even if I saw an actual crime scene instead of a body dump, there was no way I'd feel even earth-shaking magic a week later. Still, maybe I would find something the others missed.

I opened the file and immediately felt my brow furrow. Beyond the fact that it was disgusting, the picture didn't mean anything to me. The next one was the same. It was the third one that I pushed away from my face. "Gross."

Darius stepped forward to look.

I checked out the rest quickly before closing the file and handing it back. "You know what I do, right?"

Oscar hesitated, like I was asking a trick question. "We have an office here with a field of expertise similar to the one you're associated with in NOLA," he said slowly.

I shut his door, having to maneuver around Darius to do it.

"Magic," I said bluntly. A wary smile curved Oscar's lip. Like most humans "in the know," his logical mind clearly tried to pass my talents off as a joke so it didn't seem so utterly outlandish. "I suss out magic. To do that, I need to see the most recent body, where the body was dumped, and where the crime might've originally happened. Otherwise, there is no point in my being here."

Oscar studied me for a moment before looking at Darius. "Is she always this pushy?"

"Questions such as those will likely insult her, and then she'll assuredly hurt you in some way," Darius said in a bored voice. "But by all means, waste our time. It will benefit me."

He was, of course, referring to the promise I'd given him regarding my blood. "So that's why you won't actually help me, is it?" I asked.

"Yes. Next, he might ask if you are always this dim. I am starting to wonder myself."

I took a deep breath and let it out noisily before hooking a thumb at Darius and directing my focus to Oscar. "He's right about one thing. I feel a surge of violence coming on. Let's get this done, or I'm going home now. Time's a tickin', man. I need to solve this quick-like."

With a dark chuckle, Oscar came around the desk. "Have it your way, but I saw the way you looked at those pictures. The real thing is much worse."

"And I will tell you that I've seen worse still, believe me. Usually it's the smell that gets you. That doesn't make this any less gross, though."

A short car ride later, we arrived at a nondescript building without so much as a number indicating its address. Cameras pointed down at us as Oscar unlocked the door. No receptionist sat at this desk. He led us down a hall and to a back room, watched by various cameras the whole time, then unlocked the door and flicked on the lights.

I half expected a bare bulb swinging over a dirty, cracked concrete floor, and while the reality wasn't much better, it was certainly cleaner. Harsh white light rained down on a viewing table in a sea of beige. Just one table dominated the three-hundred-square-foot space, with a few folding chairs positioned around the sides. On top of the table was a pile of *ew*.

"Cozy," I said, walking up to the table. "So yeah,

skin taken off. No bones broken in the process?"

Oscar leaned against the wall by the door. "No. His face was left alone. His expression, as you can see, was one of intense pain, but he didn't have any abrasions that would suggest he'd been tied down or forced to endure the torture in any way. The skin has been put to rights in the next room."

"Gross," I muttered. That seemed to be the word *du jour*. I didn't feel any residual magic, not that I would after so long.

I put my hands to my hips and turned away, biting my lip in thought, running through all the great many spells stored in my brain. I couldn't do any of them, or, at least, hadn't tried, but I'd either read about them or seen them in action. I could usually match a spell to the effects of said spell.

Usually.

"A freezing spell wouldn't allow the mage to access the whole body." I looked at Darius, since he collected magic for his faction of vampires, which meant he knew about freezing spells, too. "They could just do sections, I suppose. Maybe freeze his upper body and one leg while working on the other...but what would happen when they took the spell away to reapply?"

"It seems as though the torso was first." Oscar pushed away from the wall and slowly made his way to the top of the body. He gestured near the neck. "You can see the cutting marks there. They're rougher than the cuts on his legs. Like the assailant was rushed, or distracted."

"Someone screaming would certainly be distracting." I eyed the wounds. "I can't tell you how many people I've punched out so they'd shut up. So annoying." I put my hands into the air. "I was not torturing them at the time, detective. It was all above board." I paused. "Mostly."

"Your humor would certainly torture them, if you lobbed jokes at them along the way," Darius said, having stepped closer to see the body as well. Maybe part of him did want to prolong the case, but his natural urge to problem-solve wouldn't let him leave this solely to me.

I grinned at him, despite his horrible put-down. I'd make a private investigator out of him yet. A grumpy, egotistical private investigator.

"Let's look at the skin," I said.

My stomach was already crawling when we entered the adjacent room. "Buffalo Bill would've had a field day with this." I eyed the man's form. "If he was the right size, he could just slip this skin suit on and go for a stroll."

Oscar started laughing.

"I don't know to what you are referring," Darius said, his eyes moving down the torso, then the legs.

"It's a movie. Never mind." I noticed inconsistencies in the thickness of the removed skin, places where it was ripped. "Definitely looks like they used freezing spells. You can see where it was applied, plus the places where the spells overlapped. They probably had a couple going at once. I'd guess our mage was not alone in this. He had people casting the freezing spells for him, while he took care of the spell to capture the energy from the actual skinning."

"They should've easily been able to peel the skin off the muscle," Darius said, his arms crossed.

"Tell me you have never done this." I shot him with a glare. "If you have done something like this, we cannot be friends. Even more than we already aren't friends."

"If you skin an animal, you cut the pelt away from certain areas, then pull it off the muscle. It comes free pretty easily. I don't know if humans are the same, but one would think they should be, at least in some areas."

"Maybe with how the spells were set up, they couldn't tug it off." I walked around to the back but didn't see anything noteworthy. "This must've been done over a day, tops."

"Why do you say that?" Oscar asked, the humor gone from his eyes now. He'd finally realized that we were no joke.

"The spell he used to capture the energy is complex.

It takes great focus. Once in place, upsetting its balance would be quite easy. I'd have to ask some friends for more details, but I've read that the spell itself is fragile. You can't touch it, no other spells can touch it, and the caster's constant focus is needed to keep it in effect. Moreover, the caster is the one collecting the energy, so he's the one who has to do the actual…crime. Clearly he couldn't keep it up with all the commotion of the victim." I ran my finger through the air, indicating the area where the thickness of the…removal mostly leveled out. "He went for the torso, probably because it's right over the vital areas, in a place where the victim could see the whole thing. That would cause fear as well as pain. Limbs can be ignored to some degree, but it's harder to ignore a knife over your heart. So then, the spell to collect the victim's turmoil would have had to be—"

"Right around his head," Darius finished for me.

"Yes, but it would need to extend in a sheet over the place our guy was cutting. Also a bit away so the other spells didn't touch it, and our perp didn't back into it… There was a lot going on. This was clearly not easy. So yes, he must've gotten whatever energy he could, but he couldn't keep up, the victim died, and he had to rush to get the blood before it congealed. I'm not sure why he kept going with the skin after that, but blood would still hold the power, just not as purely. Putting it over the circle lines would help them call a stronger demon. Why they wanted to call a high level four, I do not know, but this probably let them do it."

"It is hard to take any of this seriously," Oscar said with a straight face.

"We're just getting started, Oscar. Wait until I run into the guys who did this. You'll see some fighting you didn't think existed outside of TV." I stepped back and turned toward the door. Now that we'd gotten the analysis portion out of the way, the gravity of what was in front of me would sink in again, and I'd have another *ew* moment.

"There isn't much to see at the dump site," Oscar said. "They were pretty clean in the drop-off. We have an imprint of a boot and some blood from the body. I don't know how that would help you."

"I don't either, but it's worth a look. Otherwise, we'll be hanging around here waiting for another of these crimes to happen. I really don't want to do that."

CHAPTER 14

THE DUMP SITE was a seaport on the route from the airport to the city. Huge metal shipping containers of all colors were stacked high. A massive, empty barge rested beside the dock, waiting to be loaded. Two school buses topped with piles of strapped-down containers patiently awaited their dismissal.

As we got further in and wound through the cargo, I saw a few trucks waiting for a crane to load up their trailers. Work was slow this late at night, but some was still going on.

"As you saw, you have to go through the check-in," Oscar said as we parked and got out of the car. "But since all the containers are inspected and locked up before they get here, security isn't as tight as it should be. Tell them you're delivering lunch to your spouse and you can get through without much hassle. Not to mention there are sneakier ways to get in that skirt the cameras. This isn't exactly a closed-off location."

I wandered around the containers, all orderly, and the area, mostly clean. Nothing magical pulsed through the air.

"The dumpster is back through here." Oscar motioned to the right and started walking.

I followed with Darius by my side, his hand coming to rest on the small of my back.

"What's up?" I asked quietly, identifying the various sounds, most of which were linked to water. We were on a huge dock, after all. In the distance, the rush of cars moving along the freeway provided background noise.

"I am merely being cautious. You are unpredictable. If something jumps out, I never know what you will do. Touch allows me to keep my eyes up while monitoring you at the same time."

I nodded and swung my eyes to the right, peering into the deep shadows and looking for anything that might be amiss. Yellowed light showered the cement from poles lining the path. Up ahead was a squat building, lit with security lights.

"Behind here." Oscar squinted up at one of the light poles. "I always forget to bring the big flashlight." He extracted a small flashlight from his pocket and clicked it on. The weak white beam made a spotlight on the ground in front of him. "It'll work. They keep this place pretty clean. There's nothing to trip on. Just stay close so you can see."

He clearly didn't know that both of us could see in the dark. We didn't enlighten him. Instead, we silently followed him around a stack of containers. Not much further along, we entered a passageway between two towering rows of containers. The light from the open space cut off, leaving us in the murky blackness that criminals and unscrupulous characters favored.

That wasn't what was making my heart beat faster, though. I couldn't get over the enormity of the man-made walls to either side of us. A shipping container was big enough to walk in. Hell, one of them would be roomy enough for a makeshift office. These were stacked four or five high, towering above us. Had they been buildings, I wouldn't have worried. But something about them being movable, like building blocks in the hands of a giant, had me speeding up to get out of there.

"Giants don't exist, right?" I asked Darius quietly. "I mean, there are huge rock people in the Realm, of course—you made sure that I met one—but they aren't big enough to actually be giants. Also, are there earth-quakes in Seattle?"

"What is causing these ramblings?" Darius asked, his hand now splayed more firmly across my back. He was worried I was about to crack up. Little did he know this was normal for me.

"If these things fell, we'd be crushed." I pointed at the scarred and scuffed shipping containers. "Doesn't that worry you?"

"We would be out of harm's way before the first

stack buckled." He rubbed my back. "I am much faster than a wobbling mess of cargo containers, even when carrying a flailing creature such as yourself."

"I'm a creature now, am I?"

"I confess, being that you are so much more than human, I am at a loss for what exactly to call you."

"Here." Oscar rounded a corner and disappeared into the darkness.

I slowed, listening to the distant hum of the freeway and water lapping. Turning, I looked down the row before sizing up the container closest to me.

"A makeshift office," I said, digging through my earlier thoughts. Without a word, Darius followed me to the end of the aisle, where we met Oscar. He'd turned back to wave his beam of light in our direction.

"Stay close. It's—"

"*Shhh.*" I held up my hand. "Give me a second."

Now that we were at the end of the row, a sliver of light cut across the ground from a distant light pole. I eyed the front end of a container that served as a door. Four lines of metal ran from top to bottom, crowded toward the split of doors in the middle. At chest height, four latches—one on each strip of metal—secured it to the container. A padlock secured each latch.

"Open those please, Darius." I motioned at the locks.

"Oh no, we shouldn't break the locks," the detective

said. "Those have been—"

Ignoring Oscar, Darius waved his hand. They all popped open.

"What the hell?" Oscar leaned forward with wide eyes.

I moved forward to open the doors, but Darius stopped me with a hand on my shoulder. "Please, let me." He pulled the latches away. Metal squealed as he moved the strips down or up, depending on whether they were securing the top or bottom. A moment later he swung open the doors, revealing a mishmash of...household stuff. A black garbage bag sat on a recliner. Beyond that, a desk with plastic storage bins piled up. In the back, I saw the fronds of a plant that was hopefully (for its sake) fake. The container clearly belonged to someone moving overseas.

"That is someone's private stuff," the detective said. Clearly he was only used to breaking and entering after a crime was committed.

"Look at all the space in there." I stepped up to the edge and spread out my hands. "What is that, eight feet wide?" I raised my hand above me. "Eight or nine feet tall?"

"Closer to nine." Darius peered through the gloom. "Is it big enough for a circle to call a demon?"

I stuck out a hip, debating. "I can't be sure—Callie and Dizzy would be better equipped to field that question—but I think a high level four would *just* fit. You wouldn't have any room to work around it. But there's definitely enough room to skin a man. Again, it would be tight, but doable if they needed a place." I backed up and glanced at Oscar. "You said security wasn't great around here?"

He looked off toward the building we'd passed before turning into the stacked containers. "As far as the patrols go, they are decent for their salary range, which is on the lower side. When we questioned them, I got the idea they don't typically see a lot of action. And that's largely due to these crates being inspected and given a seal of approval before they're brought in here and shipped. That's what I gathered, anyway. The security system used to vet the actual crates is much better." He shook his head. "It wouldn't be easy to use this place as an after-hours torture chamber if that's what you're thinking, though the possibility did occur to us. There just isn't the evidence to support it. During the day people are coming and going out of here. Someone would've noticed blood. Screams."

I scoffed. "I've gotten a dead body from one side of New Orleans to the other in the trunk of a Lyft driver's car. Without the driver knowing. Mostly. If these mages have their own car, and we should assume they do, getting someone in one of these things—and skinning them in there—would be easy. There wouldn't be blood seeping out of the container. The spell would have collected it all. Within the container, sure, you'd see blood spatter, but not as much as you're probably envisioning."

His flashlight came up and beamed me in the face. "You transported a dead body in a cab?"

"I would remove that light from her face if I were you," Darius warned softly.

The vampire was right. I did not like being blasted with light. It made me more aggressive than I already was, and that was saying something.

Thankfully, the cone of light swung away. "What did you say your job title was?" Oscar asked.

"I get things done, Oscar," I said. "That's all you need to know."

"You'd have to bring an empty container into the port," Darius said. "Or empty one already here. It sounds like neither is a possibility without being detected."

"There's that," I said, chewing on my lip.

"The security would also have to be deaf," Darius said, closing up the container. "Because an empty metal box wouldn't do much to muffle the sounds of agonized screaming."

"Now who's being dim?" I asked Darius. "Do you not have spells to deaden sound within your satchel right there?"

K.F. BREENE

Darius *tsk*ed, probably at himself for asking that question.

"Let's check out the dump site," I said, motioning Oscar onward. "I assume you checked the cameras and cross-referenced the vehicles that came through?"

"We're in the process of doing that," Oscar said. "A lot of vehicles came and went that day. The dumpster where the body was found wasn't covered by a camera at the time. It had been pushed out of range and no one noticed."

"Convenient. Obviously you're checking for suspicious characters employed here?" I asked.

"Obviously," the detective said with a touch of humor. "All the security checks out, as well as any night-shift employees. Everyone has a rock-solid alibi, and no one has any priors. We're still going through the daytime shifts and any ship personnel that might've been around."

"Who discovered it?" I asked as the space opened up. A small building sat off to the side with a ramp leading up to the door. Light from a pole spotlit the closest entrance and the camera poised above it. The dumpster lurked a hundred or so feet away, a strip of police tape still hanging off the side.

"The smell was the first clue, but mostly people ignored it. It's a dumpster, after all." Oscar looked at the ground and walked off to the side. "One of the women in the office was suspicious, but instead of wading through trash, she waited for the garbage pick-up and watched it dump. The body was in a cream-colored sheet. You can imagine what the sheet looked like after being draped around a skinless person. The skin was in a trash bag. We found that after we checked it out."

"And this was a week ago, you said?" I took a tour around the trash canister. I didn't feel anything, as expected.

"Yes," he said. "If not for the suspicious worker finding this body, we would've missed it. Which makes me wonder if there have been more than two crimes and we haven't seen the evidence."

That was certainly possible.

"Where was the first body dumped? It was in an office, right?" I asked, trying to recall the details from the file Sean had shown me before I'd left New Orleans.

"A loft-style office, yes. One of six in the building. Twenty employees work there, but they'd all gone home for the day. A few people from the office across the floor tend to work late, but they didn't see or hear anything out of the ordinary."

I remembered seeing the pictures from that one. The circle was the same as the one found at the crime scenes in New Orleans, only with a few minor embellishments, indicating the mages were getting better at their craft.

"Well, super. I've got bupkis." I braced my hands on my hips. I hated dead ends.

"Did you want to speak to the local MLE office?" Oscar asked. "Maybe they'll have more for you."

"No, thank you. I might meet another Garret." I waved a wisp of hair out of my face. "I hope you didn't tell them I was coming. They won't love that."

"I didn't, no. We know all about hostility across jurisdictions." He checked his watch. Someone was probably holding dinner for him.

"Okay, well, let's head back." I started forward.

"Did you want to check in with the security people?" Darius asked, still near the trash.

I shrugged as Oscar hesitated and turned to me. "Did the local MLE office meet with them?"

"Yes," Oscar said. "They didn't find anything out of the ordinary."

"No one was magical?"

Oscar frowned. "They said no one would be capable of this crime as it pertains to a circle." He shifted. "The MLE office out here never comes out and says *magical*."

"You wouldn't think all this is so weird if they did." I turned to Darius. "If they aren't magical, there's no point. I can only figure out magical stuff, not normal people stuff."

"WHAT ARE YOUR thoughts?" Oscar asked as he drove us

back to his station.

I shook my head and stared out the window. "I guess I'll do what I always do: track down magical people within the local community and ask questions. The mage is powerful, and he's skinning people. That's crazy days, even for eccentric mages. Someone must have heard something."

"In the criminal world, someone has always heard something. The problem is, no one wants to talk to cops." Oscar chuckled. "Good luck getting anything relevant."

"I think you and I have very different ways of collecting information."

CHAPTER 15

"SO. WHERE DO magical people hang out in this town?" I asked Darius after Oscar had dropped us off. He'd offered to talk to us again back at his office, but I'd politely declined. I had all I needed from him. Which was basically nothing. That wasn't his fault, of course. This was real detective work. I was in over my head.

"They are spread out everywhere, hidden within the folds of Seattle." Darius put his hands into the pockets of his stylish jeans as we slowly walked down the street to his borrowed Mercedes. It had been waiting for him in front of the hotel, and he'd led me to it earlier like he'd expected it to be there. I'd learned not to question those types of things.

I narrowed my eyes at his non-answer. "If you want to hang out with me, you have to help me. Otherwise, get gone."

"Which type of magical people are you looking for?"

"Ideally, I need a hub where there's a variety of supernatural people, not just mages. I want to size up what I'm dealing with, see who's knowledgeable, and, of those people, pick out a few who can be leaned on for information. Any guy that skins people can't be well liked. He's probably ruthless. Or at least really grumpy."

"Sociopaths are often liked by everyone."

"Good tip. Liked by no one, or liked by everyone. Both are suspect."

"Are you hungry?" he asked as he opened my car door for me.

"I can always eat."

He nodded, like he knew that about me, and zipped over to his side of the car. My door was clicking shut as he was opening his.

A half-hour later, we parked on a street that looked similar to many of the streets I'd seen in Seattle: green, with leafy trees and clean sidewalks. I got out into the brisk night air and half missed the warm, sticky goodness of a New Orleans night. Then again, I did *not* miss the suffocating heat of a New Orleans summer.

"This place is so wholesome," I said as I waited on the sidewalk for him. The car issued a soft beep as the alarm was turned on. He put the keys into his pocket. "It's lovely, don't get me wrong, but it's so...sweet somehow, don't you think? Like...heartfelt."

"Those aren't the words I'd use to describe it, no. But it is certainly more subdued. Not as wild, despite being more natural."

"Natural, like…nature?"

"Yes. The trees you noticed."

"Oh right, yeah." I nodded in thought. "Kind of boring, though. But then, I haven't met any of the magical people yet. I might still be surprised."

"By surprised, you mean someone might try to kill you, or run from you, within the hour?"

"Exactly, yes. One can only hope."

We walked past a few businesses before stopping in front of a blue establishment. Despite the fact that it was after nine o'clock at night, I opened the red door to a packed house. What was more, a bunch of people were eating breakfast.

"*Oh,* I like this place," I said as Darius directed me toward a sign high over a counter that said *Please wait to be seated.*

A woman with rosy cheeks and frizzy hair stopped behind the counter, peering at us over her half-moon spectacles. Her eyes stuck to Darius for a moment before swinging to me. I felt the weight of her assessment, which meant she was magical in some way. She knew I was with a vampire, I could tell, and wondered if I was merely food.

I really hoped I didn't end up as food.

"Table for two, please," Darius said in a bored voice.

"Of course." I got another eyeball before she came

around the counter and grabbed two menus out of a holder. "Follow me. I'll seat you in the back. It's quieter there."

"No, no," I said, stopping her. "If you have something with more hubbub, that'd be great. We can wait."

She glanced at Darius before turning to survey the restaurant. Sheets of paper crowded the walls, all sporting handmade drawings. A small counter ran down the right and booths were stationed on the left, all occupied. Someone emerged from around a bend in the counter, indicating there was more seating back there, not visible from where we were standing. That was probably where she'd hoped to stash us. Out of sight.

"You're pretty popular, then," I said as she checked things out.

"When people wake up, they like to come in here for breakfast. Sometimes that's in the morning, sometimes halfway through the day, sometimes in the evening, like your friend there, assuming he ate food, and sometimes in the middle of the night."

"Oh, he's not my friend. He's my possessive stalker who won't take a hint."

She turned back to me in surprise. A smile flirted with her lips. "Give me two seconds. Let me clear a space."

"She doesn't like vampires," I said when she bustled away. "Did you catch that? She was not excited about a nice girl such as myself being mixed up with riffraff like you."

"You are wearing a leather outfit with a sword, gun, and fanny pack strapped to your person. What about that look says *nice girl*?"

I ignored the dig on my pouch. "Yes, fine. But I fit in. And you are still not liked. I win."

He minutely shook his head and half turned toward the door, glancing at it longingly. A moment later, he pulled his phone from his back pocket and messed with the screen.

"I've never seen you fidget. What's up?" I asked.

"I'm ready for you," the hostess said before Darius could answer. I caught Darius's apprehensive look before it cleared. His hand found the small of my back, directing me behind the hostess until we arrived at a booth some ways down. The previous occupants were headed around the bend, holding half-filled plates and not-quite-finished beers.

"You didn't need to chase anyone out," I said.

"They're regulars. They don't mind. Besides, not giving an elder what he wants can work out badly for shop owners." She pursed her lips at Darius before setting the menus down with a slap. She grimace-smiled at me. "Janette will be right with you to take your order. And a word of advice—walk away." Her eyes flicked toward Darius. "The benefits aren't worth the rewards."

Darius received another scowl before the woman moved away.

"What on earth did you do to that woman?" I took a menu.

"Her gripe is not with me. Clearly she's had an issue with one of my kind."

"What gave you that idea?" I asked sarcastically, perusing the items. I glanced up at his untouched menu. "Are you going to try and fit in?"

"No. No one here is under any illusions as to what I am."

"Super." I tapped a gigantic-looking breakfast and put the menu down.

"I can make an exception, of course, but that will ensure I need blood sooner."

"Did I say *boo*? No, I did not. Your not eating is just fine by me."

A waitress with a shock of blue hair strolled up. Her body was slight but curvy, and she had a very specific scent to her, like seaweed and salt-soaked sand baking in the sun.

Mermaid.

My eyes immediately veered to the vee of her upper thighs. The burning curiosity of how they procreated, which they could only do at sea during certain times of year, constantly tugged at me. None of them would fill me in.

She glanced at the two of us, sizing us up. To me she said, "You don't fit in with his company. You look like a man."

"Is it the boobs?" I asked, running my hand in front of my chest.

"Men do not have boobs," she said in a dry tone.

"That's my point, yes. Get it? I can't look like a man with boobs."

The waitress paused for a second. "Fine. Then you look like a man with boobs."

"Touché," I mumbled. This woman made me want to wear makeup and let down my hair.

"What do you want?" She braced her pen to her green tablet, narrowing her eyes at me. "And what is your magical scent? It's odd."

"Odd, awesome—tom*ay*to, tom*ah*to," I said. She frowned at me. "The Sunday special, please, with a side of fries."

She pulled her pen away. "Did you read how much food comes in that breakfast?"

"Yes. Which is why I'm ordering it with a side of fries. Oh, and a chocolate milkshake. Breakfast isn't breakfast without a milkshake."

She rolled her eyes and turned to Darius. "Are you going to feign normalcy?"

He stared at her with a blank face for a moment before answering. "Nothing for me, thank you."

"Say, listen," I said in a low voice, leaning her way. I glanced around us in the busy restaurant, making sure no one was paying attention to what was said. "You get a lot of people through here. Anything unusual going on lately? Anyone with out-of-control magic?"

Her brow settled low over her eyes and her lips tightened. "What are you, a narc?"

"Not at all. Just a very violent girl who wants to pick a fight with the most powerful members of the magical community. I'd even battle a mage—I don't care. Just maybe not the shifters. They're hard to shake off your leg once they latch on, hear what I'm sayin'?"

As soon she heard the word "mage," her expression closed down even more. A spark of fear lit in her eyes. That was noteworthy. But if I pushed, I'd get no help at all. Back off, and maybe she'd warm up throughout the meal.

I shrugged. "How about a really rough bar? I could go for a good fight."

Her expression turned quizzical, but the fear didn't melt away. "Is something wrong with you?" she asked.

I pointed at Darius. "I'm traveling with a vampire. That should've been your first clue."

Her huff turned into a laugh and she shook her head. "You won't be fighting anyone after you eat that breakfast." She walked away without another word.

I blew out a breath. "She knows something and it's

got her nervous. Do you think that mage is skinning magical people?"

"You would've heard if the victims were magical," Darius said. "I agree, though. She seems frightened of something. The question is whether it is the same reason we were called here."

"*I* was called here. You just gave me a lift and paid for my room."

He studied me for a moment. "You should know that the couple who got up from this seat were shifters."

I jerked around, unable to stop myself from looking in the direction they'd gone. Unfortunately, someone was walking up the aisle at that exact moment. My sudden shift spooked the man, who flinched and took a step back, right into our waitress holding two waters. The liquid splashed up between them. When he stepped away again, the glass his back had kept pinned in place was freed. It dumped water down on the waitress's legs.

"What the hell, Henry?" our waitress shrieked.

He flinched again. The guy was awfully jumpy.

"S-sorry. The girl scared me." Henry gestured, probably at me, but I hardly noticed. I was watching her jeans to see if her legs would suddenly morph into a big fish tail. It didn't seem plausible, and I'd never heard of it happening, but that Tom Hanks movie from the eighties had been pretty specific. I'd figured the writers might know something I didn't.

The waitress jammed a half-full glass on the table in front of me. "What are you looking at?"

"Nothing." I jerked my eyes up.

She scoffed and smacked Darius's empty cup down in front of him. "Better me than you, I guess. At least I don't smell when I get wet."

"You smell all the time, actually. Like seaweed. It is horrible." Darius clasped his fingers on the table and looked up at her placidly.

Shaking her head, she stomped off.

This was going well.

"You should get lost," I mumbled to Darius. "Those shifters are going to call their friends. Why else do you think they gave up their table? They don't want to battle right now, and probably assumed you would."

"I am outside of their jurisdiction. I have broken no rules."

"It's not about trying to kill you. They can make your life hell. They hang around all the time and stick their noses in your business. Trust me, that is my life in New Orleans. The shifters there are like tape stuck to my ass."

He ignored me and looked down at his phone screen again.

It was just as well. If the shifters here were anything like in NOLA, it wouldn't matter if he left now. They'd track him down and stalk him like he'd been stalking me. It might just serve him right.

"Hey," I said to the table on the other side of the aisle.

A woman with jet-black hair glanced over, confused.

"How's it going?" I asked with a smile.

The man with her glanced at Darius, and a knot instantly formed between his eyebrows.

"I'm not with him." I waved Darius away. "Say, listen, do you guys know of a good bar where people like me can get a little libation?"

I saw Darius shaking his head out of the corner of my eye.

"I'm just in town for a while," I went on, studying them for clues as to what magical creatures they might be. "Yeah, I'm here to rid the place of some skin-stealing vermin, if you know what I mean."

"They don't. You are wasting your time," Darius said.

The couple continued to stare at me like I was a strange art exhibit they'd found themselves at, but weren't quite sure how or why.

I pressed on. "The locals can't seem to get things squared away, so I've been called in to do it my way." I was so used to my sword making me uncomfortable when I sat that I hadn't thought to remove it. The woman's eyes widened and the man scowled. "So do you guys know where I can go? Hell, maybe even where I can find the skin stealer. I can take care of it—"

"They are not magical," Darius said softly.

I froze with my mouth open.

"As I said," he said in an undertone, "you are wasting your time. This is a well-known spot for the whole town, not just our sort of people. I would think you could tell the magical from the mundane a little better than that." Darius didn't bother looking up from his phone. "Very few humans are here this late, but they do tend to come in. As you see."

My smile didn't smooth over the situation, so I apologized and turned back. Zero for two.

"Unless their scent is obvious, like the waitress, I can't smell most magical species like you can," I muttered to Darius. "I usually rely on knowing people."

"Try the people sitting behind you," he said, still not looking up.

"What has you so entertained on that phone?" I asked him loudly, twisting in my seat to look over the back of the booth. I saw a head with spiky hair the color of rust. I shifted to see around him and caught the brown eyes of his female companion. Her expression crumpled into one of annoyance and—what I was getting used to in this town—confusion. It seemed that people of Seattle didn't take crazy in stride. That would greatly work against me.

"Updates," Darius said.

I smiled at the woman, who was obscured by the seat, and gave her a thumbs-up. I'd have to rise up on my knees to chat with them, and that would look ridiculous.

I sighed and turned back around. I'd have to work harder on the waitress. If she ever came back.

"Usually you have to plug the phone in for—" I finally caught on to what Darius had meant. "Updates on our situation. Got it. Anything interesting?"

"Very."

I waited for him to elaborate. When he didn't, I leaned toward him to ask, but at that moment the largest breakfast I'd ever seen arrived in front of me. The waitress set down the side of fries next to it, and had to make a second trip for the milkshake.

"You're a glutton," she said.

"And you are super observant. Well done. Hey, about that bar—"

She walked away, leaving my words hanging.

"Okay then," I mumbled. "I definitely need to try somewhere else. Somewhere I can get more physical."

"Maybe Callie and Dizzy will have better luck, since they are mages. Other mages might be more inclined to talk with them." Darius put his phone on the table and looked over my plate of food. He didn't comment.

"When we were on our way here, I got a text saying

they'd made contact with the inexperienced mage. Her mother apparently chased them away, so they were headed back to the hotel. I can send them out again, but they were up earlier than us and they aren't spring chickens. They're probably spent."

"Each moment is precious. You'll want to hurry."

I paused with my fork nearly to my mouth. "This is a change from wanting to stall. What update did you get?"

He shook his head and looked away. "I have my assistant looking into a few matters. Vlad is on the move, though. He is leaving that Northern California town."

"And heading where?"

"North."

Which was our direction. That probably wasn't good.

"There hasn't been demon activity of the same caliber up here, though," I said after I finished a bite. "Maybe he just wants to check up on you."

"His physical presence isn't required to monitor me, just as the opposite is true." He clasped his hands on the table and looked at me steadily. "I will know more in a few hours."

"Hopefully I'll have a lead by them. So far this isn't so good." We fell into silence as I shoveled food into my mouth. I really should've cut the meal short, but I couldn't tear myself away from it. It was just too good.

I could've done without Darius's staring, though.

After I'd cleaned the plate, shocking the hell out of the mermaid—which I called a win, because mer-people were hard to shock—I grabbed our check and told Darius to make himself scarce so I could pay while talking to the hostess. It was a last-ditch effort before calling this place a loss and moving on.

"Hey," I said as I stopped at the front counter where she was folding napkins. I laid the tab down and pulled out my wallet.

She glanced up. "Oh, you can pay at your table."

"Oh shoot. That's okay, it's just cash. I wanted to talk to you anyway."

There came that confusion again. You'd think I had suddenly started speaking a different language to these people.

I peeled off some bills. "You clearly know that I am magical in nature." I said the last out of the side of my mouth. Her eyes darted deeper into the restaurant, then to the door Darius had used to make his exit. "I'm not here on vampire business. Not even remotely. He just doesn't take a hint, like I told you earlier. But I am in town on business. You haven't heard of anything weird going on in this town, have you? Anything that doesn't seem right?"

Her eyes hardened and her jaw set. That was the first sign that she didn't want to get a *narc* sign hung around her neck.

Which meant she knew something, just like the mermaid.

I half lifted my hands and took a step back, quickly turning the gesture into playing with my ponytail so the patrons in the restaurant didn't read anything into it. "I totally get you not wanting to stick your neck out, but I'm not here to bring trouble to anyone who doesn't deserve it. I'm just helping your town out, that's all. I have no affiliations here."

"The Magical Law Enforcement office has been asking about mages for months. They haven't found squat."

"Clearly they are idiots."

"You an idiot, too?"

"So far, yes, I am. Here's the thing—"

"No, let me give you the *thing*. The Mages' Guild has a big presence here, and despite the MLE office trying to keep their investigation quiet, the guild has caught wind of it. They like to deal with problems concerning mages themselves. They don't like outsiders in their affairs. So their response was to lean on the MLE office so the office would clam up." She met and held my eyes. "There's a reason it worked."

"And has the guild sent someone to check into it?"

"Not as far as I know. But it doesn't matter when, or if, they ever get to it. When the guild says something is off-limits, it's off-limits or people get hurt. Do you get what I'm saying? Something about whatever is happening stinks, and it's not a stench I want coming near me."

"I know exactly what you're saying, but here's the thing. Scare tactics don't work on me. So you just waft that stench in my direction. If those mages want to see who *really* sits at the top of the power pyramid, they are free to get in my way. My friends and I have been through types like them before, and we don't mind charging through them again."

Adrenaline pumped fire through my veins. I tried to calm down, but an issued challenge, even an indirect one, always fired me up. I continued, "In the meantime, I need to find the moron who's skinning people and harnessing their energy to call demons. Calling demons is a no-no where I'm from. I mean, so is the skinning, but—" I shook my head at my slip-up and charged on. "I need to bring him in, and by bring him in, I really mean battle him and accidentally kill him, because that's how it always seems to go down. So can you help me if I promise your name will never come up? Which is an assurance I can make, because I don't even know your name—"

"Lily."

"Oh. As in, the owner of Lily's, which serves the best breakfast ever?" She nodded. "That's okay, I'll forget your name as soon as I leave. Names never stick. But I need your help. Please. I usually wouldn't resort to begging, but if I don't wrap this up and get out of town quickly, I'll have to fulfill a promise to a shifter—one that concerns a vampire—and I don't want to deal with either of those magical species any more than need be. Which up until two months ago was not at all. You can see my predicament."

She looked at me for a moment, clearly indecisive. "Satisfy my curiosity on the deal and I'll tell you what I know."

CHAPTER 16

AGNON ONCE AGAIN forced the lesser demon back down below, taking the magical summons for itself. It materialized in the same place as before, within a blood-spattered chalk circle. The same black-robed humans encircled it, trusting their magic to contain Agnon.

"What news?" the being asked, hearing the echoes of their thoughts and picking up nothing of note.

"She is in town," the human leader said. "A vampire shadows her. A powerful elder."

"The vampire is nothing. Has the girl shown her power?"

"No. She's had no reason to. She met with the human detective and checked out one of our dumping sites. They found nothing, of course. She is asking around, trying to find something to point her in our direction. I have advised my associates at the guild to allow her to continue investigating until you say otherwise."

Anger simmered within the being, but it held its

impatience in check. It still needed these ridiculous humans. They needed to run interference until the being had the answer it sought about the heir. It couldn't risk being banished from this world until then. A knowledgeable mage could make it nearly impossible for Agnon to come back on its own, which would result in its superiors stripping away its boons. If that came to pass, it would never rise in ranking. That was unacceptable.

It was time for Agnon to take a more active role. It needed the humans, but it could no longer solely rely on them.

It stepped forward until its webbed toes were barely touching the magical wall rising up from the drawn circle. A spicy blend of magic burned its leathery skin, more intricate than Agnon had expected. A level-four demon would assuredly be trapped by such a setup, forced to do its master's bidding. What a disgraceful fate.

The being pushed forward slowly, pierced with the artful mix of spells. Three, he counted, adding security to a fundamental circle. Fire licked at the being's power, threatening to tear the fabric of its essence. Bits of itself unraveled, tugging at its foundation. The mages backed away with wide eyes.

The being would need to take one of their bodies after it was through. Breaking through the circle would take too much energy for it to then create a form and exist on its own. Luckily, the one Agnon had identified as the most expendable of the group wasn't running. Stupid human.

Fire filled the cracks within its being as it kept moving through the wall. Its power throbbed like a cold, deadened thing. Energy drained from its body.

"No," the lead mage whispered. He dug into a bag at his side and extracted a cluster of herbs. The circle of mages began chanting with him, the air swirling with more spells intended to lock Agnon into their magical prison.

The being's dry laugh rattled from its throat as it kept going, feeling the magic eat away its flesh without cutting it down. The humans should've done their homework. If they had, they would've known not to use their summons again. At least not until the being had returned to the underworld, where it could no longer intercept the spell.

Fire scored its face. The fabric of its self unraveled a bit more, tearing at its center. A moment later, the pain drifted away. Agnon was through.

"That's impossible," the leading mage shrieked, throwing a spell.

The being felt the magic wash over it. It shuddered, shedding the uncomfortable feeling. Its oily black features puffed out for a moment before settling. It twisted its hawklike head, focusing on the expendable human. With a burst of power, the little it had left after breaking the circle, it speared the center of the human and filled the living shell. The human's screams cut off as the being took control. Fingers wiggled as it learned how the body worked. Feet danced. The head rolled, followed by the shoulders.

The being assumed control faster this time. It hadn't been very long since Agnon had done it before.

"Jimmy!" one of the mages shouted.

"Jimmy is dead. You may call me Agnon."

"How did you get through the circle? It was reinforced with the blood of the damned," the leader sputtered.

"It was reinforced with the blood of a human. The tortured sacrifice gave you more power, but it did not compensate for the type of offering you made. A vampire would be needed for the blood of the damned. A highly powerful magical creature might've worked as well. You know little of our kind, insect." Agnon pulled at its power in order to rise from the ground in a display of might, but the circle had too greatly weakened it. Instead, it bent back the fingers on its right hand, breaking the bones with loud cracks.

The mages grimaced. Pain flashed through Agnon's human shell, the body still reacting to its nervous system. The being followed the chemical reaction before severing the connection. Pain was not a pleasant feeling when in one of these vessels. The being did not like experiencing it.

"Now," Agnon said, taking a look around with its new eyes. The human had barely passable vision. What a nuisance. "We must put our plans into effect. I must see what the girl can do, which means we must test her." The mages stared at him with fear-soaked eyes. They were frozen with barely contained panic. That would not do. "If you fulfill my wishes, I see no reason to harm any of you."

"But I summoned a level-four demon. How did a higher level come to be in my circle?" the leader asked, standing rigid. He did not plan to let this go. Failure and the fear of humiliation pinged through his thoughts. It would cripple the situation.

"I do not need to be summoned to walk above," the being said, mustering its patience. "But I desired willing human minions, and there was no easier way to find them than to answer a summons. Humans under the illusion of safety, and hungry for power, are foolhardy. Blind. I promised you the vast sources of the under-world's power, and you rolled over like mongrels, begging for orders. You are shortsighted. It was only a matter of time before these games of yours backfired. Nevertheless, this has worked modestly well so far."

"But we didn't summon you," another of the humans said.

Agnon rotated his head, hearing the loud pop of its shell's neck bone breaking. As expected, the head became heavier as more effort rested on Agnon to keep it upright. The being shouldn't have broken that bone so early. No matter—in a day, it wouldn't be an issue.

A ruddy-faced female human shrank away from its notice, her eyes fearful.

"A demon of high power can intercept a summons once it can maintain a form on the surface," Agnon said. "Your ignorance may seal your fate. We shall see. Now. I promised you power when first I met you. I will impart that to you now in anticipation of meeting the girl. If she is the rightful princess, you will need every ounce of my help in order to survive."

CHAPTER 17

A FTER A DAY'S worth of fitful sleep, I woke up to a hovering vampire. At least I felt pretty good about our plan for the night, thanks to Lily.

Callie and Dizzy soon headed off to a watering hole that Lily had heard harbored some of the more powerful mages in the area. Members of the guild were among that crew, something that had hardened Callie's already hard bulldog expression. She wasn't a fan of that corrupt governing body. I really hoped she didn't mention that to them. Or get into a magic duel. I'd told her and Dizzy to keep a low profile. I didn't want news of my presence spreading around. That made people ask questions, and questions were bad for business.

The first item on my checklist found me and, of course, Darius outside a condo that belonged to a man Lily was nearly certain was involved with the case. She'd overheard him conversing with someone about victims and screaming. It had unnerved her enough that she'd taken his name from his credit card and put it in a little book of disreputable characters. Normally, she would've banned him, but she'd wanted to keep her eye on him. Except he hadn't come back in since.

What she'd heard was good enough for me. If he wasn't involved directly, he probably knew something about it.

"Okay," I whispered as I walked slowly up to the clean white door. My hands were out, feeling for spells. So far I hadn't encountered any. "We're just going to walk right in and get the jump on him. I'll lob a few questions and we'll see how we get along."

"Don't kill him or you'll put us back at square one." Darius drifted along behind me, calm and serene. He was using me as a shield for any magic that might unexpectedly come. Mr. Bodyguard, indeed.

"I will try my best not to kill him, yes." I reached out near the wood. A hum of magic infused my palm. I pushed my hand closer until it was actually touching the door, reading the magical current. "It's a pretty common security spell, I think, designed to trigger some sort of alarm if we cross the threshold. It's using the wood as an anchor, but it also runs along the inside. Which means…"

I blew out a breath and looked behind me at the darkened street. The streetlight closest was out, the glass broken. Someone had busted it, and I had a pretty good hunch as to who. A car rolled past, followed by another in the opposite direction. At the far end of the street I could just make out a shape wandering along. It wasn't late enough to go mostly unnoticed.

"Which means what?" Darius asked, now standing beside me. His spicy cologne mixed deliciously with his masculine scent. Unlike mermaids, vampires—thankfully—didn't smell like their other forms.

I shook my head. "Unless I use my fire to burn away the door and the spell attached to it. If there is one thing people notice, though, it's fire. Humans are drawn to it. They'd come to check it out, realize I was up to no good, then call the cops. That kind of racket would alert the mage. All bad things." I took out my sword.

"He must have heard us by now if he's home."

"We're being quiet, and he doesn't have excellent hearing like you do. We're fine. He'll hear me kicking down the door, though. As would the whole neighborhood. How annoying. I would really like to bust it in."

"I have never understood your infatuation with kicking things in."

"We all have our vices." I twisted my mouth to the side, thinking. "Trying to cut through the door would also be heard. This street is too quiet. There's no way I can get through without triggering the spell. As soon as I open the door, no matter how quickly I cut out that spell, it'll go off."

"Then after you get in, you best hurry and find him."

"Boy, you're Mr. Obvious tonight, huh? Thank goodness I brought you." I grabbed the door handle, twisted, and pushed. It didn't budge. "Can you unlock it, please?"

"Yes. And in keeping with my obvious assertions, I can also unlock windows."

I hesitated with my hand on the knob, tilting my head in thought. I hadn't considered that route because I'd figured we would have to break a window—and the sound of shattering glass would be an immediate giveaway.

"I'm not sure I realized you could do that," I muttered.

"Which was why I mentioned it," he said patiently. "Things are only obvious when you already know them. With you, there is no telling what knocks around in your head."

The window beside the door wasn't capable of sliding open. The next nearest window was off to the side with the curtains drawn.

I stepped off the stoop and threaded my way through the plants. "Opening it won't break the plane," I muttered. "The alarm won't trigger unless someone goes through it. There is an additional spell one can apply to address that issue, of course. Did our mage take the extra precaution?"

I felt the vibrations of the spell through the glass,

not anchored well because of the difference in material.

"No, he did not," I whispered. "He thinks he's at the top of the food chain. These spells are nothing more than precautionary. He's probably thinking of human burglars. Little does he know that his safety is an illusion. What a horrible surprise he'll have tonight."

I glanced back at Darius, who still waited near the door. A moment later, he nodded. The lock was ready to go.

The window squealed as I pushed it up. I ground my teeth, stopping when it was halfway open, and listened. A truck rumbled by. In the distance, a dog barked. Silence hung heavy inside the house.

I passed my sword through the open space, splitting the security spell and unraveling it. The magic winked out, leaving residue that would soon start to deteriorate. I returned to the door and eased it open, thankful it didn't also creak. Darkness greeted me, lacking even a distant glow from any light sources elsewhere in the house.

The screen of my phone said 9:08. It was much too early for him to have gone to bed, and normal people didn't sit around in the dark. There was always the chance he was upstairs, though.

There was also the chance that he'd noticed us loitering outside his house, and was currently lying in wait, using the stillness, quiet, and darkness as cover. I didn't need a magical jack-in-the-box popping out at me. I hated those things. Even though I knew it was coming, it still scared me. It could only be worse in human form.

"Okay, let's split up," I whispered, the sound barely leaving my mouth. That was the great thing about vampires. Darius could still hear me. "I'll take the—"

"No. We stay together. There is no telling what we might run into."

Arguing would just eat into time.

I started forward slowly, quietly, clearing my mind and slipping into my inner battle zone. If he was home, I couldn't afford any mistakes. One loud bang and some nervous neighbors could call in the cops. This guy was a somewhat advanced mage, so he surely had more than one loud spell in his arsenal that he would liberally throw if his life was in danger.

A floorboard creaked below my boot. Deep shadow draped down the furniture and across the floor. There were papers on the dining room table, along with a half-empty cup of clear liquid. Water, probably. People who drank vodka out of a pint glass didn't usually leave it behind unless they were passed out next to it.

A few crumbs littered the countertop. The deep hum of the fridge reverberated in the silence. A soft touch landed on my shoulder.

I jumped. I couldn't help it. I really did hate jack-in-the-boxes.

Darius took his hand away and silently pointed at the microwave sitting on a side counter.

A lone casing looked like it had been forgotten there, resting against the salt and pepper shakers. Footfalls still quiet even though my heart had lurched at the possibility of a clue, I crossed that way and let my hand hover over the orb, a half-inch in diameter. The magic in it felt zesty and packed a hefty dose of power. It wouldn't rot your foot off, but it would cause some damage. With so little evidence, I couldn't even guess what kind of spell it was, but I did know it would be useful in my arsenal if I didn't need an incantation to get it to work. It was worth a shot.

I moved to swipe the ball off the microwave, but there was a quick flash of a hand. Darius had gotten there first.

"This is no time to be greedy," I told him. "You have plenty. Let the little guy have a new spell once in a while."

"I apologize. That was not intended." He studied the casing for a moment before holding his hand out flat.

I plucked the orb off his palm. "You need to get that protective thing looked at, dude. You're falling apart."

"I need blood."

A wash of shivers coated my body. I cocked my head and forced my heart to calm down. Playing it cool, and ignoring his comment, I studied the casing. "It's bigger than the one we found on the way to the unicorn paddock, right?"

"Yes. Similar style casing, able to hold more robust spells, but definitely larger."

"These guys were in New Orleans for a time. I wonder if Tamara, the mage also calling demons, caught wind of their activities and tried to duplicate them on her own terms? It would explain some things."

"Either that or she used the same casing supplier. I can have my people check it out."

"It's worth a shot." I dropped the casing into my pouch. "Either way, it looks like we have our guy."

"You are jumping to conclusions."

"Nah, I'd already jumped to that conclusion. This just makes his guilt more legit."

"It is a wonder people employ you."

"Not at all. I get the job done. Plus a little extra if I end up at the wrong villain's house." I moved to the door off the side of the kitchen. A quick peek inside told me it was the garage, and the minimal empty space not stuffed with shelves and boxes said a car couldn't fit. Neither could a bunch of mages, a guy without skin, and a demon. This couldn't be the scene of the crime, and not just because there was no blood.

I quickly left the kitchen and angled toward the stairs. Behind us, the fridge clicked off, dosing the space in liquid, gooey silence. As I moved, the faint sound of a ticking clock reached my ears. My breath came out in rhythmic, even puffs.

I hated creeping around. Running at a madman with a sword or spell? I was *in*. But this slow, deliberate mumbo jumbo when someone I couldn't see was possibly lying in wait? Good gracious, no. It was a heart racer.

The empty staircase beckoned, closed in by walls. If someone at the top started throwing down spells, this would be a bad situation for me.

I waved Darius back, knowing he'd be in my way if I had to retreat. Also knowing that, in his current state, he'd be more likely to put himself in harm's way in a futile attempt to protect me.

He probably hated this strange situation in which he found himself.

A loud pop made me flinch. I clutched my sword tighter, ready. A few more pops burst forth like gunfire, followed by a painful groan. Just the house shifting.

Breath now coming in fast pants, I increased my pace lest I suffer cardiac arrest. Nearly to the top, and the roar of a Harley thundered past the house and up the street. I paused, wondering if someone would pop out under the cover of the noise. I would've.

All was still.

I was starting to suspect he wasn't home.

I stepped onto the top step and paused. Four doors awaited me on the second floor, two standing open. One of the closed doors was narrower than the others, denoting a hall closet or something similar. Being that I saw the edge of a toilet through one of the open doors, I suspected this place was a two-bedroom.

Ignoring the bathroom, I walked slowly toward the other open room. I needed to keep my calm and not blast his face with fire. Given that my split-second reactions were always incredibly violent, which had kept me alive so far, my goal of composure was easier made than kept.

I brushed my fingers against the wood, pushing the door open slowly. It swung on well-oiled hinges. A bed came into view, neatly made. A dresser stood against the wall, its top bare. The nightstand next to the bed had a bare top as well. This was a guest room, and clearly not lived in.

The last door awaited me. So did the vampire standing next to it, looking at me like I was going into the snake pit and he did not approve.

"Shoo," I mouthed, and motioned for him to get away. I had enough to worry about without his vampiric protective malfunction tripping me up. "Go!" I waved at him again until he grudgingly moved to the side.

The deep breath I took didn't still my raging heart. Adrenaline surged within me, preparing me for a showdown. Making me want to kick the door open with guns blazing, ready to take the O.K. Corral. I was not a subtle person.

I wrapped my fingers around the doorknob and held my breath as I turned it. The latch clicked and I froze. No sound issued from within. I slowly pushed open the door. The bottom rubbed against something. A rug.

That sound would be heard.

I threw the door open the rest of the way and jumped into the room, my sword drawn in front of me, ready to cut through a hex. Something leapt out from the right, streaking through the air. A wall of fire roared in front of me. I hadn't meant to summon it. A spire of flame shot out, raking across the back of something small and headed straight for me. I hadn't meant to summon that, either. The thing screeched and darted away, its tail on fire. I cut out all the flame, getting a grip, just in time to see the creature disappear under the bed.

CHAPTER 18

I STALKED FORWARD and swept my gaze across the room. The rumpled covers indicated someone had slept there last night, but it was currently empty. Small artifacts littered the dresser and one of two nightstands. He was single and often slept alone. Somewhat neat, but not anal about it.

My boots creaked as I sank down onto my haunches, trying to see whatever had darted under the bed.

As if hearing my unspoken question, Darius said, "It was a cat."

I pulled in a breath. "That thing jumping at me was a cat?"

"Yes. You firebombed a kitty."

"Crap. What kind of a monster sets fire to a cat?" I grimaced and got on my hands and knees. "Are you sure? I don't want some creature that you mistakenly thought was a cat to dart out at my face."

"I am sure, yes. It was a black cat."

I crawled a little closer, searching for it. The smell of burned hair tickled my nose, making me potentially feel worse. Potentially, because I wasn't fully convinced it was an actual cat, and not some vile thing with three rows of teeth that the mage had found lurking in the wilds of the Realm. I'd seen some crazy things in my life.

A lump much too close to my face shuddered and hissed. Something flung out at me. I jerked back. Flame roared in front of my face again, blocking anything from advancing.

"Of all the things to fear, a cat gets you jumpy?" Darius asked with humor ringing in his voice.

I sighed and ripped down the wall of fire. "Are you positive it's a cat? I think it threw something at me."

Darius was hunched behind me, looking under the bed. "It struck out with its paw. When you first opened the door, it was trying to get out of the room. You stopped it handily. And now it is afraid of you. Rightly so."

"At least it's alive." I took a deep breath and sat back. "Well, this makes me an asshole."

"Yes. Get out of the way. I'll bring it out."

I scooted to the side. "Vampires aren't afraid of cats?"

"Why would my kind fear a defenseless animal?"

"Well, when you put it like that..." I stood as he somehow coaxed the animal out from under the bed. He cuddled it in his arms, stroking its black head. "So, you actually *like* cats. Huh. The things you learn."

"I like ordinary cats, yes."

"As opposed to?"

"Cat shifters."

"Right." I peered closer, trying to see if I should doctor its butt. Its hiss had me backing up again.

"This animal will likely never trust you again." Darius took it toward the door, looking it over. "The burns are mild. Had she been a human, you would've done very little damage."

"That was the point. I wasn't trying to kill him, remember? I bet he would've pissed his pants, though." I took a deep breath and rubbed my chest where my heart was slowing. "The fire treated the cat like I'd meant to treat the guy, so that's good. But I didn't mean to do that. I thought I was better at controlling my fire, but clearly I'm not great when it comes to blind reactions."

"You are on the doorstep of mastery. More practice and you'll be able to control your power in both situations." Darius stepped through the door. "Since the mage is clearly not home, I will doctor this animal while you figure out what other poor, defenseless creature to bully next."

"It jumped at me! That is hardly my fault." I frowned as Darius moved away. I doubted I'd live that one down anytime soon.

I fired off a quick text to Callie, asking if they had

anything. As I waited for a reply, I approached the mage's dresser, looking through the items on top. Loose change, a wadded-up tissue (which I didn't touch), and a tube of lip balm. His nightstand had a bottle of water, a book with a bunch of dog-eared pages, and an alarm clock. The first drawer held supplies for alone time, including a bottle of lotion. The other drawers were filled with all street clothes.

His closet was divided into two sections. The first was what I'd suspect—hanging clothes, including some robes, all black except for a red one. The other half of the closet was taken up by plastic shelving.

A grin pulled at my lips.

Each shelf was stacked with several small tubs, all labeled with various kinds of spells or ingredients. I glanced over the ingredients first, finding a couple of rare ones that Callie and Dizzy would love to have. Those I pulled out and placed on the ground.

Next I pored over the spell casings, grinning harder when I saw the powerful ones at the bottom were labeled with the Latin incantations needed to unleash them. Oh, mages and their elitist use of Latin. It made using stolen spells so easy. Had it been French, or German, I would've been lost.

I pulled out all the tubs of spells. I'd be relieving him of his hard work. Assuming he was guilty, of course. If he wasn't guilty...well, I'd only steal a little off the top. Old habits died hard.

"The kitten will be okay," Darius said, re-entering the room *sans* cat. He looked down at the items I was collecting. "He is organized. Did he make all of those?"

"There are one or two that feel a little off compared to the others, but I'd say he made most of them. He might be a disgusting murderer, but he seems highly experienced. He's been at the mage trade for a while."

"Is there anything to suggest he is the one calling the demons?"

"Not yet. But I've only searched one room. I have a whole house to go." Excitement ran through me. "I love rifling through people's things. It's a personality flaw I don't apologize for."

"You should." Darius bent over the spells, reading the labels. He took a few of each, tucking them into the hyper-organized satchel he wore whenever we were on the job.

I quickly rifled through the spare room, but my original assessment had been right. It was barren of interesting things. The bathroom wasn't intriguing, either.

Back downstairs, I was just starting to look around when my phone buzzed. Callie. *We're getting a lot of shifty eyes. Most people seem to know something, but no one wants to talk. It reeks of the guild. They have their corrupt paws all over this town, the filthy bastards.*

Keep at it, I texted back. *Just remember—low profile.*

You'd probably get more done if you shook things up, Callie responded.

Only if I knew who to shake. Since I didn't, I would just create a lot of noise, get labeled a disturber of the peace, and push people into steering clear. I'd learned that much last night at the restaurant.

I missed Red. Whenever I needed information back home, he was the first person I shook down. Even if he didn't have clear facts, the rumors he collected usually pointed me in a viable direction. I was sure there was someone like that around these parts—a magical weak link, if you will—I just had no idea how to find them. It was starting to get aggravating.

Still, this guy was a good lead. I really hoped he was guilty. Not only because it would mean my work here was (mostly) done, but because it would mitigate the cat-with-the-burned-butt situation. Things like that were hard to explain to innocent people just trying to live their lives.

He had a small office downstairs. I skimmed my finger along the spines of the books in his bookcase, hunting for anything of note. Two books seemed interesting, so I took those down. "Ah ha!" I pulled a volume from the top shelf. "A book about possessions. Guilty."

"Many people have—"

I jumped and spun, the book leaving my hand a moment later. It flew through the air, only missing Darius's head because he ducked out of the way, and slammed against the wall behind him. It fell to the ground.

"Don't sneak up on people!" I said a little too loudly, holding out my hand for the book.

With a grin, he bent to retrieve it. "As I was saying, many people have books on possessions. I, myself, have one. As, I'm sure, do you."

"This guy was suspect when he spoke in a public place about the screams of dying people. These are just nails in his coffin."

"Won't you be embarrassed if you are wrong?"

"Not embarrassed so much as let down that I couldn't have all the stuff I want to steal." I stacked up the books and set them on the coffee table in the living room.

"Aren't you going to look through his computer?" Darius asked as I hunted through the living room.

"Not yet. We can take that with us. I want to seek out stuff hidden in the folds of this house." I snatched a piece of discarded chalk off the mantelpiece and held it up. "Heavily used. Smooth, too. They're doing the summoning somewhere inside. The smudges of dirt suggest it's somewhere that isn't cleaned too often. That could be a house, but judging by the cleanliness of his house, I'd bet not."

"That could be for his own use."

"It *is* for his own use, since our guy is doing this for himself as much as his crew. But let's look at the facts. He's experienced, knows how to work some pretty powerful spells, is organized, and lives in a place where the Mages' Guild has a heavy influence. Now we learn he is writing things in chalk. Many people do this, sure. I've seen more than a few amateurs in the graveyard. But not many people do it inside." I paused, connecting the dots.

"What?" Darius asked.

"Scuffs like this could come from a garage." I shook my head. "I didn't see anything in this one, but I was in a hurry. Maybe..." I cut across the house and let myself into the garage, followed by Darius.

"We've found the manufacturer of the casings," Darius said, looking into one of the stacked boxes. "He bought in bulk. Or someone else did and he is storing them."

"Ha! Guilty!"

"They could just be—"

"No way. That's super guilt, right there. He's a criminal, which means I don't have to feel bad about ransacking his house. I am definitely taking all his crap, yo. Happy days to me."

"Your moral compass is ambiguous."

"Like you can talk." I scoffed and looked at the ground, trying to find any outlines in the cleared-away space. In the dark, contrast was low, even for my vision. Still scanning, I flicked on the light and backtracked, trying to find a hint of an outline.

"Nothing," I said with my hands on my hips. "He's not practicing here."

"Hmmm," Darius said, as if I'd said something of great interest. "He—they—may have been *practicing* in New Orleans, did you think of that?" He moved toward the shelves on the side. "Maybe they wanted a space away from the guild's influence until they knew what they were doing. Or maybe the guild approves, and it sent them to another city with high magical traffic in case they couldn't contain the demon. NOLA has the best bounty hunter in the nation. If a demon got loose, there would be no better place for it to happen."

"I do love flattery, but I am far from the best in the nation. Still, you do have some valid points."

"That statement was not bent toward flattery. You are known for your prowess."

"Uh-huh." I could name five bounty hunters across the world who were legends in the business, and none of them were named Reagan. "Anyway, back to it. I want to have the place catalogued before he gets home."

"You don't have enough evidence to convict him yet," Darius said, pulling a knife out of a box.

"I'm not looking for evidence; I'm looking for additions to my magic collection. And Callie's. The evidence I'll beat out of him. That part is easy."

Darius held up the knife. "The blade has blood on it."

"There you go. You spoke too soon."

"It is a hunting knife. It could be animal blood."

"I haven't found any hunting rifles, or even a crossbow. He's some hunter if he's bagging deer without any way to shoot them."

"There are other things to hunt."

"I assume those other things just die on cue? Because otherwise, he'd need a weapon for whatever he was killing." I shifted from side to side, impatient with his slow, methodical approach to evidence collection. "I'll see you in there. You take too long."

"The treasure is in the details."

I pushed through the door and rounded the corner while brainstorming the other spots people tended to hide things. I should search a closet downstairs. Maybe look harder in the living room.

A shape caught my eye next to the front door. The *open* front door.

Shock ran through me, and I staggered to a stop, facing a man who had keys dangling uselessly from his fingers. He stared at me as I stared at him, both of us surprised someone else was in the house. That lasted a blink of an eye. Then we were action.

I dove to the side as the keys shot toward me. He hadn't thrown them. They had zipped from his hand.

What the hell magic was that?

I ripped out my sword again, having put it away after the episode with the cat, and ducked behind the couch. A swell of power engulfed the room, popping my ears and churning the air.

That was way too much power for the man who had created those spells upstairs.

I may have made a grievous error in coming here.

CHAPTER 19

"**M**Y, MY. THAT was quick," the man said. His voice was too raspy for a human, and power swirled around his words. "She has found me."

"I don't know what that means." I dug through my pouch, feeling the vibrations of the few casings I had, since I stupidly hadn't pocketed any from upstairs yet, until my fingers glanced off a spell that would work. I yanked it out and pinched, then popped up and threw it.

A sheet of air slammed into me. It threw me back, ass over end, until I knocked against the wall. The fire inside me, which usually swelled in times like these, diminished. Instead, that block of cold I'd felt while levitating grew, pulsing up through my body. A new power bled into my bloodstream, one that spread tingles across my scalp and down to the base of my spine.

A high-pitched scream sounded as the figure by the door wriggled in pain. Sparkling pink foam was burning the skin on his arms. I surged forward, sword out, ready for his counter-spell or another weird air attack.

It came when I'd cut the distance between us in half.

A block of magic sailed through the air. I cut through it with my sword. It sparked before sizzling away. Another came right after, the same intensity, but half as powerful as the ability this man had displayed with the solid air. He was using casings now.

Before I could surge forward again, the furniture bumped forward, moved into my path by unseen hands.

"Do you have the demon in you?" I asked, out of breath and not sure why. The cold thing in my stomach pounded. I knew how to work my fire. I didn't know how to work this new feeling. It wasn't responding the way my power usually did.

"I do not." The man grinned and tilted his head in an inhuman way, studying me. His laugh sounded like skeletons dancing on graves. "But I do have the power of the underworld coursing through me. It feels marvel-ous."

"It does now, sure. Wait until it starts to erode you. That won't feel as great."

His renewed laughter froze my blood. "Ah, but I will be allowed to go free if I deliver the goods to my master. You are Reagan Somerset, are you not? Here from New Orleans?"

"Who's your master?"

"Are you the girl he seeks? The heir?"

The cold hand of dread wrapped around me. "Nope. The only thrones I know of are made of porcelain. Who's your master?"

"I will take that as a...maybe." His smile could curdle milk. "Come with me. We will see if I get a big prize."

He grabbed something invisible in front of him. Air condensed around my body before lifting me partway off the ground. Huh. The demon had given him the power to move things with his mind.

"This is bad," I mumbled, reaching for my fire to break out of the air grip. It was hampered, though, overcome by that block of ice swelling within my middle and pumping out through my limbs.

"Say, listen," I said as he pulled me through the air toward him. My toes scraped the rug. "That power you feel right now, did the demon show you how to use it?"

"It is my life's blood. It is my soul. Using it is my given right."

"That didn't answer my question. What does it feel like? Is it cold? I'm just trying to compare notes, you understand."

"It feels like worlds colliding. Almighty. All-powerful. Eternal."

"Wow. No, there is no way you are getting out of this alive. I hate to break it to you, but that demon hung a *gullible* sign around your neck." I stopped directly in front of the guy, a forty-something with slightly mussed brown hair, a decent complexion, and crazed eyes. He'd probably been normal once. That ship had sailed.

The man stared at me as if waiting for me to do something.

"What?" I asked, relaxing. Nothing good came of panicking, especially in horrible situations that you had no idea how to escape.

"You are coming without a fight?"

"Maybe. I don't know. I can't really get a reading on you. Your former magic was nothing special, if what I'm sensing was yours, which I'm inclined to believe it was, but now you have this enormous power seeping out of you. How'd that happen? I mean, hell's bells, man, this kinetic magic has really thrown me for a loop. This is a first for me, and that doesn't happen very often. I'm just soaking it in for the moment. I'll tell you one thing, though. There is no way that demon is a four. No way. Fours can't impart, or even harness, this type of magic. Not any fours I've ever heard about, anyway."

"Come. I will take you to my—"

"Leader? Please say leader."

A blur of movement made me flinch. Darius appeared beside me and immediately raked the air with his already extended vampire claws. Magic crackled and sparked when his claws came into contact with it. He ripped me out of the sky and tossed me behind him. I tumbled to the ground.

He slashed at the mage. More magic sparked and fizzled, Darius's vampire magic in the form of claws, and probably fangs, able to counteract the mage's kinetic magic.

Thank heavens.

The man jerked away, back-pedaling until he hit the wall. He lifted his arms to block his face, throw a spell, or use his newfound kinetic magic.

"Keep his arms down!" I hollered, jumping to my feet. "He has to move them through the air to direct his magic."

"Stay back," Darius growled at me, pinning the mage's arms to his sides.

"Yeah, right." I stepped to the side of Darius and cocked back my fist, intending to deliver a blow to knock the man out.

The punch didn't land.

Despite Darius's vampire strength, the mage somehow managed to rip his arms up and shove his hands through the air.

Darius flew back, cracking into the wall. He rose and hissed before his body erupted into the swamp thing (a.k.a. his monster form)—faster, stronger, and more lethal. That would help, but I wondered if it would be enough. This guy had gotten a powerful gift from a mighty demon.

I felt the push of air closing around me. The man was ready to haul me away, and judging by his shifty-eyed glance in Darius's direction and his hop-steps toward the door, he wanted to do it fast so as not to battle an elder in monster form. I didn't blame him, but I also didn't intend to be taken.

I ripped my sword up. Sparks erupted from the edge of the blade, as if I'd struck it against stone, but it made it through the nearly solid air, unraveling the effect much like it would a spell. The man growled, a truly demonic sound, and jerked forward to grab me.

I dodged the grab and sliced up with my sword, intent on cutting through any newly solid air. Instead, my blade caught his wrist. His severed hand went flying across the room.

Oops.

He howled, clutched his wrist, and broke for the door.

"Don't play with air, and I won't lop off body parts," I said by way of a half-felt apology, and lurched after him.

We ran out into the night. That cold power throbbed within me again, begging to be used. I didn't know how, though. Not without focused concentration, which was impossible, given the circumstances.

Darius zipped by me, way faster in a race, and stopped further up the sidewalk, still in his ghastly form, waiting for the mage to run into him. The mage flung his hands up—or arm and hand, at any rate—and cut right, into the street. Headlights washed across his body and brakes squealed.

"No, no, no!" I yelled at the car.

The mage stopped, staring at the headlights, frozen in place.

"Run, you moron! Darius—"

Darius flashed after the man, grabbing him and shoving him to the side of the road before he could become the car's new hood ornament. I ran after them. The car had finally come to a stop, directly in my path, so I leapt up and ran across the hood. It was mighty cool.

"Let's get him out of here," I said before an invisible hand swatted me.

This time I went flying across the hood of the car, face first, and fell off the other side. That wasn't as cool.

Air closed around me like a big fist. I reached for my sword, which had fallen to the ground two feet from me, but couldn't get it before I was lifted into the sky.

The cold force within me throbbed harder, almost painful. I gritted my teeth and closed my eyes, trying to connect with it. Trying to figure out a way to lift a rock and beam that danged mage in the side of the head.

A scream rent the night. I fell, landing awkwardly and crumpling to the sidewalk. Disorientated, I dazedly grabbed my sword and climbed to my feet. Someone gasped as I shook off the pain and started forward yet again.

Darius stood in human form in the street, naked, holding the now-limp mage by the back of his shirt. Before I got there, the shirt ripped at the neck and shoulder, making the mage drop a little lower in the air. The girls from the car that had nearly mowed him down gasped again.

"Tell me you merely knocked him out," I said to Darius, limping as I worked around the hood of the car. My ankle was a little out of sorts from my haphazard landing. "Tell me he'll wake up and give us information."

"I do not like to lie to you, Reagan. I lost control when he had you in the air. I need to feed. I told you that."

"There is no way it's my fault you lost control, so don't even try to pin it on me."

"I am simply reminding you of what happens when you hold me off."

"Do you also want to be a dead body? Is that what you're after? Keep it up and I'll add you to the pile." I braced two fingers to the mage's neck.

"Is he okay?" one of the girls asked with a quivering lip. The other was already crying. Their distress was evident from their lack of questions regarding the fact that a naked man was holding a potentially injured man in the air by his shirt. With one hand. And no visible strain.

No, they weren't based in reality just now.

I deflated. "Nope. Damn it!" I turned around, seeing a row of lights and people emerging from their houses. "Well, this all went horribly wrong. Drop him and get us out of here. Fast. We don't need anyone to take pictures of our faces. Send some vampires out here tomorrow to make those ladies forget their own names, let alone the fact that they saw a monster kill a guy."

"I will not appear in photos."

"You are really hard to get along with right now, do you know that? Let's hit his house really quickly before we leave. Hurry, before the cops—" A siren wailed in the distance.

Without warning, he scooped me into his arms and raced up the street, faster than thought. We were breaking so many magical rules it wasn't funny, not to mention that we'd killed a mage whom the Mages' Guild, his circle, and—most recently—a demon might employ and/or like. My second night in Seattle and already my enemies were stacking up. I had a gift.

CHAPTER 20

"**A**RE YOU SURE this is your chosen course of action?" Darius asked me as we pulled up near the mage bar to meet Callie and Dizzy.

Instead of going in himself, Darius had given me ten minutes to run into the mage's house and get the stuff I couldn't live without. Eleven minutes later, he'd dragged me out. After that, we'd stopped by the hotel so he could get some clothes on, and now here we were, ready for a beer and hopefully some good news.

The beer was the only sure thing.

"Yes. Callie isn't great at making friends, and Dizzy is weird at the best of times. He might make friends, but he doesn't inspire the kind of intimacy that will get someone to spill their secrets. Hopefully I can be the go-between."

Darius shook his head as he exited the car. I pushed the door open and gingerly stepped on my ankle.

"Would you like me to carry you?" he asked, walking around the car to me.

I snickered. "Funny."

His expression was serious.

"The reason I let you carry me the last time was because we had to flee the scene of a crime. That was about speed, not a tweaked ankle. Give me a break."

"Do you heal at a faster rate than humans?" he asked, shutting the door for me. He adjusted his satchel around his shoulder.

"You keep forgetting that I am human."

"Do you?"

"Yes," I said grudgingly.

"Why do you detest the side of you that isn't human?"

I took a deep breath and paused at the bar door. "I'm sure my dad is a really swell guy, but he rules the land of evil. Of monsters. I don't want to be reminded of that part of my genetic makeup."

"Many demons actually do good. Spread love. Pleasure."

Oh yeah. I'd forgotten about that new knowledge.

I shrugged. "Mainly, though, I only knew my mom. She raised me. Made me what I am. I want to identify with her, and she was human."

"Human, but with the bloodline of the gods. In essence, she was more than human, more than a mage, like you. On either side, you are extraordinary. There is not one piece of you that is mundane. You should celebrate that."

"I like mundane. Mundane keeps me safe."

"You would not have been able to hide from what you are for much longer. You should be thankful you found me."

"I didn't find you, you arrogant ass. You stalked me. And why should I be thankful? Because the shifters will think I'm the enemy, or because I'll get to be a feeding trough soon?"

"Because I can protect you in a way few others can."

"Let me guess, this is going to lead into a conversation on bonding."

"Well, since you brought it up..." Humor danced in his eyes.

I held up my hand, unable to stop myself from smiling. "No."

"You say no now, but just wait. Your mind will change."

"Nope."

"I will rock your world. You will never be satisfied with that human cop."

Those damn tingles washed over me again. "You'll get blood, and that's it. I'll stand very still and rigid while I fulfill my promise. Then I'll make your life hell. Somehow."

He pulled the door open, his honeyed eyes delving into mine. "You already make my life hell," he whispered. "In the best of ways."

The man had a way with words—I'd give him that. "You probably banged your way through the nobles of France when you were a human," I muttered, entering the dimly lit interior of the half-filled bar. "Even though women weren't supposed to sleep around back then."

"Women have always had the same desires when it comes to pleasure and passion. It is society that changes," Darius said, stopping beside me. "Simply because it was declared wrong in the time, does not mean it didn't happen. I deflowered a great many behind the veil of secrecy, and they loved me for it."

"Oh, ew. Tone it down, Casanova. And I doubt they loved you for tarnishing their reputations."

"Behind the veil of secrecy, I said. I have always been discreet, and I have never lacked for partners, single or otherwise, experienced or not—"

"Please stop."

"I celebrate a woman who knows her desires, and who demands to have them fulfilled."

"Seriously, stop."

"Do you demand to have your desires fulfilled, Reagan?"

Not the tingles! "I demand that you shut it down, and to achieve that end, I'll shoot you in the leg again like I did in the paddock. Is that what you're after?"

"So violent." He gave a dark chuckle. "You have passion in spades, *ma puce*. I can't wait to experience it."

"I don't know what *puce* means, but it sounds dirty," I muttered. I pulled up my leg, snatched a knife from the holster around my ankle, and stabbed him in the side. Just as quickly, I pulled it out of his body, wiped the blade on his expensive shirt, and shoved it back where it belonged. His side would heal, but his shirt was ruined. I knew he'd care more about the latter.

He barely flinched. His reaction was another dark chuckle.

That hadn't worked out how I'd hoped.

"Ready?" I asked, stalking forward.

"Always," he replied, the velvet of his voice only easing marginally. He definitely did need blood, and if I wanted him to knock off all this *ma puce* stuff, I couldn't even flinch when giving it to him. Nor could I display all this passion he thought I had rolling around in my body. It would be like a handshake, as far as I was concerned. A tight-lipped, stony-cold handshake between acquaintances. That was all.

Nodding to myself, because I knew this wouldn't be the last time I needed the inner pep talk, I scanned the occupants of the bar for Callie and Dizzy.

"Dude, did you just stab that guy?" asked a young man with wide, disbelieving eyes. He wobbled against the wall he was leaning against, obviously drunk. That brown bottle in his hand wasn't his first, or even third.

Drunk men had a habit of flapping their gums. Especially younger drunk men when confronted with a woman wearing skintight leather. My choice of clothing wasn't only good for battle.

First things first.

I pointed at him, my hand too close to his face. "Are you human?"

"What?" He tried to move his head before bringing his hand up to bat away my finger.

"He is, yes," Darius said, his gaze moving slowly around the room. "One that badly needs a shower."

"What's your problem?" the drunk guy asked, pushing upright. His eyes found the bloodied spot on Darius's shirt. "Oh shit. Dude, you're bleeding!"

I walked away from the man because he'd only get more disruptive, and checked out the lay of the land. Tables hugged the wall on my right, and there was a small throughway between those and the barstools pressed close to one side of the square bar. To my left, more stools lined the bar, leading to a larger open area on the other side. I knew I'd find more tables back there, maybe a booth or two, and wondered if there was a pool table in the back. Judging by the crowd, the other side of the bar was more popular. It probably had more shadows and less humans. Less humans because the magical folk would scare them away from hanging around.

That was where I needed to be. With the scary folk. They didn't tattle when you hung them upside down and demanded information. And I needed to demand information at this point. Because what was up with a mage holding me off the ground with *air*? That type of thing didn't go unnoticed, not even in New Orleans.

When I turned the corner, I did indeed see a pool table with one guy bent over the green. Another guy gripping a cue stick stood off to the side, watching the shot. A few others hovered around the table with them, and several more people were spread out across the back area. Among them, sitting by themselves at a table, were Callie and Dizzy.

"They certainly did not make friends," I muttered, stopping at the top of the bar.

The bartender, a brick of a man in his early thirties, slowed when he came our way. His eyes took me in for a second before pausing on Darius. His expression hardened.

"I'd like a whiskey, please," I said. "Jameson."

The bartender leaned against the bar. The muscles on his arms bulged and his hard gaze never left Darius's face. "You shouldn't be here, pal."

"I'm going to take a wild stab here, but...shifter?" I lifted my eyebrows at the bartender. Like vampires, shifters didn't smell like their other forms.

His gaze flicked to me. "I don't work for Roger, but

I don't mind chipping in when these bloodsuckers come around."

"I have as much right to be in the Brink as you do," Darius said eloquently. "In addition, I am working in connection with the human police department. We are trying to rid your town of mages who are killing people in order to call demons. Or would you rather the death toll rise?"

The bartender scoffed. "Isn't that a little like the pot calling the kettle black? You kill humans all the time. Why should you care about a few more of them dying?"

"I do not kill them. I share a mutually beneficial relationship with them, which they are free to end at will."

I grimaced, because the ending it at will part wasn't always true. Take my situation, for example—I couldn't get rid of the bugger, and I hadn't even engaged in a mutually beneficial relationship. I'd tried not to engage in any kind of relationship at all.

The bartender scowled. "Is changing them into swamp monsters what you call a mutually beneficial relationship?"

"You've got a valid point, there, Sir Bartender." I knocked on the bar. "Be that as it may, he's not changing anyone now, and he's not feeding on humans. I spoke to Roger about this a couple months ago. Darius is helping me solve a case. Despite my hopes to the contrary, he's helpful."

"These things only look out for themselves," the bartender said.

"Usually, yes. However, earlier today he broke me out of a mage's demon-powered magical hold. How the holy hell that mage was able to suspend me in the air without his hands, I do not know, but that is not a power you want running amok in your city, trust me. There is some serious shit going down, and you can take the uncharacteristically high pitch of my voice as proof. I don't normally get rattled, but any demon that can impart that much power is…really not good. Not good at all."

I took a deep breath before continuing. I'd been constantly in motion since all this happened, so there'd been no time to think or worry. But now, explaining it, the gravity of the situation was hitting home.

That mage had wielded a power I couldn't easily counteract, and he hadn't even been possessed. That meant that the demon who'd imparted its power was definitely mighty, and quite possibly something I couldn't handle.

What had I gotten myself into?

"Anyway." I put both palms on the bar and leaned toward the guy, because he was something I *could* handle. "The vampire's claws work on that demon-inspired power, which means he needs to stick around. If you have a problem with that, get Roger on the phone. I'll deal with your alpha, not you. Otherwise, serve me up that whiskey, because I need to talk to my friends."

The bartender's face crumpled into an expression of wariness. He leaned away from me, and as he did so, his eyes flicked to the right. Without another word, he turned and went after the whiskey.

"Does your magic work on those demons because you're a vampire, or because you are an elder?" I asked Darius quietly.

"An elder of my age and experience can handle most demons, all the way up to the higher echelons of power. Vlad has tested this theory with a few level-five demons, but from what I gather, he hasn't been able to get at Lucifer's right-hand demons. I would wager that the most powerful demons and angels are beyond our capabilities."

"He is trying to work out a deal with demons, but he's testing his abilities to kill them?"

"The demons have power games, like humans. Like vampires. In order to get things done, Vlad is willing to do whatever it takes. He had to kill a few naysayers to prove his worthiness, and kill a few more who stood to oppose the plan. He is one of the most ruthless vampires living."

"Well, not really *living*, as it were…"

"You have used that joke before."

"It's funny every time."

"Hardly."

"And that is why you didn't want me to kill that demon at the mage battle?" I asked. "You didn't want to step on Vlad's toes."

"Correct. I am not at Vlad's level. Not yet. My power is nearly equal, as are my strength and prowess, but I don't have as many fail safes in place. I can't let him know that I possibly upset his plans by allowing a demon to be killed. He would take that as a personal slight, and pay me one in kind."

The bartender placed two glasses of whiskey in front of us, his gaze downcast. "I don't know what kind of magic you're wielding, but try to fit in. I don't need no trouble in my bar." He must've caught my unique scent. Thankfully, he wasn't as curious as Roger's people.

"Don't worry." I hooked a thumb Darius's way. "He'll pay for the damages."

Darius's lips thinned.

"Whatever. Look, I know a couple of the mages who like to call demons," the bartender said, sticking out his hand for money and leaning against the bar. He looked away from us, as though the very sight of us offended him.

I nudged Darius. "Thanks for the drink." He reached into his back pocket.

"They drink in here," the bartender continued.

"Usually after they do the summoning. They are always pleased with themselves. They brag about it."

"They flout the magical law by summoning a demon, and yet the shifters do nothing?" Darius said. "Do you choose which laws you uphold based on your prejudices?"

"That is also a valid point, but now's not the time." I nudged Darius again, this time to quiet him.

The bartender's face came back around, anger plain in his features. "You don't know shit about this town. If we make a move on a mage here, it's as good as declaring war with the Mages' Guild. They police themselves. I've let them know a few times that their mages are calling demons, and I've let Roger know, too. Nothing happened. You do the math."

"I have done the math," Darius said in a dangerous tone. My small hairs stood on end. "The woman standing next to me has as much courage in her pinky as Roger's entire force of shifters. She will take on the mages, the demon, and the Mages' Guild, if need be, in order to save your town. Helping her are two other mages, a human detective, and a vampire. *Not* helping her…" Darius swept his hand toward the bartender, his bar, and then made a wider, more inclusive gesture. It was clear he meant the entire town. "For a species who boasts fearlessness, you sure quiet down fast enough."

Darius took his drink off the bar, staring the bartender down, and sipped slowly. "This whiskey is subpar."

The bartender motioned at me. "She picked it."

"Okay, then. Good talk." I pulled Darius's arm. "Time's a-wastin'."

"Hey." The bartender raised his hand for me. He went to the till, showing the bar his big back. A moment later, he turned back with a few folded bills in his hand. "I may not want you here, but I ain't no crook. And don't bother tipping. I won't spend your filthy money."

It was Darius's turn to nudge me this time, even though it wasn't my change. I didn't argue.

I took the few steps closer to the bar. Darius continued on toward Callie and Dizzy's table, taking both drinks with him.

"No tip," the bartender said again, louder. Then he lowered his voice. His eyes were soft and sincere, almost imploring, as he shoved the bills into my hand. I could tell this was more than a mere monetary exchange. "That's about all I can do. Good luck. I mean that. I got kids here, a business. I can't afford to be a vigilante. But if you organize something against the guild, Roger will want to know about it. We don't have the guns against that organization, but he won't balk about lending a hand to those who do."

I crumpled the money in my fist and shook my head, playing it up for whatever spectators he was worried about. "Leaving you no tip makes absolutely no sense, you realize." I slipped the money into my pouch. His nod was slight as he leaned away. "You'll take the wage after his filthy money is laundered through your business, but you won't take it directly? That's just stupid."

His brow furrowed. "Do you know what laundering means?"

I rolled my eyes. I had thought so...

"Whatever. Suit yourself." I patted my pouch. "Also, if I don't die, I'd really appreciate you putting in the good word to Roger. Shifters follow me around about as much as that vampire does, and I'd rather neither of them did. It doesn't do much for my appearance of neutrality, you know? So, anyway, I'd love it if he heard something good about me for once. You know, like I helped out your town." I smiled at him hopefully and waggled my eyebrows. "But if you do talk to him, don't mention the vampire."

A grin slid up his face. "You're cracked."

"I know. But think about it, would you?"

"Get outta here." The bartender flung up his hand and turned away to serve someone waiting down the bar.

A moment later, I was in the ladies' room pulling out the money. The white of a bar napkin was nestled between the green bills. On it a lazy hand had scrawled two names. Nothing else, just the names.

"That'll do, pig," I muttered. Google would help me put faces to the names, no problem. But this time, I needed the dual mages on board. I knew what I was up against, and I knew I needed more power.

CHAPTER 21

I EXITED THE bathroom, planning to finish both whiskeys. Darius needed blood later, fine, but I didn't need to be sober to give it. Actually, I didn't *want* to be sober when giving it. I really didn't want any part of the whole thing.

Stupid promises and watchful shifters.

The men at the pool table were no longer hunched over when I walked out of the hall leading to the restrooms. Both were standing up straight, looking in the vague direction of Callie and Dizzy's table. I didn't think much of it until I had to push my way past a group of people, all of them staring in that same direction. In a moment, I knew why.

Three people stood at Callie and Dizzy's table, looking down on them. Darius was somewhat removed, standing against the wall, leaving them on their own. Judging by the stances of the people leaning over the table, the closed-down expression of Callie, and the worried expression of Dizzy, this wasn't a friendly encounter.

Fire surged up my middle, my power finally making an appearance.

"Where were you when that mage was trying to drag me away?" I scolded my magic.

Sure, muttering to myself made me look crazy, but when dealing with bullies, that could only help.

"You have until sundown to get—"

"What's up?" I asked, coming around the table. Out of the corner of my eye, I caught the bartender shaking his head.

A man in his sixties straightened up and swung his gaze my way. Dark brown eyes squinted at me from above a thick beard. "Are you with them?"

I picked up the nearest glass of whiskey and sucked it down. The clink of the empty glass as it hit the table drew the eyes of the woman in the middle of the group of three, mid-fifties with curly hair reminiscent of eighties perms. Residual magic saturated the air around her. She squinted at me.

Squinting must've been their go-to for conveying: *I hold the power here.*

"Yes." I lifted the second glass of whiskey.

"Are you a mage, too?" asked the far man, a pudgy guy with a serious gray mustache. It was like a mouse had crawled onto his face, lain down, and gotten stuck there.

"Well, aren't you nosy?" I leaned a hand against the

top of the chair.

"These are members of the local chapter loosely af-filiated with the Mages' Guild," Callie said with a tight jaw.

"They are more of a fan club than they are an actual apart of the guild," Dizzy added.

"It seems that we must get permission to do busi-ness in their town." Callie put the emphasis on *their* with a sharp, sarcastic bite.

"Oh." I smiled. "Well that's okay, then. You're not doing business in their town. You're visiting friends and seeing the sights. Crisis averted."

"They are working with the MLE office," Mustache said.

"You got a little something"—I waggled my finger over my upper lip—"just there…"

He frowned at me.

"Anyway, you are incorrect. *I* am working with the MLE office. Ish." I touched my hand to my chest. "Me only. The vampire back there gave me a ride to Seattle, and my friends here came along because they'd always wanted to ride in a private jet. So you see, there's no problem."

"Oh, I think there is a *big* problem," Beard said, hik-ing up his belt. I didn't miss those digits dipping into his pocket to grab the top of something sticking out of it. His hand returned to his side, holding a stick of some kind. His sleight of hand was good, but unlike me, he wasn't up to pickpocket speed.

Amateur.

"Here's the big problem." I pointed at his face. "If you are going to dye your beard, you have to dye your eyebrows, too. I mean, a deep brown beard and light gray eyebrows? Who are you trying to fool?"

"Eyebrows are a subtler job," Callie said. "He clearly doesn't have the magical finesse."

"Then use the boxed stuff at the store, know what I mean?" I asked. Someone in the gathered crowd barked out a laugh before shuffling away, eyes averted.

"We know what you're doing here, and we don't need you messing around in our affairs," the woman said, raising her chin. "All the magical people here know that we police our own affairs."

"Clearly not, since people are still dying," I said.

"The guild is working on it," Mustache said in a wavering tone. In other words, he had no idea if the guild was working on it. He turned just so until his hand was hidden by the woman beside him.

Not so subtle, bub.

Dizzy's hands drifted down to his lap.

"Keep your hands on the table," Beard barked, the muscles on his arm going taut.

"Or what?" I asked.

"Since we are mages, and they have a, however distant, relationship with the guild, they think they have authority over us," Callie said, icy but calm. "They fail to realize that since we aren't in the guild, or even a wannabe fan club, we aren't subject to their law."

"You are in our town, so you are under our law." Beard was so agitated he was spitting. It clearly made him nervous that we weren't groveling before him.

"Or. *What?*" I asked again, my voice now filled with warning. With anticipated action.

Darius took another couple steps back. He knew something would kick off soon, knew I'd get in the middle of it, and probably wondered if his primal crazy would take over and he'd kill everyone before he could stop himself. Why he thought a few steps would make a difference, I had no idea.

"They threatened to kill us," Dizzy said in an even voice. It was then I realized his hands were splayed on the table. Callie's were above the table, too, resting against her glass. The wannabe guild members clearly thought they had the upper hand.

But they didn't know the caliber and ferocity of the mages they'd decided to ambush. Even still, adrenaline roared through my body. I could deal with a lot of crap, but my friends being threatened was not on that list.

"So let me get this straight," I said, drawing my sword in a smooth, practiced movement. The fire roaring through my blood, preparing me for battle, made my movements as fast as a vampire's, something surprising in a girl that looked like a human. All three mages flinched. The woman's eyes widened. "You don't give two licks about the crazy-ass mages running around town, skinning humans and calling demons, but two tourists present a grave offense?" I shook my head slowly. "Power, unchecked, corrupts. Now get out of here. We don't bow to whack-jobs."

"This is your final warning," Mustache said loudly, for the whole bar to hear. He tensed, ready to throw whatever spell he'd palmed straight into Dizzy's face.

I sprang to action, banging Beard on the head with the hilt of my sword and dropping him like a stone. I grabbed the woman as light flashed between her hands.

Always beware the quiet ones.

The blade of my sword dropped, as though I didn't have control. I did, of course, and the tip sliced through the emerging hex, unraveling it completely. My other hand closed around the front of the woman's blouse, and I ripped her to the ground.

A bang erupted from Mustache. Red light cut through the air, heading straight for Dizzy. Before I could react, Callie's hands came away from her glass and a rectangle of blue flared to life in front of them. Dizzy's hands were digging into his satchel as the red hex washed over the blue. Both spells fizzled out, Callie having somehow anticipated what spell Mustache would use, retrieved the correct counter-spell, and hidden it against her glass in the cupped palm of her hand.

She is good.

I pivoted and kicked, catching Mustache in the teeth with my boot. Blood spurted from a split lip as he fell back, his hands going lax. He bounced off the ground as the woman climbed to her feet, her hands going for a small saddlebag-looking pouch at her side.

"Do people make fun of you for having saddlebags? Get it?" I grinned even as I surged forward and snatched her hand away. Her fingers went white on the orb she was holding before I could peel them away. "Get down!"

I swatted her hand with such force that her body whipped around after it. The spell came loose and fell at her feet. Callie jumped up, probably with some sort of shield for me, but I already had my hand in my pouch and around an empty casing. I crashed it against my blade, playing it up like I was using a counter-spell. As the woman's spell erupted, I braced myself to cut it harmlessly away, but a large, solid body intercepted and hit me like a Mack truck.

The breath gushed out of my lungs as impossibly strong arms of coiled muscle carried me to the very back of the room and into the hallway leading to the restrooms. People crowded in after us as the blast tore through the room, pushing out a concussion of air.

I finally got my breath back as the noise receded, not easy when a stone of a vampire was pinning me to the wall.

"Really, Darius?" I asked in a dry voice. "I could have prevented that."

His hard body peeled away from mine enough so he could look down on my face. I'd probably have a few bruises from that "rescue." He needed to start wearing padded clothes if he planned to keep this up.

People around us were slowly unfurling from their crouches, taking their hands away from their heads. They had clearly been expecting a huge blast. Thankfully, that mage hadn't had the power to pull it off.

"I tried to prevent this reaction," he said, stepping away. Not far enough, though. His hands lingered on my hips. He shook his head, small movements, and confusion drew a crease between his brows. "I'm not sure feeding can unseat this, Reagan. It has gone deeper than that. I don't know what's happening to me."

He sounded lost. Dare I say vulnerable? I was pretty sure those emotions were mostly foreign to him in his stage of immortality. Yet here he was, admitting them to me in a soft though urgent voice.

I patted his arm. "We'll get you that blood and see if it goes away. Hopefully it does, for both of our sakes. Because you are cutting into my cool points by saving me."

"Saving a human also cuts into my cool points, I assure you."

"I'm back to being a human in your eyes, am I? Wow. You must really hate emotion."

"Fear for your survival is distracting."

"There he is—the vampire who stole my mark." I pushed past him and exited the hall. People were checking on each other, speaking in hushed voices. The scream of sirens sounded outside the bar. The woman who'd detonated the spell lay on the ground, not moving. She'd gotten her just dessert. Beard had rolled to the side and was clasping his head. Mustache was gone.

"Where the hell did you go?" Callie demanded, rushing over to me. She checked over my face and then shifted her gaze down my body. "I didn't think you'd need to get cover. Are you okay?"

"Darius to the rescue." I shooed her away. "I'm fine. Is Dizzy okay?"

"Darius to the rescue?" Callie eyed Darius suspiciously.

"I'm okay," Dizzy said, hurrying from the bar. The bartender was on the phone. "We were prepared. They were lackluster bullies, at best. Just mad they didn't have enough know-how to get into the *real* guild. We've seen a few of those in our time. Anyway, we need to get out of here. He's going to say it was a terrorist, but their mage friends might form a posse."

"Screw their friends," Callie and I said at the same time. She grinned at me as I laughed.

"But yes, let's go. I don't want to be seen at this crime scene any more than I did at the first one." I looked back toward the bathrooms. "Let's use the back door."

"What was the first crime scene?" Callie asked.

"I'll explain later. C'mon." I ushered them along as the first policemen walked through the door. More than a few people rushed out the back door with us.

"What now?" Callie asked as we hurried along the alleyway.

"Tonight we need to get back to the hotel, but tomorrow we'll find one or more of the mages responsible for summoning the demon and squeeze the information out of him or her. I'm tired of playing this game. These last two days have seemed like a week. It's time to end it."

CHAPTER 22

I STEPPED OUT of the shower and glanced through the opened sliding doors at the windows. Blackness still coated the sky, barely allowing a few points of light for tenacious stars that would not be conquered.

I crossed into the bed area. The clock read 4:53. Soon streaks of light would cut through the night, warning of the approach of daylight.

A bottle of whiskey sat on the small table near the couch at the front of the suite. Darius must've brought it in while I was in the shower. The note said, *Get as drunk as you need to.*

I smiled. He was a vampire, which implied a certain level of selfishness, but when he let himself, he was a damned good guy as well. One who paid attention, and remembered the little things.

"Careful, Reagan," I said softly, tying the towel above the swell of my breasts. If anywhere on a mostly flat chest could be called a swell. "This is how it always starts. They're wily, these vampires. They've had hundreds of years to charm their way into bloodstreams."

I poured myself some whiskey and closed my eyes after it hit my taste buds. Darius always bought the best.

I checked my phone as I thought about my options for pajamas. They were sparse, since I mostly slept in one overworked and under-washed tank top and my undies. I did have some yoga pants and a loose T-shirt, so I supposed those would have to do. This wasn't the right kind of battle for leather.

I'd missed a text from J.M. earlier, asking how it was going. I thought about replying, since it was kind of nice that someone was checking in with me, but a glance at the clock had me putting the phone down. If he was like most people and kept the phone near his bed, and it was on, I might wake him. I doubt he cared about my day that much.

I brushed my hair, glancing at the window again. A part of me wanted to wait until dawn approached in the hopes Darius would take what he needed and go right to sleep. I knew vampires treated the days like most humans treated the nights, though. They needed sleep, but as long as the sun didn't touch them, they didn't *have* to sleep. Darius could stay up all day if he was closing in on a kill.

Me, sexually speaking.

I blew out another breath as my stomach flipped.

The days and nights with that other vampire surfaced in my memory. It was still the most enjoyable thing I'd ever experienced. The very best. Nothing could quite compare. As soon as their saliva hit your bloodstream, that was it. Your body was no longer your own. Suddenly it was a pleasure cruise taking you away, and in the past, I'd wanted nothing more than to ride that boat all the way out to sea.

Granted, my mom had just died at the time. Really, I'd wanted a seat on any boat leaving the harbor because I was not stable. Instead of resorting to drugs, I had found a vampire.

I was a different person now, though. An experienced, knowledgeable person who was mostly stable. It would be absurd to assume a vampire could still affect me the same way…

After another sip of whiskey, I dried my hair in a towel and stared at the closed door dividing Darius's room from mine. He'd closed it after delivering the whiskey. When I went over to him was completely up to me. Despite all his talk about chasing and hunting, he was giving me the control.

He probably knew that if I didn't have it, I'd tell him to get lost.

"Oh, this is a terrible idea," I said as another wave of butterflies surged through my stomach. "A terrible, bad idea." The whiskey went down a little quicker that time.

"But really, what's the worst that can happen?" I

asked myself, needing to hear a voice, even my own. "I should call Callie."

I shook my head. Another terrible idea. She'd start plotting Darius's death immediately. She didn't trust him as far as she could throw him. And if I tried to explain, she'd tell me how stupid I was for having promised such an asinine thing.

"I *am* stupid. Oh my God, I am so stupid." Another gulp of whiskey. "But again, what's the worst that can happen?" I thought about it for a second. "The absolute worst would be if I fall into a trance and start worshipping the ground he walks on. If I lose myself to him."

That wasn't helping. I shouldn't think of the worst.

"What's the best that can happen?" I asked myself as I shrugged into my T-shirt. "If I stick out my neck, give him the blood he needs, and he absolutely hates the taste, maybe it'll break the spell I somehow have over him."

I nodded. Yes. That was the best thing. I needed to hope for that thing.

My yoga pants went on, and I took another shot of whiskey, summoning my courage.

This was worse than slowly creeping around someone's house waiting for them to pop out like a jack-in-the-box. Horror movies should be made of what I was about to do.

Oh wait, they were. And for good reason.

I closed the sun-proof drapery and faced that door again. It was time. I couldn't stall any longer.

I felt like dead Reagan walking.

When I reached the door, I hesitated, then ran back for another shot. In times like these, I wished I had a normal person's alcohol tolerance. As it was, the alcohol was just taking the fine edge off. I still had a lot of stress and anxiety. A *lot* of stress and anxiety.

Back at the door, I lifted my hand to knock. Then realized it was technically my door.

After opening it, I sucked in a breath.

All of the available raised surfaces were covered in lit candles, radiating warm, flickering light. Rose petals littered the floor and the made bed. Darius sat on his sofa, dressed in a tailored suit and swirling a glass of something brown in a snifter.

As I walked in on wooden legs, he inhaled the contents of his glass before taking a sip. He turned his gaze to me. "I miss a good cognac."

"I…should change…" It wasn't quite a question, but was definitely leaning in that direction.

"Of course not. You look as beautiful as ever." He stood gracefully and waved his hand toward the bottle of cognac on the coffee table in front of him. "Please, would you care for a glass? Or perhaps you'd rather bring in the whiskey? I can also ring for anything you'd like. Name it. Are you hungry?"

I'd called for room service shortly after our return to the hotel—and proceeded to eat more than a starving pig. Otherwise I would've said yes. One thing I did love about my dad's heritage—I could eat all day without gaining a pound. *That* part definitely wasn't human. My mom used to curse me for it.

"I'll get the whiskey."

"Of course. Or I can grab it, if you'd like to sit down?"

"Yes, please," I responded meekly. I suddenly felt very out of place. I knew I should act like a lady, but I had no idea how ladies typically acted.

"Please." He held out his hand.

I avoided it like he carried the plague. Lady or not, touching him needed to wait. I contorted my body expertly enough to win a game of Twister to get around him without making contact, then sat down on the chair adjacent to the couch. He turned on the jets, zoomed into my room, and was back a moment later and pouring me a drink.

I took it with a nervous smile. He sat into his original seat and resumed swirling his cognac.

"What do you think of the events of today?" he asked pleasantly.

I cleared my throat, trying to dislodge the flurry of butterflies still flapping around my middle. "I think the Mages' Guild is suffocating this town." I crossed my legs at the knee. Then uncrossed them and recrossed them at the ankle.

"Reagan, please. Don't be nervous."

"I am extremely nervous. I don't know how not to be extremely nervous."

He smiled. "I realize I am asking a lot of you. That you are honor-bound to follow through. So in that vein, I'll share a troubled spot of my past with you, if you'd like?"

I crossed my leg at the thigh this time. It felt the most comfortable, while not feeling comfortable at all.

Why did this feel like I was losing my virginity?

"Sure," I said.

He smiled again, disarmingly. Like he knew my skin felt too tight and my legs were trembling.

"I think you know that I am very old. The last time I was human was in William the Conqueror's time." My eyes widened. That meant he was nearly a thousand years old. "You are surprised. Yes, it is hard for someone of your youth to comprehend living that long. And believe me, not many immortals can sustain their life to do so. The human world has always been turbulent. Their ways violent. It was as such when I was human, and it is so now. Magical people are the same. To make it so long is difficult. It requires skill and finesse, not just the ability."

"But...I thought you were in the French Revolution?"

"As a vampire, yes. I lived a great many of my years in France before I had the means to make my home wherever I chose." He paused, but when I left it at that, he continued. "You once asked if someone had ever tried to trap me. Tried to get me to a certain location in order to kill me."

I squinted in thought. That sounded like me, but I couldn't recall saying it. Of course, I rarely recalled what I'd said a few minutes before, so that was no surprise.

As if he could tell I needed prompting, he said, "It was when we were on the way to the unicorn paddock. You were giving me your thoughts as to why someone would wipe away their footprints. You said—"

"Right, yes," I said as the memory flooded back. I'd warned him our mark might be trying to trap us. "I remember."

"I was a landowner as a human, born to wealth. I'd lost my parents early, sadly, and at first had a hard time shouldering the responsibility. I nearly lost my fortune to gambling and mismanagement. It wasn't until I was twenty-one, an age much further into manhood at that time than it is now, that I had everything turned around. My vast estate was once again prosperous, and I was living the life meant for me. It was then I opened my eyes to taking a wife and producing an heir. There were many I could choose from who would solidify my holdings and birth strong, plump babies."

"Wow," I muttered.

"But for all the prudent choices, there was one of lesser status, a bad match, who had always caught my eye. A man's undoing is always a woman, is it not?" His smile was sad and directed downward, at his snifter. "She was as bright as the sun. As beautiful as a blooming spring flower. Her wit and charisma drew me in from the moment I met her."

He paused, and swirled the brown liquid around his glass. Candlelight glittered off the surface.

"I did not love her, but I was not far from it. I needed only a push. But even still, I would've done anything for her. As wrong as the match was, she was my beloved. Many remember their first sexual experience. Me, I remember her, even now. Her rosy lips, plump and supple. Her laugh, so hearty and rich despite her delicate features. The demure way she would look up at me through her lashes." He took a sip of his cognac, his eyes faraway. "I was eager to call her my wife. Promised to bathe her in jewels. Elevate her status. Little did I know that she was on a mission. I embodied sin, in her eyes. I did not worship every Sunday, sometimes choosing business matters instead. I did not bow my head when grace was said. Small things. More importantly, various relics she found around my castle suggested to her that I was a vampire. It was a somewhat predominant fear at the time, and if the pain wasn't still so acute, I would find that humorous, since it is what I became." His smile turned brittle. "I did not know of her fears at the time. I did not know she was a religious fanatic who imagined me akin to the devil. I let her lure me to a lovers' rendezvous, ignoring how poorly her behavior fit with her religion. I was blinded by her beauty. By her charm. Like a fool."

Silence rained down between us as he stared at nothing, lost to the memories.

After some time, he took a breath, and it was only then I'd realized he hadn't been breathing. That I hadn't been, either.

"She'd arranged for me to meet her at a carriage for an afternoon in the countryside. I arrived early, but there was no sign of her. At first I assumed she was on her way, or that she'd gotten caught trying to sneak out alone, but I was set upon by a gang of men. I was tall for the time, broad. Strong. I defended myself as best I could, but there were too many. Near the end, one of them attempted to drive a stake through my heart. It was a paltry attempt, much too high and shallow, but the damages from the beating would've ended me. The blood loss alone might have killed me.

"As I lay there, bleeding, I heard the carriage finally approach. Her sweet voice rang out. I thought I was saved." He gave a sardonic laugh. "She'd hired the miscreants. Paid them as they left. She assumed me dead—and she was happy about it. It was only then that I realized my grave error. And also…that she did not care for me. Worse, she loathed me. How blind I'd been. I blame that on youth, of course. If only blame made it any less painful."

"But you didn't die," I said softly.

"No. I lay there, waiting for death to take me under. To stop the pain. That was when Vlad happened upon me."

I sat forward. "Vlad made you?"

"Yes. He wasn't even fully middle tier at the time, but he had a cunning insight, even then. He recognized what he saw, lying there in the mud. He carried me to his quarters below ground and kept me alive until he could turn me. I reclaimed my fortune."

"And what about the girl?"

Darius's face turned away. "I could not kill her. I could not. It wasn't in me."

"I'm sensing a pattern. Except the part where I sic a gang of people on you."

Oh wait, I was thinking of doing that with Callie and Dizzy if he didn't bugger off.

My gulp interrupted the silence.

Like a soft breeze, I barely heard his next words. "I didn't feel a fraction for her what I feel for you. That should not be possible in my status of immortality."

"It was a long time ago. I'm sure the memory has faded."

"If there is one thing that hasn't faded, it is the memory of that betraying witch."

"Yikes. I stand corrected. Sore subject, clearly."

"Yes. I haven't spoken of it to anyone but Vlad, and that was directly after he'd changed me."

"Dizzy said something about someone accusing you of being a vampire and trying to ram a stake through your heart."

"Yes. What he spoke of was a misunderstanding. A friend of mine had drunk too much. Desmond has no idea of the true story. Of the depth of the pain that first betrayal has caused me."

"Yeah, I don't think Dizzy was talking about a girl."

"It is always about a girl." His sad smile made another appearance. "Our folly always has to do with a girl in one way or another."

"That's because men are dependent and can't do anything on their own. You think you run the world, and then you get sick and everything stops while you mope and whine. Let this be your warning. Quit stalking me. Nothing good can possibly come of it." I sobered for a moment. "I'm actually serious. Nothing good can come from hanging around me. I plan on killing every demon I see. If that's going to piss off your daddy, you better walk away now."

His expression darkened.

It was probably the daddy comment.

"Would you knowingly trap me to kill me, Reagan?" he asked, his eyes delving into mine.

I shook my head and shrugged at the same time, all the possible scenarios of how that might play out running through my head. "Maybe. I don't know. If I need to get clear of you and can't, sure. I might have to kill you. Like I said, you've been warned."

Unbelievably, a smile graced his lips. "There, you see?"

I felt my eyebrows crawling up my forehead. "No...?"

"You are genuine. You are a fighter. A survivor. You would not play nice to my face and then stab me in the back. You are much too honest."

"I really don't think you should hang your hat on that conclusion."

"There is something special about you, Reagan. Something...otherworldly."

"Underworldly, you mean."

"Yes." He leaned his head on the back of the couch and looked up at the ceiling. His ankle crossed over his leg. "I did not elaborate on a vampire's ability to kill demons."

I yawned and glanced at the clock. Nearly six in the morning. The sun would be up by now, probably. Or if it wasn't, it would be soon. We needed to get the show on the road.

"Only an elder can handle the fifth level, like I said," he continued. "But a middle-level vampire can handle lesser-powered demons, like you might expect."

"I can do that math, yes. Listen, do you need blood? We can chat about sabotage and fights to the death anytime."

"You wouldn't sabotage me," he said toward the ceiling.

"That line of thinking nearly got you killed the last time. You need to learn your lesson. But seriously, let's get those fangs in my neck, yes? I want to hit the hay."

His head turned toward me slowly. Hunger flashed in his honeyed eyes. "Are you sure you're ready?"

"Yep. Let's do it." I stood, because I didn't want to be too comfortable. "Where, over here?" I backed toward the wall next to the door dividing our suites because it was available wall space and also a good exit plan.

CHAPTER 23

"I F YOU WISH. Or would you rather lie down? Get more comfortable?"

"Nope. I would not, no." I pulled my hair thing from around my wrist and lifted my hands to tie my hair back.

"Please, no." Darius stood. "It is so rare I get to see your hair falling around your face. Leave it, if you would."

I pulled the band back around my wrist. I didn't care where my hair was; I cared where his fangs were.

He stalked toward me slowly, purposefully.

The expected tingles were overshadowed by an unexpected dump of adrenaline. My stomach fluttered, not because of possible sexual relations, but because a lethal predator was sizing me up. My fight-or-flight reflexes roared to life, and very rarely did I choose flight.

"This is probably the wrong way to go about this," I said in a strong voice, hot with the anticipation of battle. "If you want to actually make it to my neck, that is. I'm not the normal girl you do this with."

He smiled in a feral way, showing his elongating fangs. "Would you kill me, Reagan?"

"I'm pretty sure we covered that."

"That doesn't answer my question."

"It kind of does, though." I watched as he slowly walked parallel to me. He was looking for an *in*. Most predators did this when they were sizing up a food source, and deep in my gut, I didn't like knowing that someone was higher on the food chain than me. I didn't like being a source for anything. It felt like a challenge, and everyone knew I went crazy for challenges. Considering the way my fire had lashed out randomly at that poor cat, this might be a very bad idea, both for him and the wellbeing of the hotel.

"I am invigorated like I've never been," he said quietly, his eyes sparkling. I had to strain to hear. "Excited in a way I can't remember. Anxious. Desperate. I must have you, Reagan."

"What do you think I'm waiting here for?" I grudgingly angled my head to the right. "Get to it."

He shook his head slowly and stopped, facing me. Analyzing me. "That wouldn't be enjoyable for you. Would you rather fight and be overpowered?"

Suddenly he was right in front of me, his hands reaching.

I punched out, startled and unable to help it. My fist

connected with his midsection. I grabbed his shirt and yanked, trying to throw him away, but didn't manage to move him far. His hand nearly got a hold of my neck, and he leaned closer.

A shock of fear coursed through me. I peppered him with punches, pushing down the fire inside me that wanted to blast the whole room. In its place, that cold thing within me swelled, filling my body. Tingling my fingers. I shoved him, trying to get him away.

His body flew backward through the air. Shock smacked into his features. He crashed against the wall before falling to the floor.

I froze. I'd moved stuff before, but it had never felt like that. It had never been so easy, or so powerful.

"There is something you are not telling me," he said, running a thumb across his lips as he straightened up slowly. He eyed me, still predatory.

I shivered and desperately tried to regain composure. "Yes. It's about your personality. Trust me, you're better off living in ignorance."

He rolled his shoulders. "Could you do that again?"

"I honestly have no idea. I've moved rocks—"

"The rocks in your backyard?"

"Yes. I can usually only get the littlest as high as you just flew. But that takes a lot of concentration."

"That mage yesterday picked you up with a similar power." He stalked toward me.

"You noticed that, did you?"

"You're practicing incorrectly." He stopped a few feet from me. I flinched, ready to punch out again. The guy was making me antsy. "When it comes to fighting, you work best when under pressure."

"This isn't about fighting; it's about trying to figure out this new power. It feels and acts differently than my manipulation of fire."

"How did you learn to use your fire?"

"I studied. My mother taught me how it should work, and I figured out how it *actually* worked, which was very different."

"And how did you figure that out?"

I opened my mouth to answer that I had diligently focused for long periods of time each day, but that wasn't true at the beginning. Memories crowded in—of cold, crisp mornings when my mom would hurl things at me, willing me to defend myself with my power. If I couldn't protect myself, I'd get hit, often with wooden objects that hurt a lot, or spells that stung my skin. Of warm, humid nights when I'd walk through the shadows, my night vision doing little to protect me from her sneak attacks. The amount of spells she'd lobbed at me would make normal people cry "child abuse," but my mom had known exactly what she was doing. She'd guided me through the beginning, helping me learn to shape my abilities. It wasn't until I understood what burned inside of me that I was turned toward the more diligent, thoughtful approach, refining and manipulating.

I stared at Darius with glistening eyes, the tightness in my chest reminiscent of the pain when I first lost her. Of my sudden plunge into uncertainty. How would I learn this new power without her? I didn't even know where to start.

"We will do it together," Darius said softly, as if reading my thoughts. He was doing that a lot lately. "I can help you."

I nodded, not trusting my voice.

"May I?" he asked, his eyes dipping to my neck.

So many emotions were flying through me at that moment, with him and my mother and the sense of impending doom, that I couldn't do much more than nod.

His movements were slow, syrupy. He was taking the opposite approach this time, giving me time to adjust. To get used to his closeness so that I (probably) wouldn't fling him across the room again.

"It is a joy being in your presence, Reagan," he said quietly, his face now inches from mine. "Relaxing and exhilarating at the same time. I miss you when you aren't near."

My eyes fluttered as his sweet breath fell across my face. As the warmth of his body, so near, cocooned me.

His eyes scanned my face before stopping on my lips. I felt his hands settle low on my hips.

"Just blood," I said in a husky voice I didn't recognize.

"I am at your mercy," he said, his lips getting closer. "I have always been at your mercy."

His scent, spicy and masculine, delighted my senses. The power in his large body, the strength, made my mind buzz from his proximity.

When he bent, I was prepared for his face to dip to the side, and for the sharp pinch of his fangs as they entered my skin. I was prepared to fight the chemical effect of his saliva, as potent as the drug ecstasy. I was even prepared for my heart to thump madly, begging me to relent, to enjoy his perfect body and the rise and fall of each hard, defined muscle.

I was not prepared for his kiss.

When his lips touched mine, a jolt of sweet ecstasy cut through me. The fire within me boiled, and the excitement of battle mixed with the sweet heat of desire. I opened my mouth to him. He filled it in a rush, his tongue swirling around mine in an erotically teasing sort of way.

My moan was soft and deep. Liquid fire dripped through my middle and pooled below. Struggling with myself, I clutched his shirt front to push him off. Instead, I pulled him closer, willingly trapping myself between the hard warmth of him and the unyielding wall behind me.

His kiss increased in urgency, our shared fervency rising. I splayed my fingers across his chest, the logical side of me still urging me to push him away, but desire made me dip my hands lower.

I moaned again as his fingers slid up the curves of my hips and dipped under the fabric of my shirt. His touch sizzled against my skin and then sent a flush of goosebumps across it. The woman in me, that sensual beast who loved the feel of leather and lace against my skin, who was warm-blooded and yearned to show it, gripped the lapels of his jacket and pushed them over his shoulders.

His hands came away from me as he shed the jacket, but his mouth stayed connected to mine, his taste wild and exciting. His mastery with delicious, teasing, oh-so-sexy kisses was better than anything I'd ever experienced.

This time his hands connected at my shoulders before sliding up to my neck. One stayed there, curving around that vulnerable area, and the other glanced off my chin as his kiss deepened still.

I yanked the ends of his shirt out of his pants and slid my hands along his smooth skin, lost to his touch. To the ferocity of my desire for him. To this moment.

His hold on my neck firmed up and his other hand

dropped down to my butt, squeezing my lower half toward him. My core ached, my logic quieted, and my body keyed up, surprising me by wanting this with everything I had.

My breath came in shallow pants as his face slowly moved to the side. The hint of claw from his hand pricked my neck, sending a jolt of fear through me that I was allowing a powerful, primal being at one of the most physically vulnerable places on my body. Adrenaline dumped into my bloodstream, mixing with my raw passion to create such a potent elixir, I groaned and exhaled in sanguine bliss.

His tongue traced a blazing trail down the side of my neck. I angled my face away, giving him room to work. Melting into the moment. His body. Him.

None of this could be credited to—or blamed on—the chemicals of a vampire. He hadn't bitten me yet. It was because of my connection with *Darius*. Somewhere along the way, he'd wormed his way into my world, and now that I was letting myself acknowledge that, I realized my desperate attraction had always been there. That the need was natural, and it was based on his personality, the rough as well as the sweet. The arrogant as well as the protector.

It might not be smart, and I would have to let logic back in eventually, but for this moment, I wanted nothing more than to give in to our needs—his need of an intimate connection while getting sustenance, and mine of deep, personal contact.

The scrape of his fangs on my neck made me shiver. His mouth sucked a spot on my neck that I knew was over my artery. I was about to offer my most precious possession to him—my life's blood.

The pinch made me gasp and clutch his arms, but the following flood of ecstasy ripped the breath from my lungs. I dropped my mouth open in a silent scream, unable to handle such an onslaught of earth-shattering pleasure. It exploded, flash-boiling my body. I groaned, writhing against him, wanting him inside me to take the feeling to the next level.

His face ripped away and he slammed his hands against the wall, one on either side of my face. Paint and plaster trickled down from each point of contact. He bowed, breathing heavily. His whole body flexed. It was a pity it was obscured by clothes.

"Everything...all right?" I asked, out of breath. I was the one that was supposed to pull away, after all. We were swapping roles just now.

He began talking, aiming his words at his feet. And while the sounds were beautiful and flowing, I had no idea what he was saying.

"In English?" I prompted, resting my hands on his shoulders and dropping my head back to rest on the wall. I closed my eyes and let a smile curl my lips. A shudder of delight racked my body as his unique serum continued to course through my bloodstream. "I had no idea vampires got more potent with age. Wow, this feels good. So much better than that other—"

"Don't mention anyone else," he said in a ferocious voice. "I am not rational just now. I am completely out of control."

I grimaced, because that sucked for him, then went back to soaking in the delicious feeling of his bite. I was doing just fine, thank you very much. I saw no reason for him to ruin my high.

"I cannot describe how good you taste, *mon amour*. Your blood is truly the nectar of the gods. Sweet, spicy, complex. Better than the finest wine in all of France. Better than I could've possibly imagined. The smell does not do it justice. There is nothing on this planet that could possibly compare." He straightened up, his eyes deep and intense. "I am speechless."

"Clearly not," I said with a smile, running my hand along his jaw. I traced my thumb across his full bottom lip. "Round two?"

"If you get lightheaded, you will need to push me away," Darius said seriously, his gaze rooted to mine. He did not move toward me again. "I am having a hard time regaining control. I feel like a brand-new vampire. I am not to be trusted."

That didn't sound good. Good thing my logic was

still on hiatus.

"Question: do the chemicals in your saliva keep getting more intense, or do they diminish? Or stay constant? I can't remember with the other—" A flash of rage crossed his features. I didn't finish the sentence.

"I should be able to control it to give you whatever you desire. The chemicals, as you call them, are to counteract the pain of the bite. For tonight, however…I'm not sure I have control."

"Fair enough. And your warning is noted. Do you need more blood?"

Hunger like I had never seen before flashed through his eyes. He straightened up and moved in slowly, wrapping a big arm around my waist and jerking me tightly against his big frame. His lips crashed down onto mine, spiraling my desire to new heights.

I ripped at his shirt like a wild thing, popping buttons and tearing it off him. The feel of his bumpy muscle made me moan, smooth and warm and *man*. I felt his hands under my shirt as his tongue continued to play with mine.

Desperate, crazed, I yanked at his belt. His thumbs hooked in the waistline of my yoga pants. Soft fabric slid down my thighs and pooled at my ankles. A moment later, I was in his arms. He yanked the covers of the bed back and gently laid me on the bed.

Finally getting a clear path to the goods, I worked

his belt and pants again, getting them out of the way.

The pinch of his bite was unexpected. The rush of glorious bliss was not. I moaned, spreading myself for him. His fingers danced, so fast it felt like a vibrator, hitting *exactly* where I needed him, in multiple places, all at the same time. I had no idea how he did it, because that other vampire certainly hadn't, but I didn't really care, as long as he kept going.

The world dropped away. All I could feel was his touch and the deep draw of his bite. I soaked in the sensations, tightening up around the pleasure. Feeling it pound within me.

"Don't stop," I said with harried breathlessness, meaning both his artfully working hand and the pulling on my vein. "Please don't stop."

I rocked into him while clutching at my hair. Loud moans vibrated through my throat. Everything in me contracted. Another wave of his erotic serum surged into me, and a force of pleasure so intense I nearly blacked out pulled me under. My body shook, my teeth chattered, and my entire being fractured. I didn't know which end was up. If he was still sucking or not. Maybe he was killing me; I didn't know. All I knew was that the mother of all orgasms had swept me out to a place where there was no gravity. Where nothing existed besides this unbelievable, soul-clenching bliss pounding through every inch of my body.

"Would you—"

"*Shhh.*" I waved him away. "Give me a minute."

I shuddered with an aftershock. I knew there was more to come, and we'd get to that, but first I needed a little me time.

A moment later, I opened my eyes to Darius poised above me, his strong arms flexing as he held himself up. A delicious little smile tweaked those shapely, kissable lips. "I was right about your passion, *ma cherie*. It is all-consuming."

He lowered and softly kissed my lips, igniting the fire again. Igniting the pull to feel his skin against mine. How had I ever thought I'd be able to resist his temptation?

"I cannot take more blood," he whispered. "Even though I crave it, you'll need strength for tomorrow."

"Okay." I pulled the back of his neck, making him drop down over me. His delicious body pushed mine into the mattress. I slid my thighs up his sides, giving him access. Wanting him with every fiber of my being.

"I can't spread diseases or impregna—"

"I know," I said. "I'm not supposed to tell you how I know, though, remember?"

A feral growl issued from his throat and he thrust. I cried out with the dull ache of his size, but he immediately rose up so he could slip his hand down between us and massage me while working his way in deeper.

The pain tapered off, and a glorious sensation unfurled inside me. Small balls of fire rose from the candles, hovering in the air around us like fairy lights. The tone had changed between us, now rougher, more intense. His fingers entwined with mine, and he lifted our hands above my head as he dropped down low again, trapping me to the mattress. Dominating me with his size and strength.

Claiming me.

I knew it from his actions. From his frenzied, primal movements, intent on imparting a mark on me that I would never forget.

Strangely, without my meaning to, the fire started dancing within the room, my unspoken accent. I cried out, squeezing him tightly with my thighs. At his mercy. The feelings so *right*.

A shock wave of pure ecstasy pumped through me. I blasted apart and called out his name. The *real* mother of all orgasms shook me to the core. He shuddered above me, groaning, and wave after delicious wave of pleasure rolled over me.

In the aftermath, all of the tension seeped out of my muscles. I turned into a puddle of satisfied Reagan on the bed. His hands still held mine, but he didn't collapse over me like a human man might've done. Instead, he feathered me with soft kisses as I basked in the sensations.

"Are you ready for more?" he asked softly into my ear, starting to move again, painfully slowly.

"You've got to be kidding me."

But he wasn't. And we started again.

I could only hope that when this was over, I wasn't completely lost to him.

CHAPTER 24

A VIBRATING PHONE CLATTERING against a hard surface woke me. My phone that I'd left in my suite.

I peeled an eye open. The blurry red numbers on the clock showed five something. It was still very much light outside.

The heat of Darius's nude body was curled around me within the covers of his bed. His strong arms pulled me close, even in sleep, like I was the precious teddy bear of a sleeping child.

Good job on only giving him blood, Reagan. Way to stay strong.

I sighed within his warmth, realizing to my horror that I was perfectly content. My body fit just right, cuddled within his. It was a bad sign.

I blinked a few times to clear my vision, but I was still tired as hell. The guy had kept me up until all hours of the day. We hadn't done much resting, either, and I had sore junk to show for it.

Speaking of sore junk.

I shifted and winced, feeling the not-quite-comfortable ache in my lady bits. But wow, the guy had prowess. He should've, because of his age and situation, but still. Legendary. A little unbelievable, actually.

So that wouldn't be so easy to forget, unfortunately. Crap, I was an idiot.

The phone clattered again. Someone was clearly trying to get hold of me. And being that I was supposed to be working, and not fornicating with overprotective elder vampires, I pushed his arm away and crawled out from under it. He groaned and shifted, snuggling deeper into the pillow.

My smile at his humanlike antics turned brittle. My heart was fluttering. Actual, honest-to-goodness fluttering. This wasn't good. A heart didn't belong anywhere near this situation.

I about-faced and made for the door between our suites. It was time to get myself back under control. Thankfully, logic had returned, and I knew without a doubt that I could never go down this road again. Darius would be good on blood until we got out of here, and then he could go back to using very pretty humans who fawned all over him, and maybe I could date a human who wouldn't try to manipulate me. Or at least wouldn't succeed at manipulating me if he did try.

A pang of regret hit my heart. *Damn it!*

Back in my room, I snatched up my phone, shivering now that I was separated from the warmth of his body. I didn't recognize the number of the two missed calls. After slipping on a white, fluffy robe provided by this fine establishment, I listened to the new message.

Tiredness fled.

I shrugged out of the robe and hurried to don my leather.

Ouch. I gingerly buttoned up my pants, not comfortable in such thick, unforgiving material. Sure, the material was worn in, and therefore softer, but loose sweats would probably be more my speed after my night with Darius.

He really should've stopped after the second time. Or even the third. I would've been fine after the third.

I tied my hair up, strapped on my weapons, and ran to the door. While jogging down the hall, I tapped the missed call and put the phone to my ear.

"Detective Allen," came the gruff answer.

"It's Reagan. I got your message. You found another body?"

"Yeah. We're at the site now. The MLE office can't get here for another few hours."

"They aren't going to be of much help to you. Hold on." I stopped at the front desk and caught the eye of one of the women. "I'm with Darius. I need a car."

"Darius...? Do you have a last name—"

"I'll take care of that," the other woman said, stepping closer to the first. She nodded at me. "I'll have one brought right up. Do you also need a driver?"

I hesitated for a moment. I'd sold my mom's car so I could afford to move to the city, and I hadn't driven since. And this was a new town. "That would be great," I said. "I'll be out front."

The woman nodded and moved away, leaving the other employee blinking at me in confusion. I didn't stay to explain, but headed out the sliding glass door at the front of the lobby.

"Sorry about that," I said to Oscar as I took a seat on the bench to the right of the door. "I'm just arranging for a car. Like I said, the MLE office isn't going to be much help. They've been warned away from the case."

"Warned away? By whom?"

"It's political magical stuff. Just know that they won't be doing much. You still got me, though. I can handle it."

"Speaking of handling it, we've got an unsolved case from last night. A man got hit by a car. Another man tried to save him, but it was too late. That man, and a woman, fled from the scene of the crime. You know anything about that?"

They thought the car had killed him? "Nope. Not a thing."

"The descriptions of the two who fled sound re-markably like you and Mr. Durant."

"That right? Huh. Well, there are an awful lot of blond girls dressed in leather who hang out with tall drinks of water. It's trendy."

"The bitch of it is, the guy had a broken neck and bruising from what appears to be physical violence, but no bruising from getting hit by the car."

The Mercedes Darius had been driving pulled up in front of me. A building of a man with a stern face stepped out and came around to the rear passenger door. I waited for him to open it before sliding into the back seat.

"This is fascinating, but I don't know what you want from me," I said as the door closed.

"It was turned over to me because the witnesses swore the woman was levitating in the air," Oscar said. "Being that all you magical people assume I have a problem with demon worshipers, I put two and two together. I don't believe half of this shit, but at some point, you just have to roll with it."

"You are long past that point. Look, I don't know what you're talking about. If I did, however, I would tell you that *if* someone was at the scene of that crime, and *if* they had a hand in that whack-a-doo affair, they did you a huge favor. I would also tell you that more crap is coming your way. Whatever was going on might've amped up a notch. I don't have all the info yet, but from what I saw, which had nothing to do with a cracked neck, we're looking at a big-time demon. Much more powerful than I'd anticipated. More powerful than I am, probably."

"What does that mean?"

"It means we are up shit creek, and we better hope my mage friends brought an outboard motor, because paddles won't be enough."

THE DRIVER STOPPED behind two parked police cars with lights still flashing. People crowded on the street corner, holding coffees or just chatting with their heads close together. They kept shooting glances in the direction of the yellow police tape stretching across the sidewalk behind what looked like an Irish bar.

"Should I wait for you, Miss Somerset?" the driver asked, not putting the car in park.

"No. I can get a ride back to the hotel."

He hefted himself out of the car, probably planning to come around and open my door. I didn't wait on ceremony, and hopped out.

"Wait." The driver held out a white card. "Call when you're ready, and I'll pick you up."

"Question: does your boss employ discreet people?" I asked in a low tone.

Not one ounce of confusion or hesitation crossed his expression or bled into his bearing. "Absolutely."

His body language had been answer enough. He'd

probably seen some crazy crap, working for a vampire. Although maybe not as crazy as he was likely to see with me.

"Great." I held up the card before slipping it into my pouch and saying thanks.

The small crowd on the corner made plenty of room for me to get by, their eyes sticking to my sword, my gun, or—and this was a first—my pouch. No one questioned my weapons. They probably thought I had legit permission to have them on my person. Which, in this state, I did not.

I found Oscar on the other side of the tape, a small leather book and pen in hand. The cop standing sentinel in front of the scene put his hand out.

"Detective," I said, motioning at Oscar so the cop knew I had a friend on the inside. His gaze took in my various weapons, and a scowl flowered on his face. "Detective Allen," I said, louder.

He looked up as the sentinel cop's eyes narrowed. This cop clearly didn't like it when riffraff tried to invade his crime scene. I'd seen that look a time or two in my past.

"Yes. Reagan, great. Let her through."

The cop lowered his hand and shifted, but didn't move completely out of the way.

I stepped around him and ducked under the tape, meek as a mouse. After last night's disaster at the mage's house, I didn't need to make waves with the folks in authority.

"Come this way." Oscar motioned me on, taking me deeper into the alleyway where a metal trash bin waited to the side. Flags and hasty chalk circles on the rough and cracked cement marked evidence. A man worked from one end to the other with a camera, the flash illuminating the area in bursts.

I felt the pulse of magic and the hint of residual magic. There was a spell in the area. A strong spell. "Tell everyone to freeze."

"Freeze? Why—"

"*Now*," I said, slowly working my way around the evidence being catalogued—droplets of blood, a button, and a shoe. Next to the bin, the broken and twisted body lay in a heap. Beside it was the pile of skin. "Good Lord, this is gross."

I hunched down next to it and put my hands above the body, feeling that weak thrum of residual magic. Wiggling my fingers in the pulse, I could but guess the spells used. "It's probably like we said the other day. They froze him when alive, then used the other spell to collect the energy while they were working on him."

"Spell?" the cameraman asked. A woman with a baggie and a long cotton swab looked up from one of the blood spills.

"You should get them out of here for this," I told

Oscar. "I'm pretty sure you know why."

"You just said to freeze…"

Someone finally does what I say, and I go and ruin it.

"Walk them out the way I just came in," I said, analyzing the visible cut marks. "They hacked more than cut. They wanted to get more pain out of this one. He's a big dude, too. They were trying to find more power. Does that mean they were trying for a higher-powered demon? Or maybe they were trying to push their summons and what they ended up with was an accident?"

"Even if you had those answers, I don't know how I could use that information," Oscar said, working his way back toward me.

I held out my hand. "Just chill there for a second. There is something nasty lurking around here." I glanced at the wall behind me, the back part of the bar. I knew the spell was in that direction, but parts of it seemed to spider-web out to either side, and I had no idea how far the tendrils went. It would be easier—and safer—if the humans just steered clear.

"You can't use that information. I'm trying to get a complete picture so I can." I looked into the metal bin. Normal trash. "Why didn't they dump it *into* the bin like last time?"

"We don't know. They also left a lot of evidence.

Unlike last time."

Frowning, I checked out some of that evidence. That spider-web spell wasn't going anywhere.

"This is a woman's tennis shoe." I hunched down next to it. "It's not from the victim, and I doubt the murderer left it behind. No blood." The button was random. Something from a trench coat or large jacket. "Are you sure these are even part of the crime?"

"No. How could we know until we check them out? But the blood must be. It's fresh."

"The victim's clothes?"

"We haven't found them."

"They would've completely disrobed him before starting." I hunched down next to some of the blood. "They probably put it in a trash bin near wherever they did this."

"That would be unbelievably stupid of them. Eventually someone will notice if they keep dumping clothes into the trash bin."

"Number one, these people are murderers, but not in the normal sense. They are killing people as sacrifices, not for the joy or rage of killing. So they would be less likely to think about the stupidity of putting a victim's clothing into the trash bin. Number two, who is going to bat an eye at some ratty, old, torn clothes being thrown away every few weeks? They wouldn't have blood on them, so they'd just look like trash."

"If we can home in on a location, I'm sure we could collect enough evidence to crack this sucker."

"I'm working on that, don't you worry. Their number is already down by one."

His expression hardened, but he didn't say anything. I doubted his MLE office had any peacekeepers quite like me, and I doubted the captain of said MLE office had as much experience covering up the accidental deaths of bad people as my captain did.

Welcome to the crash course, buddy. It's going to be a bumpy ride before all this ends.

I pointed at the next bit of blood. "This was staged, as was the last. It wasn't dripped or splattered—it was poured."

"That's what it looks like, yes." He tilted his head at me. "Since when do you guys know about blood spatter?"

"Think of New Orleans as the magical Wild West, detective. We're hard-core."

"It would seem."

I put my hands to my thighs and took it all in before straightening up and turning toward the spell. "Now for the crappy part. Run and get me that chalk, would you? The one you used to mark that evidence."

"Why?"

"Why ask why?" I walked toward the throbbing spell slowly, feeling that strange coldness expand within me like ink in water. Something about the magic used here called to my other type of power—the one I'd barely glimpsed so far. Just like it had when that mage used the demon's gift of magic on me.

Clearly this was part of my heritage in some way.

I thought back to all the things my mother had said about my father. The things she'd noticed, and the things he'd explained to her, however briefly. He had often used his fire to toy with my mother. They'd make a game of it—my mother would try to hex him, and my father would cut right through it, dissolving her attempt. That was how she had come to know enough about his powers to somewhat teach me.

"You okay?" I heard behind me. "Need a light?"

The blue sky still shone above me, but the shadows had lengthened, dousing the alleyway. The deep red of the wall had almost bled away into black as the light retreated.

"No, I'm good." I put my hands on my hips and shook my head. "Just give me a minute?"

"Yeah. Can I let the others back in? We need to finish processing the scene."

"Keep them well away from here, and if I say run, make sure they do. And fast. Drop everything and run."

"Why? What are you—"

I held up my hand, getting frustrated. I really did hate working with other people. It slowed me down.

"Just trust me."

"I hate my job," he mumbled, moving away. I knew how he felt.

That cold block of power sat in my stomach, squashing the power I understood. I needed to figure this out, and now, before I faced off with the demon.

I ran over the list of passed-down powers that seemed to have skipped me. My father had been able to pluck secrets out of my mother's head, but she'd worked out a spell to keep her thoughts to herself. That had tickled him. I was stronger and faster than normal humans, like him, and I could sense magic, also like him, but he could smell where someone had been previously. I couldn't do that. At all. Then there was the whole "moving things with the mind" thing. I didn't remember my mother ever mentioning my dad doing that, but I bet he could.

My father had levitated often, sometimes carrying my mom in his arms as he drifted through the air. She'd loved doing that, and apparently, he'd done almost anything to make her smile. But he'd never divulged the difference in the various powers he used. Or maybe she just hadn't thought to ask.

Whatever the reason, I could do almost half of what my dad could do, and this demon represented the half I didn't have much access to. I was at a severe disadvantage, since the cold magic it called forth banked the power I *could* control, leaving me defenseless.

I shook my head. My bad luck, as always.

Pulling in a deep breath, I took out my sword, filled with my fire magic. Now struggling, I focused on my fire magic, fighting to bring it to the surface. I gasped as I felt the two powers swirl around each other, coexisting but not blending. I had no idea if that was right or wrong.

"Here we go," I said, ignoring one of the cops when she asked why I was getting ready to stab the wall with a sword.

Edging closer, I felt that throb, beating in time to the cold power within me. The spell was amplified by the demon's magic, dull yet vicious. I closed my eyes, focusing on the currents as they teased my senses. Getting a feel for what the spell was supposed to do. Another moment, and the intricacies of the spell revealed themselves to me.

It wasn't what I'd expected.

The spell would explode in a rush of frost. Usually it would be a blast of heat, but the demon's power had turned it wintry. So a smack of cold to the face that would result in temporary frostbite for exposed human skin.

They had dumped the body in clear view, ensuring it would be found immediately, decorated the crime scene with plenty of "evidence" for the police to fret over, and left a useless spell just out of the way so it wouldn't easily be disturbed, but would be noticed by the magical person who had been sent to analyze the crime scene.

"Shiznit," I said, backing away as a pattern emerged. I turned slowly toward the mouth of the alley where that cop still stood sentinel. "They're trying to keep me here."

"What?" Oscar asked, walking closer.

I put a hand out to keep him away. "They lured me here with the intent of keeping me busy."

"Why you?"

"Because I'm the one working the case and trying to find them." I took a few quick steps back down the alley and sliced through the spell. The magic opened up in a void, a maw of cold, potent power that raised my small hairs. It attached itself to me, like little suction cups spreading across my skin.

Fear shot through me. I hadn't expected that little number hiding within the spell. Or maybe this was the normal effect of the demon's magic. Whatever it was, it was not good.

My heart sped up and a sheen of fire rolled over my skin, weak because of the other power but thankfully still effective. Bye-bye, magical suction cups.

"What the—" Oscar half fell over himself in his eagerness to back up.

"Do you feel the suction on your…" I let the words trail away as I realized his eyes were glued to my exposed skin. He'd seen the fire. "Ah. Yeah, that. That was a spell. An experimental one that my cousin created. The Canadian cousin. Haven't I told you about him? Anyway, don't worry about it. It's illegal."

I grimaced and walked by him. I would need to disappear for a while after this. I was getting careless where my power was concerned. Also, there were too many demons and vampires in my life. That needed to stop.

Oscar yelled something after me, but I didn't catch it. I turned toward him and made my way back to the mouth of the alleyway. When I reached it, the cold power started throbbing in my middle again, increasing in potency, pushing my useable power even more.

"Not good," I mumbled, ducking out from under the tape. I put my hand on the sentinel cop, who jerked but didn't entirely move away. I'd startled him. "Keep your wits about you. Things aren't as they seem."

"What are you talking about?" he asked.

"Reagan," Oscar said, catching up. "Where are you going?"

"I was lured here for a reason, detective," I said. "I best find out what that reason is."

CHAPTER 25

T HE CROWD HAD increased as the day turned old. Shadows stretched across the street and made countless puddles of black. Someone to my right, an older woman with a canvas bag slowed her already slow pace. Her head swung toward me, and even from the distance, I noticed the inhuman glitter of her eyes.

The canvas bag fell to the ground.

A male teenager stepped out of the crowd and into the street, right in front of a car. Brakes squealed. The car careened. The teen didn't notice; he only had eyes for me.

As the old woman and teen both started my way, two more people in the crowd shifted in a creepy way, their shoulders suddenly straightening as they turned toward me and started moving steadily, though at half speed. They pushed their way forward, knocking people out of their way like tanks. Down the street, someone screamed. I could barely see a person fall to the ground. Someone else descended on the fallen, fists lashing at the person.

The sentinel cop jerked, having seen it too. His hand went to his gun, but he didn't start forward. I wasn't sure why.

The teen started to run at me, a strange glint in his eyes, a wide smile on his face. He swooped down next to one of the cop cars and picked a hammer up off the ground, barely breaking stride.

"What the hell is a hammer doing just willy-nilly behind the cop car?" I demanded.

The sentinel cop didn't have time to answer me.

"Freeze," he shouted, taking out his gun. "Put down the hammer. Freeze!"

I stepped into the path of the gun, ran forward, and ducked under the swing of the hammer. The kid's speed hadn't increased as a result of whatever spell or magic had infused him. I rammed a punch into his stomach, brought that elbow across his jaw, and then grabbed his hammer arm and knocked his wrist with the hilt of my sword. His fist relaxed, dropping the hammer. I had probably cracked his bone, but he didn't cry out. I gave him a solid punch to the nose, knocking him out cold.

The old woman finally reached me, as slow as she was, but no way was I going to punch her. That was just wrong.

"Do something about her," I said, dodging a really weak and slow slap-punch, and gently pushing her toward the cop. I didn't want to make her fall and be responsible for a broken hip. It wasn't her fault she was suddenly evil.

Someone screamed down the way. "You need to grab whoever is terrorizing people down there," I yelled as the two crowd pushers came at me, a woman in yoga pants and a portly guy.

"What the hell is happening?" the sentinel cop shouted.

"Hang with the bull and you'll eventually get the horns, my man." I did a jump kick and got the portly man in the face. He went down like a sack of bricks. The woman had stopped to pick up a stick with two nails protruding out of the end. "Someone is leaving candy for the trick-or-treaters."

I bounced on my toes, waiting for her to surge forward. I met her as I noticed someone out of the corner of my eye running around the corner with a gun in hand.

"Gun!" I shouted, blocking her downward swing. The center of the stick cracked against my forearm. I jerked my head away so the nails on the end didn't pierce my eyeball. "Get that guy with the gun!"

I punched the woman in the stomach, and she exhaled noisily. I tore the wood out of her hand and broke it over my knee. She came at me with both hands, probably trying to grab my hair like in some female playground fight. I slapped one of her hands away, resisting the urge to run my sword through her middle, and punched her in the face. Her head jerked back, but she didn't go down.

A roundhouse kick solved that problem.

The crack of a gunshot went off from behind me—Oscar. Then another from the possessed gunman who'd turned a corner. People screamed. The man sank to his knees, his gun still held out.

Another explosion of gunfire, this time from the cop next to me. I flinched away from the noise, my ear ringing. The slug hit the possessed dude center mass. He fell backward and the gun skittered across the ground. No one stopped to pick it up, thank God. No one else ran our way.

I breathed heavily, waiting for more action.

"What the—" Oscar said in a hasty release of breath. "What just happened?"

"If I had to guess, I'd say dimensional demons are responsible for this." I walked out onto the street, seeing another weapon on the curb that hadn't been picked up. "These had a purpose, though. This wasn't just a slip of power—the demon possessed these people intentionally. It's gotten personal. Unless, maybe, this ability is one he can impart to a disciple?" I pulled out my phone and looked at the screen. "I need to ask my friends. I'm not an expert on this stuff."

"A demon?" the sentinel cop said, still braced for a

war.

"I need to get a move on," I said. "Call your cop friends. Get officers in the streets. If that demon can't control its power, or worse, it *wants* to create a playground of violence, you're going to get a nasty turn of events in this town."

Oscar said something in an incredulous tone, but I didn't stick around to learn what. If something was gunning for me, I wanted it to show itself, and that would happen faster if I forced its hand.

I put in a quick call to Callie, getting her voicemail. I got Dizzy's as well, so I shot off a text. They were either still sleeping or weren't paying attention to their phones, a terrible habit they both had. A text was easier to access than a voicemail, so hopefully I'd get a response sooner. Finally, I sent a text to Darius. With the sun nearly dipping behind the horizon, he'd be out soon, and I could use the extra pair of fists if a bunch of citizens was about to come my way. I didn't want to kill these people, not if what had happened in that Northern Californian town was also happening here. It wasn't the civilians' fault some demon had decided to use them as puppets.

First, I needed to stop whoever else had been turned. I headed in the direction from which the civilians had come. Around the corner and down the street, I found someone who hadn't fared so well in the mini-apocalypse. It was too late to help them, so I continued on, seeing a broken shop window and a few people standing next to it, looking down the street with bewilderment on their faces.

I continued in that direction, but only saw a couple more examples of violence. It looked like I was only following one, max two people. That meant the demon had gone another way, or had started to control the power it radiated.

Selfishly, I half hoped it was the former. If it was controlling its power, that meant it was purposely trying to enter in a cat-and-mouse game with me. I hated cat-and-mouse games. I was no good at them. Either way, the person, or people, I was following would be taken down. That was step one.

Twilight fell as I finally caught sight of the wrong-doer. Only one. He was running into a shop with a baseball bat in hand.

I sped up, following him in. Shouting and crashes came from the back. A woman screamed. A man cursed. Above the din, a beastly yowl rose, not quite human.

I found him at the back of the store, the crazed man with the bat, battering the glass of the freezer section. An employee stood at the end of the aisle with a phone to his ear. A woman with rounded eyes stood behind him, wringing her hands.

As I moved forward, a little kid ran out from around the corner, frightened.

"Nope." I sprinted as the man with the bat caught sight of the newcomer. He turned as the kid skidded to a stop. The bat lifted.

"Nope," I said again, and launched through the air.

My shoulder hit the center of Bat Guy's back. We crashed to the ground. He writhed under me like a wild thing.

"Get that kid out of here!" I screamed, trying not to show extreme violence in front of the kid. "Get him out!"

The woman sprang into action as another female frantically came around the corner. Bat Guy tried to bite me.

"You don't have fangs, idiot. Your teeth won't do much to me." I punched him in the side, trying to do it all subtle-like as the ladies dragged the stunned kid away. I did it again.

The man growled, a demonic sound.

"Are you actually possessed, or how does this work?" I muttered, letting loose with the punches. I landed one on his head, then a second, slowing him. Using that to my advantage, I yanked him over and shifted him onto his stomach.

He still writhed, but more weakly.

"The foundation of you is still human, at least," I

said, out of breath. I pinned his arms behind his back and sat on him. "Be still, or I'll knock you out entirely. You're going to hurt when you come to, believe me."

He bucked, trying to get me off. Clearly he didn't believe me.

"Get some rope to tie him up," I shouted at the employee, punching the man again. This guy just would not settle down. "C'mon, let's go. I need to get on the move again."

Twenty minutes later, time spent tying the guy up and herding the employees like cats to calm everyone down, I finally walked out of the store. The sound of sirens crowded the air, reinforcements called in to deal with all the crazy that had recently gone down. Night had fallen, punctuated by a message from Darius asking my current location.

I glanced around for any other signs of violence. When I didn't see anything new, I walked to a corner so I could see the street signs. After sending Darius the info, I kept going, wanting to see if anything drifted my way. I had to assume the demon and/or his fan club were keeping tabs on me. You don't just lure someone to a location and then let them wander away randomly. They were probably coming up with another plan to attack. Or at least annoy, since the last attack had been paltry, at best.

Deep shadow fell over me as I passed under the cover of bushy trees, blocking the glow of streetlights. The rustling of fabric caught my ears. Shoes scuffing against the cement.

I spun, my hand reaching for my sword. Too late.

Two shapes, moving entirely too fast, zoomed at me. My hand closed around my sword hilt, but they were already there, grabbing my arms and yanking me with them.

Two middle-level vamps. Fast and strong, but not fast and strong enough. Boy, had they picked on the wrong girl.

I twisted, jerking an arm free, and crashed my elbow down on a shoulder. The vamp staggered, clutching at me. I hooked two fingers in his mouth and ripped, employing the fish hook. That was a nasty one.

He thought so, too.

He howled and clutched at his face, still keeping pace but flinching away from me. I used the few seconds of his shock to whip my legs around, throwing the other vamp off balance. I tore my arm out of her grasp but didn't drop away. Oh no. They had gotten themselves into this mess, and I was going to make sure they regretted it.

Sword forgotten for now, I wrapped an arm around her neck and swung my legs a second time, throwing myself onto her back. My feet thudded as they hit the ground, forcing her to bend over backward. She struggled to stay upright, clutching at my neck.

I swept her legs out from under her again as the guy vampire got his wits about him and his face started to stitch back together. I kicked out, clipping his chin with my boot. Bone cracked and he went whirling, back to clutching at his face.

The girl vamp writhed, but I had a swift punch with her name on it, breaking her nose. "Who sent you?" I demanded, punching again.

"I did."

That voice. I knew that musical, pleasantly pitched voice.

I kicked the guy vampire again, sending him wheeling out of the way, before turning.

My stomach curdled.

Vlad, elder of elders, stood five feet away with a pleasant smile on his face.

CHAPTER 26

THE VAMPIRE WAS so handsome that it went beyond lust inducing and straight into just plain annoying. A small smile curled his lips, and he held his hands behind his back.

I wasn't fooled. He was older, even, than Darius, and could move so fast that his fist would hit my face before I'd registered his intent to fight. The gesture was meaningless.

"Why?" I asked, monitoring the middle-level vampires as they slowly rose to their feet. They made no move to capture me again. "And where were they trying to take me?"

"You impress me, Miss Somerset. May I call you Reagan?"

"Sure, but you didn't answer my question."

"Two middle-level vampires and you were completely undaunted. That takes great skill and prowess."

"It wasn't my first rodeo. Where were they trying to take me?"

Vlad half turned, and pointed at a cafe just down

the street. "I wanted to speak with you, but first, I wanted to test your reaction speed. I have heard great things, but seeing is believing, as they say."

"You thought kidnapping me, then dumping me at a cafe, would be a good start to a pleasant dialogue, did you?"

His laugh was silky and delightful. Still annoying, though. That level of perfection so often was. "I confess, I thought I could mollify you merely with my presence. But my first impression, when I met you in our lair, holds true. You aren't afraid of much."

"I'm afraid of things, but no, you aren't one of them." It was a small lie.

"Please, will you do me the honor of having a coffee or tea?"

I blew out a breath and looked at my empty hands. I patted my pouch. "I'd really love to, but your clowns made me drop my phone somewhere along the way, and I need to find it."

"I will have it collected." Vlad barely nodded, and one of the vampires took off.

If Darius wouldn't take no for an answer, how could I assume his creator would?

"Right, okay." I glanced around, just making sure nothing else was liable to pop out at me. "It has to be quick, though. I have things to do."

"Yes. You are trying to track down a mage who is

murdering people."

"A couple of mages, yes. I think I've got two in my sights. Now I just need to introduce myself."

"I won't take much of your time. Please." Vlad held out his arm to escort me.

I didn't want to touch him. "I'm good, thanks. I don't need help."

He clasped his hands behind his back again and started walking. I fell in beside him.

"I think our interests are converging," Vlad said, ever so pleasantly.

"Our interests? I suppose this has something to do with the really powerful demon that was in Northern California—and now here?" Pure guesswork based on the dimensional demons and his presence, but it fit. Horribly so.

"The very same. I've been tracking its movements, starting with a small town in—"

"Forgive my interruption." The man kicked my politeness up a notch, what can I say? "But I heard about the demon's origins in the Brink."

"Of course. And you've no doubt heard of my confusion regarding its sudden appearance?"

"I did, yes, as well as your extracurricular activities in the underworld."

"And here I thought I was keeping a low profile." His voice was colored with humor, and he followed up the statement with a chuckle. "At first, the demon seemed to be joyriding, in a way." He opened the cafe door for me. "But murmurings in the Dark Kingdom hinted that it was sent up for a purpose. That it stood to gain an elevation in power if it found what it was seeking. What would you like?"

Vlad gestured toward the counter as fear washed through me. What did he know?

"Coffee is fine," I muttered. The remaining vampire, the girl, had trailed us into the shop, and she went to the counter to get it.

"What is the demon looking for?" I asked with an even voice.

Vlad pulled out a chair at a small table and waited for me to sit. "I thought maybe you could tell me."

I lowered into the seat as nervous flutters filled my stomach. There was no way to know if he was playing dumb or honestly didn't know. I'd heard this man made politics and manipulation seem like an art, and I was horribly unprepared for a face-to-face grilling.

My thoughts drifted to Darius. I should've waited for him on that street corner. He would have known how to deal with Vlad. This was one time I was totally fine with being saved. Actually, hoping for it.

"I came here expecting the level-four demon that had been summoned," I said. "I have no idea why a stronger demon showed up instead."

"From what we surmise, this demon intruded on the summons. It had an agenda, and by taking the summons, it had willing participants to aid it in its pursuit."

"I didn't know that was possible."

"If the demon is powerful enough to travel independently in the Brink, it certainly is. So tell me…" His smile wasn't as disarming as he'd probably meant it to be. "What is Agnon searching for?"

"Agnon? That's the demon's name?"

He nodded. There was an opportunistic gleam in his eyes, and another wave of fear washed over me.

This was bad. I needed to get out of here.

And, of course, it was at that moment that my coffee arrived. Vlad got one, too, before the vampire lackey headed outside.

At least I only had one vampire to contend with if things went sour. Granted, that one vampire was probably too much for me to handle without burning down the coffee shop, but I'd definitely give it the ol' college try. Seattle had plenty of coffee shops; they wouldn't miss one.

"I really have no idea, Vlad," I said, wrapping my hands around the warmth of the paper cup. "Like I said, I was brought here to track down a few mages who were sacrificing people in order to call a level-four demon. This new situation is as surprising to me as it is to you.

Surprising, and daunting. I'm going to have to rely on my mage friends to banish it."

He studied me in silence, his dark eyes holding mine. Suddenly, I was overcome with an intense urge to crumble at his feet and beg to reveal all I knew. I could feel it weighing on my shoulders and churning my guts. I didn't know if this was some special superpower of his, or just the desire to buckle under his obvious expectations, but it was potent.

Vlad took a slow sip of coffee before carefully setting his cup back onto the table. "What would you say if I told you that the *aswang* you defeated started its journey in Northern California, and made a beeline from there to New Orleans? Straight to your house."

I felt my brow lower as I tried to process what he'd said. "Huh?"

I didn't quite get there.

"I was sure Darius knew about that. No matter." He leaned back and crossed an ankle over his knee. "I see he has taken your blood."

I flinched, but stopped myself from reaching for my neck. A vampire's saliva healed the bite wound pretty quickly. Teamed with my healing capabilities, I knew that mark, and any others, were long gone.

"I promised Roger that Darius could take from me if he needed to, that's all," I said. "It doesn't mean anything."

His smile spoke volumes. He knew Darius and I had gotten a lot more intimate than the mere taking of blood.

That was embarrassing.

"As of late, Darius has made a habit of guarding you very closely," Vlad went on. "You, and any information about you. Any records regarding your past or present have been hidden or destroyed. Even that which should be public record. For a vampire who has always relished having no ties from which he can't immediately walk away, I find this curious. And now a demon shows up on the surface, looking for something it appears to value highly, and you just happen to show up at the same place, nearly at the same time. All these elements are a recipe for a hearty soup."

"I don't know much about soup, but Darius just wants what he can't have. That's the long and short of it. He wants to control me, and I want to stab him with sharp things."

Vlad took another sip of coffee, his eyes still glued to mine. It felt like he was peeling back the front of my forehead to get a peek at my thoughts. I felt completely naked. Utterly exposed to his prying.

If I stayed here, I was bound to reveal something I didn't want to.

How many times do you need to come to that conclusion before you stand up and walk out, idiot?

"What is it that makes you so unique, Reagan Somerset? What has this demon come to the surface to find?" He paused. His head tilted. "What has Darius stumbled upon?"

"Blood that tastes better than it smells, if he can be believed." I rose and turned toward the door.

There was a blur of movement, and Vlad was suddenly blocking my way. Someone in the cafe gasped.

His smile had turned feral. "It is in your best interest to sit back down, Miss Somerset. We are not done speaking."

Mad shivers driven by adrenaline worked through my body. This was about to get real. Where were the shifters when you needed them? "Yes, we are."

Vlad's body loosened, about to make a move. I braced myself, my power pounding within me.

Outside, a body flew across the length of the cafe window. It landed out of sight. The door swung open and in walked the best sight I'd ever seen.

"Vlad," Darius said in a quiet whip crack of a voice. "Step away from her."

Vlad's eyes crinkled and his head tilted toward me, just a fraction. Approval. For what, I had no idea.

He turned around slowly, facing a vampire taller and broader than himself. Of course, that didn't mean anything. Not to vampires their age.

"I was just speaking of you," Vlad said, not stepping

to the side. "You've thoroughly covered her in your scent. Was that by design?"

"I've already submitted the bonding paperwork," Darius said, thankfully ignoring that gross question. "Per the bylaws, she has been claimed until they come to a decision. She is under my protection. You are wasting your time here."

"I can easily deny your request," Vlad responded.

"You could try." The power and confidence in Darius's voice fluttered my insides. "Of course, you would have to wait for Winston to return from his pilgrimage. The request is frozen until such a time. You know what it means to flout our laws."

I shifted enough to see the sly grin soak up Vlad's face. "I have taught you well. Too well, perhaps." He took a step toward Darius and lowered his voice. "What have you found, old friend? It must be a diamond in the rough for you to act like this. Curiosity is eating away at me."

Darius ignored that question, too. "Have you made contact with the demon?"

A predatory gleam flashed in Vlad's eyes. "Let's step outside."

Darius pushed open the door, and both men looked at me, waiting for me to go first.

"You try to kidnap me, stalk me, threaten me, manipulate me, but oh look, you'll hold the door for me," I mumbled. "You guys are something else."

"Is that not what you desire?" Vlad asked, following me out the door. Darius moved to my side, placing himself between Vlad and I.

"No. I'd rather be left alone."

Vlad smiled like he didn't believe me. To Darius, he said, "From what I can gather, the demon is from a sect known for their ambition. They have power in plenty, and play the game well. They've sent Agnon to the surface, promising rewards if it completes its mission. That's all anyone knows, but the...coincidences are telling." Vlad glanced at me.

"How does this demon affect your plans?" Darius asked.

Vlad spread his hands. "Not at all. I am merely along for the ride."

"And the mages in the area—do they have any bearing on your intentions?"

"From what I hear, your people have already started to dabble in the politics of this area. I've granted you the professional courtesy of staying clear. I am not meeting with anyone outside of this specific situation while I am here."

I frowned up at Darius. What sort of dabbling was he doing, and why wasn't he helping me more if he had connections?

If Darius saw my questioning gaze, he didn't let on.

He nodded at Vlad. "I'll see you in the lair."

"I'll look forward to hearing about this exquisite treasure you've collected." *Yuck.*

Vlad bowed to us and then reached out his hand. The male vampire melted out of the night and handed over my phone. Before he turned away, I was the recipient of an intense scowl.

"Dude, you started it. Just be glad your face healed," I said. His scowl deepened.

"Here you go, Reagan." Vlad handed it to me. "Take care of yourself."

"Thanks," I mumbled.

Vlad's eyes twinkled as he bowed again. "Something tells me I'm going to regret passing you off to Darius. Ah well. Such is life. You can't be lucky all the time." He winked before he turned and strode away.

"Lucy, you have some 'splaining to do," I said to Darius as I pulled up the text message app on my phone.

Immediately, an outgoing message from me to Darius caught my eye. It informed him I'd meet him at the hotel in a half-hour.

The vamp must have sent it, but Darius hadn't known that.

"You ignored my text, I see." I pulled up an old group message between Callie, Dizzy, and myself.

"I knew you didn't send it."

"How?"

"It was much too polite."

I nodded, because that was a good call, as I texted Callie and Dizzy where to meet us. When that was done, I turned my attention back to Darius. "What's this about the *aswang*?"

I pointed to the right because I needed something to eat, and there was a restaurant down the way.

"Vlad knows about that, does he?" I barely heard Darius sigh.

"The question is, why don't *I* know about that?"

"I wanted more evidence. When I got it, I had other things on my mind." His touch slid down my back and across the top of my butt. I wiggled out of the way, knowing exactly what had been on his mind. "It seems my fears—our fears—are coming to fruition. The demon from—"

"I know that part. What I don't know is how the *aswang* fits into this."

"The *aswang* that you killed didn't come from New Orleans. Or anywhere in Louisiana. It left a chain of murder victims across the country. If one painted a line on the map, stringing those murders together…"

"You'd get that Northern California town." I let out a breath slowly.

"The *aswang* fed every so often en route to New Orleans, stopping and killing one person before moving along. Its first feed in town was across the street from your house."

"It was spooked off from there, I think," I said.

"Yes. But it didn't leave town quickly, as it had done on those other stops. It lingered, killing again. And again. I believe that was to gain strength. Only after the last feed did it try to infect you."

"It wouldn't have succeeded, and not because of stupid Garret firebombing my face. So then what?"

"I'm not sure. But it seems that the powerful demon sent the *aswang* to you specifically. Then it came here, possibly hijacking the mages' summons—"

"Everyone knows these things can happen but me. Why is that?"

"—and when the *aswang* failed in its duty, whatever it might've been, you were sent for. The demon is trying to suss out your power. There can be no other explanation."

"I was sent for by Seattle PD, though. And even if the MLE office had a hand in my coming, I doubt any of them hold hands with demons."

"The demon, no. The mages summoning the demon, however, had already stopped the MLE office from investigating. How hard would it be for one of the mages to put a bug in the detective's ear and call in reinforcements from your branch? Specifically, you, the number one bounty hunter in the country. The human detective would go along with that in a heartbeat. And he did."

"Except I'm not number one. I'm literally a nobody. That's a long shot."

"You worked directly with Detective Smith just once, and that was enough to make him your biggest fan."

I gave up arguing. It didn't change the situation.

"I'm not sure the demon wants to meet me face to face," I said. I told Darius about the crime scene and what had happened afterward.

"That stands to reason. It's looking for the heir to the Dark Kingdom; it must assume you are all-powerful, like your father."

"Joke is on him. Or me, I guess, depending on how you look at it."

Darius's eyes softened. He stopped me and reached up, waiting for my flinch to subside before he ran a thumb across my lips. A fierce explosion of heat blasted through me. My lady bits tightened up—half painful, half pleasurable.

"Nope." I slapped his hand away. Now was definitely not the time. I had a level-five demon on my ass. I had to stay focused.

"Together, with the Banks," he said in a low, intimate voice, ignoring my reaction, "we can defeat it. I will keep you safe, Reagan."

"I think it'll definitely be a team effort. Okay, game face. I need to find addresses for those mages the bartender named. After I scarf down a quick bite, let's hook up with Callie and Dizzy, and we'll pay them a visit." I threw up a finger at him. "And don't, for one minute, think I am ignoring the fact that you initiated the bonding stuff. We will most certainly circle back to that."

"I am looking forward to it."

"You really shouldn't be. It isn't going to go well for you."

CHAPTER 27

A N HOUR AND a half later, I was crouched in a hedge with Callie and Dizzy, staring at the front door of a house that was about a half-hour outside of Seattle. The area was on the rural side, with the next house probably a half-acre to an acre away, separated by trees and wild grasses. In front of us, a wicked spell twisted and turned, invisible to the naked eye. This wasn't a mere surveillance spell, like the one we'd encountered at the other house—it was designed for active security. Out in the boondocks, this mage wanted to make sure his homestead was protected. I bet the neighbors knew to steer clear of this whacko.

"What's the plan?" Callie asked, her hand in her satchel.

I glanced off to the right, where Darius waited in deep shadow. He hadn't wanted to join us in the spider-web-infested bush for some reason.

"Cut down the spell and charge in?" I asked. "I did the creeping around thing with the last one, and that was the pits."

"Should we go through the front, or the back?" Dizzy whispered. "The light we saw was at the back."

We'd taken a tour of the outside, monitoring the complex spell, seeing if it wrapped around the whole house. It did.

"Or we could split up," I said. "After I slice down the spell, I'll hit the back, and you come in through the front. Darius can wait at the side. At the sliding glass door. Unless the mage jumps out a window, we'll have him."

"This is probably a stupid question, but can Darius hold his own against a mage of reasonable power?" Callie asked.

"Yes, that is a stupid question." I dug in my pouch. "We can also make the spell go *boom*. That'd get him all excited. Maybe he'd do something stupid."

"Whatever we do, we'll get him excited. I doubt this guy has seen half as much power on his doorstep as what we're packing." Callie squinted in the darkness. "Judging by the complexity of this spell, its power, and the way it's set up, I'm guessing we've found the lead mage."

"I agree." Dizzy dug into his satchel before extracting a leafy plant. "A mage such as this would want to be in charge. He'd want underlings. It would stand to reason he's the lead."

"Happy days," I whispered. "Remind me to pay a

visit to that bartender and thank him."

"Joe, you mean?" Callie asked.

"I have no idea. I had Darius with me, remember? Shifters don't play nice with vampires." I blew out a breath. "Screw it. Let's do this. You guys wait until you hear a crash, then run for the door."

Callie nodded and tucked the flap of her satchel at the back so the interior was open and accessible.

I crouch-ran behind the row of shrubbery until I reached the edge and straightened up. I stuck to the deep shadows, and Darius fell in behind me a moment later. "Side door," I whispered, moving quickly.

Without a word, he peeled off.

The blood must've worked. He wasn't being over-protective. That was good news.

Fire raged within me as I jumped over a rock and made for the back door. Deep down, I also felt that pounding cold, pulsing like a beacon, yelling at me to use it. I wished it would also yell instructions.

I slipped through the gate and around the back, heading toward the porch. Stripes of light glowed between the cracks in the curtains. A wind chime lay, twisted and broken, on the ground next to a beam of wood supporting the roof.

Magic vibrated across my skin, singing the current of the spell. He hadn't encircled his whole yard, just the area around his house, and not far out. So, he was more worried about B&E than Peeping Toms. Interesting.

What did he do about pizza deliveries?

I pulled out my sword as that cold lump of power inside me started to grow. It ate away the edges of the fire, cannibalizing my power.

What in holy hades? I braced my hand to my chest.

My heart started to beat faster, and I had no idea why. Sweat beaded on my forehead and upper lip. My chest constricted, squeezing the breath out of my lungs, nearly cutting off my air supply.

The cold power throbbed now, pounding outward. Taking over. Stifling.

I squeezed my eyes shut, focusing on the fire. On the power I knew how to control. Otherwise, I'd be a sitting duck for this mage, unable to throw magic of my own, and when my sword ran out of stored power, equally unable to slice through his attacks.

"I *feel* you."

I jumped in fright at the horrible rasp that crawled over my skin like a centipede, and spun. Rocks flew out from all around me, focused in their assault. They struck a human man with a crooked smile and unusually widened eyes standing within a cluster of bamboo. The bamboo stalks bowed away from him, creaking, before swinging back and *thwapping* his body.

Did I do that?

He staggered out, his hands raised to ward the attack away, but his smile grew. He rose into the sky, feet completely off the ground, and shoved his hands backward. His shoulders popped out of the sockets. The cluster of bamboo snapped and cracked before flattening like gale-force winds had blown through it. Then the plants ripped up from the ground. Dirt clung to their roots before the whole lot was flung away by unseen hands.

Holy balls, that was a lot of power. I wasn't facing a mage, but a demon who had complete control over a human's body.

I felt my hands fist as an uncomfortable truth accosted me.

It was *the* demon. The level five. I could feel the strength of his power smacking against me, pulsing in time to the coldness within. Pushing down my fire.

"You are afraid," the demon-man said in that strange rasp that made me feel covered in crawling insects. "Are you the one I seek? I feel you."

"You mentioned that. Didn't you know it's not polite to feel people without their permission? You can't hang around with humans if you don't play by the rules." I didn't let my fear overcome me. Instead, I charged.

A push of air hit me, but I was already swinging my sword. The blade cut through the demon-man's power, my stored fire power slicing into the hard air around him. I came up, my blade aiming between his legs. He flinched as I cut up his thigh.

"What power is that?" he boomed.

I cut through another attempt to grab me, feeling the sword suck at my power. But all it could reach was the cold. It couldn't draw on the fire.

Did that matter? Could it channel this new power? I had no idea.

"Show yourself," the creature yelled. Its feet hit the ground and it waffled before turning to run. It had to be running low on power. That was good news.

"I'm right here. Quit running away, damn you." I chased it, stumbling when my foot hit a divot in the dirt.

It shoved its hand at me, clearly trying to push me away. I cut through its attempt, ripped out my gun, and fired—all in one smooth movement. Kinda. The bullet punched a hole in its stomach that immediately welled up with blood. It flinched with the knock of impact, but showed no signs of pain.

I aimed for the head this time. The gun roared, but the demon-man jerked away. Fast little sucker.

Another push of its hand, but its power was definitely weakening. I cut through the spell easily, as I had done before.

"The definition of crazy is repeatedly trying the same thing and expecting different results," I said, readying for another attack. "But can demons really be called sane?"

I rushed at him and slashed, catching his arm. The blade sailed clean through. The demon-man's flesh sizzled, the wound immediately cauterized.

I'd never seen that happen, not even with vampires.

The human face contorted into something truly heinous before stretching into a non-human, jagged-toothed grin. "Highness." The human body split down the middle, like a seam that had just been unzipped. Great black wings stretched into the sky as the skin fell away. A strange, trollish face with a protruding snout and inch-long pointed teeth gaped at me. Despite its lack of lips, it was still able to talk. "You have not learned your power. We can help you. Guide you. Prepare you to step into your intended role."

"No way." I struggled to bring out the fire, needing a good blast of it to take this thing out. It was hampered by the ever-pounding, throbbing cold seeping through my middle and infecting my limbs.

"Do not be afraid of it," it said gratingly, making me grind my teeth. "Allow it to overcome you."

Terrified of the feeling, instinctively knowing I would lose myself if I let the power succeed in overcoming me, I struck forward in terror. My blade jabbed through the demon-man's middle.

The sound of sizzling grew until it was crackling like

a campfire. The creature howled, its face contorted in pain. Three-fingered, clawed hands grabbed the hand on the hilt of my sword, freezing my skin.

A surge of power tore through me. Rocks and debris around me rose into the sky. I followed, levitating, but my inner fire wasn't giving me the power to do it. The ice had coated me in a sickly way, and like a siphon, I took the demon's magic into myself. Thoughts around me sparkled to life, but most I couldn't pinpoint. Someone was afraid that I'd know about the broken second-story window. Another was embarrassed that he'd peed himself. A gun in the car. A feeling of help-lessness. Blind terror that I would be lost, and his soul would be lost with me.

The demon howled in my face, a sound that no hor-ror movie about an exorcism could adequately portray. It writhed around my blade. I was killing it, but my power wasn't draining as it should have. Instead, it swelled, sucking the evil from the demon and ingesting it. As the viciousness took over, my humanity started to erode away.

"No," I yelled. The word came out sounding like snakes slithering across sand. "No!"

Not thinking, I raked my nails down the oily black feathers on the demon's chest. Lines like streaks of acid appeared in the wake of my fingers. A clawed hand touched my skin, and I jerked back, abandoning the sword. I needed to kill the demon, but I wouldn't lose myself to do it.

It yanked the sword from its body and let it drop to the ground. The great black wings beat at the air, taking the creature into the sky. Like a wounded bird, it faltered. Still the wings pumped, taking it higher and higher until it was an absence of light on the dark background of the sky.

I spun around, still floating. Rocks and dirt hovered with me, kept afloat by me, though I didn't know how. Nor did I know how to stop it.

The demon was gone, but that dark and sticky force I'd sucked up through my sword spread through me inch by inch. Assuming control, like a demon taking over the host body.

Clamping down, I yanked my mind away, separating myself from it. Putting everything on hold.

Fear constricted my chest. Breathing came hard. But I made myself suck in air, keeping hold of the part of me that was definitely human.

"Help me," I cried weakly. More thoughts came. Bloodied claws trying to rip through an invisible wall. Magic acting strangely. Nullifying. That window still broken. Maybe he should put something in front of it. That girl down there was clearly the one sought by the demon. She would kill, or rule, them all.

"Help," I said again, my vision changing. Usually I

saw items in the darkness like I would in the light, only with lower definition. Slightly fuzzy instead of clear. Now, however, my sight crystalized. I could see better, farther, everything sharp and detailed, with an added element of a heat map.

Two figures stood in the house, standing close together. Three other figures were off to the side, working at a magical divide. Still another sat in leafy plants or bushes out by the property line.

Who was that—

The neighbor.

The knowledge crystalized in my brain before I could finish thinking the question.

He was a male. Shocked as all hell. He'd gotten a girl pregnant accidentally. He half wished the baby would be a superhero like the one he was looking at.

Me.

"Help," I said for the third time, loud now, looking down at the ground. It took everything I had to ignore the fear and panic that it was too late. That this power, this freezing cold power spreading through me like a disease, was here to stay.

CHAPTER 28

"**Y**OU MUST BE keeping this wall intact, Reagan," Callie said. *She's fighting the demon from turning her into one of its kind.*

"Please stop thinking," I called. "I can hear your thoughts. Stop thinking. It's freaking me out."

Demons can hear thoughts?

"Yes, Dizzy. And I just said to *stop thinking*!" I swallowed past the lump in my throat. "Now, who has advice on how I can deal with this?"

"Let us near you," Darius said in a calm voice. This might've been a normal state of affairs for how unaffected he sounded. His fear said otherwise.

The figures in the house ran, moving toward the front. I heard echoes of them being called to aid their master. The demon was too weak to pass to the underworld. It needed more power.

I still had time to kill him, which I relayed to the crew. He couldn't be allowed to get his message to my father.

Of course, I couldn't do anything until I got out of

my current predicament.

"The demon must've transferred its power to you, Reagan," Callie said, her voice not as calm. Fear tinged every word. "Not the type of power—that is clearly already in you. But its actual power. The life force. You know what I mean." I did, horrifyingly enough. "You have to fight it. If you fight it, and regain control, you can…regain control."

"That's how you'll get yourself down," Dizzy said. "You'll probably fall down, but that's good, too." *Hopefully she'll also stop reading thoughts. Oh no, is she hearing this?* Dizzy stared at me, as though expecting an answer.

A thought about calling Vlad for help echoed through Darius's troubled mind.

"Don't call Vlad." I wiped my face. "Whatever you do, don't call that guy. I don't need any more turds in my litterbox."

"That's graphic," Dizzy mumbled.

"She has a right to be graphic." Callie backed away from the others. "She's stuck in midair, floating in rocks and dirt, and jeopardized by a demon. I can't believe every other word out of her mouth isn't a curse word." There was something in her hand, but I couldn't get a good look at it.

"When you practiced your new power, what cir-cumvented it?" Darius asked, pacing beside the invisible barrier that apparently I was keeping enacted.

Callie threw a casing. It flashed green before fizzling away. "Dang it," she mumbled. "Her ability to unweave spells is still working."

"I've never had to circumvent it." I wiped my face again, getting rid of the moisture. My sudden sweating problem wasn't from exerting this power. The demon had given me plenty. Too much. No, it was from the increasing difficulty of ignoring my fear. I was stalling. The hovering, the telekinesis, the wall—they were keeping me stagnant, but they were not stopping the icy, corrosive power from spreading. Its progress had slowed, but it kept soaking up my insides, turning me cold.

"Explain it to me," Darius said in a confident, commanding voice. A thought trailed away, unvoiced. *Mon ange.*

My angel. That was sweet.

I took a deep breath. "Okay." I walked him through the various phases, from stumbling upon the new well of power, to actively trying to use it, to the way the two powers had mixed like ink, and finally to the confrontation with the demon-mage and then the demon itself.

"The demon is calling forth this other side of your power," Callie said. "Like when your mother worked to bring it out in you with your training, they are bringing it to the surface naturally. I did not realize there were two halves to the whole."

"Surprise." I moved my hands and feet like a puppet.

She is on a thin rope, Dizzy thought.

He had that right.

Callie dug into her bag. "Stand back, everyone. This spell might explode."

"Wait." Darius held his hand out, studying me. "Force the fire, Reagan," he said in a soft, urgent voice. "Force the fire. Force it to take over. Get me through this barrier and I will help you."

"How are you going to help her?" Callie asked.

"Blood," Darius said, the possessiveness back tenfold. "It helped after she killed the other demon. It has to help this time as well. I will not lose her to the underworld. She is bringing back my humanity—I will not let it take hers."

"Well, that is unexpected," Dizzy deadpanned. "But unless you can get her down first, you won't be able to get blood into her."

"Force the fire," Darius urged me.

Yes, that was what I needed to do. Or just force this icy power down. But that meant dunking myself back into the sludge. I was afraid of it. Afraid of losing myself, like Darius had said.

Heat pricked behind my eyes, threatening tears. I'd never been this afraid in my whole life. This wasn't death. It was a fate worse than death. Until now, I'd thought only prison qualified for that category. The prospect of losing my humanity was so much worse. Becoming a monster.

I stared directly at Darius. "Kill me if it takes over, okay? Don't try to save me. Kill me."

His thoughts were in French this time, and his hard face gave nothing away.

"Promise me," I pushed.

"No. Force the fire, *mon ange*. Force the fire."

"Can't you do what I say *for once*?" I took a deep breath, struggling for control of my emotions. Then I reconnected with my power, feeling that dark, cold ice spreading within me. I had very little time.

"Force the fire." His voice wound around me, urging me to obey. I soaked it in, taking courage from his confidence. "Sometimes the only way out is to go *through*. You can do it."

I squeezed my eyes shut and searched for the spark. The heat that felt so good when it rolled over my skin.

Darius repeated himself, his voice like that of a commander inspiring valor and true grit in his men before they marched unto the breach.

I could do this. Both powers were my birthright. Both could be controlled, I just had to figure out how to master this new one, and later, how to manage both of them in tandem.

Gritting my teeth, I tapped into the cold power, feeling every rock and speck of dirt circling me. Hearing the excitement of the neighbor's thoughts, and the awe in Callie and Dizzy. But most importantly, I felt Darius's raw, unyielding belief that I could do this. That I was more powerful than him, than even Vlad, and if anyone could handle a trivial matter such as a demon overthrowing one's person, it was *me*.

Sometimes the only way out was to go through.

Here goes nothing.

I embodied the full force of the icy power, felt it sucking me under and turning everything black. My thoughts rolled and my breath left me. I reveled in the dark majesty of the power thrumming within my veins.

A stray thought wound through my glory.

Make her proud.

Her.

Callie meant my mother.

Emotion surged up in me. And with it, fire.

My mother had always called me her flame. She'd coaxed it out of me. She'd helped me embody it.

Now she would save my life with it.

I yanked it up and wrapped it around the horrible coldness, defusing the edges. Chopping off the seeking arms. I pushed the cold down and packed it into a tight ball, the effect lowering me in the sky, making it harder for me to keep the rocks and dirt up.

But I did.

Balls of flame sprang to life, various colors, various sizes, moving through the debris around me, making the guy hiding in the bushes do a fist pump. I rose back up and drifted forward, feeling all that horrible blackness inside me surrounded by bright light. Ice wrapped in heat.

Fire rolled along my arms and legs, but the cold stayed like a cap on my head. I'd probably still lose my eyebrows, unfortunately. You couldn't have everything.

The sweet air rushed back into my lungs. My fingers tingled with pins and needles, coming back to life. My heart fluttered, emotion surging back in.

Finally, I pushed it all back down, the fire and ice together, a knot in my stomach now, but the start of something. I'd fuse them together one day.

My feet bumped the ground and the debris in the air slowly fell. The fire winked out. The man in the bushes ran like hell.

"Someone should help him forget," I said, glancing at his retreating figure. "He was too excited for his own good."

I felt the others draw near me, but no one spoke. When I turned to them, Callie and Dizzy had their eyebrows up, as if they'd just asked a question.

Another wave of relief flooded me. "If you are thinking things, I thankfully can't hear them."

"I'm going to hate myself for saying this, but…not yet." Callie adjusted her satchel. "You can't hear them yet. But you will. We'll work on that power to help you develop it. Then hopefully control it so you don't do it all the time. I have some pretty stupid thoughts I'd rather keep to myself."

"Me too," Dizzy muttered.

Darius was staring at me with his hard face, but he didn't speak.

"Right, then, one crisis averted. Now for the second." I started toward the house. "We have to kill that demon before it can get to the underworld."

"Do we know where the summoning site is yet?" Dizzy asked, hurrying to my side. "That's probably where they'll congregate to send the demon back."

"We came here to find information, Dizzy," Callie said, tramping behind us.

"Oh yes, right."

"Let's hope there's a clue in the mage's house." The spell from earlier was gone. The mages must've taken it down before they left. They had to get through it, too. "I wonder why the demon was randomly hanging out in the yard."

"Following you, probably." Darius reached the door first and went to grab the handle. He hesitated. "Would you like to kick this in, Reagan?"

"How thoughtful. But no. Let's just go inside."

He opened the door, having already unlocked it.

"Or maybe the demon already knew you would eventually find the mage in charge. It is hard to say." Darius stepped out of the way so we could enter.

"If he got close enough to you in that ugly man's body, he could have heard your thoughts," Dizzy said. "Or my thoughts. Once that door is opened, are there any secrets anymore?"

"My mom came up with a way to block that," I said to Dizzy as I entered the house. "I'm sure you'll figure it out."

"Oh good. Yes. Very clever, your mom." Dizzy followed closely behind me.

I looked around, not sure where to start. "My only question is, can I actually kill the demon without losing myself?"

"You can. I know you can. When you've solved a problem once, that's it. You have it." Callie riffled through papers on the counter.

"But we still have all the mages to deal with," I said.

"We'll take care of the mages." Callie pushed an envelope to the side. "I'm nearly positive I finally recruited the little witch. Her mother doesn't monitor Penny's texts and calls, thank God. With her power at our backs, those other mages don't stand a chance."

"She's a mage, hon. An untrained mage." Dizzy yanked two drawers out and dumped them on the ground. "You call her. I'll help Reagan and Darius look through the house. I have an eye for picking things out of chaos. If there are clues here, we'll find them."

CHAPTER 29

"I HAVE A check stub," Dizzy shouted. "He doesn't make much at his job."

I rifled through a desk drawer in his disorganized office. We'd been at this for fifteen minutes and still hadn't found anything solid. Or helpful.

"What does he do?" I shouted.

Darius appeared in the doorway, and I jumped, knocking the rolling chair back into the bookcase.

"Jesus, man." I put a hand to my heart. "Don't just pop up like a poltergeist. I'm a little jumpy right now."

Darius held up a blue uniform without saying a word. The front resembled a police uniform, with a sewn-on patch like a badge on the arm. He turned it, and I saw *security* written on the back.

"Where did you say that skin suit was found?" Dizzy called.

"It wasn't a skin suit, and it was in terminal thirty. Port of Seattle, I think. The shipping terminal." I slipped out from around the desk and looked at the patch on the sleeve. It said *security officer.*

"Shoot," Dizzy said. "I was hoping it would be the same company."

"Perhaps they all work in security," Darius said. "It would've been hard to get a body into the terminal in the later hours without being noticed. Unless you worked there and brought it in your car."

"But they said all of the staff checked out. And yes, I realize these people probably wouldn't have any priors, but Oscar also said none of them were magical..."

How stupid was I?

"The MLE office was keeping their mouths shut." I shook my head. "They must've known a mage was responsible, and that one worked at the terminal, but they were warned away from mages, so they weren't talking." I bowed in frustration. "You even asked if I wanted to talk to the security people. I can't tell most magical species, but I know mages. I would've felt his or her magic."

"The thought had occurred to me, but I admit, it was in my best interest that you weren't thorough," Darius said. "I failed you there. I was thinking about feeding instead of covering all the bases. After hearing about the dangers in the area, we had new, more concrete leads. But this is telling."

"It is. Dizzy," I called. "What's the company name on that check stub?" I lowered my voice so I wasn't shouting in Darius's face. "They dumped one body at the port, so maybe there'll be some activity at this other place. I mean, the guy is the lead mage, probably. Maybe he uses his place of work for the summonings and leaves the scraps for the others to dispose of…"

"Torturing a body at one's place of work would probably be noticed."

I grimaced. "Unless they used a spell to hide themselves."

"What?"

Dizzy's sudden proximity, right beyond the doorway, made me jump.

"Would you guys stop sneaking around? I'm still coming down off a fear high." I rubbed my face. "What is the company name on the pay stub?"

He pushed his way past Darius. "BNSF railway," he read, looking up at me to see if that clicked.

It didn't. Not yet, anyway.

"Is it normal for mages to have jobs?" I asked, trying to weigh the significance. "I mean, the mages I get spells from in NOLA do, but they aren't particularly powerful. Which is why they are cheap and can't afford to live off their magic. This guy is clearly both powerful and experienced."

"Very few mages can afford to consistently do this full-time," Dizzy said, stalking past me and looking around the small office. He stopped at the file cabinet, pulled out a drawer, and dumped the contents onto the ground. "It isn't steady income if all you can do is make spells. You get surge months, sure, but there are also down months. Sometimes down years, depending on how many mages are trying to sell their wares. Most people need something steady, at least part-time, to cover the basic bills for the bad months."

"And you guys, who clearly don't fall into that category?" I asked, taking a hint and resuming my search. We needed something more concrete. Or, at the very least, we needed to establish we had no other options.

"Healing ointments aren't just for magical people, and very few mages can successfully do what Callie does in that arena. She can sell her stuff as beauty products, and they work ten times better than whatever the grocery market stocks. You know, because of magic. It's that business that earns us the most. Then, of course, we are reliable, hardworking, and willing to bend to strange demands, like color-coded casings. That attracts eccentric customers, like vampires who like everything *just so.*"

"One of those vampires is standing right here, you know. Listening." I grinned at Dizzy before shifting my gaze to Darius, who wore a blank face.

"All of this comes as no shock to him, I'm sure," Dizzy said, unperturbed. He emptied another drawer on the floor before shaking his head. "I don't think we're going to find anything of importance in the office. This guy isn't all that organized. He probably has the important things randomly stuffed on some shelf."

"Like you would?" I shoved a desk drawer shut, agreeing with Dizzy. I'd found zero.

"Exactly, yes. So let's move on to the living room or, better yet, find his work room." Dizzy left the mess and moved to the door.

"You know," I said, following, "the mage's house we busted into the other night didn't have a work room. He had a place where he kept his spells, but I don't know where he actually made them. That should've occurred to me."

"Why would it?" Dizzy led us into the living room, then glanced around. After a moment, he shook his head and started upstairs. "You don't cast spells, so you wouldn't think to look for the place where it's done."

It was a weak argument, but I let it go.

Fifteen minutes of searching the three bedrooms and two bathrooms, and we'd still found nothing.

"Was there a shed out back?" Dizzy moved to the window of the master bedroom, which overlooked the back half of the property. "I don't remember anything besides Reagan battling a demon midair."

"No, no shed." Darius stood in the doorway. "We are wasting time."

"We don't have any strong leads," I said, frustrated. "They are surely trying to build up power as we speak. If we head to that railway, and we're wrong, that's it. He's gone."

Dizzy gave me an apologetic shake of the head. "It doesn't look like we have anything else, Reagan. Not a key, or a leasing agreement, or a pen, or…anything. Certainly no GPS."

"Computer." I blinked. "We didn't come across a computer."

"We've got her," Callie yelled from what sounded like the bottom of the stairs. "She wants to know where to head. She's in a small town north of here, so it'll take her forty-five minutes to get into the city. At least."

Urgency ate away at me. That demon would be in a blind panic to get out of the Brink. It had what it came for and knew it was in grave peril. It would be bending the mages over backward to get everything ready.

"What to do," I said, chewing my lip.

Silence fell on the room, all eyes on me, until Callie finally yelled out, "*Well?*"

"Let's go to that rail yard." I broke for the door. "If it's a ghost town, then we'll circle back to the terminal, or maybe go hang that bartender up by the feet to see what else he knows. We're running out of time."

CHAPTER 30

"T HIS IS CLOSE to the place they dumped that other body," Callie said as she peered out the passenger window. We slowly rolled into the mostly deserted employee parking structure at the southern corner of the huge rail yard. "It's just across the freeway."

"Yes, it is." I looked at the map on my phone. "Two of the mages work within ten minutes of each other. What do you want to bet they both work night shifts?"

I tried to peer out through the opening slats of the parking structure to get a better sense of what we were getting into. Fat chance. A building stood between us and the rail lines, and if it hadn't, there would have been an abundance of crates and cargo to block our view. This was a large rail yard that likely dealt with hundreds of shipments a day. I was no expert, but I bet someone could easily get lost in the shadows if they knew where to hide. Especially if they were the security.

"I have a good feeling about this," I said into the quiet car.

"I feel sick." Dizzy cleared his throat.

As Darius parked a few floors up, a long, forlorn horn sounded in the night.

"I didn't know trains ran this late," I said softly, letting the somber feeling of the empty parking structure press on me. I climbed from the car.

"Freight carriers certainly do," Callie said, getting out the other side. She looked at her phone. "Penny is on the first floor."

"How'd you get her to come?" Dizzy asked. His gaze swept the area and his hand firmly gripped the strap of the satchel that draped across his chest. His eyes settled on the exit sign on the far wall.

"I have a way with people." Callie clearly didn't see the irony of that statement. "She had to sneak out of the house to duck that atrocious mother of hers, but the…incident a couple of months ago left her wanting to learn. She trusts me."

"She won't after this," I said, taking out my gun.

"I doubt this is going to be worse than a circle of women turning themselves into zombies, like at that mage battle." Callie sniffed. "She'll be fine. She's a natural."

I walked to the front of the car as the others started off toward the stairs. Above the wall in front of the car, which stopped at my chest, I could see a train passing below us, moving out of the vast, empty space lined with railroad tracks. To my left, on the other side of the long, low building, the tracks continued in the other direction. Leaning out, I could just make out the rail yard, lined with containers and crates similar to the ones we'd seen on the shipping port on the other side of the freeway.

"It won't tell us much, but it'll give us an idea," Darius said, waiting patiently. He never seemed to feel the urgency the rest of us did. Though seeing into his head had somewhat changed my perception of that. He was a lot better at hiding his feelings than the rest of us were.

"It's a huge space." I backed away from the wall and headed toward the stairs, which Callie and Dizzy were already making their way down. "With the buildings, and the rail cars, and the containers... If they're here, how are we going to find them?"

"They will be using large quantities of magic, not to mention the demon's power. Feeling magic is your specialty, is it not?" Darius's hand settled on my lower back. "Don't let what happened earlier make you second-guess yourself. Learn from it, and move on."

"Thanks, coach." I took a deep breath, starting down the stairs. "But it's not that easy this time. I don't know how to defeat this thing."

"We have three of the four most powerful mages I've ever met. One might not be trained, but she is a natural, as Callie said. If you immobilize the demon, they can work with us to kill it. The trick will be wiping out the mage circle before the demon escapes."

"Yes, that will be the trick, all right."

Penny was sitting in her car, staring down at her phone, when Callie knocked on her window. The girl, about my age, jumped and flung up her hands to cover her head.

"Step one, work on those reactions," I mumbled as I waited with Darius off to the side.

"As I said, untrained. Give her time," Darius murmured as Penny exited her car.

"Wait, when did you meet her? You were gone by the time we got her out of the closet at that mage battle."

"I occasionally have business in this part of the world. Like I do in many parts of the world."

I frowned. Cryptic. Or was this part of some greater design? Vlad had told Darius he'd give him the professional courtesy of steering clear of the area because Darius had something cooking...

I pushed the thought away. It wasn't important right now.

Penny tucked a flyaway strand of hair behind her ear before looking up at everyone through her thick black lashes. I couldn't get over how much she looked like a Disney princess, with her large, luminous blue eyes, little pixie features, and plump lips.

What she didn't look like was a girl who would

storm buildings, take down enemy mages, and dole out punches like they were business cards.

"Listen," I said, holding up my hand. "She might be a natural, and she might want to learn, but this is the big time. We can't bring in someone who freaks out halfway through and tries to run and hide. She could get herself, or one of us, killed."

She straightened up a little as irritation crossed her expression. When she met my direct stare, though, her spine bowed once again.

"Reagan, you're giving her crazy eyes," Callie said, grabbing the girl by the upper arm. "But she's right, Penny. This is the point of no return. There is going to be some serious danger in there."

"Assuming we're even in the right place," Dizzy muttered.

"I take it you didn't mention any of this when you spoke with her?" I asked Callie.

"Then she wouldn't have come," Callie muttered. "I definitely told her we were going to banish a demon, though."

"It's okay." Penny sighed and straightened up again, her eyes flicking to Darius. She looked away just as quickly. "I owe him, so…"

I looked at Darius, something weird and hot rising through my chest. It didn't take long for me to identify the foreign emotion.

Jealousy. Super. Can this day get any worse?

But, of course, the answer was yes, it could get worse. It could get a *lot* worse. Was about to, in fact, because either we were in the right place and were heading into battle, or we weren't and a demon with my secrets would escape to the underworld and tattle to my father.

"If you're coming, Penny, harden up," I said, walking. "Otherwise, get out now."

"You'll be fine," Callie said. I could hear pats, probably Callie trying to comfort her. "Just hex the hell out of anyone who isn't on our side."

"Hex, shoot, stab, eye-gouge—whatever." I walked out into the crisp night, a wonderful change from the sticky humidity of New Orleans. "This is the easy part. Finding some meddling mages."

"Meddling is not the term I would use for a group of serial killers." Dizzy jogged up to me. "So, Reagan, can you walk me through your method?"

"Sure. I walk around, usually quietly, and look for evildoers. Sometimes I find magic instead. So I tear down the magic and *then* find the evildoers. Generally, a battle ensues, and I kill said evildoers, often accidentally. I always blame this on them, of course."

"Yes, yes, of course." He watched my face. It was awfully distracting.

"Dizzy, why don't you look around for anything

odd?"

"The rest of the group will do that. You are infinite-ly more fascinating. Your unique approach to danger always gives me ideas for new spells."

Fabulous.

"That must be the yard office," Callie whispered, pointing at a squat, rectangular building up ahead. "Beyond it will be lots twelve through fourteen. I assume... Ah yes, there we go, various cargo. Compa-nies must rent this space out. There are other lots on the other side, but I can't remember the numbers."

"Why do you know so much about this place?" Penny asked.

"I looked at the map, dear. There are several online."

"Oh."

I paused in the shadow of a quiet checkpoint, my gaze focused on the building Callie had called the yard office. A man stood outside, just beyond the edges of a beam of light trained on the ground from a corner of the building. His gaze swept in an arc, surveying the area. Though his head was moving, and his eyes were no doubt scanning, no one was home. I could tell he wasn't taking in what he was seeing. Boredom from inactivity would do that to a person.

Continuing on, sticking to the shadows around the large check-in structure that was shut down except for one guard also asleep at the wheel, we skirted by without a problem.

I gritted my teeth as we made our way through the lot, looking at the various containers and other cargo. Nothing looked out of the ordinary, and more importantly, I didn't sense any magic.

"What's beyond this, Callie?" I whispered.

"Um." A soft glow illuminated her face as she studied her phone. "On the other side of the road, which we can't see from here—"

"I can't see anything at all," Dizzy whispered.

"—is the other lots."

"Are," Penny said. It sounded like an afterthought.

"What?" Callie looked at her.

Penny shook her head in fast jerks. "Sorry," she mumbled. "My mom always corrects my grammar. It rubbed off."

"Wonderful. A fellow wordsmith." Dizzy beamed, now pointing his phone at the ground with the flashlight function on. His jolly attitude indicated he was completely ignoring the coming danger.

"Dizzy, that is probably making it worse," I told him, pushing his phone toward his chest. "Let your eyes adapt."

"Easy for you to say. You can see in the dark."

"You can see in the dark?" Penny asked. "Is that because of…" Her gaze flicked to Darius.

"*Focus,*" I said, and not just because of what she was alluding to.

The stacks of cargo ended and the tracks cut in—a wide expanse of space occasionally lined with a train waiting for *go* time. "So far, not so good."

I crossed the road leading to the other lots. The moonlight had a better opportunity to reach us—helping the others see and allowing me to pick up the pace. We passed more cargo, but I was still coming up empty.

"How big is this place, Callie?" I asked into the hush. I'd seen it from the car, but it had been impossible to judge the size at the speed we were going.

"Big. We're not even halfway through."

"Is the walking okay, Callie? Dizzy? You guys doing okay?" I asked, worrying about hips and bunions and whatever else they might have going on. "Penny, how's the daintiness? Freaking out because you're breaking a sweat?"

"I have run three marathons," Penny said with heat to her voice. I liked it.

"Did someone fail to mention that I have healing magic?" Callie asked levelly. It was rarely a good sign. "Dizzy and I are like spring chickens."

"As long as we don't have to spring up from a crouch," Dizzy amended.

"There's the tower." Callie pointed upward.

Over the lip of the cargo lining our way rose a building that had clearly been built to overlook the goings-on of the rail yard. I instinctively wanted to be up at the top. But to what end? It hardly seemed likely the mages would have peeled up the top of their workshop of horrors, allowing me to see inside.

"Then what?" I asked.

"Let's see. The label says there's some type of repair shop." Callie squinted down at her phone. "I can't read what type. Probably a little building. It's just a speck."

"And then?"

"The line of lots we're in leads to the end of the yard. Then there's side loader repair."

I glanced into the crack between two containers to the open road. "Does that road lead all the way back?"

"Yes. It might connect with the freeway, but this isn't much more than a cartoon map, so I can't tell."

After a while, we came to the end of the lots, having passed a couple of small buildings along the way. My hope was fizzling out with each step. Up ahead, the expanse of tracks, many now filled with parked trains, reduced down into a few bare tracks leading out of the area.

"That must be the side loader repair," Callie said, pointing at a building at the end. "Which is the end of the line."

I put my hands on my hips and looked around, my

heart in my shoes. "He's not here. I'm screwed."

"We will find the shifter from the bar," Darius said, suddenly pressed against my side. "We can ask him for more information."

"Wait." Penny leaned over Callie's arm and pointed at the edge of Callie's phone screen. "What's over there?"

Callie scrunched her brow as she worked the screen. "More lots. Another checkpoint, another entrance. More railroad tracks."

I shook my head, my chest tight.

"Learn from our mistakes," Darius said insistently. "Let's check it out, then move on."

"What happens if we don't find the demon in time?" Penny asked.

Everyone fell silent. Callie and Dizzy's heads dipped to the ground. Darius's gaze turned fierce.

"No one can know for sure," I said with a thick tongue. "But judging by the number of parties trying to lay claim to me, I'd say my chances of living a quiet, uneventful life don't look so good."

CHAPTER 31

"**H**URRY, YOU FOOLS!" Agnon shouted, barely able to hold up the human's head.

The mages had furnished it with a body. A weak, diseased, aged body that was dying as Agnon crouched within it, feeding off its energy. It wouldn't be long before the human deteriorated, forcing Agnon to eject and drain precious energy of its own.

The male mage worked his knife, trying to get the correct amount of power to enact the circle.

All Agnon needed was a proper banishing spell. It didn't have to be much, just powerful enough to shove it in the right direction. As soon as it crossed the line between worlds, it could rejuvenate within the Dark Kingdom until it was ready to travel to its sect.

"Banishing a demon should be second nature to a mage," Agnon hissed, its voice filling the space. "Why is this taking so long?"

"We need a sacrifice to send someone of your strength," a woman said. "We need more energy."

"You need a better circle of mages!" Agnon roared,

lying on the ground decrepitly. "You must send me off before she finds us. She will be my death if she catches me on the surface."

But she would be Agnon's greatest boon if it could get below. The heir had both elements of the Dark Kingdom's power—something only the Great Master shared with her. Agnon hadn't seen the incendium magic, the fire, but it had felt it when her sword pierced its body. Luckily for it, the heir hadn't yet learned the full extent of her power. She was as strong as the Great Master himself, able to move worlds. Alter time. Agnon had felt that incredible might pulsing deeply within her.

And she was only in her infancy.

If Agnon could've giggled like one of those silly, tiny humans, it would have.

Its sect could train her in secret. Help her develop her power. Since she had both elements of the Great Master's power, they could bring in a neighboring incendium sect, form an alliance, and have two halves of the whole.

But first, it had to get below.

"Hurry," it yelled again.

"Master, there is no way she can find us. We are hidden from view," one of those insufferable humans said.

"She is the almighty," Agnon said. "This shack is not hidden from her eyes."

"It is not a shack, I assure you," the lead mage said in an arrogant tone. "But we are in a rural place. She'll find nothing in my home to point her here. I removed all the evidence of this location. Even if she found this place, she wouldn't know to come all the way to this removed area. Trust me—we have all the time in the world."

If Agnon had not needed this disgusting human, it would have killed him right then. How dare he disregard the heir's abilities as merely human?

"I hope she finds you just after you have sent me below," Agnon said.

CHAPTER 32

"I VOTE WE go," Callie said. "A quick look. Then we head on. Because really, what choice do we have?"

I glanced at the clock. Middle of the night. Time was flying. Chances were, if it wasn't here, we wouldn't find it tonight. Then we'd be hampered by the sunlight. Granted, the magical people could hang, but I needed Darius. He could help me take out the demon, and if not, he could help me keep from losing myself. He might be the end game.

The chances that it wasn't here were good.

I shook my head and looked back toward the distant parking garage. "There is no way they can hide in the lots. Say they were using a container, or a group of them, and hiding their freaky workshop with a spell. Humans would eventually realize there was an unnatural absence of cargo."

"Well…that's not necessarily true." Penny scratched her nose. "In addition to making something invisible, you could use a spell to distract the human mind so they don't recognize the gap between things that aren't invisible..."

"I know, but—" I started.

"The eye wouldn't notice it, no," Callie trundled over me. "But the mind, eventually, would catalog it. The mind isn't so easily fooled as the eyes. It'll put up with a difference in data for a while, but eventually, it'll catch on. Then it'll start forcing the eyes to *see*. You have to switch the spell, or switch the setup, or switch...something to change things up. Spells wear off, and that isn't just because the magic escapes. It's also because human perception gets more intelligent."

"That. Yes." I made a circle with my finger, like a coach running out of time. "But now's not the time to walk the newbie through spells. I think we're looking for something more secluded. On your map, is there anywhere for a disguised building to go? Or even an electrical station or something? Anything with four walls and a roof?"

Callie brought the phone closer, squinting. "Granted, this probably isn't to scale. And though it has been accurate so far, that doesn't mean—"

"Answer, please," I said.

"It doesn't look good, but it isn't improbable."

"*Isn't improbable.* Double negatives don't save lives, Callie." I frowned and shook my head, hating how slowly we were going. Feeling the urgency deep in my gut.

As if hearing my thoughts again (he was starting to make me nervous), Darius said, "I can carry you through the park." He grabbed my arm. "You should be able to detect magic at accelerated speeds."

His insistence made me pause. No doubt he was feeling bad about not pressing at the start of this whole mess.

He'd been right before.

"We all go together," I said in a split-second decision. "We'll move fast. If it's not here, Darius, you run, get the car, and pick us up."

"How are we going to get across?" Penny asked, staring at the void that was the tracks.

As if on cue, a speck of light came from around the bend. The train became visible shortly thereafter. It slowed as it rumbled into the rail yard.

Callie rolled her eyes. "You're telling me that a marathon runner can't dodge a slow-moving train?"

"No, I meant, how are we going to get around all the trains parked in our way? Going through the places where they join together will be tough. And probably greasy. You don't want to get that velvet suit all mucked up."

"Hopefully then she'd throw it away," I muttered. "Come on, we'll go around the end. It's not that far."

Like a bunch of teenagers, we waited until the train passed—one engine and only a few cars—and then hurried across. The lights of the checkpoint blared not far away, since we'd had to cross in a somewhat public place. To save us time, and sneakiness, Darius took the lead.

The guard lay in his booth by the time we walked through, passed out with a serene smile on his face.

That horrible hot feeling rose in my chest again, my reaction to Darius biting someone else. I was losing my mind.

"Let's hurry." I started to jog, not caring if I left the others behind. More cargo containers rose up around me, the same as the ones we'd seen before. Already having lost hope, I just wanted to get through here as quickly as possible and move on to the next thing.

A couple of tracks split off, leading off to the side and down the middle of the cargo areas, and both tracks were currently occupied by train cars in different stages of being loaded.

"No magic," I said, nearing the end. Dread pierced my gut. "Absolutely nothing."

"Just up here there is an emergency…thing. I can't make out what kind, though." Callie pointed ahead.

"Darius, go get the—" A faint feeling of magic tingled my skin as I neared the end of the cargo area. "Wait."

"I feel magic," Penny said, just a little behind me. "Evil magic."

K . F . B R E E N E

I glanced back at her, surprised.

"There is no evil magic. Or good magic. Just magic," Callie said in a hush. "It is the caster's purpose that defines the spell."

"The caster makes this magic evil," Penny amended. "It is dark and clingy and...sticky." She wiped at her arms.

I peeked around the corner. A large space existed beyond the cargo lots before the land became industrialized again. To the naked eye, it was empty but for a small building that sat near the edge of the graveled area. A small, out-of-the-way shack that didn't seem maintained. Next to it, however, was a moderately sized area cloaked in a heavy invisibility spell, shot through with spider webs of different kinds of eye distractions.

"Holy crap." Relief and fear washed over me in turns. This had to be it. This had to be the site we were looking for.

And that meant I was about to confront a really powerful demon for the second time.

"Someone put a lot of time and effort into this collection of spells," I said in a hush.

"What kind of spell?" Callie whispered.

"Invisibility and multiple types and power levels of distraction spells. It has all the bells and whistles. What I don't understand is how come no one missed the loss of a structure this large?"

"How large?" Dizzy asked. "Does it fill the whole space?"

"About three-quarters of it. You can see where people have been walking around it." I pointed at the lines of foot traffic in the gravel. I doubted the humans even knew why they didn't make a beeline to their destination, instead arcing around what they thought was absolutely nothing.

"The moonlight isn't bright enough to see whatever you're pointing at," Callie said. "But a distraction spell would make the fact that something used to be there, and now isn't, slip by the brain for a while. Something of this magnitude wouldn't fool people for long. The mages have probably taken down and put up the spells several times, which explains the need for a few mages, even if the summoning didn't."

"Whatever the reason, there it is, and we need to get going." I patted my various weapons. "Where to start?"

"Rip that spell off like a Band-Aid," Callie said, pulling out items from her satchel. "Then we'll take the mages and you work on the demon."

It would take too long to slice through each of the components with the sword. No, this required my fire.

"But it'll take time to get the various parts of that spell unraveled. Otherwise it'll blow up in our faces," Penny said, picking at a button on her shirt while studying the spell that she could clearly see. She was one in a million as far as mages went, which worked out for me. She wouldn't think I was horribly unique. Not for a while, anyway. And hopefully by then I'd be out of the public eye again.

"First I have to kill that demon, though," I said to myself.

"What?" Callie asked.

I shook my head. "Give me a screen, Callie. We don't want anyone to see this."

"It is highly volatile." Penny was still picking at her button, analyzing the spell. "They did a good job with it."

"Take one last look, because it's about to go boom." I nodded to Callie, who plucked at Dizzy. They walked a ways to the side and started muttering, pulling items out of their satchels.

"Should we get closer so they can make their spell smaller?" Darius asked.

I judged the distance before glancing at Penny. "No. You can withstand the heat, and I won't feel it, but my fire shield after it takes the spell's energy would be too hot for Penny if we got closer."

"Shield?" Penny asked, blinking those luminous eyes.

"Do we need to do all sides?" Callie asked as Dizzy muttered an incantation. A rudimentary sheen of red tumbled down from the sky like a curtain—a unique and somewhat on-the-nose way of enacting that particular spell—blocking the view and probably any sound from the other side.

"No. Just where humans might be wandering around." Fire filled me in a rush, spreading heat into my limbs. For now, I ignored the pulsing coldness deep in my gut. I would be confronted with that soon enough. "In reality, he did us a favor by putting this thing way out here."

"We're sure it's him?" Darius asked.

"Nope. But we're hoping for the best." I waited for Callie and Dizzy's spell to meet the ground before moving my hands through the air, fingers spread.

Fire licked the gravel around my feet. Penny inched back.

I pushed my hands forward and the fire responded to my unspoken command, crawling toward the structure before pausing at the base. The spell was well rooted.

"This mage definitely knows what he's doing," I said, the words no more than a whisper in the hush. "Get ready for some potent and aggressive attacks."

"I've been working on it since I saw you in New Orleans and I can't seem to come up with a way to make fire do that," Penny said, having inched up again. "I've tried everything I can think of."

"It's my cousin," I said quickly. "In Canada. Experimental spells."

"Cousin?" Dizzy asked.

"Oh yes, he is crazy, her cousin," Callie said. I heard Dizzy grunt. He'd probably gotten an elbow to the side. I hoped so, at any rate. "Never does the same thing twice. Totally unpredictable. Don't try to duplicate that; it could kill you. Reagan lives on the wild side."

"But you don't have a casing." Penny pointed at my empty hands.

I lifted said hands, making the low-heat fire coat the outline of the spell.

"She started with the casings." Callie cleared her throat. "I'll explain it all when you come for training. It'll be fine. Let's just focus on the here and now."

I half smiled, because Callie clearly needed some time to come up with a good lie. My humor dripped away, though, as I felt the vibrations of the spell turn angry.

"Here we go." I increased the heat, crackling through the spell. Like snapping strings on a violin, pieces of it kept breaking away. *Pop, pop, pop.*

I threw up a curtain of fire in front of us for protection. The protection and concealment spells sizzled violently, unraveled or eaten away entirely by my power. Without warning, they burst, reacting exactly as Penny had predicted. An explosion of magic slapped against my wall of fire. Sparkles of color spread out across the flame curtain before I ripped it to the side, exposing a medium-sized warehouse with blackened windows and a plain door.

The door flew open and a shock of magic blasted out at us.

CHAPTER 33

I CAUGHT THE attack in fire and ate away the spell, making the mages' eyes go round in astonishment. My return fire was exactly that: a thin stream of heat-intensive flame directed right at them.

It hit the first mage dead-on. He screamed and patted at his black robe before running off the steps and onto the gravel. Clearly he had forgotten the stop-drop-and-roll technique. The flame grew, about ready to burn him alive.

Gross.

I tore the fire away and jerked my head. "Darius."

The vampire was there in a moment. Two strong hands wrapped around the mage's head. Penny flinched at the *crack* that followed.

"What are you?" one of the mages yelled, staring at me with a slack jaw. Next to him, a female mage bent to her hands, her lips moving. They'd shut the door behind them.

A blast of green shot from the female mage, headed for Dizzy. He didn't have time to counter, but a sheen of black rose up in front of him like a net, catching the mage's spell like my fire might've. Unlike my fire, however, the sheen of black didn't eat away the magic, or even unravel it. Instead, it wrapped around the spell, making an outline like a comet. It looked about ready to implode.

"Uh-oh," Penny said. Clearly she'd thrown up the netlike spell, trying to mimic my magic. It was not wise to experiment on the fly.

"Run!" Penny screamed, throwing up another layer of magic.

"Penny, you'll only make it worse," Callie yelled before hurrying over to Dizzy, her hands full of supplies.

"I can undo it," Penny replied, moving her hands through the air.

The spells fizzed and shook in midair, frozen in place but not subdued.

"Reagan," Callie yelled. Penny was damn near the most powerful mage I'd ever seen. Dealing with her magic gone rogue would be too much for even dual mages of Callie and Dizzy's caliber.

I created a sphere of fire around the mess of magic, and not a moment too soon. The cocooned spell reversed Penny's intended goal. Spikes of magic shot out in all directions, pounding at my sphere from within. A few spears broke out, incredibly powerful from the merged energy of both casters. It punched divots in the ground and shot through the wood of the warehouse.

"Bad idea, Penny," I said, out of breath. I felt the drain of power. "Don't try to mimic my magic. It doesn't work like yours."

She nodded with an ashen face. "Okay." She swallowed hard. "Okay."

"Go, Reagan." Callie motioned me away. "I got it from here."

The female mage had run down the few steps while I was dealing with the magic, splitting up from her stunned male counterpart. She'd probably hoped the man would snap out of it and guard the stairs. Or maybe she just figured her chances were better on her own.

Leaving her to Callie, I charged the door, feeling that now familiar cold throbbing in my middle. The demon was in there, and I was about to drop in and say hi.

Darius got there before me. He grabbed the still-stunned mage out of the doorway and ripped him away, leaving the door for me. I kicked it open and ran into the warehouse.

Hundreds of candles glowed around the floor, illuminating boxes stacked at the back and around the sides. In the middle of a cleared space stood three mages, all in black robes, making a triangle around a circle drawn on the floor. Beside them was a pile of gross, not human this time. An animal of some sort.

"You guys really don't have the hang of sacrifices, you know that?" I said, inching forward slowly. I didn't know what spells were brewing in that circle. One wrong move, and I could accidentally give the demon enough power to ride the magic home.

None of the mages glanced my way, all of them hunched in a troll-like way, completely focused on the circle and what was in it. A homeless man sat within the circle, bent and crippled in an inhuman way. The demon must have taken over that body, eating away anything that had once been human.

This demon needed to die, like all the people it had killed while on the surface.

I gritted my teeth, reining in the surge of fire that roared through me.

Don't be hasty. You have to approach this delicately or you'll be screwed.

Something exploded outside, shaking the warehouse. Still, the mages didn't seem to notice.

The homeless man's head swiveled until his gleaming eyes took me in.

"You are too late," he rasped as Dizzy and Callie hurried through the door. They immediately slowed down, as I had done, taking in the scene. Penny came in after them, hanging back. "It is done."

"You're still here," I said, feeling that aching cold-ness expand within me, threatening the fire. I made sure my sword was stocked full of fire magic before it was too late. "I can still break into that circle and peel you out of there."

Darius stripped off his clothes. Penny's eyes wid-ened in shock, and she jerked her head away. A moment later, he molted into his monster form.

"Can we get rid of those mages, Callie?" I asked, walking around the edge of their stooped, muttering forms. They weren't in control of themselves anymore. However the demon had done it in its weakened state, it had assumed full control.

"Not...yet. Give me a minute to look at that circle." Callie went the other way, squinting at the chalk on the warehouse floor.

"It's an intricate one, hon," Dizzy said. "Magically fortified, structurally sound... It'll take a minute to disentangle. They've gotten better at this. They're masters, really. I'd love to get a picture."

The demon's laugh was like a swarm of locusts. "They are under my control. Any tampering with the circle will grant me a free ride home."

Sometimes I hated being right.

"So, what, you're just going to sit in there until hell freezes over?" I asked, stepping beside one of the mages and feeling the hum of magic in his spell. Intricate, indeed. Not like anything I'd experienced before, and certainly not like anything I'd ever seen in a book.

The cold within me pulsed, pushing at the fire. The candles around us flickered.

The demon-man's smile widened. "Oh, but you are powerful. You are creating a flux in the fire element. Can you feel it?"

No. But I wasn't about to admit that.

"Come with me," the demon-man said. "Let us train you. You need a guiding hand, or your magic will destroy you. We can help."

"I've been good so far." I walked over to the next mage, feeling a different hum. Good Lord, this demon had some very interesting ways of working this circle. If I hadn't been so scared and angry and all around put out, I'd be fascinated.

"Yes. Somehow, yes," it rasped. "But luck always runs out." A chunk of skin peeled away from the man's face.

"Yuck. And here I thought the vampire monster form was gross. It's got nothing on you, homeboy." When I reached the last mage, I felt the slightly different hum, getting a feeling for the three corners of what the demon was orchestrating. It was awe-inspiring. And more, I knew it was within my power to set such a circle—and to unravel it. It was like listening to someone speak a language you hadn't conversed in since childhood: you couldn't quite grasp what was being said, but you felt the rightness of it in your bones. All I needed was time to sit and study what was happening, and I knew I could come up with a way to circumvent it.

Unfortunately, time was something I did not have.

"Penny, can you read anything off the mages?" I asked, circling the mages once more. I could feel the circle gaining power, which meant the demon was becoming more powerful, too.

"Yes. But their magic is…"

"Odd, yeah. Analyze it. See if you can't find a way to cut them off without infusing the circle with more power."

"Okay," she said in a tiny voice.

The man's skin was turning translucent, showing black feathers underneath. The demon was about ready to emerge from his cocoon.

"Whatever move we make, we have to do it soon," I said softly, closing my eyes as the hum of the circle vibrated my skin. I stood right next to it now, clearing my mind and letting the magic whisper to me.

The cold throb grew, as I had known it would. It tried to push my fire down.

Blend your heritage, ma bichette. Blend your heritage. Blend your heritage, ma chere. Blend your—

"I got it, Darius. You can stop repeating that now."

Fuse—

I tilted my head, staring at the creature in the circle. That thought had reverberated from it. The demon had cut it off, and now it was either shielding its thoughts or not thinking at all, but it had been there.

Fuse.

Fuse my magic.

"How?" I asked it, not meaning to. Then, hoping for another slip-up and a free lesson, I asked again, "How do I fuse my magic?"

Its smile stretched across its face, and not in the theoretical way, like in books. This was inhuman and horrible, showing black fangs and a thin tongue behind them. "Come with me, and we will show you."

"How can you show me if you don't have the same type of magic?" I asked, raising my hands to the invisible wall of the circle. The cold bit into my skin. The feeling was unpleasant, but if I had to be honest, no more painful than the fire. I realized now that my hatred of the cold was related to the fear of what it would do to my fire.

I needed to push beyond this; I just didn't know how.

"How are we coming, Penny?" I asked, giving in to the cold. Letting it rise up through me like I'd done earlier that night.

"I think… I think I can create a kind of bridge, but

only for a moment." She exhaled noisily. "You'd have to kill the demon within a very short amount of time. If you don't succeed, he'll be banished. We're not trying to banish him, right? We're trying to kill him? Because banishing would be very easy."

"Kill, yes." I grimaced at the demon's laughter. "Sooner the better."

"You have the capacity for greatness, but you are not there yet, heir-child." It laughed again.

"I hate you." I closed my eyes as the cold overcame me. Suffocated me.

The candles around us dimmed and then went out.

A shower of bright white light shone down on us. Darius had turned on the warehouse lights.

Everyone, including the demon, squinted and raised their arm against the unexpected glare.

"There goes the romantic atmosphere," I said as the sludge rose up within me. Freezing my limbs, like at the mage's house. This time, though, I was prepared.

With everything I had, I pulled at the fire deep in my gut as the circle throbbed even colder against my hands, inside me.

"This has to happen now, or he's gone," Penny said. "He's nearly got the power he needs. He's draining it out of the mages."

"Told you so," I muttered to the mages, wrestling with my fire. "Never trust a demon."

Thoughts of my mother floated through my mind. Of Callie and Dizzy's blind faith. Of No Good Mikey and the gang, welcoming me into the neighborhood even though they gave side-eyes to most everyone else. My thoughts even lingered on Darius and his soft caresses. Darius, who had tried his damnedest to protect me, and look after me, when he ignored most everyone else.

I welcomed the flutter in my heart this time, reminding me that I was human. That this cold power would not steal the parts of me that could feel, any more than the fire had.

The heat crept up, encircling the cold. Blending. But not fusing.

For now, it would have to do.

"Go, Penny," I barked. "Darius, take down the mages. Callie and Dizzy, work with Penny in any way you can, and protect Darius from the mages' attacks."

"You can do this, Reagan," Callie said.

"Go!" I shouted.

CHAPTER 34

I FELT THE strength from Penny's magic, threading light and buoyancy through the demon's dark, dank magic. Cracks formed, shattering the cohesiveness of the pyramid of the spell. The circle flickered, one moment a self-imposed cage with a one-way trip to the underworld, and the next, nothing more than some lines and characters drawn on the concrete floor.

My power burst forth, grabbing the demon in a concussion of air and raising it up. Darius ran around the circle, easily dodging a battery of spells. He broke a spell casing he'd been carrying and threw it at one of the mage's feet. Sickly green smoke enveloped the mage, making him convulse. Callie and Dizzy threw something at another one of the mages. The final mage met Darius face to face as he came out of his trance. He shot off a stream of red, but Darius easily dodged it. A moment later the mage succumbed to the elder's strength and power.

I crawled fire down the borrowed body of the demon, shedding the shell he'd made of the homeless man, and exposing the oily black feathers beneath. I pushed my hands forward and felt the rush of fire fill me, rolling over my arms and out through my fingers. The spicy heat raked across me in a way I'd grown to love, even as the hollow coldness pumped in my stomach. A stream of hellfire tore through the air and splashed across the demon's front, melting half of him away.

Orbs of light popped up around us. Boxes floated up from the floor. I didn't worry about controlling either hallmark of my power.

I gritted my teeth from exertion as sweat dripped down my face.

The demon howled and writhed, trying to break free. A blast of air slapped my body, jolting me backward. Boxes flew, aiming for me.

None of them made it far.

Magic pulsed from all around us, my mages putting up spells to block me from being struck.

"Die, you bastard," I yelled, squeezing the demon in place with air while pushing forth another blast of hellfire. My limbs shook with the effort. Weakness clutched at me.

The fire tore at the creature right before something cold and solid hit my face and sent me reeling backward. A pile of char sank to the floor in the middle of the circle as the power radiated through the room.

"It's sending it down," Callie shouted, throwing a spell at the circle. The energy melted in, fueling the banishment spell.

"It's done," I said, panting. I held up a hand. "It's done."

The pile of burned black feathers disappeared from the warehouse floor, sent down to the underworld.

"It got two full-power blasts of hellfire." My legs gave out and I fell to the ground. Darius was there a moment later, hefting me up into his arms, in human form again, thank bejeebus. "It was nothing but a puddle of a former demon. Nothing could come back from that."

"Are you sure?" Dizzy asked, analyzing the circle.

My head felt unbelievably heavy. I let it fall to Darius's shoulder. "I saw it right before it went down."

"That was close." Callie glanced around. Exhaustion deepened the lines around her eyes. "That was really close. Thank God you can find a needle in a haystack, Dizzy. We almost didn't get here in time."

"Oh, that was nothing." Dizzy took out his phone and held it up to take a picture of the circle. "The pay stub was lying there, clear as day. I just had to pick it out from under a pile of his junk. He probably forgot it was even in there."

"Darius, you need to get dressed," Callie said, scowling at him with her hands braced on her hips. "No one needs to know what urges you are having right this second."

"We need to erase this evidence." Darius lowered me to the ground, ignoring Callie. "And to do that, you need to burn this warehouse to the ground. It is the easiest approach. Do you need some blood?"

"No, no." Callie marched over. "No way. She's in it thick enough where you're concerned. Don't think I haven't noticed. No, Penny can take care of that."

Penny stood off to the side, wringing her hands and looking anywhere but at the fallen enemy mages. "Yes, I can do magical fire. I mean, you know, not like Reagan. I can't control it like that. But I can set a fire well enough. My mom still doesn't know what happened to our shed."

"Atta girl. And don't you tell her, either. You're better off." Dizzy nodded matter-of-factly. I noticed that he very consciously didn't glance at the glowering Callie. A few questions had probably just been answered for her regarding some destroyed items in her house.

"Let's get going." I struggled out of Darius's grasp.

"You're staggering like a drunk." Callie grabbed my arm to brace me. "Vampire, cover that thing up and then go get the car. We'll get this place burning in the meantime."

In as little time as it had taken her to say it, Darius was dressed and looking impeccable. It boggled the mind.

I squealed like an idiot when he scooped me up and took off, leaving Callie shouting behind us. I let my head drop again and held on tightly.

"Today is Saturday, right?" I asked.

"Yes."

"I forgot to text J.M. that I was working. He probably figures, but still. I should've texted. I'd much rather be out to dinner with him instead of battling a demon."

"I know," he said as we tore through the lots. Dawn was a few hours away. We had to get back to the hotel. "Can you still read my thoughts?"

I let my eyes flutter closed. "No. That's only when the other power overcomes me. You know, I vaguely remember that happening with the fire when I first learned to use it. Well, not like that, but I remember feeling the fire rage through me, and having the uncontrollable desire to burn everything down. Just burn it all down. I just remembered that when I was wrestling with my magic earlier. My mom had a way of talking me through it. I can't remember how, though. I was never in my right mind."

"We will figure it out." Darius zipped past the office building. The security guard, who hadn't moved much since we'd walked past earlier, blinked in our direction. He didn't even unhook his thumbs from his belt.

"How are you on blood?" I asked, then wanted to

knife myself. "I didn't mean to ask that."

"I do not need blood, but I long to revel in your body. Stay with me today."

No was on the tip of my tongue, but it wouldn't exit my mouth. I'd spent so much time fighting to keep from losing myself to the demon, to that cold power, that I didn't have any energy left to fight the allure of the vampire. I didn't even want to.

He set me down next to the car and opened the door before handing me into the seat. He filled the driver's seat a moment later, and then we were on our way.

"They'll notice the car rolling through," I said as I put on my seatbelt.

"By the time they check it out, we'll be gone."

It turned out we were both right. The guard started as we drove along the road, moving much faster than the posted speed limit, but no one had shown up by the time we'd loaded up the mages.

"Why'd you put up a more intensive invisibility spell?" I asked in confusion as Darius turned back to the road. We'd forgotten about Penny's car. *Oops.*

"Penny's magical fire wouldn't have burned much of that place before someone noticed the fire." Callie massaged her thighs.

"It seemed a lot stronger before I saw Reagan's fire. I'd love to speak with your cousin, Reagan," Penny said.

We passed a security truck, and the driver slammed on his brakes when we zoomed by.

"He's a recluse," I said, rubbing my eyes. "He lives in a shack in the woods. I only see him once every so often. He just randomly sends me spells to try out."

"Maybe the next time you get some, you could let me know?" she asked hopefully.

"Yeah, sure. If I do. Who knows, he might be dead."

A grin curled Darius's lips as he pulled into the employee parking lot.

We said thanks and goodbye to Penny (and Callie and Dizzy promised they'd call her) before pulling away. She got into her car and pulled out behind us so quickly that one might've thought she was a vampire herself. Clearly she didn't want to get caught by the security guard who was patrolling around, looking for us.

"Give me a moment," Darius said as the security truck pulled across the road in front of us.

I watched in vague fascination as Darius exited the car, put on the jets, ripped the door of the security truck open, and bit the driver. That hot jab of emotion pierced my chest, and I looked away. This was getting out of hand.

When he entered the car a moment later, his eyes lingered on my face.

"What's up?" I asked, not meeting his stare.

"I saw your expression just now. You are losing the battle, as I have. You are realizing that *forever* between us would be the unbreakable bond humans speak of, but could never fully understand."

"No," I said, and crossed my arms. Why did he turn me into a juvenile with my responses?

"I don't like the sound of that, young lady." Callie leaned toward us.

"I was only wondering why you bit him instead of just knocking him out," I said, trying to dig myself out of this sudden hole I'd found myself in. Callie and Dizzy would find a way to kill Darius if they thought my mind was lost to him.

"This will be a positive experience he won't quite believe," Darius responded. "He will be less likely to share news of it."

"We should get going before someone else comes," Dizzy said, peering out his window. "I hope there aren't any cameras. You didn't kill him, did you, Darius?"

"I didn't, no." Darius's gaze lingered on mine for a moment longer before he turned back to the wheel.

THE RIDE BACK to the hotel was quiet as everyone decompressed. Darius parked out front and helped Dizzy and Callie out of the car before holding out his arm for me. He didn't insist on carrying me, thankfully, even though I leaned heavily on him. When walking through the lobby, a dapper-looking man in a tailored suit glided up to us.

"Mr. Durant." The man, who was surely a vampire, based on his flawless face, nodded at Darius. "It is a pleasure. I apologize that I haven't been able to properly greet you until now."

"Mr. Regent," Darius said in greeting. "We have been busy. Thank you for accommodating us."

"My pleasure, as always. I look forward to the critique." His smile was a whopper—charming, disarming, boyish, and devilishly handsome all at once. He was a panty melter, for sure. "Please, can I interest you in a drink?"

"Not just now, I thank you," Darius said, starting forward again. "We've had a long night. I do wish to speak with you regarding some matters in the area, but that can wait until tomorrow."

"Of course, sir." Mr. Regent flashed that mouth-watering smile again. "Can I send something to your room?"

"I'm hungry," I mumbled with my hand on my stomach.

"Yes, darling. You are always hungry." Darius nodded at Mr. Regent. "Surprise her. She'll eat most anything."

That was true enough.

"Of course. And you?" Mr. Regent glanced at Dizzy

and Callie.

Dizzy turned up the wattage of his smile. If he'd hoped to compete with Mr. Regent, though, he had a long way to go. "We'll place an order in a little while. Thanks so much."

"Of course," Mr. Regent bowed with a soft chuckle. "At your convenience."

Back in my room, I heaved a sigh of relief and collapsed on the bed. The last trembles of fear worked their way out of my system. That had been a helluva fight, and most of the battle was against myself. I had so much to learn. I knew that now. There was a gaping hole in my knowledge about my power that I needed to close up. That I needed to fuse with what I did know. The demon had seemed so certain I was powerful, and being what it was, that it had been sent up to find me, it probably knew. I needed to look into that.

Tomorrow.

Or maybe the next day.

I was too tired to worry about it now. The threat was gone, and that was good enough for the moment.

My stomach rumbled. I heaved myself up off the bed and stripped. I needed a shower and food. Then I needed to really ponder if heading over to the vampire's room was a good idea.

My stupid heart fluttered again. This time it wasn't as welcomed. I was in great danger here, and not like I'd originally thought. I wouldn't lose myself to Darius because of his species, but I might in the way a woman loses herself to a man.

The hot water falling over my skin felt good. The absence of the hollow, cold magic felt good. And when I got out, wrapping myself in a white, fluffy towel felt great.

I stood in the center of my room, looking at the white door leading to Darius. He wouldn't come in to pressure me, I knew. He wouldn't open the door and ask if I was coming. He would wait for my decision, and respect it, whatever it was.

I heaved a sigh, tried to resist, and walked to the door.

On the other side, I smiled at the fresh rose petals littering the ground and bed, then cocked my head in confusion at all the unlit candles.

"Afraid of a fire hazard?" I asked as I stepped into the room, officially making my decision.

He was dressed in a robe and had draped a big arm over the back of the chair.

"I thought you could light the candles," he said. He stayed where he was, waiting for me to come to him.

"You're not playing those hunter-and-prey games you said you liked, huh?" Heat infused my body. Concise balls of flame sprang to life around us, then drifted toward the candles.

"No." Darius lifted a hand to stop me. "Light them with a thought, not with that method."

I snuffed the little balls of flame. My fingers curled into fists as I concentrated, imagining all the different little wicks spread across the room. With a push, they lit as one.

Darius smiled. "Perfect. And I already told you, I hunt until my intended fully succumbs to our joined pleasure. As you did last night. When that happens, I fully succumb as well. We are past games, you and I. We are equals, and both of us are completely invested."

"That's heavy." My instinct was to meander around the room, trying to get comfortable or work up the gumption to leave. I knew where I would end up, though. I knew that when I'd walked through the door.

So I just cut to the chase. And dropped my towel.

"When's dinner coming? I'm starving," I said, heading toward him as my body surged with need and my core tightened in desire. I'd fight it tomorrow. Tonight, I'd succumb, as he'd said.

"Soon," he whispered, his eyes feasting on me. "But first, let me worship you."

CHAPTER 35

A HARD KNOCK sounded at my door.

I frowned, because I didn't think J.M. was the type to pound, but I wasn't expecting anyone else.

I sprayed a bit of hairspray on my newly styled hair and headed out of the bathroom.

It was Monday. We could've returned yesterday evening, but the whole crew had decided it was a great idea to take a day to recuperate, sightsee, and actually enjoy the town. Oscar had been shocked when I told him it was over. He'd began asking questions about the specifics, but just as quickly backed off and decided to investigate the remains of the site. Half of the information he got from me he wouldn't be able to explain anyway.

Little did we know the guild mages would be stalking us the whole time. Looking menacing for long periods was actually harder—and more exhausting—than I'd expected. It kept the idiots away until we could make it back to the Edgewater Hotel, though, a place the guild didn't seem to want any part of, so I wasn't too put out.

I'd asked Darius what was going on between the mages and the vampires in that area, and how he'd come to know Penny, but he hadn't given me a thorough answer. What I could deduce was that he'd helped out Mr. Regent the month previous, but didn't have any direct dealings in Seattle. From his vague answers, I figured that the vampires didn't like anyone having jurisdiction over them. They had to tolerate the elves in the Realm, since no one could unseat the elves' power, but the vampires had decided they would no longer tolerate the guild. Somehow, Penny and some other mysterious mage were the reason. Darius wouldn't say how, or who this other rogue mage was, but I had a feeling it had to do with a massive amount of power.

I'd quickly decided that it wasn't my problem. In the last couple of months, I'd had some pretty close calls. I needed to lie low for a while. I hated it, but Garret would stay the king of the NOLA MLE office for a while longer, the douche.

Tonight I would connect with J.M. to see if he'd made any progress on dealing with magical people, because I'd made a promise. Truth be told, I didn't really care. I'd help the guy out if he needed it, sure, but after everything I'd dealt with recently, I would just as soon stay in with a bottle of wine.

I opened my door to the surly face of No Good

Mikey.

"Hey," I said, leaving the door open and heading to the kitchen. A glass of wine while I waited sounded like just the ticket. "Want a drink?"

"Am I supposed to come in, then?"

"What was your first clue, the opened door or the offer of a libation?"

"Her and her fancy words," I heard him mutter. He appeared in the archway to the kitchen and promptly leaned against the side. "What do you got?"

"Wine, beer, whiskey, cognac, vodka, Baileys—"

"A beer, thanks. Any kind, doesn't matter."

"Good. Because I only have one kind." I grabbed out a bottle, popped the top, and handed it over. "What's up?"

"Where you been?"

"Seattle. For work."

He grunted before taking a sip. "Smokey said it was quiet while you were gone. You know, for the stuff he watches. The normal crime in the area went up, though. Some thugs are trying to throw their weight around. Expand their territory." Mikey huffed and took another sip. "I figured I'd let it roll until you got back. Let them try and mug you."

"Mug *me*?" I poured myself a glass of red. What type specifically, I had no idea.

"Yeah. A pretty blond girl like you—when you have

hair—walking all alone in the dead of night? They'll think you're easy prey."

"That won't be a nice surprise for them."

"Like I said, I'll wait until they try and mug you."

I motioned for him to go back into the living room. He peeled off to the side to allow me out, then followed me. I plopped down on the couch. He hesitantly took the love seat, the first time he'd dared to get comfortable in my house.

"So what's up?" I asked, because he always had a reason for coming around. I didn't think he was the type to casually hang in someone else's space.

"I'm not gonna lie—I'm still not easy about all that stuff I saw." He threw an arm over the back of the couch. "That shit ain't right."

"Either you get used to it, or I kill you."

His laugh said he'd like to see me try. "The other thing is that someone has been coming in here. I ain't never seen him, or heard him, but Smokey said someone's been going in through your back door when you aren't home."

"Did he see just one person?"

He squinted at me.

"There have been a few people coming in," I said. "Or I think so, unless they sent reinforcements the other day when I was messing around with them. A friend of mine, who has more money than a single person should, has his minions stock my fridge and clean up and stuff."

Mikey's eyes widened. He glanced around and slowly nodded. "It is always clean. Does this guy pay for it?"

"Of course. There is no way I'd pay for someone to bust into my house when I wasn't home. I don't even need half the stuff they stock. But he's hard of hearing when I tell him to get lost."

"You don't seem like the kind of girl to let someone get away with that."

"Trust me, you don't know what I'm up against." The doorbell rang as I took a sip. "I have a work thing tonight. Kinda." I pushed myself off the couch. "This guy is in the same position you are with the magical stuff, but he works for the police and has to deal with it professionally."

"With the police?"

"Yeah. Detective. I met him at my old job."

"I wondered why you was all done up. It is that swank lookin' dude who always comes around?" Mikey followed me to the door.

"No, he's the one who stocks the house. And does a whole lot of illegal stuff. Definitely not a cop."

Mikey shook his head. "Why would you, of all people, try to wrangle with a cop? I'd stick with the illegal dude. That's a more comfortable setup, if you don't mind me saying."

"Trust me, it isn't more comfortable, and also, I'm not wrangling. Just being nice for a change. It's annoying."

"I'll say. I don't bother. It makes my life easier."

I huffed out a laugh as I pulled open the door.

J.M. stood there in jeans and a blue button-up, attractive by human standards, but unfortunately plain compared to what I'd been looking at for the past week or so. It was hard to compare anyone to Darius, and no one could compare to Vlad.

"Hey," I said, pushing the door wide.

J.M. was about to say *hey* back, but his smile dwindled as his gaze snagged on Mikey behind me.

"Oh, he's my neighbor." I got out of the way so Mikey could leave the house. "He just stopped by."

"I got nothing to do with this, bro." Mikey held up his hands, one still holding a mostly full beer, and scooted by J.M. "Take my advice, though. Don't put a move on her unless you know she's into it. She is not one to mess with."

"Lovely, Mikey, thanks," I said sarcastically. "See ya."

Mikey saluted with his beer and started down the street.

"Didn't you say he was your neighbor?" J.M. asked, watching Mikey.

"Yeah. That house." I pointed at the house on my

right, in the opposite direction Mikey had taken off. "He wanders around the neighborhood sometimes. It's fine. It's all very normal."

J.M.'s confusion said he wasn't sure about that. He turned back to me and his eyes took me in. "Wow," he said as his gaze roamed my face then dipped to my body. "You're..." He shook his head. "You're beautiful, Reagan."

I smoothed the red silk fabric over my legs. It was one of the many dresses Marie had bought for me, and the most casual of the bunch. I'd done a little makeup and tried mildly on my hair. All this because J.M. had texted that we'd go somewhere *nice* to eat, his treat.

Now, seeing him in a pale blue button-up with a pair of jeans, I realized my error. *Nice* in Darius language meant at least a four-star rating. It meant fancy, but to his tastes, still somewhat mediocre. I was in the real world now, where people weren't made of money.

"Thanks," I said.

"Sure, yeah. I think I'm dressed too casual."

"Oh." I hooked a thumb behind me. "Do I have time to change?"

"God no. No way. You're gorgeous. Every guy in the place will be jealous. Come on." He stepped aside so I could exit the house.

I stepped out and locked the door behind me. At least it would keep non-vampires out.

J.M.'s midnight-blue Mustang waited at the curb. He clicked his key fob and the lights flashed. I stepped to the passenger door and waited as he walked around to the driver's side.

"You okay?" he asked, opening the door.

I rolled my eyes at myself. I had to remember J.M. was from a different time than the people I traveled with lately. He wasn't hung up on opening doors.

"Yup. Sorry, I just needed to check my phone really quickly." I dove into my handbag, pushed my gun out of the way, and grabbed my cell. There was a message, thankfully, so I totally looked legit.

I opened the door and sat into the car before reading the message from Smokey. *A human is watching your house. Nicely dressed. Slicked-back hair. Should I tell Mikey?*

I looked around as J.M. pulled away from the curb but didn't see anyone. Or Smokey.

Did Smokey even sleep? The guy seemed like he was up at all hours.

I texted back, *No. Try to get a picture if you can. Even from a distance.* I needed a new hobby, and messing with Darius's people might need to be it.

10-4, came the return message from Smokey.

"So how was your trip?" J.M. asked as he turned the corner.

We talked about pleasantries during the car ride, any holes in the conversation quickly plugged with useless info. A while later he parked the car across from the brewery in the French Quarter. I'd caught a cab in almost this same location while I was working with Darius.

I blew out a breath as a pang hit my heart. It had been a little over twenty-four hours, and already I missed him. It wasn't even the glorious nights wrapped in his body, or the witty dialogue we always shared, but the comfort of having him by my side. Content that he had my back, and I had his.

Man, I just wanted to see him again. It was really annoying. Especially since I wasn't good at reining myself in.

"Reagan?"

"Hmm?" I blinked as J.M. held the door to the restaurant for me. "You okay?"

"Oh yeah. Sorry." I laughed. "Head in the clouds. It's been a long week."

"I'll say." He followed me into the restaurant and then up the stairs as the hostess led us to our table. After we were seated, he said, "I heard the case was filed away, but you didn't bring anyone in. So it was a dead end?"

"Oh." I stalled, not really sure what to say. Telling him my friends and I had killed the whole lot of them was probably the opposite of my duty as a friendly ear to help him through his transition to the magical world. "It was resolved, but not traditionally. You'll probably learn more about that from Sean."

"He seemed happy enough with the result." J.M.'s brow furrowed. "If you didn't bring anyone in, though, I'm not sure how you could call that a win."

"The crimes will stop. That's the win."

He nodded slowly.

"Speaking of, how's all"—I made a circle with my forefinger—"this going? The magical stuff?"

"We solved that case you helped with." He beamed.

"Oh yeah?" I looked up from the menu. "Who did it?"

"The daughter." His grin was triumphant. "We found the sword at her house. She hadn't even cleaned off the blood." He shook his head. "She butchered her own father. We're not sure what she was after yet."

I tsked and resumed looking over the menu. "I'd find that out before you close the case. If it's magical in nature, and valuable enough to kill someone over, more people will try to get in on it. Magical people can be ruthless scavengers."

"Doubt it. It was a family spat."

I wiped the sudden crinkle from my brow. I didn't work for the MLE office anymore. Their lack of thoroughness wasn't my problem. "Right. What are you going to have?"

The dinner passed with stilted conversation, largely due to my continual dropping of the conversational ball. My mind kept wandering, and try as I might, I couldn't keep it rooted to the conversation. Finally, the dinner was over and we found ourselves outside.

"What's next?" J.M. asked, standing too close.

I took a step away, not wanting him to get the wrong idea. "You know what? I think I'm going to head off. I have a friend I want to visit."

"Oh." His expression fell, and he looked around. "Here?"

"Just"—I motioned—"up the way."

"Oh. Well…okay. Are you sure I can't take you for a drink?"

"No, but thanks for dinner. Good luck with the transition. I think you'll do great." I put up my hand for a high five. His immediate compliance was a childhood reaction that required no thought, if his obvious confusion was any indication. I threw him a wave and headed away.

CHAPTER 36

T HE HOT, STICKY night embraced me. I'd missed
New Orleans. Sure, Seattle was green and mild and
beautiful, but it didn't have enough crazy for my taste. It
didn't have enough old-world and deep magical tradi-
tions. Hell, it didn't have enough nudity. What was the
fun in that?

Jazz music clattered out of the bars and people
danced on the streets as I made my way to my destination. Shouts and laughter filled the night. Empty plastic
drink containers and discarded wrappers littered the
curbs. I found the man I was looking for where I always
did, leaning against the wall smoking a cigarette.

I slipped behind a group of people walking in a
mostly straight line until I was near him. Then, for old
times' sake, I stepped out suddenly. "Hiya, Red. What's
new?"

Red flinched and froze, his eyes wide as he stared at
me.

I covered his bony shoulder in heavy pats, making
him flinch with each one. "Did you miss me?"

He shook himself out of his fear-induced coma. "Reagan. You're back." He did not sound happy about it. "I don't know anything."

I knew that tone. He did know something. Something good.

Red was the guy I could always shake information out of in this town. If he didn't know it directly, he always knew a rumor that at least gave me a direction. It took the trip to Seattle for me to realize how much I relied on him.

Lucky for him, I was off-duty. Would be for the foreseeable future. I did not care about his gossip. The opposite, in fact—I didn't want to know. This visit was for payback.

"C'mon, let me buy you a drink." I yanked him toward the bar.

"You know I don't drink."

"When has that ever stopped you from sitting and watching me drink enough for the both of us?" I pushed him ahead of me and into a booth at the back of the dark bar. After I'd gotten a double shot of whiskey for each of us (I'd be drinking both), I sat down in the booth with him, recognizing his trepidation.

No, I didn't want anything, but it wouldn't do to let him get too comfortable. Just because I was leaving the bounty hunter gig for a while, didn't mean I needed to close the door on information. Insurance, and all that.

"So you heard I went to Seattle, huh?" I sipped my drink, watching him.

"Roger got a call from a shifter named Joe in Seattle. Joe said you did Seattle a service of some kind. Roger didn't say what." Red licked his lips, still nervous. Usually he settled down when he realized I wasn't going to hurt him. He clearly had a really good secret. I still didn't want to know. "Our orders on you are on hold. We were told not to track and report."

"Roger had you guys on track and report with me? That explains why you were always hanging around." I shook my head. That was annoying, but good on the bartender for fulfilling his end of the bargain. "But that's on hold?"

"Yeah."

"Not called off for good?"

Red shrugged helplessly. "You're...you. You cause trouble."

"I clean up trouble, actually. That's what bounty hunters do."

"You cause it in order to clean it up."

"Well now, that's just confusing." I let it go. "Listen, you've helped me out a lot over the years."

He eyed me warily.

"You made a lot of marks really easy to find," I continued.

His brow lowered. He expected the shoe to drop,

and equally expected to be under it.

My manic grin probably wasn't helping matters.

"So I'm going to give you a whole bunch of gossip." I waited to see his reaction. It was still one of mistrust.

"About what?" he asked.

"My foray in Seattle. What went down, the mages' involvement, and how I helped. How Joe's bar was blown up. You know, a bunch of stuff no one knows but…well, me. And soon, you."

Distrust crossed his features. "Why would you tell me?" Then the wariness kicked in again. The guy's face was like a comic book. "Because I don't have any information to trade. I mean it."

"Stop taunting me with your secrets. It's making me want to drag them out of you, and I don't want to know." I nearly rubbed my eyes until I remembered I had makeup on. "Why you? Because I'm giving back. But if you don't want to know, that's cool. I couldn't care less." I made a move to leave.

"No, no, no, no, no!" Red held out a hand. "I'm listening."

With a smile, I told him the things that were fine for him to know—things that could be spread around and gossiped about without stirring up a lot of drama. Things that would damage the reputation of the guild and make the vampires and shifters look good. Also make the mages of NOLA look good. Sure, there was an ulterior motive—bringing magical people together to combat that corrosive magical force—but Red got to have all of it for absolutely free. It would give him something a small-time player like him rarely had: Roger's undivided attention.

When I was finished, I leaned over to pat him again—I loved making him flinch; my bad—and headed out. "Good luck, buddy."

He watched me go with a bewildered expression, probably amazed that I honestly didn't want the golden egg he was sitting on. My phone buzzed with a text as I exited the bar.

I got a high-dollar case if you want it. It was from the captain. *Big money. Dangerous.*

Impulse had me unlocking my phone to reply, but I kept from typing *yes.* The captain's case was probably directly linked with whatever Red was hiding. And while in the past, the intrigue alone would've had me agreeing, not this time. I had gotten too close to unspeakable horrors in the last week. For my own safety, I needed to take a back seat for a while. I needed to train.

No thanks, I typed back. *I quit.*

Good. Get a hobby.

I smiled as I headed away, not paying attention to where I was walking, just going wherever my feet took me. It wasn't long before I blinked up at the large corner house in the French Quarter. A ghost tour had stopped kitty-corner, staring up at it in awe and hearing a tale about the vampire who'd once owned it when New Orleans was young. Little did they know that a vampire owned it now, and he was just as suave and debonair as the one in the guide's story. Less obvious, though. Probably.

I ran my fingers through my hair, probably fraying the loose curls I'd worked so hard on creating, ruining the hairstyle. Why did it matter?

I chewed on my lip and looked away.

Because I want to look pretty for him for once.

My stomach fluttered as that damning thought curled around my head.

What was I doing? He was a vampire, for criminy sakes! Callie would *kill* me. Then she'd start talking about ways to kill *him* without being found out. Dizzy would just nod in agreement with her.

I needed to forget about Seattle. Forget about Darius, and vampires, and the whole thing. The dual mages could rig something up to keep Darius's minions out of my house. I knew they could. It was telling that I hadn't asked them to before now. But I should. This had gotten out of hand.

With a heavy heart, I kept on walking, blindly, pretending it was the humidity that made my eyes sting with unshed tears.

Once I was tired of touring the town, I took a Lyft

home and had it drop me down the street from my house, where Mince idled, staring at his phone.

"Hey," I said, climbing from the car.

He glanced up, a big guy with pulpy features and a thick nose. He'd been a boxer back in the day, and had the face to show for it. "Hey." He gave me a rare smile. "I haven't seen you around in a while. Smokey said you went to Seattle."

I leaned against a stranger's banister as I looked at the cemetery wall. "Yeah. The weather's really nice there at this time of year."

"I'll bet." He put his phone down. "What were you doing there?"

"Working."

"You have a job? Huh. For some reason I thought you were unemployed."

Mince always confused me with the old white lady up the street. "Not really. I'm going to lie low for a while, though. Hang around."

"Good." He nodded and went back to his phone. "Mikey relaxes more when you're here, which means the rest of us don't have to bounce around on egg-shells."

I laughed at his unique take on the saying. "Anything else going on?"

"Nah." He gestured down the sidewalk. "Smokey is watching your house. You had a break-in."

My mouth dropped open. "Really, Mince, you couldn't have started with that?"

"What?" he asked my retreating back. "You always have break-ins!"

That was true, but still. The guy needed a lesson on what was noteworthy.

I crossed the street hurriedly when I spotted Smokey's skulking figure in the entrance of the cemetery. He was harmless, but boy did he put out the *creepy* vibe.

"Hey," I said, nearing. "Did you get any pictures?"

"Yes." He dug out his phone, touched the screen, swiped, and then angled it toward me. "That's the human."

He was talking like a magical person. That probably wasn't good, since he was human and technically shouldn't know about the supernatural.

The picture showed the back of a man's head. Smokey swiped. The side of the man's face. Smokey swiped. A blurry shot of the front. No help.

"Cool, thanks," I said, leaning away.

"Do you want me to text them to you?"

Why, so I could memorize the mundane haircut? "I got it right up here." I tapped my temple.

He nodded, like he had figured that was the case. I was magical, after all. I should be able to do superhuman things like remember blurry pictures. Little did he know, the images were already forgotten.

"He was the one that broke in?" I asked, turning to face my house. A window glowed.

I hadn't left any lights on.

My stomach fluttered again.

"No. He left right after you did. Were you followed?"

I frowned. "Not that I noticed. I looked when you texted."

He grunted. I wasn't sure what that meant.

"Another one walked in through the front." He swiped and showed me a picture of my open front door. Then another. Then the door mostly closed.

"Cool," I said again. Because really, what else was there to say?

"I took a picture of the person walking in. Then of him facing me dead-on. Then of him closing the door behind him." Smokey's eyes held a special twinkle, and also traces of fear.

"Vampire," I said softly, knowing that was the cause of the twinkle. Also knowing that his mind had quickly moved on to the *aswang,* a supernatural creature that *didn't* excite him.

He nodded slowly and glanced around, as cautious as if the cemetery had ears. And maybe it did, though Smokey would know best, since he practically made a second home of it. "I wasn't supposed to mention who it was, but my loyalty is to you, not *him*." Smokey lowered his voice. "It was the one who always hangs around with you. He let himself in, stayed in there for an hour, and then came out to speak to me."

I breathed through my mouth, trying to still the flip-flopping of my stomach. I needed to seriously cut that out. "Oh yeah?"

"A gentleman. Very influential, I can tell. He seems important." Smokey puffed up. "He asked me to watch over you and inform him if you are ever in any danger. He gave me his card." Smokey patted his pocket. "But I'll burn it if you want me to. Like I said, my loyalty is to you. Not to him."

I smiled to myself and glanced away to hide my pleasure. Darius didn't need Smokey's help—he had a horde of people who could do the job better. Darius had approached Smokey for me. He knew that, even though it was strictly forbidden to bring non-essential humans into the fold, I threw a bone to ol' Smokey now and again where it concerned the supernatural. Clearly he had spotted Smokey watching over my house and, knowing his importance to me, decided to make the old man's night.

"You might as well," I said, not able to stop the smile bleeding through my expression. "Just in case the house falls down and I get trapped under a beam, or something."

Smokey nodded and patted his pocket again. "That's what I was thinking. It's probably good to have backup in case something comes around you can't handle." His expression crumpled again; his thoughts had definitely shifted to that *aswang*.

"Okay. I'm going to head in. Thanks for your help." I thought about patting him, then thought better of it. He was still oozing creepy, after all. There had to be a reason for that.

I let myself into my house. Fresh flowers greeted me from a vase by the door. The living room light was on, and sitting in the couch, reading one of the books he hated but couldn't stop reading, was none other than Darius.

CHAPTER 37

"Hi," I SAID, suddenly out of breath.

He closed the book and stood. "Wretched book. Wretched series. I don't know why I keep picking it up."

"What are you doing here?" I asked, dropping my keys into the bowl.

He put the book back and surveyed me. "I wanted to see you. Also, I have something for you that I wanted to deliver in person." An air of menace crowded the room. "How was your date?"

"It wasn't a date. And it ended early."

He glanced at the clock.

"I had a few other things to do in town."

He nodded, analyzing me for a moment. "You are stunning, Reagan. Your effulgence steals the breath from my lungs."

I exhaled with a smile. The man was too suave for his own good. Knowing what three-syllable word to say in times like this was his superpower.

"Want something to drink?" I asked.

"A cognac. Shall I get it?"

"Well, since you offered, I don't mind if you do." I lowered onto the comfortable couch.

His lips tweaked into a grin and he zipped into the kitchen. No time later he was back, handing me a glass of wine and sitting down with a snifter.

"First." Darius reached to the side and picked up a large, thick binder. He handed it over. "For you."

I scowled at it, because that was what I did when I saw something that resembled schoolwork, and opened it. A picture of a warehouse amid empty fields and a parking lot greeted me. Turning the pages, I saw a lot of documents that looked confusing.

"Uh-huh." I closed the binder. "And what's this?"

"Your new warehouse. You need someplace out of the way to practice. It has ample space and is removed from the next property. It should work."

I felt my eyes widen as I opened it again. "Mine?"

"Of course. Your name is on the deed. Your false name, of course. We can sell it to your various identities as we need to create them. But it is yours. You will also need a car. I nearly bought one, but know that your neighborhood has particular idiosyncrasies."

Basically, he thought it would get stolen. "Thanks, but I can buy a car."

"Choose whichever one you would like and inform Mr. LaRay. He'll take care of the paperwork."

"I can buy my own car, is what I meant."

"Don't be silly." He waved me away.

I didn't argue. I'd just do it when he wasn't paying attention. It was easier that way.

"Now." He swirled the brown liquid in his glass, his eyes downcast. "I wanted to discuss a sensitive matter with you." He took a slow sip of his drink. "Reagan, for the second time in my life, and the first time as a vampire, I am falling in love. I didn't think it could happen after I changed into...what I am. I have never heard that it could. But here I am. I was seeking a solution to undo this change in me, but after Seattle...I have gone too far. I no longer want the antidote. I want to lay claim on you. I want you to let me. And for the first time in my history, I want to feel what happens when love fully matures."

I stared for a moment, my mouth hanging open in what couldn't possibly be an attractive expression. The warmth in my chest swelled until it overtook my body. I felt light, and full, and cherished.

Oh shit. I was in big trouble.

"Okay, but," I said, needing to keep my wits, "I live by human rules, and in this place and time, that's monogamy. I'm not going to consent to falling for a guy—not to mention a vampire—who sexes up women all over the world every time you need blood. I'd have to crack a skull, and the first one would be yours."

A smile graced his lips. "If you remain available to me, *mon ange*, I will agree to being solely with you. Exclusivity is much easier for a vampire than a human, or a more-than-human, as you are."

I licked my suddenly dried lips as warmth pulsed in time to my heart. Was I seriously entertaining the idea of starting a relationship—a *relationship*—with a vampire? An elder vampire, no less, the most dangerous kind?

"Oh man, I don't know," I muttered.

He stretched out his hand and took mine, grazing my knuckles with his warm lips. "I didn't expect to end up in this situation either, Reagan. But here we are. Let's embrace it. What have we to lose?"

"A lot. Each of us has a lot to lose."

He smiled, a lovely sight, before pulling me closer until I was resting against the heat of his body. "That makes it more special."

His lips dipped, connecting with mine. Unable to help myself, maybe not wanting to, I wrapped my arms around his neck, deepening the kiss. My toes curled and my stomach flipped. Oh Lord, this man had a hold on me. Even if he wasn't completely a man.

"Let's just…be friends with benefits, maybe?" I murmured against his lips. Compromise. That was the ticket. "Or maybe a relationship, but a secret one. Those are a ton of fun. How does that sound?"

"Don't tell Callie and Dizzy, you mean?"

"Them, or anyone who will try to talk me out of this—" *very bad idea.*

His chuckle was low and dangerous. "Whatever you want. But remember, vampires can be possessive creatures. Our primal sides uphold the verbal or, in this case, emotional contract. I will not see humor in anyone hurting you, or anyone trying to have you."

"In contrast, I probably *will* see humor in someone kicking your ass. But I promise to avenge you right after I stop laughing." He stood, and I held on tightly as he swung me up into his arms and carried me toward the bed. A thought occurred to me. "This situation has nothing to do with a blood bond, though. I'm not agreeing to that. So you can stop that paperwork, or whatever is happening in the lair. The only reason I'm not making a bigger fuss is because it's keeping Vlad away. But it's not going to happen."

"We'll talk about that in the future."

Maybe I was jumping into the deep end with dating, but I would not shackle myself to a vampire. I didn't say that, though. Not right then. I would save the bad news for when he returned to being a butthead. It was only a matter of time.

I kissed along his jaw. "Make love to me, Darius, and don't make me regret this."

"My pleasure, and you have my word."

EPILOGUE

V LAD STALKED ALONG the lower hall in the lair, thinking over the things he'd seen. It had been truly unbelievable. From the moment Reagan had made her way down into the lair, he had known she was special—an impression heightened after he'd watched her take on two middle-level vampires in Seattle—but never in his wildest dreams could he have imagined how special.

In Seattle, he'd interrogated a man who had seen her battle a demon while hovering in midair. Later Vlad had seen her eat away a spell with fire, manipulating the flame in a way no mage on earth could. He would've thought them fools, especially Darius, for not having sensed his presence in the rail yard, but now that the pieces had clicked together, he completely understood.

The entire crew had been terrified of what it would mean for the demon to make it back to the underworld. That could mean one of a few things, but after looking into the types of demonic power, and hearing the details of power only Lucifer himself could wield, the unbelievable had become a reality.

Darius had possibly found the most valuable being in the world. He had found her, gained her trust, and tied himself to her.

Vlad had known Darius would yield greatness. That was why he'd arranged for the young man to be fooled into a precarious position—and then beaten within an inch of his life so he would be grateful to Vlad for turning him. It had already paid off ten-fold, but this…

This was everything. This was the key to tearing down the elves.

"Vlad."

Vlad turned patiently as Sabrine paced toward him. Her stiletto boots, completely impractical for a woman of action, but something she deemed a necessity for reasons he'd never questioned, clicked on the hard ground. Her leather duster flared out behind her, revealing a tight red bustier that was also completely impractical.

"Yes?"

"I heard back from our contact in the Dark Kingdom. The demon from Seattle was not killed."

Vlad stilled. "Elaborate."

"The demon is in bad shape. Hellfire ate most of it away. It has some essence left, but very little. It seems as though it was an extremely narrow escape."

Vlad curled one hand into a fist before relaxing it.

"Where is the demon now? Can we finish the job?"

"It is in the Edges. Those who saw it appear are trying to coax it back. You know those in the Edges. They hate humans, having seen a great many summonings gone wrong."

"They are also mistrustful of us."

"They do not have love of vampires, it is true. We can lie in wait, but will have a small window in which to grab it if it recovers and tries to cross the river."

Vlad felt the exhilaration of ruined plans course through him. It meant there was work to be done. He had the golden key to Lucifer. To all the power of the Dark Kingdom. That would be ruined if he, himself, couldn't present Lucifer with the uncrowned heir.

"Find out about an heir," Vlad said, his mind whirling. "Find out all you can. No detail is too small. Most importantly, keep this as quiet as possible."

"And Darius?"

"Darius doesn't think anyone knows about his pet. Keep it that way for now. First we need to know where we stand. Only then will we take future steps."

Vlad waited until she stalked away before slowly heading back to his room. There was no need to be hasty. Not yet. That demon might perish, in which case, they had all the time in the world. If it didn't, they would make a grab for it.

All else failing, Reagan would have to cross the river

into the Dark Kingdom to kill it before it reached its sect. There would be no other option, not if Vlad (and she) hoped to keep her a secret. Through Darius, she was now one of Vlad's greatest assets.

The End